SWORD
of the
GOLDEN STUD

by

Ashley Carter

A FAWCETT GOLD MEDAL BOOK

Fawcett Publications, Inc., Greenwich, Connecticut

SWORD OF THE GOLDEN STUD

© 1977 CBS Publications, The Consumer Publishing Division of CBS, Inc. All rights reserved.

The material for this book has been prepared for publication by Ashley Carter through special and exclusive arrangement with the Lance (Kenric L.) Horner Trust.

ISBN 0-449-13842-9

Printed in the United States of America

10   9   8   7   6   5   4   3   2   1

For Harriet, and for Howard,
with love . . . .

Between two worlds, one dead,
One powerless to be born

—Matthew Arnold

SWORD
of the
GOLDEN STUD

CHAPTER I

Salt spray blown across him with trade-wind savagery stung Jeff Carson's face. He set his long legs apart, bracing himself on the narrowest uppermost plankings of the forecastle deck as the sleek brig shuddered. The three-masted vessel was like a living creature under sail, canvases bellied pregnant with the wind, the sea purling frothy gray from her bows, the deck riding gently across pummeling sea swells. Slipping free from the grip of the vast green embrace of the Gulf of Mexico, she glided through the tide-ripped narrow passage into the safe harbor of Barataria Bay. They rode in on the tide between Grand-Isle and Grand-Terre islands, those two green natural fortresses that had served Jean Lafitte so stunningly as fortifications against enemy, predator, pursuer.

Jeff breathed deeply. He had slowly learned to endure, if not to cherish, the sea, and this was the moment of every journey that he loved best—the hour they sailed within sight and smell of home port. It was good to be back here, to end a long sea voyage, thrilling and re-assuring to know he could soon report to Lafitte the successful accomplishment of a dangerous mission—without bloodshed or loss of a man.

He watched the distant quay on Grand-Terre take shape —golden sunlight flooding rich green palms, mangroves, moss-fringed live oaks, deeply scarlet flowers growing

11

rampant everywhere. A cresting sun silvered the bay and brilliantly illumined the sea, beaches, and primitive bayous.

His pleasure was tempered by an old sense of apprehension. Coming into Barataria Bay always stirred nameless dread and unburied panic inside him. He'd never been able to lose that uneasiness of entering an unknown, forbidden world, an alien place. Sure, he was accepted as an equal here, welcomed. But would he be if Lafitte and his men knew the truth—about Bricktop the fugitive slave? Would they drink with him and share their women with him if they knew he was a nigger masquerading as a white man? Here were gathered the toughest men from the meanest ports of the seven seas. Here all invaders were repelled casually and without advance inquiry or admonition. If a stranger survived, he was often questioned as he hung by his heels, screaming his answers between lashes of a bullwhip. Few unwelcomed guests survived. No survivor ever lied very long about his origins, motives, or connections. These men had their own strange code of ethics, and Lafitte himself stayed alive, affluent, and healthy by running a tight ship—aboard or ashore.

Jeff shook his broadcloth jacket up on his wide shoulders. He remembered his own arrival at Barataria two years ago. He'd come then, living the old lie, pretending to be white. Thank God, he'd come in one of Lafitte's own schooners, at Lafitte's own request and escorted by Helen Latimer—a very intimate acquaintance of Lafitte's from his days as a young hellion and rascal about New Orleans.

He pushed his fingers inside his starched white shirt and touched the now bent and misshapen diamond-encrusted gold cross on its thin, long gold chain about his neck. Helen had given him this good luck talisman— in appreciation for a long, long night in her bed at Poinciana plantation, north of New Orleans. She'd promised him the charm would bring him good luck. He believed superstitiously that it had saved his life more than once. And like the golden talisman, the wealthy widow Latimer had been his guardian angel, guaranteeing a warm welcome in Lafitte's headquarters at Barataria village on Grand-Terre.

All that seemed to belong to another lifetime, and the memory stirred old hurts, the anguish of his love for Chloe and the violent way he'd lost her. He forced it all from his mind.

As Captain MacFarland's ship cut through the breakers that pounded the brig—the Gulf's backslapping farewell—the first silhouette of the pirate settlement materialized. The town—controlled heart, skin, and soul by Jean Lafitte—was not a ramshackle or temporary stopover. It was substantially constructed, a cluster of wooden houses like fiefs kneeling in obeisance before the mansion—that three-story red-brick chalet which dominated the other dwellings, the island, the bay, this whole world apart. The only other building that dared rise above a single story on Grand-Terre was the watchtower on the quay, from which lookouts could scan the gulf, bay, rivers, and bayous for miles in every direction.

A beguiling and misleading atmosphere of blue-hazed calm pervaded this place. Jeff exhaled heavily. There was calm here, but it was underscored by tension; a quiet purchased at the cost of constant vigilance, the exercise of total authority, the almost divine control over life and death by one man—Lafitte.

As the distant piers took shape, seeming to ride out on the sanguine bay to meet the swift, silent *Sainte Teresa*, one sensed a Spanish flavor in the village architecture: in the presence of many steps gracing the façades of most buildings, the moorish flare of bays, gables, and tiled roofing. Lafitte's background was believed to be French, though he operated legally in his plundering of merchant ships under letters of marque from the Republic of Cartagena that permitted him to prey on all ships flying Spanish flags. Admittedly, he never took captured ships to Cartagena to claim them as prizes. This was unreasonable, too far away, so he convoyed them in to Barataria, near the mouth of the Mississippi.

Lafitte also admitted he sometimes mistook an English, or even a French ship for a Spanish vessel. Once captured, he claimed them as prizes of war and brought them too to Grand-Terre, where he maintained a settlement, only sixty miles south of New Orleans, which was home port of his privateers, the base of his operations. But Barataria was no lawless community of cutthroats. Leading merchants of New Orleans frequently came there to buy merchandise. They were treated with respect and guaranteed every safety.

"Hey, me bucko!" Captain MacFarland called to him from the pilot's cabin amidships. The old salt's basso-profundo voice needed no megaphone to amplify it. "Got you back home safe to land after all, eh, me lad?"

Jeff glanced over his shoulder and laughed. "Aye, skipper. Despite your best navigation, we made it—one more time."

"Watch your tongue, you lubber!" Captain MacFarland bristled. Where his authority and seamanship were concerned, he was totally without humor. "You ain't ashore yet."

The imposing sight of that enormous-bellied man standing on the shining white deck brought back to Jeff his first encounter with the skipper. There had been raging conflict between them from the first—the dour, intimidating MacFarland intent upon impressing his indisputable authority upon every stranger aboard his ship as the first order of business. Only the fact that both Jeff and the captain answered to the same man, Lafitte, settled their differences without violence. MacFarland's men called the captain a devil with a beard reflecting hell's own fires. His burring voice came right off the high tors and wild moors of heather-swept Scotland. He wanted no seaman to like him. Affection was effeminate, a sign of moral weakness. He wanted to be feared, and he was.

Jeff stared across the middle deck at Captain MacFarland, stripped to the waist, sweating like a mule, sweat glistening in the gray hairs of his chest. The battered uniform hat set jauntily over one ear bore grimy, indecipherable insignia that Jeff had never yet been able to identify. Why had MacFarland left the service of some mighty empire to sail for Lafitte's freebooters? Had he slain a superior officer? Seduced some admiral's daughter? Stolen? Fallen asleep on watch? The captain never talked of his past, of better times. That was a closed logbook.

"You might run aground, even in Barataria Bay," Jeff taunted.

The red beard shook. "I'm still captain of this here tub, lubber, and until you dock, you best speak to Cap'n MacFarland with your mouth full of respect. . . . You can lord your handsome self around the women from here to San Domang, but aboard my ship, I'm the nearest thing to God almighty you'll ever see, laddie. And don't you forget it."

"How can I forget it, you old pelican bait? You yell at us twenty times a day through that megaphone, telling us who's in charge."

MacFarland laughed. "For y'r own good, laddie. And don't you doubt it. If you learn to step lively aboard MacFarland's ship, you won't forget to heel-and-toe it when you go to see Lafitte with your lyin' version of how you backed down his old friend Morgan Roy and carried out his little mission for him—and no mention, I'll wager, of how good ole Cap'n MacFarland pulled your tail out of the shark's mouth."

Jeff watched the wind-borne racing sloops speed out, circling the three-masted brigantine like tiny terriers harassing a mastiff. These lightweight crafts, which could cross Barataria Bay like gulls in a downdraft, were an invention of Lafitte's. They resembled the Mediterranean felluca—from which Lafitte may have borrowed the narrow, lateen-rigged lines. The shells were used to reconnoiter, deliver messages, spy, and simply to run when running proved to be the better part of valor.

Captain MacFarland hated the lithe little racing crafts, and he pressed the megaphone to his mouth, cursing them with every foul oath he could remember or invent. "A disgrace to the art of sailing!" he raged. "Get them trash buckets out of me path or I'll run ye down."

The men manning the small craft yelled, waved, and made obscene signs. Finally, like some great dane surrounded by yapping poodles, the captain ignored them.

"Something amiss—on the pier yonder," MacFarland called across to Jeff. "Or can your eagle eye that never misses a tart on the street, pick out objects at such a distance?"

Jeff squinted, studying the strangers gathered along the sun-stabbed quay, the flat-bottomed riverboats riding at anchor. A dozen red-coated state militia men formed two stiff-backed lines, supported by another dozen men in less formal khaki. All were armed. They stood rigid, quiet, unmoving. It was easy to see why they remained stationary even at a distance. The forces of Louisiana law found themselves silently but effectively checkmated by the motley crew of Lafitte's rascals who appeared to be lounging, loitering, sunbathing along the docks, perched atop cotton bales, leaning against posts, or simply watching the sea. In reality they were taut drawn and ready for action. One word, one wrong move, one overt mistake could trigger trouble, and the troopers understood this. These seadogs, disreputable, bearded, greasy, in all stages of undress, scarred of face or body, tattooed, were men whose very smile could chill an adversary's blood, diminish his will, dissolve his courage. A man gripping a flintlock in sweated fist could well feel unarmed and helpless facing these privateers.

Jeff admitted he had himself experienced this fear at first among these freebooters. It had taken him a long time to earn their grudging respect. He believed that now, after having dealt with the pirate Morgan Roy down at Cap François, he merited a place of responsibility and authority in their organization. If a man didn't get his throat slit, he could get rich in Barataria, and this was what Jeff Carson—once known as the fugitive slave Bricktop—had been seeking as long as he could remember.

Jeff shivered. It seemed to him he'd spent his life runing toward something, looking for a place where he could *belong*. At last, he believed he'd found it here at Barataria among the scum of the seven seas. Hell, his own beginnings were none too fancy, pimping for third-class whores in Louisville, running for his life when his masquerade failed in Mississippi, living by his wits. The kindest thing people said about Jeff Carson was that he was a rogue, a rascal. Like water, he was seeking his level.

Looking back over the past two tough years at Grand-Terre, Jeff decided he had been happy learning the ropes as a slave trader, apprenticing in Lafitte's organization. On the first assignment Lafitte gave him, he had delivered 300 blacks and 14 fancy wenches from Cuba though he'd had to ride out the hell of a hurricane at sea to do it. But he'd done it! In every job handed him, he'd succeeded beyond his wildest fantasies. He had never worked harder, faced more danger, or been happier in his life. Once, in another existence, he'd lived in roseate anticipation of wedding and bedding Minerva George and becoming an accepted member of the landed gentry. That had blown up in his face. He'd been tied down, the huge brands scarring his back exposed to Minerva's horrified eyes, and he had run to save his neck. Here at Barataria he learned to test, grade, inspect, and handle niggers. He could almost forget that he was black except at those moments when some vicious cruelty to the helpless slaves made him sick at his stomach. Working with the miserable Negroes made him feel entirely white. He learned to choke back and deny any compassion. He worked as René Beluche's assistant. They processed blacks from the mid-passage of the slave ships, through Barataria barracoons, to the auction vendues upriver at New Orleans.

He fared well. No young agent for the most affluent New Orleans or New York firm lived better. Every time he delivered slaves at a lower price than Lafitte anticipated, Lafitte paid him an extra bonus. As a fringe benefit, he was furnished his own house in the village. A plump German fraulein kept house for him and slept in, when he let her sleep. His house and clothes gleamed, starched and immaculate, and Gretchen was an excellent cook. Finally, she had learned there was more to sexual adventure than lying passively on her back to accept his advances. She had come to love all the new ways she had discovered to rouse and sate him. He had a good life, and he felt that his victory over Morgan Roy had secured it and cinched his place of trust in Lafitte's organization. Hell, when he told Lafitte the full details of how Morgan Roy—fat bellied, one eyed, hog jowled, violent, mentally unstable—had backed down, Lafitte might consider a promotion. At least, he had a hellish good commission due on the blacks he'd recovered from the slave-stealing Roy.

Jeff walked aft, going amidships, where he saw Vincente awaiting him near the gangway. MacFarland's seamen scurried around Vincente, brushing him, running past him on both sides, hauling in sails, readying for docking.

Land was so close now Jeff felt he could almost stretch out his hands and clutch up fistfuls of the beautiful soil. Land! A place to walk that didn't roll beneath your feet, a place that didn't smell of tar and paint and urine! He wanted to leap overboard, swim to the pier, scramble up on it and plant his feet firmly on *terra firma*. He was back home—the only home he had—and the ugly little village had never looked lovelier.

Abruptly, now that he'd returned aft, and with some small shift in the wind, that incredible stench from the hold struck him like a blow in the face. His steps slowed involuntarily. From below decks, he heard that strange, haunting, and deeply disturbing keening of the shackled slaves. Something in their plaintive, whispered wailing stirred long-forgotten, inborn terror and sadness from his own ancient past, from generations long dead. He didn't understand it and yet he went ill hearing it. His lips felt suddenly parched, and the cottony dryness of his mouth extended far down into his empty belly, and the throbbing inside his head made him feel as if his skull might crack. But worse than the muted crying, the smell of the slave

18

ship suddenly enveloped, attacked, and nauseated him. If he made a hundred trips, he would never grow accustomed to this evil stench. The musk of unwashed black bodies combined with smells of crusted blood, open wounds, sweat, sickness, and excrement to assail his nostrils.

With difficulty, he swallowed back the acrid bile that gorged up in his throat and forced himself to smile as he joined Vincente near the gangway. Damn it, nobody got anything for nothing. Everything had its price tag. He was willing to pay whatever it cost him to trade in slaves, to deny his own blackness, to hide his guilty secret, to build his fortune. Once he was rich enough, he'd go where he'd never have to smell another nigger. But even as he thought this, he admitted wryly, he could never escape his own skin or the branding-iron wales scarring his own back.

"Anxious to touch ground, are ye, lubbers?" MacFarland's bass voice, amplified by the megaphone, battered at them.

"I've been ready to go ashore since the minute I learned you were to skipper the *Sainte Teresa*," Vincente shouted defiantly, knowing the captain could never hear him in the caterwauling of sounds.

Vincente was tall for his fourteen years—wiry, with the slender, dextrous hands of a pickpurse and the huge black eyes of a choirboy. Fourteen? Vincente had been born with native wisdom few ever acquire in long, misspent lives. He had been under twelve—and looked nine—when he audaciously took over Jeff Carson's life in Cuba —a bilingual shoe-shine boy, a pimp for his sister, the bastard son of one of Havana's gentry. The adolescent curves of his body were firming, stretching into sharply defined musculature. Already he carried himself with the unconscious, faintly arrogant manner of the Latin aristocrat. In his mid-teens he was taller than the average Cuban male adult and his frame promised additional height. He held his head high, his thick black curls growing down over his collar. His short straight nose, high forehead

19

defined by widow's peak, and thick black brows, made him exceptionally handsome, almost pretty. His lips seemed carved, darkly red, parting in his easy smiling to reveal white, even teeth. There was inherited hauteur even in the tilt of the strongly cleft chin.

He was a handsome young devil and made daily more aware of his comeliness by feminine attention. Already, mature women turned discreetly to eye his curls, his carriage, his animal arrogance, his youthful audacity, his innate self-confidence. He grinned up at Jeff and spoke with a long sigh of relief. "Well, *señor amigo*, we made it. Once more."

Jeff laughed at him. "You sound like you thought we might not."

Vincente did not smile. He shrugged. "I took few side bets, Don Jeff."

Jeff put his arm about the boy's slender shoulders. "Hell, Vincente, the world's our oyster. From here, it's all downhill."

They fell silent, attracted by the docking operations of the huge vessel. No matter how often one watched the battle of man's mind and muscle against ship and sea, it never grew old; it was like action never seen before because each time could be different, depending on the men, the tides, the wind, and a hundred imponderables.

They watched as the *Sainte Teresa* hove to, her wings clipped, her sails secured. A longboat came gliding out under half a dozen oars to intercept them. It was manned by bare-chested sailors, grunting as they pulled furiously on the long sweeps, muscles swelling and tautening across their shoulders and backs. When they drifted near the bow, one of the sailors stood up and caught a line tossed from the ship and made it fast to the stern of the long boat. Then the heaving, straining seamen dug in with their oars and towed the brig in to its berth at the long pier. The dock detail shouted and cursed as they secured the ship to the pier with fat hawsers.

Jeff frowned, watching the unmoving red-coated and khaki-clad lawmen remain at rigid attention on the pier, sweated down in the merciless blaze of the sun. The long quay was piled with crates and boxes, barrels and casks from most of the market places of the world—some of it legitimately unloaded here from registered merchantmen. But much of it—most of it—comprised booty taken by Lafitte's pillagers. Lafitte was a respectable business tycoon now—with a blacksmith shop and a huge merchandise mart in the *Vieux Carre* at New Orleans. Lafitte's days of piracy were behind him, but not that far behind.

Vincente caught Jeff's arm. "Look, Don Jeff." Excitedly, he pointed to the crowd gathered at the foot of the gangplank, which was being swung into place. "Look who has come out in this heat to welcome us home."

Jeff grinned and leaned out over the ship's rail waving toward Captain Dominique You. Dominique was his oldest, most-trusted friend, his sponsor in the organization. It was Dominique to whom Helen Latimer had addressed her cologne-scented letter that led to Jeff's being accepted in Lafitte's company. It was Dominique You who, with Madame Hortense at the madame's Riding Academy in the *Vieux Carre*, had secretly watched Jeff's copulating with Chloe and thereupon decided that the young redhead had the thrust and drive Lafitte and company could profitably employ. That was the first time Jeff had made love to Chloe, and though she was a paid whore, until her tragic death theirs had been the kind of total sharing that must have exalted intercourse in Eden. He'd not suspected Hortense and Dominique You were spying on their lovemaking through holes in the ceiling. He had long since forgiven Dominique. He had never forgotten Chloe. He never would.

He scowled now when Dominique You did not respond to his greeting by so much as a nod of his bald head. Jeff yelled his name and waved again.

Dominique You half crouched at the base of the gangplank, ready to spring upward on the ladder the instant it was secured. His face was cold though he gazed directly upward at Jeff. The size and Falstaffian corpulence of the man, his round red face and deep-set ebony eyes, along with that fringe of white hair decorating his naked pate, gave him a grim and forbidding appearance.

"Dominique! It's me, you fat old bastard!" Jeff yelled.

The gangplank was barely set in place when You jerked aside the restraining halter and strode up the ladder with the agility and speed of a man half his age and 200 pounds lighter. Extending his arms, Jeff went down the steps laughing and shouting. Even the rigid lawmen turned to stare.

Three of the sourest-faced thugs Jeff had ever seen this side of nightmares followed in Dominique You's wake. Though each carried gear—white canvas roll, ropes, line—Jeff ignored them. He was glad Dominique was down here to greet him, pleased that he would be able to boast of his victory over You's old enemy, Morgan Roy, to his respected friend even before he reported to Lafitte in the red-brick chalet.

They met halfway up the gangplank—the young stallion and the huge grizzly. A sense of terrible wrong struck Jeff, a combination of wrongs—the lawmen, armed pirates lounging too casually along the quay, You's scowling face. You looked as if he didn't even know Jeff Carson, and if he knew him, he hated him with unremitting passion.

Jeff forced a laugh and reached out for the enormous man with both arms. Dominique You shook his head. He raged at Jeff in a voice once well heard above the thunder of storms at sea, "Get back on that brig, you bastard!"

Jeff's smile died, his mouth sagged open. He felt as if his heart had slipped its moorings, as if he'd taken leave of his senses, or as if the rest of the world had. "What?"

"You heard me, Hengst!" There was no compromise in You's tone, no friendliness in his voice, only chilled hatred.

"Hengst?" Jeff stared at his old friend, now totally convinced the world had gone out of control. "Hengst? Dominique! Have you lost your senses? It's me. It's—"

"We warned you, Otto Hengst!" You's thunderous

voice rode over Jeff's, drowning it. "We warned you never to come back here to Barataria."

"But—" Whatever protestations Jeff might have voiced were cut short, driven back down his throat by Dominique You's hamlike fist rammed straight into his face. His nose crushed under the impact. He tasted his own hot, salty blood. He almost choked on it. His eyes glazed, the pier and the sky changed places. Pain wheeled and soared like sea gulls across the vacuity of his brain. He wanted with all the rage moiling inside him to hit back and to keep hitting until the world straightened and made sense again. But he could not even lift his arms. Messages from his nerve centers were short-circuited. He staggered.

Vaguely, he heard Vincente wail in protest from the head of the gangplank where he halted, locked in horror and disbelief. Jeff hoped that Vincente would have sense enough to stay out of this unequal battle. One pile-driver blow from You's fist would destroy the young boy. It hadn't done a great deal for his own sense of equilibrium.

Dominique You did not even hesitate to set himself on the narrow ladder. As Jeff, stunned and weak-kneed, clutched at rope sidings to secure his balance, Dominique You struck him twice with his fist, once in each temple. Lightning flared white inside Jeff's skull. He felt his stomach walls disintegrate, his mind go blank. He was barely aware of the short chopping right cross that caught the edge of his chin, drove his jawbone upward under his ear, dislodging his reason and plunging him into semiconsciousness.

He was physically paralyzed. He sagged forward. Dominique didn't even attempt to catch him or break his fall. You sucked in his huge belly and, with his men, stepped aside and let Jeff plunge down the ladder to the dock plankings. Jeff dove headfirst in a terrible kind of slowness and unreality where only pain was real.

"Tie the lubber up in the canvas jacket," he heard Dominique You order. Vaguely he was aware of being lifted and trussed in an ill-fitting strait jacket, but in the warm, half-world where he floated, it did not matter.

From some incredible distance, he heard Dominique You shouting in a fragmented voice, telling Vincente to stay aboard the *Sainte Teresa* under pain of death.

Then in that same broken voice, Dominique You was talking to a khaki-clad man with snake boots, four-inch belt, and massive beer belly. "A troublemaker, M'sieur High-Sheriff Bourett. A thief named Otto Hengst. We ran him out of Barataria. No rat hole on earth would accept him—so he came back here—despite our warning. . . . Don't let it upset you, M'sieur High-Sheriff. We'll handle it all—in our own way. You've got your hands full with your own grave and deplorable matter. . . ."

And then Jeff was faintly conscious of being toted by three men, roughly, going along the crowded pier. He struggled, raging, and then he plunged deeper into the warm occluding pool—and the world receded into blackness around him.

CHAPTER II

Jeff fought upward through the dark and blinding fury. He struggled against the restraining lines on the canvas strait jacket and managed to free himself. He strung together the vilest epithets he'd learned at Barataria, in Cuba, aboard slave ships, and among the pimps and whores of Louisville.

He thrust the jacket aside. There was some sense of release, and a kind of moral victory, in hearing his own voice raging, venting his spleen, but he wished devoutly that Captain You were there to hear him. Perhaps he needed an audience because what he felt was mostly self-pity. Damn their eyes! He had successfully completed a villainous task—at least as well as Jean Lafitte himself could have handled it. He'd recovered the stolen property, and he'd avoided a battle that could have cost lives, and maybe even a sailing ship. How could even Lafitte have improved on that performance? And this was his thanks! To be attacked in a *coup de main* from the one man he had always trusted above all others! Smashed full in the face by a battering ram of a fist! Paralyzed by blows to each temple—and *there* was pain and loss of bodily control! Dominique You knew all there was to know about fighting dirty, about incapacitating an enemy before he even knew he was an enemy! Damn them all! He wanted to howl out his despair, his final loss of faith in even the dregs of humanity. He hurled the canvas jacket from him furiously and sat up, looking around.

He was not certain at once just where he was. Gradually, he became conscious that he was not alone. His voice softened, faltered, died away, and he stared at the two voluptuous young women who gazed back at him with open admiration and sensually whetted appetites. This attention alleviated slightly his wounded ego, the ache of his bloodied face, his towering rage.

The girls smiled, tipping pink tongues against full-lipped mouths. They were new to Barataria since he'd been away, and he noted with some pleasure that they were a better grade than most of the women who gravitated here. He'd learned at once that the women who came to Grand-Terre were likely to be tougher than their sisters in the Tchoupitoulas Street cribs. Hell, what other kind of woman would be attracted by these sea vermin, gathered from the evil holes of the earth? These men were murderers, pirates, thieves, no matter what Jean Lafitte called them. Grand-Terre was a step down from the cribs of New Orleans. But these girls looked young, fresh and pretty—they had been scrubbed, hair brushed, dresses cleaned.

He managed a faint, fragmented smile. He found their attentions and admiring glances curative and restorative. He hoped he never got so damned old that a pretty woman's smile couldn't eat through the acid of whatever hatred was roiling inside him. They looked at him and they liked what they saw, and this appeased him slightly.

He smiled, letting his eyes graze across them. He had always been made supremely aware of his extraordinary good looks and uncommonly attractive body—the brightening eyes of approving women were the best mirrors of all. They showed him his reflection in its finest image—the slender, tall body, the bigness in the chest, the wide shoulders, the tapered hips, and the audacity at his thighs that not even clever tailoring could conceal or diminish. And he had proved himself smart and sharp minded a hundred times—simply by staying alive against incredible odds—a hunted, fugitive slave in a white man's skin, the bastard son of an octoroon slave wench and a passing stranger, masquerading in a white man's world where one drop of Negro blood branded a man black forever, living among them, drinking with them, and laying siege to their white women! If he had a flaw, it was the stupidity that kept him fighting to go on living free—and living well—in a jealously guarded white society where all odds were stacked totally against him. But be damned if he'd surrender. He might die in the next ten minutes, or the next ten years, but when he died, he'd die free! Nobody would ever again enslave him. He'd never chop cotton, cut sugarcane, hoe corn, or tend animals, or live like an animal again. Never would a white man force a "yes, masta" from his lips, unless those words bubbled out with his dying, retching globules of blood. He was almost twenty-one, and by God, if he died at twenty-two, he'd die free, die fighting for his freedom.

Remembering how he had come to this place—wherever it was—he swore again, savagely. Not even scantily clad beauty was enough to obliterate the fearful injustice in his mind.

Pausing in his railing to catch his breath, he moved his gaze across the faces of the two girls. They smiled uncertainly, and the smaller one was trembling slightly. His rage frightened them, but his comeliness intrigued them, adding spice and heated liquidity to the thrill of their titillated terror and attraction. Yes—goddamn it— he could see mirrored in their eyes that he had a healthy, handsome body. He had a good mind, ambition, and boundless energy too. Yes, even as a prisoner in this place, he possessed everything any young twenty-year-old could want. Except . . . There was one thing he could not escape in this life—and the fearful truth was brought home when he suffered injustice such as he had at Dominique You's hands—he could never extricate himself from the bonds of those invisible stripes of imprisoning slavery. No matter who else he deceived, he *knew*; the blood of blacks flowed in his veins.

Yes, damn it all, he could live like an emperor, if only his blood were not—in these times and this place!— fatally tinted with traces of Negroid blood. How much? He didn't know. His mother was an octoroon, but he hadn't the least inkling in the world who his father was, except that the red-haired son of a bitch had moved in swiftly, pestering one of Baxter Simon's precious virgin wenches that Simon had been saving for his own deflowering, usurping Simon's *droit du seigneur*, his right to first entry with his slave wenches. Jeff's father had moved out quickly, just escaping the rage of the cuckolded Simon.

The hell of it was, few entirely white men had skin as smooth and clear as his. But probably *no* white man had a huge *W.O.* branded between his shoulder blades— welted, scarred, and immutable in his flesh. His right palm bore the seared scars where he'd caught at the branding iron, vainly trying to wrest it from the grasp of the enraged "Masta" Simon. The son of a bitch got him good—he was forever branded, like any of the other Willow Oaks plantation animals, property of Baxter

27

Simon, marked as a "runner" for life. Anyone who glimpsed that brand knew him for what Baxter Simon's branding iron had stigmatized him: a black runner, a runaway slave, *a nigger!*

Hell, admit it, he was a nigger. This meant that by legal definition he had Negro blood, no matter how miniscule an amount.

He tightened his jaws so fiercely that a small muscle worked in its grim squared line. He never permitted anyone to see his naked back. To be safe, he never fully undressed—even with a passionate and pleading female—except in the dark. If female hands, clutching him closer, struck upon those telltale brand weals, he could lie—in the dark. Nobody would see that brand and live. He couldn't let them; it would be like signing his own death warrant. Let the women drool and suckle and salivate over him in the darkness. What they got from him with the lights out, few other women got with other men in brightest luminosity. No, nobody could be allowed to see him naked! Nobody could be suffered to know he was legally a Negro—and go on living. As long as he was careful, no one could tell; his red hair, his tanned, classic-featured face swore he was Caucasian, purentee white!

"What are girls like you doing in a place like this?" He looked around, still unsure where he was, though he watched gulls soar on updrafts beyond an open window.

The girls looked at each other and giggled.

"Did you make somebody in authority mad?"

They giggled.

"Did you perhaps refuse Lafitte himself? Is that why they threw you in here?"

They giggled.

"Did you break a law? Kill somebody? Lie? Burn the biscuits?"

They giggled, hugging each other.

"Do you like to fuck?"

They giggled. They looked at each other and both nodded simultaneously, giggling. He laughed, reaching for

28

them. "How do you feel about a *ménage à trois?*"

He felt them quivering with delight and they pressed closer. He felt their hands meet at his crotch. He wanted to laugh! Obviously, while he'd been unconscious, they had inspected him, and now they couldn't wait to prove to themselves their eyes had not deceived them. He heard their pleased little gasps. He closed his hands on their breasts. At his right hand, the breast was more than he could hold, squeezing between his fingers. On his left, he felt a firm young grapefruit. How delightful! What was more pleasant than variety served on the same menu!

He turned his head to the right and kissed the full upturned lips. She opened her mouth, parted her teeth, took his tongue as deeply as he could thrust it, sucking at it hungrily. They came up gasping for breath. "I'm Nicole," she whispered.

"Nicole," he repeated.

She shivered with delight as his fingers fondled her and she nodded again, licking at her lips with the tip of her tongue.

Nicole was in her late teens, and still maturing. One could almost sense the conflicts between the extraordinary bulge of her high-standing swollen mammaries and the fabric that covered them. Her lips gleamed, the saucy amoral red of a whorehouse lamp, and her eyes were the same golden brown as the high-piled curls crowning her shapely head. Except for her breasts and hips, Nicole was slender, but her thighs were ample, curving downward to smoothly sculpted calves and ankles.

The minx squirming on his left tightened her fingers on him, digging in her nails as if to remind him of her presence. In retaliation, he squeezed her breast until she gasped aloud in anguished delight. He turned reluctantly from Nicole's lush beauty and looked down at his other partner.

"I'm Zilla." She turned up her face, eyes closing like a sleepy child's, mouth parted to receive his probing tongue and the fierce pressure of his lips. It had been a long sea voyage and he did not disappoint Zilla, nor keep her waiting. He felt her body wracked with a delicious shudder, and her hips worked almost involuntarily against the cement hardness at his muscular thigh.

"Zilla . . . you're a minx, aren't you, Zilla?"

"Does that mean I'm crazy for it?"

"That's what it means."

She whipped her hips, breathless, her cheeks flushed.

Jeff bowed over her pixy face, letting his tongue linger after he withdrew from thrusting deeply into her throat. He licked slowly at her inner lips until she quivered helplessly.

Jeff grinned. Nicole was the beauty, with those elegant breasts and high-piled hair, but little Zilla was the sexpot, the unquenchably thirsty. She was pretty, impish, with turned-up nose, wide-lipped mouth, slanted eyes, and soft tea-rose skin. Possibly fifteen, or at the most sixteen, she wore her dark brown hair cropped close about her face. Her dress, of some fragile flowered fabric, had nothing beneath it. Her femininity was outlined, fevered, against his thighbone.

"Why are you girls in this place?" he said.

"For you." Zilla smiled and lowered her eyes as if afraid to let him read the raw desire smoking deep in their brown depths.

Neither of the girls had released her locked grip on him. Excitement coursed upward through him. It was delightful having two eager hands vying for possession. Despite his rage against You, the sense of outrage at the treatment meted out to him, his need to confront Lafitte, this was going to be one of the most pleasurable imprisonments in recorded history. He felt himself engorging with blood, bristling against the tightness of his trousers.

Pressed against him, Zilla worked his belt buckle loose and Nicole jerked open his fly. His towering erection flared into view like a falchion unsheathed. Both girls drew in their breath, held it. They knelt forward, gazing raptly at the colossus, clinging to it jealously.

Zilla, the minx, pounced upon it first. Wild because she had been outmaneuvered, Nicole cried out like a wildcat. She grabbed Zilla's chopped hair in her fist, trying to pull her away.

Jeff laughed, fondling them. "Don't fight. There's enough for both of you."

"There's too much," Nicole gasped. "But I don't care. I want it first. I've got to have it . . . now."

Nicole and Zilla lost no time in extricating themselves from the restraints of peasant dresses. They were naked underneath those brightly printed shifts. Their breasts, the taut melons and the ripening young fruit, were four globes promising a world of varied pleasures, each crowned with a bright ruby.

Jeff laughed aloud. They had turned an alcoholic loose in a winery!

They came to him, unself-conscious as does in their nakedness. Nicole, her face faintly contorted with her rising passion, lay back, reaching for Jeff. "Do it, do it, do it," she whispered in frantic urgency.

Jeff hesitated, wondering what the minx Zilla would do if he turned away from her. He dropped his tight-fitting trousers and stepped out of them. Both girls waited but he kept on his shirt. Not even these sex-wild little animals would share his deadly secret.

He knelt before Nicole. Breathing wildly, Zilla caught him in one hand and guided him into the other girl.

Jeff grinned. This kind of service could be habit forming. He reached over and pushed his hand between Zilla's thighs. He found her burning hot.

The girl beneath him pumped frantically, crying out meaningless words and chewing at her lips. Her large breasts quivered. He became aware that Zilla had pressed herself up under him, driving him frantic with her tongue. But when her nervous hands strayed over his hips to thrust his shirt aside, he jerked his head up and spoke savagely across his shoulder. "Don't do that! Leave my shirt alone."

He felt Zilla tremble. Damn it! Those weals criss-crossing his back were his guarded secret. He had stayed alive to this moment because he trusted no one, not even

31

the most excited female. Often, women pleaded for his total nakedness to match their own, but he had been obdurate, and under his stallion's servicing they had forgotten his strange modesty.

Nicole cried out, shivering as she reached a climax. She sagged under him. He lifted himself and Zilla slid into place. She was quickly wracked by orgasms, but kept pumping her hips, locking her ankles about him.

Watching them drove Nicole wild. She lay on her back, her legs wide, playing with herself, her fingers whirling madly. Seeing Nicole's helpless excitement roused Zilla, and she flogged her hips against Jeff until they both sagged, trembling, clinging to each other.

Jeff fell away from her but Zilla was not content. If one girl playing with herself excited him, two girls playing with each other would be a show to fascinate him. It was. Zilla began by nursing Nicole's large breasts until both girls were quivering. Then, slowly, Zilla drew patterns with her tongue across Nicole's rounded belly and downward to her thighs. Jeff found himself erect and bristling and he reached for Zilla.

Jeff wanted to laugh—or weep! This *ménage à trois* would have been farcical had it not been so totally exhausting. He was being figuratively and literally whipsawed between these two delightful little marauders.

Nicole was quickly spent but even more quickly renewed and driven to rampant rapture by everything Zilla did—to her, to herself, to Jeff, to both of them. Nicole would sag, sexually destroyed after only a few strokes. She left him in the worst kind of lurch, rising swiftly to a climax that left her trembling, sweated, and, she swore, sated. But Zilla's lascivious activities quickly restored Nicole's cravings and she was grabbing for Jeff again—only to be too swiftly transported beyond endurance and into new and final agonies of exhaustion.

His hand closed between Zilla's thighs. The minx Zilla amazed him. Her indefatigability, her tenacity, her ability to prolong every coupling astounded Jeff and threatened to annihilate him. Zilla was inventive, creative, insatiable.

This was fascinating; but her avidity continually renewed and refreshed Nicole, and Nicole's brief but debilitating flings whet Zilla's ravenous appetites beyond control. Zilla knew every trick to rouse him once more when he'd have sworn the camel was dead.

Finally, Nicole rolled away, turned her back, and was almost instantly asleep, breathing deeply, exhaustedly, through parted lips. Looking at her and having already performed far past his best previous efforts, Jeff envied her. To sleep! Perchance to dream!

But Zilla remained overheated, reaching for him in breathless greed. She cried out, kissing him, "Never have I had—or even beheld!—one so lovely, so huge, so—so rock hard! I must enjoy it while I can—in every way I can! You do not know the lack in so many men—the things one must do, simply to keep them erect enough to use at all."

She pushed him down into a cane-backed straight chair and knelt between his knees. She came down upon him at last and writhed her hips, content to keep him sheathed inside her indefinitely. As she pumped, she watched the battered cross on the gold chain about his neck bounce violently—a pendulum gone out of control.

Zilla caught the little diamond-encrusted pendant in her fingers without missing a beat of her hips. The talisman was badly bent, misshapen, but he wore it as proudly as when the widow Helen Latimer had given it to him—in lyrical gratitude for his favors.

"Where did you get this?" Zilla whispered.

He grinned. "For service—beyond the call of duty."

"Why is it so battered?"

"It's a long story," Jeff told her, breathless, "and not the long story you're interested in."

Smiling, Zilla kissed him and he resumed his pistonlike stroking of her slender body upon his. Through his mind raced the memory of the way Helen Latimer had written the letter which had introduced him to Dominique You—that bastard who until recently had been his most-trusted friend. Then she'd insisted that a letter—the one that had changed his life—was too little payment for the excessive delight he'd given her. She'd reached into the bodice of her dress, dipping into that mellow, sweet-scented cleavage, fumbling for a moment until her fingers drew out the fine chain of gold, upon which hung this gold cross of intricate workmanship, set with small diamonds. She'd unclasped the chain and cross and placed them in his hand, the metal still excitingly warm from her voluptuous body. She'd called the gift a talisman, saying it would always bring him good luck and should serve to remind him of her. She had circled the chain about his neck, unbuttoned his shirt collar, and tucked the cross inside against his chest. He felt its warmth from her overheated body against his own skin.

Recalling Helen's insatiable desires—her willingness to do anything that might rouse and gratify him—replenished Jeff. He caught Zilla's hips, working her faster. He watched her face go pale, her lips part, a bright ecstasy flare in her eyes.

He felt her rising to a fevered orgasm, but he himself was beat. He was a stud who had often sold his favors to women, grateful women who never left him unsatisfied. But he'd never found himself in the amorous clutches of such an insatiable little vixen as Zilla.

Despite the pain in his body he continued to respond to Zilla's covetous lovemaking until, in incredible savagery, she battered herself uncontrollably upon him, demented by unendurable delight. She gasped, digging her finger-nails into his shoulders. She sank her teeth into his throat, and then, like a hurricane force suddenly spent, terrible quiet followed her destructive frenzy. She fell away from him, staggered to the bed, and sank upon it beside Nicole. In seconds she was snoring contentedly.

Jeff grinned tiredly. His record remained intact. He'd never left a lady less than totally satisfied. There, sprawled on that bed, lay two young girls who were completely exhausted. He felt a surge of pride, though the backs of his legs quivered and he was afraid to attempt to stand up at the moment—even when he heard shouting and violently pitched voices outside his window. He was beat but proud of himself. Why shouldn't he be proud of that with which nature had endowed him, and which he had learned to use to its ultimate value? Maybe, in its way, it had been intended to balance the evil brands scarring his back and the faint but telltale markings of Negroid blood across his flat belly. Anyhow, he was proud of his manhood and of his prowess. Goddamn proud!

He looked down at himself, limp, bruised, and discolored. He laughed. "You're a heller," he said. "That's what you are—a heller."

CHAPTER III

Jean Lafitte stared at the cold-eyed man standing across his desk from him. Lafitte's mouth twisted into a bitter smile, as if he were sucking a lemon. "And what do you propose to do with M'sieur Carson—if I should agree to help you find him?"

Baxter Simon hitched his jacket up on his shoulders. For almost the first time in his entire life, the slave breeder was less than comfortable, less than totally self-assured. He accepted without question his exalted position among all men; he was accustomed to being treated with respect by white men, and obeyed instantly and without delay by black. But it was clear to him that he had entered a strange, exotic world, unlike anything he had ever known. He forced his chilled tone to match his host's. "Well,

Mr. Lafitte, it's real simple what I plans to do with that friggin' runaway nigger once I catch him. . . . I'm going to de-cod him, suh. That's what I'm aiming to do first. You castrate a bad nigger, he stops runnin'—'cause he's got nothing to run to anymore. I'm plain goin' to cut off that nigger's balls."

"That's certainly plain enough." Lafitte gazed up at his uninvited guest from beneath heavy black lashes, a hooded look that concealed all his own thoughts and emotions. Lafitte sat back in his swivel chair—the kind invented by old Thomas Jefferson, he'd been told. His curly black hair wavered in the breeze from a ceiling fan operated by a naked black boy in a corner.

Lafitte compressed his dark lips and studied Baxter Simon under veiled eyelids, appraising him. His first impression was one of stomach-churning hatred. Any man who came charging into Barataria Bay making demands upon Lafitte was already in danger. This man Baxter had compounded the unforgivable by arming himself, bringing a squad of red-coated state militia from the governor's office and a detail that included the high-sheriff of the parish. To come in here uninvited was intolerable, to display strength and political power was outrageous. Lafitte was outraged, but no one could have guessed it from his quiet tone and calm manner.

One might have thought Lafitte a most congenial host, attentive, courteous, and genial to a fault, unless one read the truth from the exaggerated politeness in his cold voice. Lafitte was a rugged, virile man, toughtened by the brine of salt spray in every trade lane of all the oceans. Although he was only of average height, his sturdy build and wide shoulders made him imposing. His dark hair, silvered at the ears and temples, curled close to his head in ringlets. He was clean shaven but a blue shadow lay along his tight, squared jaw. A small, ill-healed scar under his left eye pulled his face into a permanent devil-take-you expression. His deep black eyes, under thick lashes, were sharp, watchful, keenly alert. One shuddered to think of Lafitte as an enemy.

"As for your helping me find Jeff Carson—or Bricktop, since that's the black stud's real and only name—I don't ask that. I don't even ask for your permission, suh. I have here a warrant from the highest court in this here state, giving me the right to search," Baxter Simon said.

Now Lafitte leaned forward bracing himself against his desk. He peered up at Baxter Simon. Lafitte had encountered powerful, deadly, and conscienceless enemies in his life, but he found the slave breeder something new in his experience. There were rights in Baxter Simon's world, obviously; but just as obviously, all rights accrued to Baxter Simon. The man was second- or third-generation land and slave owner. He accepted his personal superiority as divinely ordained. Heavy-shouldered, barrel-chested, in his middle thirties, Simon was handsome in a hard, disciplined way. Travel-weary and driven by obsessive hatred for his escaped slave, Simon stood straight, booted legs placed solidly apart. His belly was as flat as that of a man many years younger, and he looked as if he'd been born a self-reliant aristocrat, square jawed, with tilted left brow expressing his arrogant disdain for lesser human beings, which included most of the human race, and for all blacks, whom he considered not human at all. He had unyielding brown eyes, strongly hewn features, and a wide downturned mouth. His dark hair was brushed back across his high forehead and trimmed along his collar. His body was tempered by rough work and long hours in the saddle. He was a man most people found imposing and somewhat intimidating. Lafitte let Simon's ringing challenge die in the quiet, cool room, and when he spoke, his own voice was more modulated than ever. "I advise you to forget the warrant, sir—"

"That warrant came through intervention of the governor himself. It is backed by the strength and power of the state of Louisiana."

"Yes. Well, let me say this, sir. If you thrust that warrant toward me one more time, I shall rip it to shreds and stuff them singly up your asshole. Is that clear enough?"

37

Baxter Simon retreated a step under the impact of the pirate's softly murmured words. He felt as if Lafitte had struck him across the face. Yet Lafitte seemed to relax in the deep chair, which bore the ornately carved initial *L* on its back. Another man might have apologized, remembered suddenly a previous engagement elsewhere, or turned and fled. Simon was a driven man and he recovered quickly. "I ain't *askin'* anything of you anyway, Mr. Lafitte. If you'll be kind enough to turn over to me my property, I'll get back upriver to N'aw 'Leans."

"You have come in here making charges, demands, waving some sort of warrant. But I have yet to be shown that I have any property that belongs to you."

Simon's voice quivered with suppressed rage. "I know it is ludicrouslike talkin' to you about stolen niggers— I know you make your millions off stolen niggers. That's why I brought this here warrant." He kept it at his side. "The nigger Bricktop—callin' hisself Jeff Carson—is here. He is my property, and there is a penalty of fine and imprisonment for harboring fugitive slaves. I bring that to your attention because I have not come here without knowin' who you are, what you do, and how you deal. I can perhaps put us on more equal footing by telling you the governor himself has agreed to enforce the law on harboring slaves—unless you do return my property to me forthwith."

Lafitte nodded as if considering this. "How very interesting."

"Listen to me, Lafitte. I know you're a hero to these Cajuns and Creoles down here. They think you helped save the nation in the War of 1812. Hell, we both know if you did, it was for the personal profit and enrichment of Jean Lafitte, and talk of patriotism is so much shit."

That self-mocking smile again lightened Lafitte's face. "You don't hold me in the highest regard, eh?"

"Let's say I know who you are, what you are. This appearance of respectability you're wrapping yourself in lately don't change my opinion one whit."

"Then why did you think you could come in here and

walk out with a valuable Negro—if I admit for sake of argument he is here?"

Baxter Simon managed to suppress his rage and keep his voice level. "I told you why. They's a law against harboring fugitive slaves. They also happens to be a law callin' for hanging for nigger stealing. . . . I intend only to invoke the first one, but by God, I'll see you in prison."

Lafitte exhaled. "There are people who just won't let you escape your past, will they?" he inquired, almost plaintively. But his dark fingers opened and closed on the steel letter opener on his desktop.

The fact that he owned a blacksmith shop on St. Philip Street near the cathedral in New Orleans, and a large merchandise store on Royal Street with the finest stock in the country did not impress Baxter Simon.

Like many others, Simon regarded him as a pirate. But Lafitte saw that his greatest crime—as far as the slave breeder Baxter Simon was concerned—lay in his traffic in slaves. Since Congress had passed a law forbidding further importation of slaves into the United States, Lafitte's greatest profit now came from his selling of contraband Negro slaves who had been confiscated from slavers plying the sea lanes from Africa to Havana. Business was so good, the traffic in slaves so brisk, that Lafitte was even *buying* slaves from barracoons in Cuba and making up to $800 profit each at New Orleans vendues.

He'd found plantations of the South avid for slaves, and they didn't care where they got them. It was becoming daily more difficult to supply the market, and Lafitte was making more money selling slaves than he'd ever made in piracy or in merchandising fine laces, satins, and other European goods which passed through Barataria to his fine shop on Royal Street.

Lafitte smiled, a chilled twisting of his mouth. "You are truly obsessed to have this slave back, aren't you, Mr. Simon?"

"He's my property. A man ain't successful raisin' slaves for the *legitimate* slave markets if he lets runners get away from him. He has to bring them back. Has to make 'zamples of runners."

"And too, this little trip to Barataria is your opportunity to put a crimp in my tail, isn't it? I'm a rival of yours, eh? That also eats your entrails, eh?"

Simon shrugged. "I can live with your rivalry. Don't say I approve. It takes me up to fifteen, sixteen years of risk and expense to bring my coffle to vendue. It galls me to get there and find my niggers up against niggers that you took from some slave ship, stole, got free, or bought a few weeks earlier in Cuba for maybe $100 each. That there kind of competition is unfair, but it's just about what a man might anticipate from a *pirate*."

Now Lafitte laughed. "You don't get the sense that this is the pot calling the kettle black, Simon? For hell's sake, we're both *slave* traders!"

"I raise slaves. Breed 'em. Breed the best grades. Fancies. I don't steal 'em off slave ships."

"Hell, man, you're overlooking the only important fact —we both deal in human beings, in enslaved men, women, and children."

Simon winced and peered at Lafitte with a new contempt. "Nothin' wrong with dealing in niggers—any more than it's wrong to sell horses, cattle, sheep, hogs, or any other animals. It'd take a man like you to think of *niggers* as *human* beings."

"A man like me?" said the soft voice.

"A nigger ain't human. He's nothin' but an animal even if'n he's got a lot of human blood in him. Even as much as this Bricktop that you calls Carson. Don't make a fuckin' bit of difference how much human blood a nigger's got. He kin be white as me. Or you. White as Jeff Carson. But if'n he's got one drop of nigger blood, he's a nigger— a animal. Kin sell the whitest mustee just the same as the blackest *bozal* straight off the boat from Africa. An' sellin' Bricktop Jeff Carson is just what I aim to—an' soon as I cut his balls off."

"You don't believe he's earned his freedom?"

"Earned? What earned? He's a nigger! That sure hell

40

ain't goin' to change, no matter what. An' he's my slave for life—less'n I sells him, or sets him free through manumission, which I ain't nevah gonna do. They ain't *no way* a black can *earn* his freedom, or *earn* anything else. He's born a slave, and he dies a slave. That's God's way. You can't make a friend of any nigger, but he can be a pet—same as a horse or a dog can. But *nothin'* ain't gonna make 'em human. That son of a bitch Bricktop has run free long enough, and I means to take him back to Willow Oaks—"

"And cut his balls off."

"Yes, suh. For a start."

"And why do you feel you can charge in here and demand that I turn over to you a man I believe to be white?" Lafitte sat back in the chair, peering up at Baxter. If Simon had been more sensitive, he might have seen the way the privateer's cheeks had grayed out, grown pallid, though the voice remained cordial, if tauntingly chilled and chilling.

"Because, goddamn it, Bricktop is a nigger. And he's *my* nigger!"

"Barataria happens to be my province, sir."

Simon straightened, outraged. "I am a landowner. A breeder of fine-quality slaves. A respected citizen. I have a right to go anywhere to hunt me down my own fuckin' renegade niggers."

"Almost anywhere." Lafitte tapped his desk with the steel letter opener.

"I came, law-abiding, with a warrant. I came with the law on my side."

"That's where you made your gravest error, sir. Perhaps you would have done well to have come alone— as one gentleman dealing with another."

Color flushed up under Bax Simon's tanned cheeks. His dark eyes hardened. "A gentleman? Alone? To deal with the cutthroat pirate Jean Lafitte?"

Lafitte shrugged. "Even so. It has not yet profited you a great deal to storm in here as you have. I am making every effort to remain a cordial host. Words—like cutthroat, even pirate—make it difficult."

"If you're not a pirate, I apologize," Simon said with a sardonic smile.

"I assure you, we operate legitimately under letters of marque from the Republic of Cartagena. My trading in slaves is as legitimate, and equally as morally indefensible as yours."

"Then, as one *businessman* to another, may I plead with you to turn my property over to me so that I may start back across the bayous? It's a long trip to Carthage, Mississippi. You are hiding my property. But I am willing to forget every legal technicality if I am returned my property."

"It's not that simple, sir. The Jeff Carson who came here—highly recommended by a most-respected gentlewoman, the owner of Poinciana plantation, Mrs. Helen Latimer—that Jeff Carson has been accepted as a white man. There's been no question about his race—"

"Hell. There'd be no question now. Bring him out. We'll strip off his shirt and I'll show you my brand. He's branded with the letters *W.O.*—Willow Oaks. That means he's a Willow Oaks animal. That brand means I had to brand him because he's a runner. And that all means he's a fuckin' nigger—and he ain't no human."

"That's very interesting."

"You goddamn right it's interesting. I can see how you might be feelin' softhearted toward this fellow callin' hisself Jeff Carson. You ain't the first people that has been fooled by him. He was almost married to a lovely lady up at The Georgics plantation—a Miss Minerva George—until I turned up and showed them the brand on my nigger Bricktop's back."

"You had him in your hand, and you let him get away?"

"Somebody loosed his spancels and his shackles. He stole a horse and he run. That's almost two years ago. I tracked him to a shack outside New Orleans. Had him trapped. But I killed his nigger doxy, and he got away again. But this time I know he's here, and I mean to claim my nigger."

Lafitte stood up, lithe as a puma, and as dangerous. He stretched. "You make a most forceful case."

"You sure hell I do. Right is on my side."

"That's always most convenient, to have right and God on your side. Why don't we walk down to the docks? My lieutenants are there. Perhaps we can deal with your problem in a manner satisfactory all around."

Baxter Simon grunted, laughing in a self-satisfied way. "That's better. Figured you'd see it my way." He slapped his planter's hat atop his head.

Lafitte merely bowed, indicating the door with his head. As they left the room, Lafitte spoke to the naked slave in the corner. "Keep that fan stirring the air, Elijah. I want this room as cool as it is right now when I get back."

On the docks, Lafitte introduced Baxter Simon to Captain Dominique You, to René Beluche, and to Captain Correau, who headed the small fleet of racing sloops that patrolled the bay at speeds of up to forty miles an hour.

"Mr. Simon swears he can prove that our young lieutenant Jeff Carson is a Negro named Bricktop. A slave owned by Mr. Simon of Willow Oaks plantation. He demands that we turn Jeff Carson over to him. He says he has the strength of the law, the power of right, and the blessing of God almighty on his side. How do you feel, should we turn Jeff over to Mr. Simon?"

Captain You, Beluche, and Correau each shook their heads silently and negatively. Lafitte smiled and shrugged. He started away, then turned and spoke over his shoulder to Correau. "Keelhaul the son of a bitch," Lafitte said.

CHAPTER IV

From where Jeff stood at the double windows—naked except for cotton undershirt and gold cross—he could see the village, the entrance to Lafitte's red-brick chalet, the small cottage where he had shacked-in with Gretchen, the docks, crowded with lawmen and freebooters, the dark bay, the bayous, and the open sea beyond.

He'd been astonished at first to find himself in an upper-floor room of the watchtower. Obviously this was a room where the lookouts sacked out between watches. At the moment, it was his prison. He grinned crookedly. He had done all in his power to make it a memorable imprisonment—something Nicole and Zilla could tell their grandchildren.

He'd found out it was a prison quickly. With Nicole and Zilla sprawled in exhausted sleep across the bed, he'd gotten up on shaky legs, walking for a moment like a newborn calf. He inspected the room, glanced out the window, realizing he was near the top of the watchtower. From up here, he could look down on the airborne sea birds, the soaring gulls, the diving pelicans, the graceful heron, the flighty little terns.

Knowing where he had been thrown—like a croker sack of potatoes—didn't improve his disposition or lessen his raging need to get back at Dominique You. In fact, as soon as he determined where he was, his next thought was to find a way out, the quickest escape possible.

Strengthened by his rage, he crossed the room, walking more steadily—as if the floor were the rolling deck and the watchtower a storm-tossed vessel on the high seas.

He caught the doorknob and rattled it. He earned instant, if less than promising, response. He heard the butt of a gun clatter on the flooring beyond the bolted door, the pound of heavy boots. A man's voice said, "What do you want?"

"I want to get out of here."

A snarl of laughter stung him through the doorway. "What's the matter? Two wenches too much for you?"

"They're both sleeping," Jeff said in a mild tone. A brief, incredulous silence ensued. Jeff said, "Come on, let me out of here."

"You get out, stud, when M'sieur Jean Lafitte say you get out."

Jeff swore, mentioning Lafitte's antecedents most unflatteringly, and turned from the door, frustrated and raging. Shouts, rising on the wind from the docks, brought him striding back to the windows, where he stood staring down at the sun-bleached street.

At first, it seemed the crowd had increased down there, but then he saw that the men had simply knotted in closer. He saw why. Jean Lafitte himself was on the pier, magnet drawing all attention.

Jeff caught his breath. The man with Lafitte was Baxter Simon. His heart lurched. Though Lafitte had always treated him fairly, his first thought was of betrayal. The privateer had betrayed him.

Jeff shuddered involuntarily, his whole body wracked with chill. If Lafitte refused to return him to Baxter Simon, wouldn't he still end up on a New Orleans auction block, knocked down to the highest bidder? Jean Lafitte was no sentimentalist. Money was the only thing that made Lafitte cry. Mammon was his only god. Somehow, he had to get out of here. Never again would he be a slave. He would die first.

Staring at Baxter Simon's broad back, the arrogant

set of his head, brought back vividly to Jeff all the fearful images of the slave cabins, slave food, slave existence, and the denial of all human dignity to the blacks of Willow Oaks. He remembered the night Simon had branded him; the same night he'd vowed to run one more time, and to keep running until he died. Now it was time to run again.

Raging inwardly, Jeff glanced over his shoulder at the two naked women sleeping in exhausted bliss on the rumpled bed. So that was why Lafitte had You knock him unconscious and transport him to the top of the watchtower. The doors and stairs were barred by men with guns. It was almost a hundred feet straight down if he tried to go out the window. But the clever Lafitte and You had it all figured out, eh? Give the redheaded mustee a couple of women to play with when he wakes up and he'll be right there the next time you go looking for him. Damn their eyes! They were right about him of course. He was a stud first—a nigger and fugitive slave next—and anytime you set a hair trap for the redhead, you knew you had your quarry. At that moment Jeff wasn't sure whether he hated Lafitte for his cleverness, or himself for what might yet prove to be a fatal weakness.

He swore. The worst of it was that, even realizing what a predicament he was in, he found himself glancing toward Nicole's nudity, at Zilla's tea-rose flesh, and something stirred deep in his loins. For hell's sake! How could he even think about pestering wenches at a moment like this?

He thrust the girls from his mind. He had to think. Merely to go over in his mind that he was trapped in what might be terminal trouble wouldn't do it. He had to figure a way out of here, and then a way out of Barataria Village, across the bayous, and up sixty miles of swampy river. . . . Oh, hell, impossible! And worst of all, when he ran this time, he'd no longer have only Baxter Simon on his tail, Jean Lafitte would be hunting him down too. He could think of no rat hole on earth deep enough to burrow into where Lafitte's men wouldn't ferret him out if they wanted to.

He sweated. He stared down at the crowd on the pier. Frowning, he saw Lafitte start away from Simon, pause, and say something across his shoulder. It was too far away. Jeff couldn't hear the words, but he did hear the rousing shout that went up from the sea marauders. This sure hell bode ill for somebody—nothing but evil evoked such spontaneous response from those hellions.

He watched Lafitte smile grimly and then stride away, his shadow bouncing ahead of him as he crossed the cobbles toward his chalet.

The shouting brought Jeff's gaze back to the men on the dock. Baxter Simon was suddenly surrounded by a knot of Lafitte's men. The militia and sheriff's deputies who'd accompanied Simon here remained taut, silent, and unmoving.

Stunned and disbelieving, Jeff watched the freebooters rough Baxter Simon up. The big slave breeder fought back, but only briefly. He was no match in dirty fighting for the weakest of Lafitte's sea rats.

Jeff watched as Simon's wrists were secured behind him, his ankles tied together. Simon yelled protests until somebody snatched Simon's own sweated bandana from his pocket and crammed it into Simon's mouth. Simon tried to spit it out but it was swiftly secured with line. The gag line was so tautly wound that it pulled Simon's mouth and lower jaw awry. But Simon was effectively silenced.

So entranced was Jeff with what was happening down there on the sun-seared pier, he was unaware that the two girls had wakened and were whispering and giggling together on the bed behind him. Their voices brushed at his consciousness like flies, darting in and out, but he went on staring out of the window.

On the pier, three men caught Simon as if he were a pine log, and with Captain Correau leading the way, they toted him off the pier into one of the racing sloops. The men tied a rope about Simon's waist and secured the other end to a deck cleat in the stern of the sloop.

Jeff trembled involuntarily, suddenly aware of the two girls on their knees to him. Nicole pressed her full-bosomed body between him and the wall. But it was the little fox Zilla who brought Jeff's attention zinging back from the docks and wholly within this tower room. She wrapped her arms about his legs, her hot little tongue darting.

Sweated, Jeff fought to keep his mind and his eyes on that strange scene unfolding in the bay beneath him, but even as the sloop shoved away from the pier, with Simon Baxter poised defiantly astern, he admitted he was waging a losing battle. His breath quickened and he found his hands clutching Zilla's short-cropped hair. With his other hand he cupped Nicole's head at its crown and forced her closer.

Damn him! No matter what peril threatened, he was never too busy to put everything else aside to mount some woman—and two women exercising all their charms and tricks upon him made it doubly difficult to resist! He had been so certain that he was finally and completely spent, whipped by all the wonders these two succubi had performed upon him on that bed, but he had the certain sense now that he was never going to tire of what these two minxes were capable of doing to him. He did glance out the window, saw the sloop's sails snap as they caught and bellied out with the breeze. But he didn't really see anything clearly out there. He stared through an occluding haze, his eyes glazed by his own smoking emotions. His life lay on the line and yet he was thinking that he was going to have these two women one more time. His need was almost as great as his jeopardy. Hell, the pagan Romans were probably right—the threat of death in the arena was the most distracting aphrodisiac! His own life hung precariously in the balance, yet never had he wanted two women more.

Zilla thrust herself upward against him, her lips nuzzling, driving him out of his mind.

"Come back to bed," Nicole whispered, staring up at

him from her knees. Her eyes were reddened, her lips swollen.

He shook his head. "I've—got to see—what's going on down there."

Nicole kissed him, her tongue skimming. "We can't do what we want to do for you—not here. We must have the bed."

They caught his hands, leading him toward the bed. He did not resist. He could not. He cursed himself but admitted the truth: one woman or another was always going to be more important to him than his own life. What a way to die. . . .

Baxter Simon stared in horror at the dark waters of Barataria Bay fleeing past in the wake of the brightly polished racing sloop. The lithe craft skimmed across the water like a fishing snipe. He heard the crew yelling and talking behind him but he did not turn to look at them.

Simon's attention was turned totally inward. He boiled with hatred, with outrage—against the lawmen who had stood idly by while he was attacked and trussed up like an animal, as much as against Lafitte, who had ordered this unconscionable act, and the brigands who carried out Lafitte's bidding. Damn them all. He wasn't dead yet, and as long as he lived he would remember in rage and violent need for reparation, and they would pay. Somehow they would pay for this treachery.

Suddenly, Simon felt himself caught from behind by two sailors. They snagged his bound arms, half lifting him. He shook his head furiously, his dark eyes murderous. He was unable to speak. But it would not have mattered. They would not have listened.

He heard Correau yell from behind him. "Heave. Heave the son of a bitch."

The sailors lifted Simon and hurled him over the stern of the sloop. He felt himself sailing through spray and then he struck. The water was harder than a brick pavement. The long rope played out and he spun and twisted

49

like a lure on a fish line. Abruptly, the rope caught, and he felt as if his legs were being yanked off at the knees.

He spun, twisting, riding against the savage run of the sloop's wake. He tried to keep his head up. He gasped for air every time his head cleared the foaming water. He cursed helplessly and silently against the pressure of the soaked bandana which was being forced down his throat. He tried to push it back with his tongue aware that it was going to choke him to death.

The sloop slowed as his weight played against it initially, but then it picked up speed, riding across the top of the water gracefully, tipped so far that the sail almost skimmed the surface.

Simon's head began to spin as his body was being spun on the end of the line. The sky and water changed places. He was no longer conscious of when his head was above the water or below it. He sucked water into his nose. He felt himself choking, but mostly he choked on his own choler. God help these bastards if he lived through this.

It seemed to go on forever. He was dragged in a wide sweeping circle inside the bay. It seemed to Simon they were trying to drown him. Goddamn them! If they had good sense, they would drag him until he was drowned. He couldn't live with the rage flaming inside him, and he knew damn well they couldn't. His last rational thought was of hatred, of vengeance.

He sank into terror as the water filled his nostrils, burned his eyes, weighed down his clothing. He was only vaguely aware of being played in at the end of the line like some giant tarpon. He was dragged feet first over the sloop's stern and thrown prostrate on the deck. Somebody untied the line and jerked the sodden bandana from his mouth.

Simon lay unmoving. Water spewed from his throat, leaked from his nose, stung his eyes, rolled in salty rivulets from his hair. He shook uncontrollably, but he was not cold, simply overwhelmed with outrage.

He felt the sleek vessel slide into its berth at the pier,

but most of all he heard the spewing of derisive laughter that assaulted him. The freebooters lined the pier staring down at him. Weakly, he lifted his head. In mounting rage, Simon saw that even the lawmen and the red-coated militia men were smiling. Sons of bitches. All of them, sons of bitches.

They got him on his feet and half carried him up to the pier. He was still more than half-drowned, but he forgot his weakness, his illness, and his wetness when he saw Jean Lafitte's sardonically smiling face through a red, occluding cloud of unadulterated hatred. Lafitte watched him with the casual interest one might pay any trophy from the sea.

By some supreme effort of will, Simon straightened and stood unaided. He spat globs of snot and salt water upon the dock at his feet. He raised his salt-reddened eyes and met Lafitte's gaze levelly. "You son of a bitch," he gasped. "You got everything your way—this time . . . but you should have killed me. You son of a bitch, you should have killed me."

"Perhaps next time, *m'sieur*." Lafitte gave Simon a mocking bow.

"You're a thievin', nigger-stealin' murderer, Lafitte," Simon raged, choking on salt water and his own rage. "An' I promise you, an' we meet on neutral ground, I'll gun you down for the swine you are."

"Perhaps. But I see I have failed to teach you a lesson it might have greatly profited you to learn. Maybe your head is made of stone. Maybe you are incapable of learning anything."

"A filthy pirate like you. What could you teach me?"

Lafitte shrugged. "I realize you are an arrogant aristocrat, *m'sieur*. I understand you have lived perhaps forty years believing in your own superiority to other human beings. But if you wish to go on living, you might well have learned this most important lesson of your life."

Simon spat. "And that is?"

"Something you'd better learn well. Heed. When you come into my province, you come on *my* terms, not yours.

51

Rules are my rules. Laws are my laws. If you come again into Jean Lafitte's territory you will come only on Jean Lafitte's terms." He shrugged, bowed again, and gave Simon a chilled smile. "This was simply my warning."

"All right, you thievin' bastard, now hear my warning." Simon's voice shook, but no one was fool enough to think weakness caused its shaking. His salt-reddened eyes blurred with tears, but not a man-jack among them found weakness in his tears of rage. Lafitte's pirates moved in closer, their faces chilled, but Simon was not aware of them, or if aware, unconcerned. The high-sheriff of the parish, M'sieur Bourett, looked ill. His face was gray and pallid. His deputies and the militia had shrunken into an ineffectual knot. If they were thinking anything, it was to pray they got out of here, soon, and alive. Simon was not concerned with them either. They had come in here as his support, swaggering, full of promises about what they would do to back him up in reclaiming his runaway nigger. Well, they were clabber-assed lilies, and to hell with them. He gazed into Lafitte's chilled eyes as if the two of them were alone on the sun-struck dock. "I tell you this, Lafitte. I'll be back. As long as you harbor my nigger here, I'll be back . . . and by Jesus, I'll keep coming back. But you won't take me again like this. You won't take me again."

Lafitte bowed slightly and shook his head. "Ah, well, m'sieur. So be it. A man who refuses to learn from his mistakes is doomed to keep repeating them, eh?" He shrugged. "Meantime, may I wish you—and your friends —a pleasant trip back upriver?"

CHAPTER V

Jeff was wakened roughly by heavy hands grasping his shoulders and shaking him. Exhausted as he was, he came slowly and unwillingly up from deep sleep, remembering his last waking image—the little vixen Zilla pleading for one more pleasuring. She hadn't cared that he was fagged, all she'd wanted was to demonstrate her loving appreciation. Perhaps she had done it. He didn't know. He had pitched into stunned sleep. For some moments now, his eyes opened, he remained disoriented, not even sure where he was. Crimson-tinted sunlight of late afternoon streamed through the panes of the wide window. His flailing arms encountered the heated flesh of his slumbering companions. He turned over, yawned, and stared up into the ugly face of the guard. "Let's go, Carson," the fellow said. "M'sieur Lafitte wants to see you at the Big House."

Jeff sat up, smiling weakly. The sailor spoke to him but was staring in fascination at the delectable bodies of the two naked wenches sprawled asleep beside him.

Jeff hoisted himself up from the bed. He walked unsteadily across to the window and stared down at the streets and quays of the village. The docks were empty, a few pelicans loitered on posts. The *Sainte Teresa* lay at anchor, like a dead lady with sails reefed and her crew absent. There was a faint sense of sadness about the silent vessel.

Jeff felt a release of the tensions that had wound him taut. The flat-bottomed riverboats were gone, and with them the khaki-clad deputies and red-coated state militia. He prayed this meant that Baxter Simon had been sent away too.

"Get your pants on," the guard said. "Lafitte says to move fast. On the double."

Jeff grinned because the guard spoke loudly, hoping to waken one or both of the little foxes. The bulge at the man's crotch showed plainly where his mind was. But neither Nicole nor Zilla stirred. Overwhelmed by fatigue, they lay dead to the world. The guard stood the temptation as long as he could. He reached over and caressed the full globes of Nicole's breasts and pushed his hand between Zilla's thighs. Zilla automatically rolled over on her back, spreading her legs and smiling without even waking up.

Jeff stepped into his pants. He smiled bitterly, thinking of the confrontation with Lafitte ahead of him and, after that, the uncertainty of his future. He buttoned his trousers, buckled his belt. He sat on the bed to pull on his boots. Movement of the mattress brought Zilla awake. At first, the hand on her mons veneris thrilled her, but when she glimpsed the tattooed arm and scarred face above her, she cried out and lunged away as if caught in a nightmare.

Awake, Zilla watched Jeff dress, her eyes stricken, her wide-lipped mouth drawn down. She shook Nicole awake as Jeff buttoned his shirt, stuffing its tails inside his trousers. "Wake up, Nicole. Our stallion is leaving us."

Both girls, their eyes brimming with tears of loss, reached for him. They pleaded with him to come back to them. Jeff shook his head. He was afraid they had been a last supper for the doomed man. He kissed them lightly. "I wouldn't wait up," he said.

The guard went ahead of Jeff on the long winding stairwell down to ground level. When they came out onto the street, Jeff blinked against the sharply stabbing brilliance of the afternoon sun. All breezes had died down; it was hot and humid on the swampy island. Jeff paused, looking around. The village was quiet, with a stunned kind of silence, as if the sun had sucked the last drop of energy from the citizenry. Even the animals drooped, listless in every square of shade. A fat man, naked except for ragged cotton underpants, slept in a big wingback wicker chair on a shaded cottage stoop. A young girl, completely nude, was curled in his arms, sleeping with her head on his shoulder. Anywhere else on earth this might have been a picture of a grandfather and grand-daughter, but Jeff knew it was something else at Barataria.

"Let's move," the guard prodded him. Jeff preceded the armed man up the sun-brazed street from the water-front. They walked in the middle of the rutted road where not even the shade of live oaks protected them. People moved inside most of the houses, but all seemed only semiconscious in the stunning heat of late afternoon. He sighed. Barataria didn't look like much, a rat's nest in the bayous, and yet he'd been happy here. It was over.

Jeff felt his heart slugging faster, assailed by more than a nagging fear that the fantastic dreams he had permitted himself about his future as a slave dealer with the Lafitte organization were fragmented. Hell, nothing lasted. Damn it, he'd worked hard here; he'd given it everything he had, and with René Beluche as his tutor, he was swiftly learning all there was to know about peddling nigger flesh.

He glanced down at his sweated hands. In his right palm the small weals of that branding iron reminded him forcefully of those larger weals burned into his back. He was a nigger. Now that Baxter Simon had been here, there was no doubting that Lafitte knew the truth about him. Had Lafitte sold out to Simon? He doubted this, not because Lafitte was sentimental—he was not. But returning Simon's fugitive promised no profit for Lafitte and Lafitte's life was informed, directed, and channeled by profit.

He shrugged his sweated shirt up on his shoulders. This short walk in the sun, along with the fear and panic, pasted his shirt to his body. If Lafitte knew he was a fugitive slave, he could be sunk lower than the Bartlett Deep. On this trip they'd sailed across that bottomless trough in the Caribbean that extended from the Gulf of Honduras to the Windward Passage between Cuba and Haiti. Old Captain MacFarland had ticked off names of old friends and old ships that had gone to the bottom. "They'll be there, lad, so far down the Angel Gabriel can't even pipe 'em home." Jeff sighed. He himself might as well be at the bottom of that canyon as far as Jean Lafitte was concerned.

Jeff slowed involuntarily and the guard prodded him in the back with the gun barrel. Run, he told himself, and then reason prevailed and he asked himself, run where? There was nowhere to run—the bayous, the river, the open gulf.

He lengthened his stride. He had no hope that Lafitte would accept the fact that he was legally a Negro and suggest they continued as they were. He didn't know Lafitte well, but he knew him better than that. The moment Lafitte saw Jeff Carson as Bricktop the mustee slave, he saw him as a black animal to sell on the auction vendue for a profit. What the hell that he had worked his tail off for Lafitte and his organization. What in hell was loyalty to a pirate? Lafitte's loyalty was to gold, and an extra fancy mustee, heavily hung as Jeff Carson was, would fetch eight to ten thousand dollars in the slave mart. Was that why they had trapped him in the tower with the two foxes, Nicole and Zilla? You had knocked him senseless before he'd learned that Simon was at Barataria. They were certain Jeff wouldn't run as long as he was being entertained by two little sexpots. They'd baited the trap well and he'd lain there contentedly, awaiting his doom.

When they reached the red-brick chalet, the guard stepped aside and nodded toward the front door. Jeff stared up at that wide brass-studded entrance to the Big

House. He sweated, his heart pounding erratically. He banged the heavy brass knocker, breathing as if he'd run a mile. The door was opened almost at once by a black servant in a rust-colored suit. Jeff entered the cool foyer and sat in the straight-backed chair the aged Negro indicated. A nude black boy lay on his back in a corner and slowly lifted and dropped one leg, working the ceiling fan by a light line attached to his ankle.

The old servant hobbled back into the room and bowed toward Jeff. "M'sieur Jean say he aspectin' you, masta suh. Say for you to come right in." The aged man led the way to a half-opened door and held it open until Jeff entered. Then he closed it behind him. Jeff had the sensation of being shut in a cage from which there were no exits, that whatever his life had been to this moment he had shed it and left it all behind him outside this heavy door.

He looked about the dimly lit, fan-cooled room. It was immense and elegantly furnished with the best La-fitte could steal. Costly Persian carpets that had never made it to their legitimate destination, carved and gilded arm chairs from the master craftsmen of France, crystal chandeliers. As imposing as this edifice was from the out-side, its palatial exterior barely hinted at the interior elegance.

Jean Lafitte sat behind a broad, intricately carved mahogany desk. He gazed intently at Jeff but did not get up or extend his hand. He remained seated in the chair with its large *N* ornately carved on its back. Jeff saw that René Beluche and Captain Dominique You were also reclining in deeply upholstered chairs. Dominique was enormous, his shoulders stretching the seams of his coat, his gross weight threatening the ornately carved legs of his chair. He was a man more at home on an open deck of a ship than among dainty furniture and tables decorated with porcelain bric-a-brac. René Beluche was a flat-bellied, youthful tiger of a man. He and Jeff had once shared Helen Latimer in a memorable *ménage à trois* during one of his first nights in Barataria. There was no recollection of shared friendship in the dark, clipped-bearded face. Neither Beluche nor Dominique You offered any greeting.

Lafitte did not invite Jeff to sit down. Jeff's exhausted legs threatened to buckle under him as he went on standing, nervous and taut drawn. But as the three men discussed him and his recently completed mission—talking about him as if he were not even present—Jeff was able to relax slightly. From Lafitte's first words of praise, it was obvious he was pleased with the way Jeff had handled the violent and mentally unstable Morgan Roy.

"Captain MacFarland says our young redhead had Morgan Roy eating out of his hand after the first hour."

"Aye," You agreed. "Said they went in there prepared to fight their way out, maybe losing a dozen men. But they were permitted to load the stolen blacks, take on water, lemons, and provender for the slaves—and then leave peaceably."

"Admirable," said René Beluche.

"Clever to simply tell Morgan Roy his ships could never ply a sea lane in sight of a Lafitte ship without fighting for its life," Lafitte said. "That is masterful diplomacy. Because the other side of the coin is a spirit of cooperation. I wonder if I myself would have thought of that. I think I would not have. I was filled with rage against Morgan Roy when I sent Carson down to Haiti. I expected Roy to fight back—I hoped he would. I meant to go in there and crush him once and for all."

"But we might have lost the *Sainte Teresa*," You pointed out, "if Carson had merely made threats. No man a-sail knows Morgan Roy better than I—and I know him to have a violent, insane temper. If he were an ordinary man trying to live in an ordinary world he'd be behind bars in a madhouse."

"And most of all, MacFarland says, Carson never once let Roy get the fool impression that Lafitte was timid, or afraid to fight for the stolen slaves. They even joked, MacFarland said, that Lafitte had stolen them too. The technicality was—and Carson kept quietly stressing this—

that Lafitte had stolen them first, and Roy's piracy—against pirates—was going to make him suspect wherever his pennants were spotted at sea," You said expansively.

Jeff felt his anger rising. If they were pleased with him, why didn't they include him in their conversation? Why didn't they bother to glance once in a while in his direction? Why in the hell didn't somebody invite him to sit down before he fell flat on his face? Damn them, they were treating him like a *nigger*. His face flushed hot, and his belly went empty. That was the answer. They *were* treating him like a nigger. Yesterday, he had been an equal, and they would have treated him as an equal. Now he was known to be legally Negroid—of no value to the Lafitte organization except as an extra fancy stud on some New Orleans vendue table. His fists tightened, his nails biting into his palms. He wanted to rage at them that he was the same man today as he was when he backed Morgan Roy down in the old pirate's home base. In what way was he different, in what way less intelligent, in what way less worthy of their respect? Damn it, in just one way. There was black blood in his veins—he was a nigger to them. He wanted to smash the prejudice from their faces. But what would this buy him? A quick death and an early grave. He warned himself to go on standing there—as long as his quivering knees would support him. It was far more important to stay alive than to vent his rage against these three men.

At last Lafitte swiveled slightly in his chair and looked up, his black eyes lightened by his cordial smile. "Congratulations, Jeff, on a job well done."

"Our best to you, boy," Beluche said.

"I know you thank me," Jeff said with some sarcasm. "My face still aches where Captain You showed me his appreciation."

The tough men might have turned totally against him at that moment—he *was* black and his tone was insolent—but instead, Lafitte put his curly head back and laughed. "We knew only two ways to keep a stallion like you quiet." He shook his head laughing. "We chose the less violent."

Jeff dared to smile with the buccaneer. "May I say, sir, I deeply appreciate your choice of weapons?"

Lafitte's mouth twisted wryly. "I trust the—uh—dueling was satisfactory?"

"It would be ungallant of me to answer, sire. . . . May I humbly suggest you ask the—uh—ladies?"

Lafitte put his head back laughing again. "Oh, I shall! I shall!"

Beluche spoke with just a tinge of envy edging his friendly voice. "Those two doxies were brand-new merchandise, and Lafitte insisted you have them first—in payment for your services."

Jeff smiled and inclined his head toward the leader of the organization, thanking him.

Lafitte no longer smiled. He said, "I am afraid, Jeff, that particular kindness was almost the very last I shall be—permitted—to show you . . . as much as I personally love and esteem you."

Jeff kept his voice coldly polite. "I am grieved indeed to hear that, sire." He used the exaggerated title of respect in heavy irony.

Lafitte nodded, but did not smile. "So am I. You have been a real asset to our organization. You learned your lessons well. You handled every assignment far better than any of us dared hope you would. . . . I hate to lose you."

"Because Baxter Simon told you I am black?"

Lafitte shrugged. "Because Baxter Simon says so does not make it true. I ask you. Are you a black man?"

Jeff's heart lurched. It was almost as if Lafitte invited him—pleaded with him to deny Simon's allegations. The intimation was that if Jeff called Baxter Simon a liar there would be no further inquiry; he would be accepted at his word.

Jeff drew his gaze across the faces of the three men. He wiped the back of his hand across his mouth. There was even more underlying the implication that his word

60

as a gentleman—a *white* gentleman—would be accepted here. He had often seen in the past two years what befell men who lied to Jean Lafitte. They were destroyed, or they withered as useful arms of the organization because Lafitte never again trusted a man who lied to him once.

His breath quickened. The feeling in this room was that these three men—Lafitte, You, and Beluche, the very upper echelon of the organization—were prepared to accept his denial of his black blood. They would not demand to see the brand marks. If he said he was white, they would take his word. He could go on working under René Beluche, learning until he was *non pareil* among slave traders. He could become rich. One day he might sit in this very council with these men. But his whole future would rest on his lie. Why not? Hadn't he lied to stay alive this long? But staying alive, and trying to deceive the very emperor of thieves were unrelated matters. If he lied now to Lafitte, the privateer would accept his lie—for what it was—but his trust would erode, disappear, and next time there might not be an alternative to death as a way out. And Lafitte had until now been honest with him—he was being honest with him at this moment. No matter what happened, he respected and admired Lafitte, he owed him the truth.

"Legally I am a black, sir," Jeff said.

A stillness settled in the room. Jeff remained staring straight ahead. He did not want to look at Dominique You who had welcomed him and paved his way for a ranking position in the organization. He didn't want to see the expression in the face of René Beluche who had shared Helen Latimer's charms with him through a wild orgiastic night. He did not want to see as much of the emotions as Lafitte would permit his hooded eyes to reveal.

Lafitte stared up at Jeff. He smiled, but it was a cold grin and not meant to be shared. "So. You deceived us?"

"I worked hard. I gave you the best of my body—of my brains. The best I had to offer."

"But you passed yourself as white. You wanted us to believe you were white."

"I let you believe what you wanted. I am white. As white as any of you. I am white."

"You dance along a thin line, my young friend. The blood is what we speak of—and the blood—she is Negro blood, eh?"

Jeff hesitated, then shrugged. "Part of it. I won't lie to you, sir. My mother was an octoroon. A slave—servant for life—of Baxter Simon of Willow Oaks Plantation. May God help me, I know only that my father was a redheaded white man—in a hurry. He didn't even hang around long enough to give me a name."

"But Baxter Simon gave you one, eh? Bricktop? And you are a Willow Oaks slave?"

"No." Jeff held his head rigid, staring straight ahead.

"Baxter Simon says he owns you."

"He says he owns me. But let him prove it."

Lafitte smiled wryly. "By law?"

"By taking me back to Willow Oaks, sir—alive. When he does that, then he has proved he owns me."

Lafitte laughed genuinely and heartily. You and Beluche joined him. Lafitte said, "That's good enough for me. As you boast, your skin is white. But your heart, young rogue—she is black, eh? Blacker even than mine."

Jeff did not try to smile, but at the warm tone of Lafitte's voice, his eyes stung with tears. This was unanticipated kindness.

"Yes," Lafitte said. "You are a young rascal after my own heart. . . . That's why it is so sad to tell you you cannot remain any longer at Barataria."

"Is not my work satisfactory, sir?"

"Excellent, my boy. That's why it grieves me to lose you. But it is not my luxury to be able to do always just what I want to do, eh? I must think first of the organization. What is best for the organization? It is not best to permit you to stay here at Barataria, or yet to allow you to work for us anywhere else."

"May I ask why, sir?"

"Of course. There are many reasons. First, this man Simon—he is a man obsessed where you are concerned. He tried to kill you two years ago outside New Orleans, no? Instead, he killed a young girl you loved, eh?"

"Chloe." Jeff whispered the word, chilled at the memory.

"We could kill Simon. But this would raise a swarm of hornets. He is a man of the landed gentry. With much political support here in Louisiana as well as in Mississippi. As long as you are part of our organization, Simon will hound us. He will harry us, within the law, any way his mind conceives—because he is a maniac on the subject of returning you to Willow Oaks in slave chains. . . . We run a legitimate operation here at Barataria, but I won't have the law snooping around at inconvenient times. This is what Simon is capable of having them do. As far as I am concerned, if you were once Simon's slave, you have more than earned your freedom. He does not see it that way. He never will. For that reason, we must ask you to leave—Barataria and the organization."

Jeff felt his heart slip its moorings. In many ways this was what he'd anticipated, but it was less horrible than being sold on a slave mart vendue.

Still, the regret went deep, and it was bitter. He had been happy and busy and—damn it!—successful, here at Barataria. He had served himself and the organization well. He liked his work. Though he dealt with black slaves in their miserable middle passage, he often forgot he was not entirely white. And he had the fantastic dreams of the wealth possible to him from the commissions on sales he would effect for Lafitte. He liked René Beluche as a man and friend, and he enjoyed working with him. There could be no more dedicated, congenial teacher on the subject of slave flesh in this world. It had been wonderful, too, having a home of his own for the first time—with plump, Nordic Gretchen there to keep him well fed and happily bedded. After two years of René's superb tutelage, he had become an expert judge of slave quality. For the first time in his life, he *belonged* somewhere, he could put down roots. He could stop by René Beluche's on his way to the slave barracoons in the mornings, have coffee and gossip with his good friend. He could go home to Gretchen. Home. God knew, nothing ever lasted.

He bit back the bile. It was doubly evil to be ripped up and thrown out just when he had successfully completed his toughest mission, earned a place of respect and responsibility in the organization. He wanted to fall on his knees and plead for an opportunity to prove his whiteness, his worthiness, his value. But he knew better. These men had once been his friends—they had accepted him as equal. Now he would be talking to them across that unbridgeable gap between white and black. There was no way to communicate across that impassable gorge.

"I am sorry," Lafitte said. "I was prepared to accept your lie that you were white, even when I knew better. But I admire and respect you because you did not lie to me—though the truth costs both of us a great deal."

"And I," René Beluche said. "You were a *bon élève, mon ami*. I shall feel your loss far more than the others."

"I doubt that, René." Dominique You's deep voice had an unaccustomed catch in it. He gazed up at Jeff. "You won my respect, lad—both as a humper of women and as a worker. . . . You are a real man, lad, though you are," his smile was wan, "easy to hit with a right."

Jeff smiled. Tears welled into his eyes. At that moment he forgave Dominique You for smashing him in the face, for any wrongs he might perpetrate against him now or in the future. It had been good to know Dominique, his great and trusted friend.

He moved his gaze to Lafitte who toyed with the steel letter opener on his desk. Ironic that now he was parting from Lafitte because he was a Negro. When they'd first met, Lafitte's leading question had concerned blacks. "Tell me, Jeff," Lafitte had said that day, "what do you know about niggers?" Well, he had delivered an answer from whole cloth that day, but now Lafitte knew the truth.

The brand weals burned and throbbed on his back as if suddenly infected and fevered. He hoped his face had not flushed red to match his hair. He stared at the floor to conceal the rage and disappointment smoldering in his eyes. He knew about niggers because he was a white nigger. A mustee. Hell, if he'd lied to them, they never would have found out the truth. He was smarter than the smartest white man he'd ever met. What did the whites say about a mustee? Just enough human blood to make him tricky and untrustworthy. Well, that was the kind of mustee he was, damn it. The smart kind. Smart enough to have fooled them. One thing he shared with these three white men—and every white man who judged him, as they did—human intellect. His mind was sharp, keenly honed by constant and desperate use. He had learned to use his brain often and to better advantage; he'd had to, just to stay alive.

"You were right, sir," he said in a cold, formal voice. "I could not have stayed. I worked well. But I am black." As he spoke, he unbuttoned his shirt, peeled it off. Then he pulled the sweated cotton undershirt over his head, the golden cross battering his chest. He turned his back so they could see the brand marks—the *W.O.* Baxter Simon had burned into his flesh more than six years ago.

He saw Dominique You wince. René Beluche had seen many scarred black backs. He showed no expression. Lafitte's voice was gentle. "There is one last reason why we must send you away, Jeff. For your own safety. You would not be safe here now that Baxter Simon knows you're here. He might have you ambushed. You'd have to be on guard constantly, just to stay alive. If he offered a high enough bounty, you might find yourself betrayed from within the organization. I recruit good men—but tough—and unsentimental. I have heard too, when you have a hundred hounds, one of them is bound to be a son of a bitch. Eh? You are no longer safe here. That is why you must leave—and why, under no circumstances, are you to return to Barataria, or to the Lafitte company in New Orleans—the break must be total and clean."

Jeff nodded. "When do you wish me to leave, sire?"

Lafitte was calm, businesslike. "Instantly would be most satisfactory. Safest for you. You can get together your belongings—perhaps you'll want to say good-bye to your woman?"

Jeff sighed and nodded again, though he had small desire to say good-bye to Gretchen. He hadn't seen her in months; he had been allowed time to walk in the house they'd shared and tell her he would never see her again.

"Your immediate departure will be best. No sense giving Simon time to set some trap. I have a final and urgent mission for you. When you have completed it, you will end forever your association with us. You'll owe us nothing; we will have no obligations to you—and you must never return here."

Jeff nodded. "And the mission, sir?"

"The mission is a simple one, a delivery. But it must be handled with diplomacy and tact. I want you to deliver papers and $10,000 in cash to a plantation called The Laurels. The papers and cash go to a Madame Margarith Morceau—widow of André Morceau. He fought bravely at the Battle of New Orleans in 1815. But he died—only recently—on a secret mission for the Lafitte organization. Not even his widow knew he worked for us. No one—including Madame Morceau—can know that these papers and money come from Lafitte."

Jeff stared at the privateer. Lafitte was sending him away from Barataria, exiling him, and in the same breath trusting him with important documents and 10,000 in cash! "Why do you trust me, sir?"

Lafitte laughed. "Because you're a good nigger, Bricktop."

Jeff winced, unable to smile though he knew Lafitte meant the jibe kindly. Lafitte added in a serious tone, "I trust no one more, regret losing no one more. This mission will carry you from here. From the estate of Madame Morceau, you must find a new life."

Lafitte handed a thickly packed saddlebag across the

desk, along with a map marking the direction of the plantation known as The Laurels. Jeff took the saddlebag and the map. He inclined his head in a quick bow to Lafitte, Beluche, Dominique You. Then he turned and walked out, no longer Jeff Carson, respected member of Lafitte's company, but once again a homeless fugitive slave named Bricktop. Just like that, he thought emptily. This part of his life was over.

CHAPTER VI

The old Negro servant closed the wide brass-studded front door of Jean Lafitte's Big House. Jeff stood outside, painfully aware of the finality of the sound of that closing door.

Jeff paused, hesitating outside Lafitte's closed door for a beat longer than was healthy—when Lafitte said good-bye, or made a request, they were commands to be executed immediately on pain of death. Loitering might suggest opposition, or at least the questioning of his authority, both equally reprehensible in those fiery black eyes. The violent-tempered pirate's six senses were acute. A man lingering outside his door might signal treachery. Lafitte had learned to listen for the diminishing tread of boots—upon such small details were founded his longevity in a hazardous trade.

For Jeff, this was a moment of hurting sadness. He felt the painful sense of loss, the dismaying prospect of a fortune slipping through his fingers. He had never belonged anywhere for very long. Even here at Barataria village, his time in residency had always been brief. Brief, yes, but well served and happy. Damn it, he'd been delighted, both with the quality of his life and his prospects for great wealth! His most fantastic dreams had loomed just ahead, almost within his grasp! Hell, he should have known better than to count on permanence, even among other fugitives. He should have known better by now—a woods colt had no stall.

Just the same, that closing door, thick, huge, and forever barred against him, had a special and disturbing significance. It was not the first time a door had been slammed shut in his face. But he'd become accustomed to luxury, to that special gratification of belonging to a vast, far-flung organization that offered huge rewards as well as protection. Now that was all stripped away. He had one more mission to fulfill for Lafitte. The heavy saddlebags reminded him. He tossed the strap across his shoulder and strode out into the sunshine. He appeared as devil-may-care, as self-assured as ever, but inside he was quaking. Where would this new road take him? He knew only that it would have to be away from Barataria, somewhere Baxter Simon couldn't find him or he'd be dead or enslaved. He'd be dead because he was damned if he'd ever be enslaved again.

For the first time he felt abandoned as well as alone. He'd always made friends easily—his red hair and easy smiling charmed people, and he was surrounded by sundry mortals, even when he couldn't always trust them.

He walked along the sun-strapped street, afternoon shadows jabbing huge fingers at him in his loneliness. The village was larger than it had looked from the deck of the brig this morning. This morning? A thousand years ago this morning when he'd been Jeff Carson, a trusted Lafitte lieutenant. People ventured out into the streets as the day cooled slightly. The population numbered somewhere between five and seven hundred; the town was adequate to serve their needs, from food to women. He passed the large drafty building that served as dormitory where new wenches were stabled until they were chosen by some townsman or found a mate for themselves.

He himself had found Gretchen in the dormitory. She had not been the prettiest woman there, nor yet the ugliest. But most, he'd been warned, were fireships, ready to infect the man who touched them. Gretchen was large, plump, Nordic, knew how to cook, if not to fuck—and she was clean.

He passed the general store where groceries and provisions had been issued to Gretchen on presentation of chits issued to him. Yells and obscenities rose from the red brick calaboose as he passed. Faces of obstreperous or drunken men and women pressed against the barred windows. He crossed the promenade, passed the storehouses, which were stacked to the rafters with fine fabrics, foods, and hardware from every port.

Hell, it wasn't much of a town. Sixty miles south of New Orleans. Cut off from the rest of the world by open seas or treacherous bayous. It was isolated. A hot corner of hell. And yet he could not stifle the emptiness inside him at the thought of being exiled from the purgatory that had become his own Eden.

He stopped outside the cottage where he had lived well, if not ecstatically, with Gretchen for two years. The snug little house hadn't looked like much, hot and stuffy and unkempt the first time he saw it. Gretchen had changed all that. He winced at the idea of telling her it was ended—once he was gone they would take this place from her and she'd be returned to the dormitory to await some other man. The courtesy veranda was thickly hedged by blooming jasmine and hibiscus Gretchen had planted two years ago and tended so lovingly. Casement windows stood open, white curtains billowing in breezes from the bay.

"Jeff! *Mein herr!* Jeff! Jeff! You have come home to me!" The front door was thrown open and Gretchen ran through it, arms extended.

He caught her in his arms and kissed her violently.

Their neighbors crowded out on their stoops, or stuck their heads through their windows, to watch, shout, and laugh. Gretchen was laughing and crying at once, and Jeff became aware that her body was shaking visibly.

Jeff cupped her round face in his hands and looked down at her. Indeed she presented a far different—far improved—appearance from that time when he had seen her first in that dormitory two years ago. She was plain, still, but her delight in life gave her an inner glow that erased the plainness and showed how freshly vital, clean scrubbed, and healthy she was. She had learned to use *maquillage* to advantage. She had experimented until she discovered the most becoming way to wear her hair. Large cornflower blue eyes glowed with her inner pleasure at having him safe at home again. Her short, uptilted nose, her Nordic-pink cheeks, full red lips, and white, strong teeth—her whole face glowed with excitement at his return. He realized that every change she had made was in the plaintive hope that she might please him. What in hell was a girl like Gretchen doing among the whores and privateers of Barataria? Everything about her screamed out for a faithful, hard-working, preferably Teutonic husband, and a farm somewhere. Everything, except the deep shadows swirling in her eyes. Though she'd never talked about it, Jeff knew Gretchen was a driven girl—running from something, looking for something she had never found until she came to live here with him. It was a hellish thing, having to tell her it was over.

She pressed her magnificent mammaries hard upon his thick chest as if trying to crush them against him. She was a tall girl, junoesque, with ample hips and well-turned legs. Maybe Gretchen wasn't plain at all, or else that sea voyage had been longer than he'd realized. She looked *good*.

"Oh, *mein* Jeff," she whispered. "We can have dinner now—if you like. Or we can go to bed—for a rest—and eat later . . . if you like."

Jeff enclosed her in his arm and went up the steps.

His legs were just beginning to feel strong enough to support him. Nicole and Zilla had drained him dry. There was no way he was going to be able to bed Gretchen, no matter how wild for it she was—and he could feel her full hips writhing against him.

He was almost relieved to find Vincente sitting in the middle of the kitchen floor. Vincente was polishing Jeff's boots and his own. Jeff laughed at him. "How many times have I told you, Vincente, you don't have to shine boots any more? Not even mine. Not even your own. We've servants for that." Under his breath, he amended it, we *had* servants for that.

"No servant can get the exact, correct gloss on Don Jeff's boots," Vincente said. "Nor on mine. Only I am so expert at polishing our boots."

Jeff smiled and shrugged. No sense in arguing about boots with Vincente. The boy was obsessed with the love of boots. Jeff understood this passion—Vincente must have shined literally thousands of boots on the docks at Havana, but until Jeff bought him a pair, Vincente had never owned his very own shoes. Now, Vincente spent every extra *real* for boots.

Jeff's first encounter with Vincente had been with his boot on the boy's shoe-shine box within his first hour in Havana. Jeff had rested his foot on the box while Vincente worked with black liquid and brush, adding a copious amount of spit because, he claimed, spit made the finest shine. And Jeff had had to admit he'd never had boots shine so brilliantly before. He'd praised Vincente, and this had amounted to letting the camel get his nose in the tent.

Jeff winced. Well, that was all over too. He exhaled, thankful for Vincente's presence. He would tell them both that the old life—built around Jeff Carson—was over for both of them.

He dreaded parting with Gretchen. He hated to lose Vincente who had become a loyal confederate—a sharp-minded rascal. But he had known from the first it was wrong to bring Vincente away from his native Cuba. The boy had a brilliant intellect. He should be in school, not chasing around with a fugitive slave whom he revered as the totally white Don Jeff! Well, he'd been looking for the opportunity to return Vincente to Havana where he would be at least technically under the protection of the illustrious aristocrat Don Cipriano—who was, as a matter of fact, Vincente's natural father, though the fact was *no que importe* in Havana. This was the moment—bitter but perfect—for breaking all ties with the past, cleanly and finally.

He dropped the saddlebags loudly on the dining table, wanting them to see that he was prepared for travel. If they realized he was being sent away, it would lessen the pain for all of them. He could play down the fact that it was permanent. "I am being sent on another mission," he said, not looking at Gretchen or Vincente. "Orders of Lafitte."

"He is sending you so soon?" Gretchen wailed.

"When do we leave?" Vincente poised, ready to leap to his feet.

"Yes. Today. A flatboat is being readied to take me upriver to a trail out of the bayous. They will bring a horse here. And I'm sorry, Vincente, but you will have to stay here this time." He smiled, lying. "Lafitte's orders."

"The hell with Lafitte," Vincente raged. "I work for you."

"Keep your voice down, if you want to stay alive," Jeff said. "No one says the hell with Lafitte—not in Barataria—not aloud."

Gretchen was sobbing, pressing her apron against her eyes to absorb the flow of tears. "Oh, Jeff, *mein* Jeff, I can't let you go. Not so soon—again."

Jeff bit back his own tears that threatened to choke him. He was not going to lie to Gretchen further. It was one thing to have Vincente learn after he was away from here that Lafitte had not ordered Vincente left behind. It was another to let this desolated girl believe he would ever come back to her, or to Barataria.

"This is good-bye, Gretchen. Forever. I am being sent away from Barataria. I will not be permitted to return."

"Then I'm sure hell going with you," Vincente burst out.

"Shut up, Vincente. I'll deal with you later," Jeff said.

"Please, Jeff, take me with you," Gretchen begged. "I won't need a horse. I'll walk. I'll eat very little. I'll be no trouble. Please God, Jeff, take me with you. Don't leave me here."

"I can't take you, Gretchen. I don't know where I am going. I do know that I am in deep trouble. That man Baxter Simon who was here—he claims he owns me, Gretchen."

"Owns you? How could such a man own one as you?"

"It doesn't make sense, but it's a legal fact. I'm sorry, Gretchen, I've lied to you in more ways than one. I am not a white man, and I hid that from you—"

"Oh, no, Jeff!" Gretchen shook her blond head, sobbing. "I have known—from the first."

He stared at her, eyes wide. "How could you have known?"

"Oh, *mein* love, I had to know. I was too curious. You never took off your shirt, even by candlelight. I had to know why. Once when you were sound asleep—I lit a candle. I saw the terrible brands in your back. They broke my heart. But I knew your fearful secret—from the first."

He shook his head. "And it didn't make you hate me? Lying to you? A black man—a nigger—pretending to be a white man?"

"Oh, no. No. It made me love you more. I admired your great courage. Before you had seemed an arrogant, devil-may-care man. But then—knowing the truth—I saw how brave you were. How troubled. How you lived always in danger of losing your life. I had always felt great love for you—from the moment I saw you. But now I loved you with great depth, because I felt great pity for you in your loneliness and your bravery."

Jesus, Jeff thought, I'd have never closed my eyes for

73

an hour in this place if I'd known she knew my secret! It was not that he didn't trust Gretchen, but he had learned the way to keep a person from revealing a secret under duress was to keep that person unaware of the secret—what she did not know, no one could force her to tell. He drew her against him, tenderly and gently for the first time since he had known her. He kissed her heated, damp lips, tasting the salt of her tears.

"Oh, Jeff," she pleaded. "Come to bed with me—one last time. Please! Something I planned, I dreamed, I learned—to please you! Please!"

She caught his hand, pressing it to her breasts. Her mouth was pulled, her tear-filled eyes agonized with longing and loss. He nodded. The hell with fatigue. The hell with Lafitte's orders to get out instantly. He owed Gretchen at least this final attempt to gratify her needs. She had dedicated her every waking thought to him for two years—how many legally wedded wives could make such a claim of fidelity and adoration?

He managed to pull off his boots without losing his balance and falling. He tossed them to Vincente. "Polish my boots, boy," he said. "And we'll talk—later."

Vincente caught the boots but did not look up. He said, *"Sí, señor,"* as if he were speaking to a stranger.

Gretchen had divested herself of her clothing by the time he entered their bedroom and closed the door behind him. She came to him, nude, her full breasts gleaming. Her hands caught at his belt, removing it, unbuttoning his fly. He tried to respond; he wanted to; it was gratifying in this terrible moment of loss to see how badly this young woman wanted him. He had performed for older women, for women he didn't want at all, women to whom in Louisville he had sold his favors. If he could grow hard enough to please those customers, he would not fail Gretchen now, exhausted and sated as he was.

She let his trousers fall below his knees. When they toppled about his ankles, she sank to her own knees and worked them over his feet. Then she caught his hips tightly in her arms and pressed her mouth hungrily to him.

He responded to the ministrations of her heated mouth and he sighed, relaxing. It was going to be all right. He was not going to fail her. Gretchen would have the doomed woman's last meal!

He stared down, watching her frantically loving him— she had planned a surprise for him! She, the phlegmatic Nordic, was wilder than the little minx Zilla, more passionate than the overheated Nicole! At last he bent down and took her up in his arms. She did not demur but let him carry her to the bed. The windows were flung open, the curtains billowed with the first evening breezes from the bay—and only the air was cool in that room. She cradled him in her arms, pressing him into the luxurious depth of her mammaries. Her hands stole down his back and closed tightly. She drew him into her with all her strength, digging her fingers into his flesh. He lunged with pain and she gasped with the pleasure his pain afforded her. He responded to her grasping fingers and she continued to pump her hips beneath him, using all the strength in her arms to press him closer until, crying out, she began to buck her body in uncontrollable delight, then sagged beneath him, quiescent.

She went on clinging to him, holding him inside her. He truly wanted her, perhaps for the first time since he'd known her. He threw off all restraints, determined to lift her to new heights of excitement, to force her to surrender completely to him. Her passion equaled his. For these moments he saw nothing, thought nothing, wanted nothing but the woman struggling beneath him to get ever closer, as if she could finally be happy only by becoming physically part of his being.

She had kindled this raging fire in him and he was going to see her consumed in its heat. Despite her little moans of agonized delight, he drove harder. She trembled all over, whispering unintelligibly, clinging to him. Her desire, her lips, her hands, her fiery passion had stirred him to heights he had not approached with Zilla or Nicole.

Her passionate appetites in turn kindled an overwhelming craving in him for her—for Gretchen.

Gretchen gave herself more fervently than she had in all the nights before with him, and she had believed then that Jeff was driving her out of her mind. She cried out, thrusting her hips upward, sobbing for breath. They mounted the heights together until the very act of breathing in that rarified atmosphere was painful, and then they plunged into warm, sated softness of semiconsciousness together.

He must have slept, perhaps for only a few moments. He came awake abruptly to find her gently kissing his lips, tracing their outline with the tip of her tongue. Her tears splashed on his cheek. "Please don't cry," he said. "We had a good life together, Gretchen. You—are much smarter than you were—now you'll make some lucky man a hell of a wife."

She nodded, sniffling. "Yes . . . thanks to you . . . but after you—thanks to you—will any other man ever please me?"

CHAPTER VII

Jeff held Gretchen until she subsided into an exhausted slumber, whispering that he had left her drained, that she would be all right as soon as she had a small nap. She would be like new, and she would fix him a dinner he would never forget. And then her voice trailed away, and she slept.

He got up as quietly as he could and dressed. He stared down at her, his eyes stinging. He didn't love Gretchen; he had never pretended to; he had been honest with her about that, at least. But damn! he'd miss her. His life had worked itself into a pattern of using people and then walking away from them. He took 500 in bills from his savings and commissions and pushed them gently under her pillow. If Gretchen wished, she could buy her way out of Barataria; she could find her stolid German boy—and her farm somewhere. . . .

Vincente had lighted a lamp. The boots were all polished, gleaming. Vincente insisted that Jeff sit down in a wing chair and he put the highly shining boots on his feet. As he worked, he told Jeff that the horse had been sent from the Lafitte stables, was tethered to the balcony railing and probably eating Gretchen's jasmine. The boy who brought the horse said to tell Don Jeff that the flatboat awaited his convenience, but they would like to get upriver and back before too late—those river arms and bayous could be treacherous in the dark.

"I'm ready to go," Vincente said.

"I've told you." Jeff shook his head. "You can't come with me, Vincente. You heard Gretchen. I am not white. I am a fugitive slave. I don't even know where I am going."

"Hah! I do not care about so unimportant a matter as what blood is in a man's veins. The blood of Don Cipriano means I am the son of an aristocrat. Yet, until you came along, I shined boots and pimped for my sister Perla—an outcast. In Cuba, it is less than important what blood a man has—it is what a man is here—in his balls. And there, *amigo,* you are *mucho machismo!*"

"You are still young, Vincente. With schooling, you can be a great man—perhaps greater than your own father, Don Cipriano. But you will not learn the things you need, running—God knows where—with the likes of me."

Jeff shook his head violently. He had made his own way in life through pretense, lies, subterfuge. But his lies were a matter of life and death with him. For him to live honestly would mean death or a return to slavery. Vincente was different. He was Don Cipriano's son, even if, like Jeff, he was the aristocrat's woods colt. Vincente was accepted as white by society and would never face slavery. With a good education there was no limit to the accomplishments possible to Vincente. He could not be weak, or sentimental. The time to be tough was now. He had to send Vincente back to Cuba, back to school, back to the casual but real sponsorship of Don Cipriano. His uncertain life ahead offered nothing for Vincente.

"If I knew where I was going, Vincente. It might be different—might."

"Have we ever asked ourselves such questions before?"

"Stay here." Jeff hardened his voice, making his words a command that did not permit questioning. But he was pleading. He was tired, exhausted, defeated, not up to the job of showing a young boy the error of his ways. "I have nothing to offer you, damn it. Can't you see that? I am a fugitive slave. I'm masquerading as a white man, but I'm as black as any slave in that barracoon!"

Vincente's voice was calm, chilled with its reason. "We are all masquerading as something we are not."

"I'm on a dangerous mission." Well, perhaps the delivery of money and papers to a war widow would be less than hazardous, but staying alive was certainly a real peril.

"We've been together on a few of those."

He winced. He could not deny that Vincente had rendered invaluable aid in Havana when Lafitte sent Jeff to buy slaves. Without the shoe-shine boy that trip might have ended disastrously. Vincente had stowed away on the slave ship, had lived through the hell of a hurricane at sea with him. Vincente had been with him when Chloe was killed by Baxter Simon's gunfire. Vincente had recovered the golden cross from the dead girl's hand where Jeff had left it as a parting gift for his deceased love. It

78

had been Vincente who reminded him that the dead past buried its dead, that for the living, life went on. The talisman could do nothing for the dead girl—even misshapen it could be pawned for bread and wine to keep them alive another day. Damn it, it was time for Vincente to go back home, back to Cuba, to school.

He spoke as calmly, as reasonably as Vincente had. "Always before, Vincente, we had someone behind us to support us. You had Don Cipriano. We had Lafitte. We had this safe harbor into which we could run when things got too hot. . . . I have been warned I cannot even come back here, Vincente."

Vincente shrugged. "Then it is no place for me."

Jeff shook his head, spoke in a cold tone. "No. I have made up my mind. I'll travel faster—and farther—alone."

Vincente stared up at him, scowling. "But why should you leave me?"

"Because you are a young boy! Because you need an education. You should be at home in Cuba, not chasing around the edges of hell, on devils' missions."

"Take me with you," Vincente pleaded. "Am I not as much good luck to you as that broken gold talisman you wear around your neck? Can it fire a gun, wield a knife, see what is happening behind your back?"

"I grant all that, and I love you as a younger brother, Vincente—"

"Then take me with you!"

"—as a meddlesome, bothersome kid brother, always underfoot. You've saved my life. I thank you. It was one thing for you to travel with a young *white* man. But it is something else to be *running*—with a fugitive black man. Can't you see that?"

Vincente shook his head stubbornly. "I see you only as you have always been. You have always been what you are at this moment, no matter what you pretended. The dangers were always as great—no less. . . ." He was on the verge of tears. "I have no wish to return to Cuba. You *are* my brother. You are *mi familia*—only my sister, a *puta* in Havana, is as near. You need me more.

79

A busy whore in Havana has no need for a younger brother hanging around."

"You're right about that. . . . Your pimpings days are over! Just as mine are—I hope. . . . Closed chapters. But you—with an education—"

Vincente was openly crying now. "Those are only words, my brother! What better education could I have had than in your company. In any situation, I am the master, because I have been taught how to stay alive— by you!"

"There's more to living than simply living by your wits." But Jeff hesitated, wincing. He had no desire to leave Vincente behind here in Barataria except for the boy's own welfare. Vincente was his right arm. But . . . again he hesitated. It was time to stop thinking of himself, his own comfort. Vincente was a young twig who yet could be bent toward the light of salvation, toward a golden future, instead of the ragged life as the friend of a fugitive nigger—with a life expectancy no longer than cock length.

He shook his head, spoke in finality. "No, Vincente. I can't do it. You've run free long enough. It's time for school, for security, for discipline. My God, boy, I'm thinking about you, what's best for you!"

"I will not agree it is best that I be sent away from you."

"But I say so. . . . If I had a place to hang my hat, a place to call home, I'd share it with you, Vincente. But I'm damned if I'll take a kid like you into what's left of my life."

Vincente stared up at him through tears. "So this is the way you would treat a friend?" he whispered.

"That's the way with us niggers," Jeff said. "You can't trust us. That's the way it is, Vincente. Be thankful you learned it now—instead of on the brink of hell somewhere. . . . Go back to Cuba, Vincente. We've had one hell of a time. But that's over. Past." He counted out money, gave it to the boy. "Take this. It'll help you start in school. Become a respected politician—a pirate, but respectable. When you're wealthy—and safe—drink a toast to old Bricktop, the runaway slave who wouldn't let you throw your life away."

Still crying, wiping at his nose with the back of his hand, Vincente looked fourteen. He took the money Jeff offered and stuffed it inside his shirt. Jeff drew the boy against him and held him tightly, roughly. But Vincente shook free and refused to shake hands. "Go to hell, *señor*," he said. *"Vaya al infierno."*

He turned and ran, sobbing, from the room. Empty-bellied, Jeff stood and watched him go. He tried to shake off the overwhelming sadness, but he could not. He loved Vincente. It saddened him to know he would never see the boy again. Now he was truly alone, friendless. Another door had closed in his face. Vincente was gone.

Jeff took up the saddlebag and the carpetbag, which had not been unpacked. He went out to the horse awaiting him at the front stoop. He forced himself to shake both Gretchen and Vincente from his mind. He had nothing more to offer them than he had given them— their freedom. He must not mourn Vincente. The boy would be better off in Cuba. He himself had to look forward, not back. He was destined to forget people who played a part in his life, even those who had loved him, or helped him most. Minerva George was no more than a name to him now, though he supposed he had loved her once. He had used Helen Latimer, and ridden away without looking back. Chloe had loved him and because of it lay in a grave—seventeen years old and dead. . . .

He secured the saddlebag and the carpetbag and swung up into the saddle. The horse was spirited. Silently, Jeff thanked Lafitte for this last gift—a fine mount to carry him into his new life. He turned the horse and headed downslope toward the piers. He heard Vincente and Gretchen at the door of the little cottage, but he did not look back.

Hurricane lanterns glowed to lead him to the flatboat that awaited him at the pier. It was almost fully dark, the night seeming to smoke up from the clotted jungle that encroached hour by hour upon the village and the bay—the million tendrils of the banyans, the wild cabbage palmettos, the thickly twisted mangroves. The world around him seemed strange, gone out of kilter. A silence deepened that not even the noisy drunks in the dockside tavern could dispel.

At the pier, he looked back. The houses and shops bunched along the street like some village lost out of time, from some remote century, the provincial architecture transplanted to this bayou country, and losing much in the translation.

"That you, Carson?" A savage voice lashed out at him from the deck of the flatbottom. "Lead your horse aboard and let's weigh anchor. I got no love for these treacherous arms of the river after dark. . . . If orders came one level less than from Lafitte himself, I'd tell them and you to go to hell till come morning. But the old man said we go, and go we do, if you'll stir your ass."

Jeff led his horse aboard, tethered him, and stroked his nose and neck to soothe him as the awkward flatbottom moved out into the bay. The wan lights of Barataria receded in the darkness. His last glimpse of the pirate village was winking lights, dark squares and rectangles choked in jungle growth.

The complaining skipper moved the boat out of the bay, making an awkward turn across a carpet of hyacinths. It entered an inlet where the night silences deepened oppressively. The water of the inlet lay flat and still, coated with green slime. Moss dripped like choke chains from live oaks, bays, and magnolias massing the banks of the dead lagoon. Cypress and mangroves reared, a wall of constricting closeness.

Beyond the dead inlet lay the dank bayous. The flatbottom moved forward cautiously, following the faint beam of the hurricane lamp up forward on its bow, as if searching across the bile-colored lagoon for swift-moving currents that would show the river just ahead. The boat plowed through the clogged water, pulling abruptly out into a deepening channel. Jeff heard the skipper cursing, but the oaths were relieved, and it was as if the crew breathed fully for the first time in an hour.

Mosquitoes clouded in over the boat, even in the wide main stream. The night seemed breathless. Because his legs threatened to buckle under him, Jeff sank to the deck and put his head back against a bulkhead. He might have slept. He heard shouting, orders and curses mixed. He got to his feet and watched the wide flatboat maneuver into a landing.

Jeff saw an ordinary with a single lamp glowing over its front door, a couple of other buildings, and then a narrow lane pointing north through the clotted bayous. The log road out. The skipper came back to him. "Well, here you are, Carson. We made it in spite of hell—the same way we'll make it back, as though you give a damn. Arrogant young upstart. Got a message from Lafitte for you."

"Thank you, skipper."

"Don't thank me. I don't even understand it. But Lafitte said you'd understand. He said you should keep alert—on the log road out of here—for your friend."

Jeff nodded. The plank was tossed from deck to pier and Jeff led his horse across it.

The gangplank was retracted almost instantly, and slapping mosquitoes and swearing, the skipper headed the flatboat down river. Jeff stood on the small dock, watching it turn, suddenly wafted along like a leaf on the current. He waved, but supposed they didn't even see him.

Jeff stared at the ordinary sourly. The inn looked like what it was, a decrepit, sodden, mildewed fleabag on the brink of nowhere. The glow of the lamp over its door showed him how roach-infested it was. Jeff had encountered and suffered poor taverns and overnight stops before, but none possessed the ugly, forsaken air of poverty of this unpainted structure, this miserable and primitive shack. But he was weak with exhaustion, lightheaded with weariness. He decided he could sleep even sharing a bed with bedbugs.

He walked the horse toward the ordinary where moths

and mosquitoes batting at the lampshades were the loudest sounds in the settlement. But something happened, unrelated to anything else, like a fragment from a nightmare that brings you fully awake, and sleepless, for no good reason. At the sound of his boots on the boards of the dock, the three or four horses loop-tied at the leather-slicked tie rail outside the tavern across the road wickered and stirred. The three men came out silently and stared without speaking out into the darkness. It was as if they'd been sitting inside listening for any sounds of approaching hooves or boots.

Troubled without knowing why, Jeff swung up into the saddle. The hell with the ordinary. He could hardly sleep worrying about getting his throat cut during the night. He sank his boots into the horse's flanks and raced past the tavern, going out of the town, headed north through the bayous on the rut-pocked log road.

He rode fast in the darkness, a dangerous thing to do; a twisted ankle and he lost a horse in this godforsaken country between Barataria and nowhere. When he'd gone about a mile, he slowed the horse, stopped and sat listening. There was no sound behind him. It was as if the world of the bayous held its breath along with him.

He urged the horse forward along the dark trail. He passed no houses, at least none he could see from the road. These people built rickety structures on stilts at the brinks of bayous—huts that could be written off when the river washed them away. It wasn't a way of life that attracted him. These Cajuns asked nothing except to be left alone to fish, hunt, and skin alligators. They lived on rice, red beans, and shrimp, cooked with plenty of cayenne pepper, and they were content. Hell, even the word bayou was a corruption of *boyau,* the French word for gut. Bayous were gutlike, ox-bow lakes in these low flatlands, formed in poorly drained areas by old rivers with high and low tides. Water backed into these lagoons during floodtide and died there under rafts of water hyacinths, surrounded and strangled by moss-clotted oaks, stark skeletal cypress, palms, huge ferns, wild magnolias, bay trees, all strung together with the thick webbing of dank vines and mangroves.

He slapped at a mosquito on his neck, the sound like a rifle shot in the darkness. Twice he almost fell from the saddle, sinking into sleep despite his efforts to keep his eyes open. The night became haunted. There was the unreal sense of hearing horses' hooves behind him. The sound had to be in his own exhausted mind because when he stopped to listen, the sound behind him ceased. He shuddered and kept moving in the darkness, letting the horse follow the tortuous twists of the trail.

At the first bright fissures of false dawn, Jeff felt his heart lurch with exultance. He felt as if he had won a victory, over the dark night, the black bayou, the wild imaginings of his own mind. Daybreak. He saw a clearing, an open pool where a doe sipped daintly. He swung down from the saddle, led his horse out to let it drink. He sagged to his belly on the shoreline and ducked his head all the way under, hoping to wash out the last wisps of sleep.

When he came up, he saw them. They had come in swiftly from behind him. The first thing he saw was their horses, then the guns in their hands.

"Get up, friend. Slow and easy."

Jeff got to his feet. Water dripped from his hair and face down his collar. He was no longer sleepy, but he wished to hell he were closer to the gun sheathed on his saddle.

"Just nice and easy, friend." This first man was Creole dark, his voice flavored with the accent and inflections of the bayou French. He was toadlike, small astride the huge horse. Evil smeared his bearded face, almost as tangible as bayou mud. Along with the ugly cruelty there was savage weariness—the all-night pursuit from the landing had exhausted and outraged him. This traveler had inconvenienced him and his confederates, and his temper was short. He swung down from the saddle and approached Jeff.

The second man was even darker, but he was a huge

brute, looking powerful and thick shouldered sitting in the saddle. Holding his gun like a toy in his massive fist, he swung down. He towered over Jeff's own six feet. His expression was dour, dull, and humorless, as if no giant intellect glowed behind his small black eyes. "I watch him, Fabio. You check for gun. Yes."

"Git his goddamn money and le's git out of here," the third man said, and Jeff glanced toward him. These were three creatures from a bad dream, only this was a waking nightmare. They had been stalking him all night, waiting impatiently for him to make camp where they could slit his throat quietly.

The third fellow slid from his saddle. He vaguely resembled the little man the brute had called Fabio, with the same thin, hatchet face and thick beard, scraggly hair dripping almost to his shoulders. He was only slightly taller than a dwarf, his body pulled askew by a hunchback. He gripped a gun in his left hand and clutched a cruel-looking bullwhip in his right—as if this were the weapon of a real, even if misshapen, man. "Search him, kill him, and let's git out of here."

"Reckon you're always nervous like this early in the morning—before you've stolen your first cup of coffee," Jeff mocked him.

"Shut yore mouth, less'n you want me to shut it for you." The hunchback tilted his gun.

"Stop it, Philippe," Fabio ordered. "Don't use a gun—a knife is quieter. You don't never know who's around the next bend."

Fabio moved closer to Jeff, wary. Jeff used the moment to edge toward his horse. Fabio stepped along on the bias with him. Jeff took one more step before Fabio's curses stopped him. "You ain't gittin' back on that horse anymore in this life, friend."

"Don't call me friend," Jeff said. "Or I'll break your face."

"Oh, is it going to be a *plaisir* to slit your throat, *m'sieur*." Fabio trembled in anticipation.

"Get the money first, goddamn, an' le's get out of

here. I got no stomach for workin' in broad daylight."
The big man's voice shook.

Fabio holstered his gun and patted Jeff's body roughly.
He came up with gold pieces, a long knife, a few folded
paper dollars. In the meantime, brother Philippe had
yanked the saddlebags from Jeff's horse.

For the first time, Jeff felt true fear. It gorged up
through him. He had felt he had some chance to fight
his way out of this. Simply leaping into the creek might
put him out of reach of their guns and knives. But the
$10,000 and letters in that saddlebag made the difference.
He had to stand and fight. If he lost Jean Lafitte's $10,000
he would be better off dead! Lafitte would never buy a
story of road agents following him all night.

He sucked in a deep breath, held it. These swamp
rats had pushed him into a corner; they had driven him
to the place where he had to die or they had to die. He
could lose his own money—and the few thousand he'd
amassed in commissions and bonuses at Barataria comprised his entire stake. But he could lose that and be no
worse off than he'd been when he arrived at Barataria—
as long as he was alive. But Lafitte's money was something else. Losing that money was simply writing his
own death warrant, and damned if he'd let these three
thugs do that for him.

Moving suddenly, he drove his fist in deep under
Fabio's belt. The twisted little man buckled forward,
retching and moaning. The other two remained unmoving for a long breath.

In that brief span of time, Jeff leaped for the gun at
his saddle. He would have made it smoothly and successfully, but the frightened horse, unused to him, already
tense, spooked and leaped away. Jeff tried to use the
horse as shield, putting its body between him and the
road agents. But the fractious horse danced away from
him, quivering and jerking its head. He managed to get
his hand on the gun, and he pulled it free of its holster,
but he was left vulnerable and open to the bandits.

Philippe made some strangled crow sound deep in his

throat. He did not fire his gun. That whip cracked like a pistol in the morning stillness, and the leather snaked through the air. Jeff's right wrist went numb. His fingers were paralyzed. He watched his gun fall from his lifeless hand, unable to do anything about it.

Still vomiting, Fabio leaped toward him. He backhanded Jeff across the temple with his gun. All the new agony of the heavy metal cutting into bone and flesh flared through Jeff's brain, along with the residual pain from Dominique You's great fists. He crumpled to his knees, for the moment helpless.

This moment was all the three needed. The big man caught the bridle of Jeff's horse, claiming it. Philippe said, "That's a mighty fine-looking hat. I want that. And that shirt."

Fabio laughed. He tossed the planter's hat over his shoulder to Philippe. He ripped Jeff's shirt from him and threw it to Philippe who chattered in frenzied delight at his presents. The gold chain was ripped next, the golden cross rammed into Fabio's own jacket pocket.

On his knees, Jeff shook his head trying to clear it. He heard the big lout say, "Them high-polished boots are mine."

"Sure they are, Elice," Fabio said. He struck Jeff again with the gun and Jeff plunged forward on his face. He was aware of Elice's huge hands yanking off the boots Vincente had polished so lovingly, but it didn't seem to matter in the pool of pain where Jeff's mind simmered. Fabio laughed, "Might as well take his pants too. He ain't goin' to need fine-lookin' pants like these where he's goin'—doubt that bayou gators fancy pants anyhow."

Jeff was aware they ripped off his trousers. Then his undershirt was torn away. A long, stunned silence followed it. He heard Fabio screech at last. "Well, well, will you look at this here. This fine bucko ain't no white man after all. He's a friggin' nigger—and a runner at that. Will you look at that brand on his back? You ever see anything like that? Now who would ever have thought a fine-looking, elegant man too nice to be called a friend of Fabio Belmon, is nothin' but a friggin' nigger. And worse than just a nigger, a bloody mustee! He ain't neither black nor white."

Jeff struggled up from the darkness of pain, wondering why they didn't kill him. But even as he figured why, he heard Fabio putting it in words. "Maybe we got us a real prize here, *mes amis!* A extra fancy mustee nigger. Stoled money and a horse—and run. Somebody would pay us pretty, I vow, to git him back. Don't think we ought to slit the throat of this one. . . . We take him back to the landing. Man through there just yesterday with the law, looking for a runaway mustee buck."

"Don't favor havin' no trash wid de law," Elice said.

"Nor me. Ordinary times," Fabio agreed. He ripped away the last of Jeff's clothing. "But this here spotted calf is something else. I tell you, he'd bring more'n seven, eight thousand on the slave market. I know that! I seen it time and again! We ast for a reward—we git one big enough, we turn him over to the law. We don't, we suddenly very sorry, *m'sieur,* the poor black man pined away and died—and then we takes him to a slave auction in New Orleans."

"You takes him," Elice said. "I want no part of that."

Fabio screamed at Elice. "Stop being stupid, you great bull! This is a fortune in our hands! So we've had trouble with the law. Fuck them all! This escaped slave will make us all rich. For hell's sake, Elice, look at the way the bastard black is hung! Why, I never saw one like yours, Elice, but this bucko's is bigger on a soft than yours at its hardest! Never seen anything like this before in my life. Here he is—naked as the day he was born, and built like a jackass—just waitin' to make us all rich. And you worry about the law. Come on, tie him across his horse and let's get out of here."

The huge Elice knelt to hoist Jeff's naked body upon his horse, but Philippe's strangled voice, making unintelligible noises, stopped them. He danced around them, holding the saddlebag open, exposing the stacks of money.

Fabio gazed at it, incredulous, laughing, shaking his head, and laughing again, uncontrollably. "Look at that! The heavy-hung nigger comes riding into our lives to make us rich. More money than I ever saw, plus a nigger to sell at auction. He hated me to call him friend, but the heavy-hung nigger is so dear to me, I swear to you I could kiss him. . . ."

CHAPTER VIII

Vincente came upon them stealthily, almost as if he materialized from the blue mists that wreathed in from the inlets and smoked across the narrow road.

Fabio worked, totally absorbed in his newly acquired riches and in the size, heft, and probable selling price of the heavy-hung mustee. When he looked up and glimpsed the slender Cuban boy standing in the middle of the road, gripping pistols, unmoving horse at his back, he didn't even believe it at first. A jest of the gods, a trick of the morning fog, a bad joke. He continued exulting over his great good fortune for a full breath before he jerked his head up, checked again, and croaked, "Look out, *mes amis,* a-hind ye!"

Lying naked in the sodden bayou mud, Jeff stared, dazed, at the apparition in the mists. He thought dazedly, *What are you doing here, Vincente? Why aren't you safe at school in Cuba?*

Jeff pulled himself up to his knees, but none of Fabio's

thugs gave him a glance. They peered in horrified fascination at the silent, cool-as-ice youth holding guns fixed on them.

Jeff whistled silently between his teeth. Vincente was armed better than these road agents, with their single-shot rimfire pistols, suspected. The two guns Vincente held had come from an Havana *armería*—the best gun-smith in all Cuba, the boy had boasted when they bought them.

They had come away from that gunsmith with a brand-new type of flintlock—a gun said to have been invented by an American living in England. The revolutionary pistol fired a number of shots separately and consecutively. Bullets were contained in a cylinder that was rotated by hand—an ingenious weapon. They had seemed expensive at the time, but Jeff saw them now as cheap at half the price!

"Why, hell's balls," Fabio raged. "Will you look? Hit's just a kid—fresh from its mama's tit! Drop them guns, boy, and ride fast out of here, and we'll let you go alive."

Vincente's smile remained chilled. "I count badly, *señor*. So *hagan ustedes el favor*. For your own safety, do not force me to attempt to count past three before you have dropped your guns and all articles taken from the poor helpless man wallowing *alone* in the mud."

Jeff grinned inwardly. Vincente was giving them all hell, him included. He was being castigated for having dared venture into bayou country alone.

Fabio's designating Vincente as a callow boy prodded the dwarflike Philippe into an error. Barely tilting his gun, Philippe pressed the trigger. The explosion was loud, the gunsmoke curled up, thickly, into the fog, but it was the second explosion. The first came from the gun in Vincente's left hand.

The impact of Vincente's bullet, striking dead center into Philippe's constricted chest, drove the misshapen predator lunging backward. He struck on his humped shoulder, rolled there oddly for a full beat, and then spilled facedown, his nose only inches from the black-water pool. Philippe was dead.

Fabio stared first at Vincente, unscathed. Then, incredulous, he whirled to look for his brother. At the sight of the twisted body sprawled facedown in the mud, Fabio broke into uncontrollable sobs. He howled out in an agony that rattled across the silent sweeps of the bayous. The cry was the primal scream of beast-man bereft and alone in his cave. The sound got inside Jeff and shook him. Herons, cranes, and small birds took wing from fern, grass, and inlet.

Still sobbing, tears streaming down his dirty, bearded cheeks from his reddened eyes, and mucus running from his nares, Fabio wheeled back and crouched, turning crablike to fire. But again, the brigands were too slow for Vincente. The gun in his right hand exploded.

Fabio dropped the gun and grabbed at his right arm, badly ripped by the bullet from Vincente's gun. Fabio forgot everything but the pain in his arm and sank to his knees. He clutched at his bleeding arm, sobbing.

"Looks like you done shot your wad," Elice said to Vincente.

Vincente bowed, using his left hand to rotate the cylinder of the gun in his right. "If you think so, *señor,* come and take me."

Elice's wits ground more slowly than the mills of the gods. But the big man had seen many guns. He recognized something new and dangerous in the weapons the boy held. He hesitated.

Behind him, Jeff shook the mists from his head, took up his own repeater from where it had fallen. He said, "Stand easy, Elice. It wouldn't take much to make me kill you."

Elice did not remove his fascinated gaze from the strange new guns in the boy's hands, but he heard Jeff and he nodded. He let his own gun fall into the mud of the road. Jeff went up behind him. He took the guns from Fabio, Elice, and the dead dwarf and threw them out into the pool. The splashes were loud—a beautiful sound to Jeff. He was still hearing sounds—he was still alive—thank God and an insubordinant Vincente. . . .

"Get your clothes on," Vincente said to Jeff. "Suppose a lady came along?"

"I'd be ready," Jeff said. But he pulled on his trousers, shirt, and sitting beside the wailing Fabio, he pulled on his boots. Dressed, he took his time reclaiming the valuables Fabio and his men had stripped from him. The gold chain had been broken; he dropped the cross into his pocket. He recovered the saddlebag, his own money, knife, and papers. He replaced his belongings on his horse as they had been earlier. All this time Elice had stood locked, unmoving.

Jeff knew that sooner or later, the big lout's slow-cooker mind would conceive some attack, no matter how crude. The better part of valor was preventive action. Using the lariat looped on Elice's own saddle, he tied Elice's ankles and then secured the man's wrists between his shoulder blades. The big man grunted in pain and discomfort, but Jeff said, "You'll grow accustomed to it, Elice. You'll like it—once you realize the alternative is to join your friend Philippe."

Elice ceased grunting. He bit his mouth, standing straight. He tried to protest when Jeff turned his pockets inside out.

"No wonder he complains," Jeff said, awed. "The big gorilla is carrying more than $500." He tossed the wad to Vincente. "Buy yourself a trinket—when you get home to Cuba."

Despite the pain and bleeding in Fabio's right arm, Jeff trussed him up exactly as he had tied the huge Elice. Fabio cursed and wept until Jeff took Fabio's own bandana from his hip pocket and thrust it in the bearded man's mouth. He secured it with rope, making an effective gag. He then gagged Elice, using his own underpants, which Fabio had stripped from him.

Fabio's pockets proved to be a greater treasure trove than had Elice's. Jeff tossed more than $1,000, rings, and golden earbobs to the pile at Vincente's feet. The dwarf had only a few dollars. Jeff took the money and crammed it into his own pocket.

"Are we about ready to go?" Vincente asked.

"I don't think we should leave our friends here, where they'll be found so easily," Jeff said.

Vincente shrugged. "What do you suggest?" He walked over to where the contorted body of the dwarf lay beside the water. With the toe of his boot, as if the dead thug were vermin, Vincente rolled him into the water. The ugly little corpse floated outward, trailing blood from his bullet wound.

Vincente knelt to gather up the booty taken from the captives. Suddenly, Fabio began to writhe and twist on the ground as if in an epileptic attack. Turning, Jeff and Vincente saw why. A ten-foot alligator, which might have been mistaken in the still water for a dead log, surfaced and then closed its huge mouth on the dead body.

Fabio strangled trying to wail out his horror as the huge reptile spun over and over, its tail and body lashing the pool white as it dragged its prize underwater.

Jeff found a tree some distance from the road. An ancient live oak, it was shielded from the lane by thickly matted mangroves, huge ferns, and palmetto palms. Catching the two men by their boots, he dragged them across the road and down the embankment. He looped two ropes over an oak limb. Securing the ropes to the ankle ties of both men, he pulled them each about two feet from the ground and tied them off. They swung there, facing each other, unable to speak.

Vincente watched from the shoulder of the road in admiration of Jeff's handiwork. Both brigands were making unintelligible sounds, wailing behind their gags.

Jeff walked up the incline to the road. He took up the reins of the three horses, tied them together, secured the tie to a length of rope which he fastened to his saddle horn.

"All right, Vincente," Jeff called. He swung up into the saddle, viewing the trampled, bloody scene of their recent violence with a shudder. "Let's ride."

Vincente bowed toward the two thugs, hanging by their ankles from the live oak limb. Only fate would determine how soon they would be found by passersby. Vincente spoke in a most courtly tone. "We leave you, gentlemen, victims of your own greed, of your own native mosquitoes, the natural isolation of your remote home region, and your own tiny little consciences."

CHAPTER IX

They rode out of the bayou jungle. There was little difference in the surrounding country—but the water plants grew less profuse, the shell-paved road was wider, and infrequently they passed other travelers. Men sagged in ox-drawn carts, sweated in the humid heat. Horsemen passed them warily; they themselves were alert to any unusual or covert actions of the riders they passed. It was not a time when a man trusted strangers. One stayed alive and fed his family the best way he could. Sometimes what was best for him proved fatal for his adversary.

With the three saddle horses in tow, they made poor time. But, Jeff thought with some bitterness, for the first time in two years, there was no hurry, no true destination, only uncertainty around the next bend.

A pale disc of cresting sun blazed whitely, burning away the last wisps of morning fog and beading sweat across their faces, darkening the armpits of their shirts.

Jeff tried to listen to Vincente, but he found himself stifling yawns with his fist; he had passed a sleepless night, a violent morning. He recalled with pleasure yesterday's enchantment in the clinging arms of Gretchen, Zilla, and Nicole. But he looked forward to a clean bed, even a bed less than clean—a quiet haystack somewhere.

Exhaustion was overtaking him, his mind seemed to be going fuzzy.

Some miles above Lake Salvador, they rode into a settlement called—Jeff was certain, in irony—Paradis. They rode first to the town stables and blacksmith shop. Here, Jeff haggled sleepily with the owner over two of the horses they'd taken from Fabio. Both he and Vincente had discussed the possibility that the bandit's horses might be known in the entire territory, but if the bearded hostler recognized the animals or tack, he gave no overt sign. He agreed he had buyers for two good animals, finally ended up giving Jeff a fair price for three saddles and two horses. The least of the animals, the horse ridden by the hunchbacked dwarf Philippe, they kept as a pack animal. Vincente transferred the small chest that had been secured behind his own saddle on the long ride through the bayou country. "What you got in a chest that big, young fellow?" the stable keeper wanted to know.

"Boots," Vincente told him with a smile.

The hostler and the stable hangers-on were so sure they were being gulled by the boy that Vincente had to unlock the chest and show them the highly polished boots.

"Great balls," one of the men said. "You sell shoes, young fellow?"

"No, *señor,*" Vincente said with a warm smile. "I buy them."

Jeff yawned again, staggered by fatigue. He said, "Where would a man get a good meal in this town?"

The stable owner squinted, staring up and down the single street of Paradis. "Well, if he's smart, he'd find a good cook, marry her, settle down, and go home for his meals." All his friends, the hangers-on, laughed and

96

agreed. "Failing that, I reckon the only thing left is the tavern yonder."

Leaving their horses at the stable to be watered, fed, and rubbed down, Vincente and Jeff walked along the sun-blasted street, angling across it to the tavern. The area was stalled into stunned silence in the heat. They entered the tavern, found it clean, swept, dusted, with red-checked tablecloths on tables set with large candles in beer steins. The food proved that gourmet cooks, like prophets, are unappreciated in their own countries.

A stout girl attended them. Walking away from them, she reminded Jeff of Gretchen, but she was darker and younger and lacked Gretchen's hidden, smoldering look. She brought them a hot creole gumbo that was better, richer, and tangier than anything Jeff had tasted in the finest restaurant of the *Vieux Carre*. Both he and Vincente put away two bowls of the crab, okra, tomato, and sea-food broth, along with two small loaves each of rye bread with carraway seeds. Then the girl brought them catfish, hot and steaming, crispy and savory. By this time Jeff had encouraged the girl to admit her name was Evangeline. This was a less than uncommon name in this parish, she told them. Many Cajun girls were named Evangeline. Jeff told her he would wager the name fit none as it did her. But when she also admitted she was thirteen, he abandoned her to Vincente.

After devouring two of the flaky, creamy tortes for dessert, Jeff felt as if he had been drugged. He needed sleep, badly. He said, "Why don't we just check the rooms upstairs? If they're clean at all, we'll spend the night."

"I'd like that," Vincente said, watching Evangeline's bottom twitch as she walked away from them.

"Damn it," Jeff said. "You are only fourteen years old, Vincente. You're too damned young to be sniffing after wenches."

"I wish only to follow in your great footsteps, *mi amigo*," Vincente said in his politest tone.

"And that's another thing," Jeff said. He yawned. He

was too tired, too grateful, and too filled with delicious food to be angry. "I thought I told you to go home to Cuba, and not to follow me."

Vincente watched Evangeline's unfettered breasts bobble under her peasant's blouse. The girl knew he watched and she increased their bobbling for his enjoyment. Vincente's voice was almost chilled. "Who was following you, *señor?*"

"You were, you damned young rascal."

"No, *señor*. I was not following you. I was merely traveling to Cuba—in my own way, my own fashion—and our paths just happened to cross."

Jeff laughed despite himself. "Just happened to cross, eh?"

"*Sí, señor.* Just happened to cross—to your great good fortune."

"All right, damn it. All right. I thank you. You saved my life. But I'm going to get you back to Cuba if it's the last thing I do."

"I hope it is at least the last thing, *señor,* unless you agree to accompany me."

"Why not?" Jeff said. "At least it would get you back home and under the wing of your natural father, Don Cipriano. It would get you back in school, you young hellion."

Vincente watched Evangeline glide across the room, bosom bouncing under her dress. He shrugged. "As you say, *señor*. But we are going to spend the night, aren't we?"

Jeff yawned almost helplessly. His eyes would barely stay open, but he did not miss the way Evangeline looked at Vincente from beneath thick, lowered lashes. "I ought not to. You're liable to get us both in trouble. What if her father catches you? She's thirteen. He'll kill you."

"Ah, *señor,* you forget. I learned from the master. From you. Caution was one of the first lessons I learned from you."

"Oh, go to hell. But I can tell you this. If you plan

any adventures with that underaged Circe there, you'll have a room of your own."

"Ah, *señor!* You are most understanding. I was wondering how to broach that subject—without hurting your feelings."

Jeff swung at him but missed.

The tavern owner and his wife were delighted to learn that Jeff and Vincente would spend the night. They handed keys to rooms adjoining Evangeline's. "The girl Evangeline will show you the way, gentlemen." Her father smiled. Jeff pitied the man. Unlike most tavern keeps, this fellow was most trusting of transients. He was, as a matter of fact, a hell of a poor excuse for an ordinary owner—he served excellent food in clean surroundings and, Jeff found, the bed and bedroom were spotless, the mattress of shucks cool and deep.

He fell upon it. He heard Evangeline and Vincente whispering together for a long time after the girl should have returned downstairs. But he sprawled across his mattress, too exhausted to care. From a great distance he heard her father bawl up the stairwell, "Evangeline! Get your lazy ass back down here. There's work for you to do." She answered, "Yes, father, at once." But she was still giggling and whispering with Vincente in the next room when Jeff plunged into deep, stunned sleep.

Jeff remained restless though sunk in exhausted slumber. Even while he slept a nagging awareness of imminent danger constantly simmered in the back of his mind. As Lafitte had warned, Baxter Simon was on his trail, somewhere out there now. He could come unexpectedly upon his bitter and implacable enemy around the next bend in the road, beyond the next hill, in the first gathering of nightshade. Bax Simon was a busy man, with slaves to whelp, grade, and market—a huge, rich plantation to oversee—but first, Simon was a driven man, obsessed by the need to balance all accounts. Few men ever stirred Simon's hatred as had Bricktop, the runaway slave. Nobody got the best of Baxter Simon for long. No fugitive slave could be permitted to walk free. The very freedom of such an animal was an affront to Simon, and a rogue nigger gave other niggers rebellious ideas. An owner made an example of renegade blacks or he lost control; he was soon out of business. This was never going to happen to Bax Simon. He would devote twenty-four hours of every day to insure that it never happened. As far as Simon was concerned, Bricktop was a doomed runner . . . it was only a matter of time.

Jeff shrugged deeper into the mattress. It was not his nature to look forward in fear or to look backward with longing. He never hurried to be hung, but he met his problems in their season. Dread was debilitating, despair self-defeating. He figured himself at least as intelligent as Baxter Simon, and he was younger. Pursuit kept his wits honed. He didn't look for trouble, sometimes he ran from it; he stood and faced it when he had to. Simon was an unequal foe—everything stacked in his favor. But in one way they were equals. His hatred matched Simon's, breath for breath.

The next morning Jeff awoke a little after eight o'clock. He felt renewed, rested, refreshed, reinvigorated. Some of his native optimism had returned. He lay for a moment in the bed, orienting himself. There was activity in the street; sounds of heavy dray wagons, men and equipment, rose to his open window. The light curtains bulged with an errant breeze. Despite his predicament, the world looked good. The sun streamed in past the pregnant curtains, its yellow shafts almost reaching his bed.

He joined Vincente at a red check–clothed table in the dining room downstairs. Vincente looked like the cat who had eaten the canary and appropriated its cage. He was enjoying his third cup of coffee, served by a sad, tear-choked Evangeline in a fresh dress and white, crisply starched apron.

"You rascal," Jeff teased when Evangeline went into the kitchen for their order. "So you raided the hen house last night?"

"She brought the whole nest to me, *amigo*," Vincente whispered, describing in glowing terms the way Evangeline had crept along the roofing in the darkness from her own room and entered his chambers through the window. "Like a cat, Don Jeff, like a soft, sweet little pussy cat."

"And you feel no compunction at violating a virgin?"

"She was not a virgin," Vincente said. "Though barely used. She did admit she had never had anything as wonderful as she had with me."

"There's a lot of that kind shared," Jeff said. He broke off, changing the subject as the red-eyed little chick returned with a large tray from which she served them light, golden brown pancakes, eggs cooked precisely right, fresh ham, and fingers of fried fish to dip into small vials of oil and vinegar.

Jeff ate ravenously. He did not know when they would find food so lovingly prepared again. As he settled their bill with Evangeline's father at the bar, he congratulated him on his excellent cook and asked that the cook be commended.

"Raoul is a wonderful cook, *m'sieur*," the tavern owner said. "He is a mustee, you know."

"Oh?" Jeff's head jerked up.

The tavern owner was counting out his change in gold. "Yes. His father was a Cajun, and his mother an octoroon servant here in town. Some of these mustees—when they've a lot of human blood in them like Raoul—are almost human, almost as smart as a human being."

"Yes," Jeff said. "Some of them."

"Some of them are indeed," Vincente agreed with a faint taunting smile.

Jeff glanced at the boy, troubled. He was certain Vincente would die before he would betray his guilty secret, but on the other hand, Vincente's taunting smile reminded him forcefully of the old adage: when two people know a secret, it is already shared by twice two many. . . .

It took Vincente a long time to tear himself away from the sobbing Evangeline at the kitchen door of the tavern. Jeff collected their horses, Vincente's chest of boots, and his own carpetbag and lashed them to the back of the pack animal. He walked them into the sunlight, strolled to the side of the tavern and whistled. Vincente kissed Evangeline brutally hard on the lips, squeezing one of her breasts furiously as if hoping to impress his memory in her mammary forever. Then he broke away, running, and leaped up in the saddle—to impress the little waitress, Jeff realized.

Vincente continued to chatter for miles about his nocturnal rendezvous with the daughter of the innkeeper. He insisted upon describing it all in detail, a kind of blow-by-blow description. "She said she could come to me early," Vincente said. "I thought she meant around midnight. I was prepared to stand the waiting. But her father won't let her work in the tavern after supper. She is too young, the men too rough. So as soon as it was dark, she came in my room through the window. She barred the door. Then she came to my bed. She had on nothing but the shift. She pulled it off, dropped it on the floor, and then crawled into my bed, reaching for me."

"I hope you didn't disappoint the lady."

"I am not the heavily endowed stud, Señor Don Jeff Carson, but this is the vow I make every woman who takes me in her bed—I will die trying to satisfy her."

"And you satisfied the little kitten without dying, I see."

"She was so pleased, she begged me to marry her."

"She's thirteen! And you're fourteen! My God!"

"Even so. She said her father would be happy to have me work at the tavern with her. That the day would come when we could own it all together. Anything, if I would stay with her."

"Did you tell her you are on your way to Cuba to learn to read and write?"

Vincente drew in an outraged breath and was silent for some moments. But his news was too wonderful to keep. "All the things I learned—by spying on you and Gretchen, and others—I thoughtfully taught my little Evangeline."

"What do you mean, you spied on me?"

"What better way to learn?" Vincente inquired. "She was a most willing pupil." He described in detail the many positions of love, the way he had taught her to use the tip of her tongue to tickle, rake, inspire. He spoke with such attention to every action in fact that Jeff found himself growing aroused. It seemed longer than one day since he had been emotionally and physically drained by Gretchen, Nicole, and Zilla.

He changed the subject. The middle of the bayou country was no place to suffer overpowering lust. He said, "One thing you have never told me, you little scamp. How did you get to the landing from Barataria?"

"On the same flatboat you used."

"How could you? I didn't see you—or your horse."

"Oh, no, we came on a second trip. I was waiting at the dock when the flatboat returned, with my horse saddled, my bags and chest packed. I gave the flatboat skipper an order signed by Jean Lafitte himself. The order stated that I was to be transported to the landing at once, that I had to reach Jeff Carson in all haste with the most urgent of messages."

"The hell you did."

"The hell I didn't, *señor*."

"Do you mind telling me how you got that order?"

"That was easy. I wrote it."

"You! You can barely write. You can't do forgery—or write well enough to copy Lafitte's hand."

Vincente smiled like an imp of Satan. "I write well enough to deceive a man who cannot read at all, *señor*."

The pound of horses' hooves, the clatter of coach wheels, harness and gear thundered behind them. They rode off the road, one on the left shoulder, the other on the right. A few hundred yards ahead was a fork in the road.

They slouched in their saddles, Jeff holding tightly to the rein of the packhorse, and sitting in the shade of moss-hung live oaks, they watched a rich coach race past them. There was much to mark the coach as unusual: its excessive speed, the fact that it was being driven by a well-dressed young dandy who was straining every muscle to keep his wildly racing team under control, the way the window flaps were drawn as if something hidden and secret were concealed in its tonneau.

The man driving the coach barely glanced at them. Jeff was thankful they'd had the foresight to clear the roadway. The young fop, pretty, faddishly dressed, slender, could not have stopped his horses nor turned them.

Using all the strength in his back, arms, shoulders, and legs, the young exquisite blade managed to head the horses left at the fork in the road.

They sat unmoving, without speaking for some moments, watching the coach until it disappeared in thin dust along the left trail. Without speaking, Jeff nodded his head forward. He and Vincente rode to the fork and sat reading the signs. The sign to the right promised New Orleans in the distance. New Orleans! *Vieux Carre!* Bourbon Street! The St. Louis Hotel! Madame Hortense's Riding Academy—for men who hated horses. Jeff was sorely tempted.

The left fork pointed north and west to Ascension. There could be little to compare between the village and the most cosmopolitan city in America.

"Why don't we flip a coin?" Vincente suggested.

"Because," Jeff searched his saddlebag. "I have a map. The road to The Laurels Plantation. We can pray it's east—toward New Orleans." But when he'd shaken out the small map Lafitte had marked for him, he saw their trail led to the left. He didn't have to speak; the way he sagged in his saddle conveyed the bad news to Vincente.

Before they could speak, they heard a horseman approaching from behind them. He rode as pell-mell as the coach. When he saw them slouched in their saddles at the crossroads, he pulled so hard on the reins that his lathered mount reared, trying to escape the cruel pressure of the bit. The man struck the horse viciously with his crop to quiet him.

He was a Creole, handsome, dark, with small clipped mustache and pointed goatee. His black eyes surveyed the world arrogantly, and the very tilt of his head invited a man to hate him. "A coach just raced past here," the man said, glaring at Jeff and Vincente as if daring them to oppose him. His dark eyes searched both roads. They stretched silent and hot. "Which way did it go?"

"Why?" Jeff inquired.

For a moment the young Creole aristocrat looked as if he might strike Jeff with the same crop he'd used on his horse. He despised insolence in lesser human beings—which comprised the whole of the human race, Jeff saw.

"It's none of your damned impudent affair," the Creole said.

"Then go to hell," Jeff said.

"You, boy." The man jerked his pretty head around, staring at Vincente. "I'll give you a quarter to tell me which way that coach went."

"And I'll give you a dollar to go fuck yourself," Vincente said.

The dark man looked as if he might explode with the pressures ready to erupt inside him. By some terrible exercise of discipline, he managed to keep his voice under control and to twist his mustached mouth into an unaccustomed smile. "The woman in that coach is my wife. The libertine driving that coach is her lover." His lip curled and his black eyes flashed. "Her latest lover. I would deeply appreciate it if you would tell me in which direction they went."

"Of course," Jeff said. As one, both he and Vincente pointed to the right, toward New Orleans.

The dark-skinned man's mouth twisted. "Of course. They are headed for his plantation. The stupid fool—thinks he can hide my wife and my coach from me." He gave them the briefest nods, heeled his horse viciously, struck it with the crop, and raced off on the wrong road, headed east.

Jeff watched the fleeting figure a moment without compunction. There had been no question in his mind about which direction he'd give the husband. All the world has ever loved lovers. And besides, though marriage is an honorable estate, fornication is a much older, holier, ordained activity—the normal, natural, God-given, uncomplex, simple right to take it where one found it.

CHAPTER X

Jeff halted his horse in the middle of the sun-braised road. They had followed the left fork only a few miles when he held up his hand to signal Vincente to stop.

Vincente drew alongside Jeff's mount and the packhorse in the lacy stitching of shade under a wide-reaching bay tree. Ahead, down the dusty road, they saw the carriage that had earlier rocketed past them like a gooney bird in frantic flight. The fashionable equipage was still splendid, expensive wooden exteriors highly burnished, door and window frames brass gilded, team sleek and fat rumped and decorated with rich leather and shining metal harness. But the coach tilted crazily—its right wheel had spun off under the battering of the road, the deranged mishandling of the reins, and the distracted swaying and rocking of the tormented vehicle.

The lover—so designated by the irate jealous husband back on the road to Paradis, and so recognized by an uncritical Jeff Carson—was struggling to lift the front axle in order to replace the wheel. Even from the distance, it could be clearly discerned that he was totally shaken, sopping wet with sweat, frustrated, and half-crazed with fear of being overtaken by his light-o'-love's jealous husband. He had discarded his bottle green jacket, rolled up his laced sleeves—and he still looked helpless.

As Jeff and Vincente approached and rode alongside the coach, both doors of which were now flung open, the woman's voice was wailing, beseeching Jacques to hurry. "You know, Jacques, Kevin can't be more than a mile behind us."

"Goddamn it, June! Oh, forgive me, *ma chérie!* But goddamn it, June, I'm doing the best I can."

"I know that, Jacques lover! But if Kevin overtakes us here on this road—we will be destroyed."

"Goddamn it, June. *Pardon, ma chérie!* But goddamn it, I have more to lose than you. *You* will be destroyed socially—I will be *killed.* I am as anxious to get this wheel on as you are—but I am helpless!" He looked as if he might weep. When he dragged his dirt-encased hand across his eyes, he left a ludicrous trail of black mud.

"Perhaps we might be of some small service," Jeff said.

So engrossed in their own terrifying predicament, so wrapped up in each other and their own plight, neither goddamn-it-June nor Jacques-lover had seen or heard Jeff and Vincente ride alongside the coach.

June screamed, and Jacques cried out in involuntary terror. Jacques spun around, no doubt looking for his bottle green jacket and perhaps the small single-shot derringer many gentlemen carried. June quieted much quicker than her sweated, harried lover. She recoiled only slightly against the polished panel of the carriage. She stared up at Jeff, and even in this moment of anxiety, he recognized the faint swirling of interest deep in those exquisitely almond-shaped eyes.

"Who are you?" she said.

Jacques spoke, voice shaken. "We have no money with us. Neither of us. We are in a sad predicament— not even road agents would take advantage of such travail as ours. Please?"

Jeff ignored the lover. Jacques was not much, less even than that. He stood perhaps five-six in his high-heeled boots; his pantaloons revealed scrawny legs and sorry thighs. His hips were slightly plump, a plumpness that would have sent many of Lafitte's seamen into a thrall of oestrus. His belly was flat, he was pigeon chested and narrow of shoulder. Only his stiff neck displayed the courage of arrogance. His sharply cut features gave him a look of weakness, his cheeks were pale, but there was his curly hair rampant about his forehead, curling over his ears and collar to stir the heart of superficial females.

June, goddamn it, was something else! Jeff bowed in the saddle toward her, letting his eyes linger upon hers, on her swollen, murrey lips, the white rise of full breasts exposed at her décolleté bodice. She was, Jeff admitted, the loveliest creature he had beheld in many a month; there was about her much to rouse a man to violence and depravity, to drive a gentleman like Jacques to defy a jealous husband. Jeff admired Jacques no more, but understood him better! Possibly eighteen, or at the most twenty, June had crisp black hair parted severely in the middle and drawn back into a loose roll across the nape of her neck. Her skin was the smoothest Jeff had ever seen. The flowered muslin dress she wore accentuated all her curves, the upthrust of those saucy breasts, the powdered whiteness of throat and bosom.

In that breath of time, Jeff determined that he wanted, more than anything else, to join that nonexclusive club in which Jacques was presently presiding officer. He wanted her.

"I'm sure we could help you," Jeff said. "Perhaps we could do—a great deal for you."

Jacques was still shaking his head, fearful of attack from robbers along with the imminent arrival of June's mindlessly jealous husband. He kept shaking his head, but obviously June was smarter. She shared Jacques's mistrust of strangers on a lonely road—it was the curse of the times! But she was also pragmatically aware of their desperate need for competent assistance.

And there was one thing more. Jeff had smiled at her.

When Jeff Carson smiled, few could resist his charm; he looked at you and invited you to share the exuberant joy he found in simply being alive and free! Perhaps his heightened pleasure came from the precariousness of his own existence; every moment *was* precious, to be enjoyed to the hilt. Tomorrow he might be dead! But no matter! Come laugh with me now in this vital moment, his youthful, yet worldly smile importuned. He realized he could give others pleasure, find excited gratification in doing so, and being doomed, had no time to waste in nonessentials.

"I'm sure you could help me," June said. "I'm sure of it."

"We don't need your help," Jacques protested.

"Jacques lover." June's voice broiled him on the spit of her disdain. "Don't be a complete ass."

Jacques winced and retreated a full step under the impact of her contempt. He sweated. He had wasted their time talking when he should have been mounting her. When he did mount her, he was driven to such frenzy of delight that he could not control himself. He had left her far from satisfied. And now, when he had run the wheel off her carriage, he was totally helpless to replace it. He wanted to cry. His lower lip did quiver slightly, but he tilted his head higher and murmured, "As you say, *madame*."

Jeff jerked his head at Vincente who swung down from his own saddle and, as if reading Jeff's mind, began removing his boot chest and Jeff's carpetbag and Lafitte's saddlebag from the packhorse.

"What are you doing?" Jacques demanded. "We can't go away and leave this coach here—it would be tantamount to an admission of guilt."

"I know nothing of guilt," Jeff said. "I was going to suggest that you take this horse and ride across country—in all haste—to your plantation."

"A splendid suggestion," June said.

"Totally unacceptable," Jacques said. "I can't leave Madame Levaux—abandon her here with strangers. No." He shook his head. "I can't leave you here, June, with total strangers."

"I'll be all right, Jacques. We're less than two miles from Baiser."

"And even if I could, do you expect me to ride bareback?" Jacques said, shaking his head.

Jeff shrugged. "I don't care what you do. But I can tell you this. We met a man at the fork, looking for a wildly racing coach with a handsome young white man handling the horses. We sent him to the right, but he may have already turned back."

"Kevin," June whispered in an ecstasy of terror.

Jacques made unintelligible little sounds in his throat. He stared at Vincente, at Jeff, back along the road, at June. Clutching up both her hands in his, he kissed them frantically, turning the palms up.

"You're wasting time, Jacques," his lady said.

Tears streaming through the mud about his eyes, June's lover swung up on the bareback of the pack-horse. He was at home, even without a saddle, astride the animal. He nodded at them, punched the horse in the flanks, and galloped off north on the roadway.

They wasted no time looking after him. Jeff found an axe in the toolbox at the rear of the coach. He chopped down a sapling and walked back to the road, clear-cutting limbs and branches. Using Vincente's boot chest, padded with saddle and saddle blanket to protect it, he slowly levered the front axle up from the ground. Staring at his bulging muscles in arms, shoulders, back, and thighs, June cried out in delight. While he held the axle aloft, June aided Vincente in shoving the wheel back on the shaft.

Quick inspection showed Jeff the bolt had sheared away, but he found a disc and pin in the tool box from which he fashioned a reasonable lock-nut. "It should hold for two miles—if we travel slowly," he said.

When he turned to look at June, he found her

smiling, nodding, but her gaze was fixed on the prominent bulge in his trousers. She said, in a breathless voice, "Why don't you tie your horses to the back of the coach? Your boy could drive the team, could he not? I do wish you'd sit inside the coach with me. I've been through a trying experience, I feel on the verge of hysterics."

"An excellent suggestion," Jeff said. He thought, this is an ideal quail! Her husband on her trail, her latest lover racing across country bareback and running for his life, no possible way to explain this situation, and she was entranced with the quality of his manhood. "I know how nervous and upset you must be."

He tossed the boot chest, saddlebag, and carpetbag into the baggage compartment of the coach. Vincente replaced saddle blanket and saddle. They secured their horses to the rear grips of the coach. Vincente swung up into the driver's seat and took up the reins. Both Vincente and Jeff checked the road behind and to their relief found it still empty—hot and silent. Turning back, he found that June had not taken her gaze from below his belt buckle. "Take it easy, boy," Jeff called up to Vincente. "Slow. I don't know how long that wheel will hold up."

June put her head out the window. "Yes, boy, please be careful. Don't try to—hurry."

She sank back into the coach and Jeff found, with excited pleasure, that her taut little hip was pressed against his. Jeff was thankful for this opportunity. He loved the directness of those almond-shaped eyes beneath those thick lashes, the oval face with its suggestion of squared cheekbones to give her just that faintly imperious look that added spice to complete surrender. And this he would have from her! Had she ever bedded with a real man—or had her lovers been of the style and quality of her Creole husband and her pigeon-chested lover?

He smiled at her again and her eyes held his for a long hungry moment. Jeff apologized and reached across her to slam the coach door. He leaned so close to her that his cheek caressed the silky fullness of her breasts. He breathed deeply of the heated sweetness. She did not move away but smiled her thanks and let her hand drop between their legs. Since there was no space between their legs, her overheated fingers rested palm up upon his thigh, inches from his fly. He held his breath, waiting for the movement of the carriage, or her own need, to bounce those fingers against him.

He shifted painfully, glancing around. The interior of the coach conveyed the wealth indicated by her manner, her dress, and her team.

"I don't see *how* I can ever thank you enough for all you and your boy have done for me," June Levaux said. "You have saved me from disgrace."

"We're not home yet," Jeff reminded her, watching her fingers on his thigh, less than an inch away now. He could turn slightly and she would either have it in her fist, or she would draw away in real or pretended shock. This was a crucial moment, and he didn't want to spoil it. He would wait for her movement, or at least some further overt sign of encouragement. He wanted so much and there was obviously so little time, but he would not rush her and thus lose her.

She laughed. The jiggling motion of the coach bounced the backs of her hot fingers against his rigidity. She jerked her hand away, let it fall back less than an inch from its painful prominence. He sighed, emboldened. She had touched him, and she meant to touch him again—quite by accident, but assuredly. "But Jacques Archet is at home at his plantation. All the power will be gone from Kevin's foolish raging."

The coach struck a pothole in the road. Jostled, June laughed lightly. Her hand fell against him with the skimming touch of a butterfly and as quickly gone. But the impact of her heated hand was like the blow of a sledge hammer. "You have such lovely hands, *madame*," he told her. He covered her hand with his own on his lap, forcing her palm with gentle touch to encase his rigidity.

"Thank you." June caught her breath audibly but she left her hand there. After a moment, her fingers tightened, measuring, testing, inflaming.

"One thing troubles me, Madame Levaux." Jeff tried to ignore the agonized aching under her seeking hand. "What is your husband going to think when he returns to find *me* beside you?"

"He will think nothing," she assured him. Her hand relaxed, gripping him overtly now, but she was not relaxed. He was certain she had never encountered a cannon of such caliber in all her campaigns. Her pale cheeks, her glazed eyes assured him she had not. The way she fought to remain calm and in possession of her faculties underlined her delight with him. "I will permit him to think nothing. After all, you were a good samaritan. You fixed my carriage. Oh, you were so— muscular! You did it with such ease . . . you quite turn a young woman's head, *m'sieur*. . . . Is it terribly hot in here, or is it my imagination? . . . And, after all," she babbled, "we are chaperoned—by your boy. Is this not true? . . . Oh, my dear, I don't know how I shall ever repay you for all you have done for me."

Jeff gazed down at her. His heart thundered. Her hand clutching him fiercely now, every bound of the coach, every turn of the wheels on the rough road was agonized delight.

"Perhaps one kiss would be total payment, *madame*," he suggested. "You are by far the loveliest woman I have had the delight to meet. One kiss from your lips would be a memory to carry with me to the corners of the earth—and rich payment for any meager service I may have performed."

"If you wish a kiss, *m'sieur*," June said, breathless, "you have earned it. But you'll think me so forward . . . we are strangers."

"No. We are not strangers. Not you and I. Not anymore." He did not by glance or tone indicate the grasp she had on him down there. Her fingers tightened almost involuntarily. She clung to him. She leaned against him, placing her head in the hollow at his wide shoulders, and turned her face up to his.

Jeff closed his lips over hers. Something like the charge of static electricity surged through him at the contact of her mouth. He pressed her sweet-scented lips apart and pushed his tongue between her teeth. Kissing was never going to satisfy him. He slid his hand into her low-cut bodice and spilled her pink-tipped breasts into view. His fingers closed, caressing, fondling. Her mouth opened wide and he drove his tongue deep.

As if obeying irresistible impulses from outside himself, Jeff reached down and drew her skirts and crinolines above her knees. She sighed and sagged heavily against him. His fingers moved at her thighs. Her body shivered in delighted little spasms of ecstasy and then thrust upward to him in a total surrender. In that moment he could have possessed her—in bright daylight, on an open road, in a moving carriage, but in that precise moment, sounds from outside the coach penetrated his consciousness, brought him jolted and shaken back to reality. He became aware of young black voices screaming. "It's her! It's my lady's coach. Mis June home! Miz June home!"

And then Jeff heard Vincente call down a warning from the driver's seat. "We're at her plantation."

Finally, June too was able to control the wildness inside her heated mind. She managed to pull herself straight in the carriage seat. She brushed her dress down and sat up straight, poised, if pale and unnerved.

Agonized, Jeff stared out the coach window at the plantation. They had turned in between monolithic stone gates and moved along a lane of live oaks that led to a French Colonial–style home, palatial and imposing on a small knoll. The whole estate was immaculately kept, its boxed hedges, green lawns, and decorative plantings carefully tended and closely manicured. The drives were swept clean of leaves and litter. There was that atmosphere about June Levaux's plantation home of all that money could buy—money in prodigious amounts.

"We grow sugarcane." June managed to speak in a conversational tone as if nothing had happened between them. "And cotton. Cattle too. And we have extensive lumber."

Jeff smiled. "What you are saying is that you have too much—of everything."

Her eyes met and held his, going weak like a sleepy baby's. "No, *m'sieur*. All I am trying to say is that until this last hour, though I had not realized it, I have nothing at all."

"You are most kind."

"I trust I can prevail upon you to spend some time here at Baiser de France. My father named it Kiss of France, but I call it French Kiss—you know?"

"Of course," Jeff said.

CHAPTER XI

They were enjoying delicious cold mint juleps on the shaded veranda more than an hour later when they heard the thunder of a horse's hooves on the lane from the public road. Gravel clattered in the driveway as Kevin Levaux rode furiously up to the front steps and slung himself from the saddle. He tossed

115

reins to small black boys who looped them through the metal rings on the horse-head hitching posts at the side of the house.

Levaux strode up the steps to the magnolia-shaded veranda, slapping his riding crop against his thigh. He was tall, with some remnants of manly good looks showing through the hypertense, frustrated face and rigid lines of his young body. His clothing was of superb quality, streaked with sweat and road dust. His black hair grew deeply indented at the temples and curled over his collar most fashionably.

He stared, almost shocked to find June relaxed and at ease on the veranda. She sat in a pillowed, wingback wicker chair between Jeff and Vincente. Jeff's long legs were stretched out before him, and the wicked bulge at his crotch only served to enrage the already embittered and bellicose man. Beyond them, he saw the two horses hitched beside his own trembling, lathered mount. He knew he had seen them somewhere before, but for the moment he could not place them. He jerked his head around, searching the premises for his rival, the hated Jacques Archet of Arrow Ridge plantation.

"Where is he?" Levaux demanded. He glared down at his wife. "Where is the pusillanimous bastard Archet?"

June remained relaxed in her chair but her quiet voice lashed him. "Must I remind you, Kevin? We have guests."

Levaux stopped searching the shaded, magnolia-scented veranda. He brought his malevolent gaze back to the dark-haired Cuban youth and the heavy-hung red-head. "Who are you people? Where have I seen you before?"

"We met you on the road from Paradis," Jeff said.

Levaux slapped his crop against his leg. "Ah. You two scoundrels! Sent me on a wild chase to Archet's plantation—and all the time the treacherous pair were here."

Jeff shrugged. "You asked us, *m'sieur,* which way a racing carriage had gone."

"And you lied to me."

June's voice interposed. "I must ask you to remember, Kevin. These are my guests. In my house."

Her young husband winced. Her reminding him that the money, property, slaves, and bank accounts were all in her name alone was the cruelest blow. Jeff felt no qualms of conscience. His rogue's sympathies were ever on the side of an erring wife rather than with her wronged husband. He shrugged negligently. "Perhaps I erred. It seemed to me that a coach had recently turned right."

June sat forward. "I demand, Kevin, that you apologize at once to Mr. Carson and to young Vincente. They are my guests and we are deeply indebted to them."

"Oh?" Slightly calmer, but still provoked beyond reason, Kevin peered again at Vincente, at Jeff, and then at the two horses hitched beyond the jasmine hedge. Something was wrong, something flitted to the rim of his consciousness which would put everything in perspective and finally settle the matter of his wife and her lover—her latest lover!—but he could not pin it down. "And what service have these two *gentlemen,*" he made something bad-tasting of the word, "performed which puts us so deeply in their debt?"

"If you'll calm down, I'll tell you," June said. She indicated a fourth wingback chair. "Sit down. Janus will bring you a julep." She rang a small bell at her side.

Resentfully, obstinate still in his unsettled rage, Kevin continued to pace the veranda for some seconds like a caged animal. He scrubbed with his thumb knuckle at his solar plexus as if he were afire inside. At last, he flung himself in the chair and accepted the chilled glass from the black slave at his elbow. "God knows, I need a drink." He took a long swig of the liquid. He belched, his face contorting with some pain. "My God, June, you're killing me—as surely as though you hold a gun to my head!" He drank again. "Well, go on, what lies are you going to tell me now?"

117

June caught her breath. "I shouldn't even speak to you," she said. "You are behaving abominably."

"I?" He laughed, a rasping, half-sobbing sound. "I have been racing half-crazed across the countryside looking for you—and your lover—in your assignation. Oh, my God! And I am behaving abominably."

"I owe you no explanation," June said. "But because I want this to be a pleasant day for our—for my guests— I will try to put your suspicious, unreasonable mind at ease. . . . Toth and I were returning from the Church of Our Blessed Mother—"

"The church?" The words were a strangled cry.

"The church." Her voice chilled with a deadly calm. Jeff stared at her in admiration. She was unprincipled. What a perfect confidence woman she would have made! "I go there Wednesdays for Mass—"

"This is not Wednesday." Kevin whispered it, on the verge of choleric tears.

"I go to confession when I may," she continued in her easy manner. "When I need to pray for you—for us— for our marriage. . . . On the way home, a wheel came off our carriage. Alone, Toth was helpless—"

"Toth? Toth was with you?"

"Toth is my coachman, dear." Her tone was one she might use with a retarded child.

Kevin put his head back and bawled, "Janus! Hell take your black hide. Get out here."

The front door opened and the butler came, bearing mint juleps on a tray. Levaux raged, "Put those goddamn things down and get Toth up here. Now! You tell that black Toth I want him up here on this front veranda in two minutes or I am going to take the hide off his worthless back."

"Yassuh, masta." Janus backed away. "I sho' tells him." He placed the tray on a table and fled, going around the side of the house.

Levaux slumped in his chair, long legs extended before him, dark gaze fixed on the parquet flooring. His hand quivered on the frosted glass.

June's quiet voice pursued him. "Don't you want to hear the rest of it?"

"Yes, goddamn it. I want to hear about Jacques Archet. Meeting you in the hammock. Pulling down the shades at the coach windows. And you—like some cheap slut off the streets. That's what I want to hear."

"Then I'm afraid you will have to take your contemptible, evil mind somewhere else. My story is very simple. I went to church—driven by my coachman. Returning, I lost a wheel and these gentlemen kindly repaired it. This is the truth. If you want something else to stew in your suspicious mind, you'll go elsewhere for it."

"Oh, I'll go elsewhere, all right. I'll go back to Arrow Ridge plantation. I'll pursue that cowardly Archet into his chamber and drag him from under his bed. Oh, I'll get the truth."

Her head tilted. "Yes. Why don't you do that?"

Before either of them could pursue the acrimony further, Janus returned with a youthful black man. Toth was built like a professional athlete: thick shoulders, narrow hips, and muscle-corded legs in cotton pantaloons, which revealed the outlines of his considerable manhood, but which were of ideal weight in this humidity. Toth looked to be between eighteen and twenty, but anxiety had aged him in the past five minutes. He shook, sweating as he trod fearfully up on the cool veranda. He stopped, head bowed, near Kevin Levaux's chair. Jeff pitied the poor bastard. *There, but for the grace of God . . .*

"It's all right, Toth," June said in a gentle, reassuring voice. "You have nothing to fear."

"Yes'm, Miz June, ma'am," Toth said. But he did not look up. He went on sweating; he went on trembling.

"Toth. Do you want to feel the blacksnake across your back until you're bleeding—and in shreds?" Levaux demanded.

"Oh, no, masta. Please don't whup Toth! Toth's a good boy, masta."

"You know what happens if you lie to me, don't you?" Levaux persisted.

"Yassuh, masta, the whips . . . but I don't lie. Toth don't lie."

"Where were you this morning, Toth?" Kevin leaned forward in his chair. His goatee quivered, his black eyes seemed to slice into the black slave, ripping him open.

Toth looked as if he might vomit. "I with Miz June, masta."

"There," June said. "That's enough. You may go, Toth."

"Yes'm." Toth shook in visible relief. He turned to lope away, but Kevin's voice crackled like thunder, stopping him.

"Stand still, damn you! Where did you and Miz June go, Toth?"

"I drove mistress to de church, masta." Toth gulped, obviously swallowing back the bile gorging up in his throat.

"Get out of here, goddamn you," Kevin said. "This is not over, Toth. You go down to the stables. You take my horse with you. You send me a fresh horse, saddled. At once."

"Now what fool thing are you going to do?" June inquired. The tone of her voice revealed she didn't give a damn.

Kevin lunged upward, so embittered and envenomed that he knocked over his chair. "Oh, this little matter isn't over. These fellows—" his gaze raked across Jeff and Vincente and then returned, troubled. "These fellows have lied for you. Toth has lied for you. But I know one bastard who hasn't the guts to lie to me when I start beating him with this crop. I'm going to Arrow Ridge plantation, my love, and when I return, with your lover held by the scruff of his neck, we'll have a showdown once and for all."

A black boy, wearing only lightweight white pants, came running with a fresh horse saddled and ready. He came to the foot of the steps and waited. Kevin turned toward the steps, then glanced across his shoulders, staring at Vincente and Jeff and then at their horses. "Something's bad wrong—about you two. I can't pin it down. But I will. By God, I will. . . . Don't worry, my love, I shall be back."

"That's the hell of it," June said under her breath. "You always come back."

They watched Levaux climb into the saddle, whip the horse, and go racing along the lane toward the road. Jeff said, "What will you do? From what I saw of M'sieur Archet, he won't stand up well against your furious husband."

She shrugged. "It will end as I want it. In the end, Kevin will believe what I want him to believe. I will make him believe it. He will have no other choice. Let him ride across the country. It might help to calm him down."

Jeff smiled. "Isn't there a chance he might find out the truth?"

June Levaux took a long sip of her chilled mint julep. "What is the truth, *m'sieur?* At Baiser de France, the truth is what I say is the truth . . . I am June Antoinette La Fourche–Levaux. The plantation is *mine*. Every boll of cotton, every stalk of sugarcane, every slave . . . I inherited all this from my darling, deceased father. I am June Antoinette La Fourche–Levaux of Baiser de France."

"This must be very comforting," Jeff said in some irony.

"The truth, my handsome young friend, further is that my husband is a Creole. A poor but handsome man— an adventurer, actually an opportunist who married me for my money—My darling father—far wiser than I— hated Kevin. In order to protect me and Baiser de France from Kevin's profligate character, my father arranged his will, ironclad. Kevin can touch nothing, unless I give it to him. This has twisted Kevin's character even more than it was before. He is savagely jealous, murderously resentful of any man who looks at me. He demands to be master of this house, this plantation, and of me, even though he knows all three are impossible to him. I under-

121

stand the poor devil, though it makes me despise him no less. I realize he feels emasculated because I control the money, everything—and he can only stand impotently by."

"Why doesn't he relax and enjoy it?"

She smiled. "Perhaps because he is not so clever. And there is more to upset him and make his rage more virulent. . . . He cannot satisfy me . . . in our bed. He leaves me always—when I allow him to touch me at all—in the lurch. Do you understand what I mean by that?"

Both Jeff and Vincente nodded simultaneously. "That must indeed be fearful on you," Jeff said. He felt her eyes fixed on him once again.

"You don't know how bad it is," she said. "No man can know. . . . It would be bad enough—once in a while—but always to live with nothing else, it is unbearable. My nerves are affected, my humor, my disposition—sometimes I feel I am losing my mind. . . . Yes, I've had lovers since Kevin and I were married. God knows I have looked for release—for love returned in the way I am prepared to give it."

She laughed suddenly and stood up, brushing all unhappiness aside. "Come. Let me show you my calves. They alone give me direction in life. They are my pride."

As they walked in the sun toward the cattle pens outside the feed barn, she told them how she'd become interested in buying day-old calves and raising them for the market—as breeders or as beef. Young bulls were usually knocked in the head the day they were delivered. This was done to get more milk from the cows and keep a herd from being overrun with bulls. She had sent out word to all neighboring plantations, farms, and cattle ranches. She paid five dollars in gold for every day-old bull she could buy. She sent her slaves to pick up the animal. She fed them in pens at the barn. By the time they were six months old, there were buyers coming to look at them. Her profit had been enormous.

"But, even if it had not, this has been the only pleasure in my life in these past months." She laughed and touched

Jeff's arm. "If it were not for my calves, I'd go quite out of my mind. . . . I'd be as crazy as Kevin."

In the pens inside the barn she walked among the dozens of tottering calves. In pens beyond these, the animals from three to six months were caged, and in the open were the larger bulls, which she had raised from the first day of their lives. She told the slaves to show her guests how her calves were fed. A mixture of feed and milk was placed in a bucket from which a phalliclike oilcloth nipple extended ten or twelve inches. They watched the feeding for a while. As they turned away, June whispered to Jeff, "The size and shape of that nipple —the way the calves nurse at it—drives me wild, even when I see it every day."

When they returned to the veranda, Vincente said, "Don Jeff, I believe we should ride on."

Jeff nodded. He agreed. From the first moment he had seen this lovely young matron he had wanted her desperately. But how would they get together in this house under the suspicious nose of Kevin Levaux? Jeff had no wish to be killed by her husband, nor did he want to kill Levaux. This would appear to be the only alternative if he stayed here overnight. She would come to him. He could see her planning this already, waiting impatiently for nightfall. He would not resist her, because he could not.

She cried out. "But you must stay tonight. . . . Why, I had hoped you would like it here at French Kiss— perhaps you might extend your visit, a week or more." She looked at Vincente and smiled. "We have some delightful young bed wenches—black, quadroon, octoroon— virgins if this appeals to you. From ten years old up past your age. I plead with you to reconsider."

They sat again on the cool veranda. Janus served fresh mint juleps, small flaky lady fingers and wedges of cheese. As if speaking casually on some matter of no import, June said, "A most interesting medication—a tranquilizer —has made my life with Kevin easier. . . . This delightful Doctor Fabrett, in New Orleans, prescribed an opium derivative to calm Kevin and put him to sleep. . . . Kevin and I were visiting in New Orleans soon after we were married. Kevin was on edge, tense, nervous, almost out of his mind most of the time because he was almost impotent—no matter how desperately he tried. I was advised to see Doctor Fabrett. The good doctor talked to me and Kevin and then prescribed laudanum as a calming agent, a relaxant and sleep inducer for Kevin. . . . It has been a godsend to me. A dosage as prescribed by Doctor Fabrett for Kevin has a most calming effect upon Kevin no matter how upset or restless he may be." She smiled, reached out, and placed her hand on Jeff's thigh, high above his knee. "I have found that by doubling Kevin's dosage, we are *both* calmed. I am relieved by his quiet sleeping, and he is placed in a state of total slumber for the whole night—sometimes until the middle of the following morning."

CHAPTER XII

During the entire time he loafed at Baiser de France, Jeff was restive, feeling obligated to set out for The Laurels and the completion of Lafitte's mission. But this urgency was wholly counterbalanced by his restless compulsion to bed the luscious Madame Levaux. Not even the fear that Baxter Simon might be closing in on his backtrail, or the realization that the jealously unhinged Kevin Levaux might kill him altered that pulse-charging desire. Only those driven by overpowering inner compulsions could empathize with his passion; those fortunate beings not so impelled would never even understand. He wanted her. He needed her. He had to have her.

She came boldly into his second-floor bedroom a little past nine o'clock that night. She carried a glass-shaded lamp, which illumined her erotically in the enveloping darkness. Her fragile, transparent gown clearly outlined her full, pinkly tipped breasts, rounded hips, and that dark triangle at her mons veneris. Her black hair tumbled free almost to her waist.

Jeff shivered. That compulsive desire to have her at all costs suddenly erupted into reckless and unheeding necessity. He didn't give a damn about anything except having her as he had dreamed since the first moment he'd encountered her on that road—completely, to her total surrender, and beyond, as often as he could manage. He swung up out of bed and reached for her. . . .

Her coming to him had been accomplished with such casual ease. He had envisioned an agonized wait until past midnight. No. He should have known. Her fierce desire matched his. She had directed all her thoughts, every action toward reaching this room and his arms as speedily as possible. After four chilled mint juleps on the magnolia-textured veranda, both he and June had become reckless and indiscreet. She'd laughed too much, touched him too often and too intimately. Frequently, her eyes would glaze over and she'd stare at him in stark, raw need, not giving a damn who saw it, as long as he did. Vincente had shifted nervously in his chair, sweated and uncomfortable.

They were in the sun room when Kevin finally returned at dusk. Levaux rode swiftly, cruelly pushing his horse past its endurance. The animal faltered on quivering shanks and fetlock joints as the stable boy led it off toward the barns.

When Kevin stalked in, June was playing a love song on the spinnet. Jeff and Vincente relaxed on overstuffed lounges in the spacious and elegantly appointed sun room.

Highly glossed pieces of French Empire furniture, up-holstered in fabrics of bright tintings of green, yellow, and orange brightened the room, like islands on the patterned, pastel lime handwoven carpeting. A tall white mantel encased the wide fireplace, which was ornamented with burnished brass andirons. Fragile curtains billowed at ceiling-tall windows. A single painting dominated the room—a lively, decorative work of broad, flashing strokes and brilliant colors by Fragonard. The atmosphere of the bright room precisely epitomized June's spirit, verve, and love of color and excitement. How oppressive Kevin's attempted subjugation must be to her! Jeff pitied her. He felt compassion for Kevin but his sympathy was tempered and adulterated with wholehearted dislike. His empathy for June, on the other hand, was underscored by his growing and overwhelming need for her.

Janus drifted about the parlor with a long taper, lighting tall candles and crystal lamps against the encroaching dusk. As Kevin entered from the foyer, the black servant scurried from the room, taper guttering.

Levaux was strangely subdued. He strode toward the piano, then stopped, as if troubled and disoriented, in the middle of the room.

Sipping brandy, Jeff felt Kevin's eyes upon him. He met Levaux's dark gaze over his glass. He found no rage, only puzzlement. Kevin's eyes moved on to Vincente, and he studied the boy with that same questioning glance.

June stopped playing. The fragile sounds faded, replaced by an oppressive quiet. Distantly a black baritone sang mournfully to the dying sun. Servants hurried about the house, the sounds remote and unreal. "So you decided to come home?" June said. "I hope you learned all the evil you looked for."

Kevin winced. He shook his head. His voice sounded empty, incredulous. "No. You all say the same things. The sniveling Jacques Archet swears he was in his fields with his overseer. His overseer supports him with the straightest face. Toth backs you. These two fellows insist you were with Toth—and not Archet—when they came upon you on the road—that it must have been another fast-racing coach they saw turn right at the forks toward New Orleans, but of which I found no signs. Your priest at the Church of Our Blessed Mother. He tells me—with his hands tented in prayer before his chin—that you were there, at confession."

"Surely, Kevin, you're not accusing the poor priest of joining the rest of us in a conspiracy of lies." Her voice raked him like talons.

He shook his head and laughed self-deprecatingly. "No. Why should the priest lie to protect you? Let's ask what he would stand to lose if he opposed you? An annual tithing which buys his cassocks, and surplices, his sacramental wines, and his parish smoked hams. He has almost as little reason to lie as—say Jacques Archet."

"You're letting your unreasoning hatred of Jacques unsettle you," she said in a scathing tone.

"Am I? It's these two fellows who trouble me. Why should they join in lies? What will they gain? And yet, the answer lies with them. I know it. Something skitters on the rim of my consciousness. Once I find it, I'll know the truth—and I can rip apart your damnable fabric of lies."

"Well, I hope you find it soon, my love," she said. Her mouth twisted and her eyes despised him.

He flung himself into a chair and chewed at his mouth. After some moments, June resumed playing, but she made mistakes, repeated, lost the theme and the flow of the music. When Jeff looked up, he found Kevin's sick black eyes studying him, deeply troubled, probing.

Janus announced dinner. June waited, but Kevin went on slouching in the chair. She shrugged and walked into the candlelit dining room between Jeff and Vincente. Kevin followed. He sat morosely at the table, taut, watchful, without appetite for food.

The succulent dinner went begging. Only Vincente ate voraciously, eyes fixed on his plate. Mild, well-seasoned mutton, served with halved potatoes toasted in butter, tiny green peas and asparagus, followed an extremely hot clear broth. In turn, this was followed by creamy pies, chased by green crème de menthe. Kevin ate nothing. June pushed her food about on her plate but actually ate little.

Jeff might have eaten, despite the way his stomach was drawn in knots by his overactive glands, but June had seated him to her right and almost as soon as they were seated, he felt the heated, fierce pressure of her knee. After a few moments her hand slid over, probing at his lap, finding the object of its search, fondling, caressing, stroking. Her face, though slightly pale, was the image of innocence and chastity. . . .

After dinner they repaired into the well-lighted living room. Here, a gilt-framed portrait of June's father overwhelmed the heavy French Provençal furnishings, the other less ornate portraits. Kevin staggered slightly as he entered the room. He yawned almost helplessly.

Jeff's gaze leaped to June's face. She smiled and nodded almost imperceptibly. She had administered the distillate—the laudanum was already at work in Kevin's system.

Jeff felt a distinct twist in his loins. He was pleased when Kevin said, "It's been a fearful, grueling day for me. I'm tired. I'm going to bed." He almost glared at June. "Are you coming with me?"

No one could have been more astonished than Kevin when June replied meekly and submissively, "Why, of course, darling. . . ."

Kevin paused in the wide foyer doorway. He glanced malevolently back over his shoulder toward Jeff and Vincente, but his malevolence was fragmented by a yawn. "The matter of my wife's coach . . . it's not settled, *mes amis* . . . something is wrong . . . and I shall find it. . . . Meantime, I bid you good night."

Vincente was led away to a second floor bedroom by a dainty high-yellow maid. Janus motioned for Jeff to follow him. It was scarcely full dark but Jeff knew most rural homes were dark by nine o'clock. Tonight he was pleased to retire early.

In his incredibly polished and glistening bedroom, he undressed, leaving on only his cotton undershirt. The spread was turned back on gleaming white sheets. He lay down on his back, sinking sensuously into the down mattress. Jesus. This was the way to live. What if he instead of Kevin were June's husband? Like Kevin, he would be making a bargain, trading what he had for a share of June's immense wealth. But perhaps he'd have delivered more in return for value received. Could he relax and enjoy the easy luxurious life of the parish squire? Could he—or any man—keep June Levaux satisfied and faithful?

Hell yes, he could keep June occupied, happy, and sated. Barefoot and pregnant! He'd never leave her—what had she said?—in the lurch. He'd learned the secret of satisfying women from women themselves. The innermost desires and fantasies of females would astonish most of those men who believed they knew their women best! He'd enslave June, as he had every other woman he had bedded. Enslaving a female simply meant playing her game her way—it was almost like shooting doves in a baited field.

He enslaved the women who loved him because he became a slave to them! He probed for reactions, fantasies. He thought first of arousing the wench out of herself, eroding away her last inhibitions and transporting her from the reality of caution and codes to a sublime paradise where she tossed, writhed, and panted her way to total satiety. Women were rendered complete, but never exhausted because he sparked their imaginations. This was where their responses lay. They remained always more than a little hungry—for him! Discomfited when he was too long away from their arms. Few men took the time to draw a woman out of the mold into which her training and learned repressions had compressed her. He knew how; he did it; he enjoyed his labors; he profited.

When June entered his bedroom and he came toward her, she gasped in delight and anticipation at what she saw. "My God," she whispered. "You are as wild for it as I am."

"I'm wild for you." He laughed, taking the lamp from her and setting it on the bed table.

"And I—"

"Since that first moment—"

"On that road—"

"When I looked at you—"

"When you came near me—I knew."

She pulled the fragile fabric of her gown over her head and threw it behind her into the darkness. Jeff gazed, spellbound, at her bewitching beauty. She came toward him, gleaming, naked, reaching for him with both hands.

"Oh," she whispered. "You don't know how long I've waited—for this. . . ."

"And I—"

"Such a long, interminable day—"

"All my life—"

"Yes. And mine. . . ."

"So much to make up for."

He lifted her in his arms and laid her down across the bed. He turned to lower the wick and blow out the lamp. Her voice stopped him. "Wait. Leave it on for a while. I want to *see* you. All of you. Take off that foolish undershirt."

He shook his head. "No."

"You must! You're so beautiful. So rugged and beautiful, I've got to look at you."

He forced a smile but remained adamant. "Sorry—it's a peculiarity. . . . If I take off my shirt—I can't do it."

"You're joking."

"I wish I were."

She frowned, then brightened, smiling. "I understand. I do . . . I've heard that many men have—strange fetishes."

"It won't matter," he promised. "You won't care."

"You're so beautiful—the most beautiful man."

He smiled. "Maybe we were made for each other."

"Come to me. Come to me, Jeff . . . my Jeff . . .

please . . . oh, come to me now."

Jeff blew out the lamp and returned to the bed, pulling her close against him. It had been a long, eternal day, but now at last, the waiting proved worthwhile. He kissed her for a long time, as if assuaging a terrible thirst. She parted her mouth wide and accepted his tongue deep inside. His hands explored the warm softness of her body and she reached upward, drawing him into her.

Jeff came down upon her. She tilted her hips, accommodating her body to his, and when he thrust himself into her, she cried aloud, gasped, and then wailed in an unintelligible keening.

The fiery excitement of her mindless murmuring, the soft firmness of her fever-hot skin, the wild pumping of her hips intoxicated him. He thought of nothing, heard nothing, remembered nothing, desired nothing more than her total submission.

She responded with a savagery he had seldom encountered—even among those paid professionals at Madame Hortense's Riding Academy in the *Vieux Carre*. June was wild for it, she was starved for it. Nothing existed for her outside this bed, this darkened room. He delayed his own climax until he felt her quiver helplessly. In mutual delight they clung together, shaken.

He lay close beside her. He was quieter now inside, for the moment freed of that unsettling passion which had raged through him all day. While she panted in exhaustion, he amused himself by learning her body, by committing it to memory through his searching fingers. Soon she was whispering in a frenzy of need. He forgot reality, time, space. He was not even astonished when the room was suddenly illumined in brilliant orange.

Vaguely at first, and then with a chilling recognition of imminent danger, he heard movement behind them in the garishly lighted room. He lunged upward and away from June. Crouched on his knees, he stared over his shoulder at Kevin Levaux.

Levaux stood just inside the corridor door. He held a large candle aloft in his left hand. He held a gun in

his right. He raged, "I remember, damn you, Carson. . . .
I know now what was wrong—different. . . . You and
that damned boy. So honest. So innocent. So helpful. You
had *three* horses when I saw you first on that road. Three
horses, goddamn you . . . not two . . . so that's how
that bastard Archet was able to race across country to
his place. Damn you. You lied. You all lied."

Staring at the wild-eyed Levaux, Jeff saw two things.
The tall man, in silk pajamas, was still reeling under
effects of the tranquilizing drug. And he had not yet seen
June Levaux writhing under Jeff on the guest bed. Levaux's mind was completely absorbed in the discovery
of how they had tricked him earlier today.

Grabbing up a pillow, Jeff threw it as hard as he could,
striking Levaux high and snuffing out the candle.

When the guttering candle failed, the room was plunged
into darkness. Levaux yelled. Beside Jeff on the bed,
June whimpered, reaching for him.

Jeff sprang from the bed and ran to the window. He
glanced back at the cave-dark room. Dimly he could
make out Levaux's tall figure lunging across the flooring
in pursuit.

Jeff went out the window. He slid down the courtesy
roofing, slowed himself with his heels. He clung with his
fingers to the roofing edge, then let himself drop to the
grass. He heard Levaux's struggling through the window
behind him and then toppling along the roof.

Jeff glanced around in the darkness. He whistled shrilly,
hoping that Vincente was still awake and not previously
engaged with some high-yellow wench.

A match flared for a brief beat across the yard at the
barn. The light was instantly snuffed. Jeff ran toward the
glow, rocks and grass chewing at the soles of his bare feet.

Behind him, Levaux struck the ground hard. He grunted
helplessly as the breath was knocked out of him. After
a moment he pushed himself up, patted around until he
recovered his handgun. Then he ran after Jeff in the
darkened yard.

"Don Jeff. Here," Vincente whispered from the stygian

darkness inside the feeding barns.

Jeff ran through the door into the space where they'd visited June's calves in the afternoon. Vincente touched his arm.

Kevin ran into the barn behind Jeff. Jeff and Vincente pressed deeper in the shadows of feed sacks, leaning against the rough plankings of the wall.

Kevin moved quietly. By the time they realized why Levaux was so quiet, it was too late. Kevin fired a match, lit a lantern. He heeled around them, gun in hand, searching the interior stalls for them. The awakened calves bawled, startled.

"Come out of there." Kevin held the gun unsteadily but fixed on them. His eyes were dilated, with the strange, wild look of a man half-drugged but determined to exercise discipline over mind.

"Take it easy," Jeff said. "I know what your beef with Vincente and me is—but you don't want murder on your hands."

"You're going to tell the truth—about my wife and her lover," Levaux said. "Or I'm going to kill you both."

Jeff kept his voice level with a calm he did not feel. "You won't get away with murder, Kevin. . . . The parish priest won't support you. You might make one killing look like an accident, but not two."

"Shut up. Damn you. You're going to admit—in front of Archet, the priest, Toth, and June—that you lied, that you gave Archet one of your horses so he could get away from me."

Jeff drew a deep breath. The half-drugged man, intent upon his discovery of their treachery, had not seen June in Jeff's bed. He doubted that Levaux wanted to commit murder because they'd lied to him. He stepped suddenly to the left, moving away from Vincente.

Muddle-minded, Kevin jerked the gun around, tracking him. Vincente made a standing jump. He struck against Levaux. The tall Creole staggered. The gun flew out of his hand. He dropped the lantern.

Vincente caught up the lantern. Jeff leaped forward

and kicked the gun beyond Levaux's reach. The confused man turned, grabbing for the gun. Calmly, Jeff cracked him across the nape of his neck. Kevin sprawled out on his face.

"Get rope," Jeff told Vincente.

Vincente nodded. He brought lines looped on pegs. The bawling calves wailed. "Those damned calves are going to wake up every slave on the place," Vincente said.

Jeff looked around—sacks of grain mash to mix with milk and small casks of cane syrup were stacked against the wall. "I think we can quiet the calves," he said, "and teach M'sieur Levaux that it is more blessed to give than to receive, at the same time."

They stripped the silk pajamas from Kevin's body. Jeff secured ropes on Kevin's ankles and wrists. As he was tying him, Levaux regained consciousness. Seeing that he was nude and being tied up, Kevin became hysterical. "Don't kill me," he pleaded. "I meant you no harm. I swear . . . listen to me . . . I've been saving money— a great deal of money—from slave sales that June doesn't know about. . . . I've hidden the money . . . here in the barn. . . . You can have it all. It's yours, if you spare me."

Jeff went on tying him. Kevin nodded frantically. "There. It's there—in a chest, behind those syrup casks— if you'll let me go."

"Got to teach you a lesson," Jeff said. "Never saw a man yet that was weak in the sex department that didn't steal from women and children. . . . You got to see that you've got to give in this life—and keep giving— even when you don't feel like it anymore."

Kevin wailed, protesting until Jeff used the man's silk pajama shirt as a gag, tying it tightly. Kevin went on raging but now his voice was muffled. Jeff and Vincente hefted Kevin and carried him inside the calf stall. They spread his arms wide, securing the ropes from his wrists to high pegs driven into the wall studs. Kevin watched them in mounting terror. They spread his legs wide, tying the ropes off securely, leaving Levaux spraddled-legged against the wall.

Jeff found old paint brushes. They broke open casks of syrup and poured the fluid into the sweet milk-and-meal mixture. Then they dipped in the brushes and slathered the syrup, milk, and meal over Levaux, from his navel down to his knees.

Watching them, eyes wide with horror, Kevin shook his head, grunting and groaning helplessly against the silk gag in his mouth. Jeff and Vincente retreated from the calf stall and Levaux watched the small animals stagger toward him. He shook his head, screaming deep inside his mind.

Jeff blew out the lantern, set it on the floor. He and Vincente walked across the yard, Vincente leading their horses. "Why were you out in the barn?" Jeff asked.

Vincente grinned. "I saw that Mrs. Levaux going to your room—her gown was thin, revealing almost as much as her eyes. And her eyes were wild. I decided I'd better dress and get our horses saddled."

Jeff laughed and nodded. "I'll be with you—as soon as I dress and collect my bag."

He climbed the stairs and strode along the upper corridor to his room. His door stood ajar as Levaux had left it. Jeff stepped inside the guest bedroom and closed the door behind him.

He caught his breath. Across the room, in the shadowy dark, he saw that June still lay as he'd left her, nude, her hips writhing on the mattress. He heard her frantic, distracted whisper. "Jeff . . . please . . ."

Jeff crossed the room. It would take longer for him to leave Baiser de France than he'd indicated to Vincente. He lay down beside June, whispering, "It's all right, my love. . . . I'm here. . . . Never let it be said that M'sieur Jeff Carson *ever* left a lady in the lurch."

CHAPTER XIII

They rode north, prodding their horses to a gallop along tree-arched lanes. Finally, they let their horses slow to a canter and then to a walk. The night crowded in upon them, velvety blackness gleaming with a misty star shine. They did not talk much. Vincente was thoughtful. Once he said, "Maybe when I get a stake, I'll ride back to Paradis." When Jeff didn't answer, Vincente lapsed into silence.

Jeff sighed. He hadn't answered Vincente because he caught himself in time, biting his lip to remain silent. He almost warned the boy that he'd be sorry if he ever went back anywhere looking for the *same* girl he'd left behind. People changed, even when places seemed the same. If the girl remained unchanged, he himself and his needs and outlook would have altered. You left old happiness alone—in the only place where it wouldn't tarnish, in memory. No sense burdening Vincente with such a cynical thought distilled from his own bitter experiences even though the boy was mature for fourteen. Let Vincente learn from his own mistakes; he might even get lucky. Some of his own pleasantest dreams had been wrapped around the impossible fantasies of *going back* to places where he'd been happy, to girls who had been unforgettable. He'd forgotten them eventually, as Vincente would. Meantime, let the boy learn his own lessons of the heart . . . and heartbreak.

The scrape of leather, the motion of the horses, the clop of unhurried hooves on the hard-packed road were the only sounds in the deepening night. The farthest dome of heaven was vaguely illumined by stars that glittered like far-flung sequins. Jeff found himself wishing for a woman he could believe in, a life he could trust, a place where he could build some security. That wasn't to be his fate. His destiny was to run in the night, to take hurried love where he could find it, like some transient gulping at cool water in a spring he'd never visit again. He was doomed to find his women loving, grateful, and quickly gone.

He pushed his hand into his shirt and closed it on the battered gold cross given to him so long ago by one of those grateful evanescent loves. He drew out the gold talisman. The chain had been easy to repair. Staring at it in the starlit dark, he knew Helen Latimer had been right. The cross had been his good luck charm, his only amulet against evil.

He smiled tiredly. He was getting superstitious. A life like his would render any man superstitious. He gazed up at the winking stars wondering if they held the answers to his rootless existence. Tired like this, he felt terribly alone and vulnerable. He belonged nowhere. Like a bird in passage he could stop to rest for only a few moments before he was hurtled along on some errant wind draft. Home. He could have no home as long as he fought against what he was inside. The only place he could rightfully call home was that plantation where he'd been born—and reared in hell. No, he'd die before he'd go back, or let anyone return him in chains to Willow Oaks.

And yet in his exhaustion he could almost wish he were all black. Even black slaves *belonged*. They had a security he would never have. White men thought for them, worried about them, fed and cared for them. And because mistreatment and cruelty were economically unfeasible, fiscally unsound, for the most part white owners treated their blacks well. Sometimes one wondered who was the slave and who enslaved? Blacks were enslaved for life, but they slept at night, they had exciting wenches to fire their dreams and heat their beds—wenches so fascinating that the white men chased them, preferring them to their own white-skinned wives. God, how he pitied white men who'd never savored black female flesh.

Spurred by pride in his own black blood, he wished that he were all black. Black, he could relax for a little while. He could work as a man, love as a man, rest as a man.

The hell he could! He straightened in his saddle as if waking from a bad dream. What in hell was wrong with him? What on this earth was more vile and inhuman than the enslavement of one human being by another. That slavery was older than history didn't alter a damn thing. He'd been a slave, subjected to the whims and vagaries of whites. Never again. No, he'd keep running, even if he found rest only beyond the grave. He paid the price. He ran. He belonged nowhere, but by God, he was free!

He rode, sitting straighter in his saddle. The cost of his freedom had been high, he didn't deny that. He'd existed in a state of unceasing terror. His own mother had been thrust into a coffle headed for the slave market when he was fourteen. Where was she tonight? Under what conditions did she exist? And his pusillanimous father? What of that hasty fornicator? Where was he? What was he? Who was he?

Daylight showed them this delta country was far more prosperous than the jack oak and pine regions up around Willow Oaks and Carthage. Vast estates, imposing chalets reared against the pink sky of false dawn. Jeff grinned. No matter what he might consider in exhaustion, he was *not* black. He was white. He could ride up to the front door of any of those mansions, stranger that he was, and receive a gracious invitation to dine, to spend the day and the night.

He did not want to stop. The early morning emptiness before breakfast affected his thinking, that was all. Clear-headed, he saw these godforsaken crossroad towns and the huge farms for what they were: empty, remote, and isolated, nests of red-necks. But to the people who lived in them, they were the center of the universe, and the sun itself revolved around them. Little people, small-minded, who seldom traveled more than twenty miles from their home in their lifetime, nor wanted to. The narrow mentality obsessed with itself—I and me and my own—the inbred littleness that fed on itself behind a façade of cordiality and hospitality. He had nothing to say to them.

About eight that morning, Jeff figured they should stop for breakfast. They loop-tied their horses outside a cross-country ordinary and carried their saddlebags and collapsible suitcases inside with them.

The interior of the tavern room was smoke-hazed and dark even in the brilliant morning. It smelled hotly of grease. A few rough tables were set about the floor and thick tallow candles burned and dripped upon them. There were no other guests at this hour.

The sleepy-eyed tavern keep took their order and repaired to the kitchen to help the black cook prepare and serve it. Since they were alone in the unpalatable dining room, Vincente stealthily counted the money they had appropriated from their attackers in the bayous.

"Almost $2,000," Vincente said. "Hell, we're rich. We could buy a stake in some business that would make us wealthy. With the 10,000 Lafitte gave you, we could become business tycoons. . . . I have always longed to be richer and more influential than my dearly beloved father, Don Cipriano."

Jeff laughed coldly. "Would you like Jean Lafitte on your trail for the rest of your life?"

Vincente laughed and shoved the saddlebag away from him on the rough bench. "Even without Lafitte's money, we're well fixed for a start, Jeff."

"Do you really think I can ever settle down somewhere?"

"You've got to someday."

"Someday. I can't think about someday—"

"The richer you are the safer you are, I've learned that for sure."

"—all I can think about right now is delivering that money Lafitte entrusted to me."

"Oh, you're right." Vincente nodded emphatically. "We should get it to the widow with all haste—insist she count it—and demand a receipt, signed and notarized."

Jeff laughed. "Now you're getting smart. Very smart."

They choked down an unappetizing breakfast of greasy ham, greasy fried eggs, and warmed-over sour-milk biscuits with chicory-flavored coffee. Afterward they fed, watered, and rubbed down their horses. In less than an hour they were on the road north again.

Noon found them at a weather-beaten crossroads store where they ate rat cheese and soda crackers washed down with sugarcane juice. By nightfall they entered a world light-years removed from the rich Louisiana delta estates. They stabled their horses and spent the night at a ramshackle tavern.

Jeff and Vincente shared a corn-shucks mattress on a rope-supported bedframe. Jeff sagged quickly into exhausted slumber. He had no idea how long he had been asleep when something disturbed him. He lunged up in bed, chilled and shaken.

He hadn't realized he'd yelled in his sleep until Vincente said, "What's the matter? What are you yelling about?"

Jeff shuddered. He was cold and he could not say why. He realized he'd gone through a terrible nightmare, but when he tried to recollect it in the chilled reasoning view of wakefulness, he found it fragmented, lost. Nevertheless, he remained cold; he could not sleep again. At last he got up and dressed. He prodded Vincente with his boot. "Get up, get dressed. We're going to hit the road."

"Forget it, you crazy *nigger*," Vincente said. "I had one hell of a long day on that horse. I'm dead. I got to get—"

Raging, Jeff caught the front of Vincente's shirt and

140

hoisted him two feet in the air. Jeff's voice shook. "God-damn it, boy, don't you ever call me *nigger* again!"

"My God, Jeff! I was joking."

"Not joking. Not when you think we're alone. Not ever! You stupid little bastard. This is my life you're making jokes with."

Vincente pulled himself free. He shrugged his shirt up on his shoulders and sighed heavily. "Well, at least we can get started on the road. I sure as hell ain't sleepy anymore."

"Then get up, damn you. Get dressed. Let's go."

They rode all night, Vincente slumped half-asleep in his saddle. Jeff pitied the exhausted boy. At the same time, he was filled with this nameless dread and—regret. Fear. How long before Vincente betrayed him, even un-wittingly? A fugitive could trust no one. His fists gripped the reins tightly, his knuckles gray.

To conceal his fears and the troubled direction of his thoughts, Jeff bought Vincente a double-sized breakfast and let him sleep three hours in the stable hay before they set out on the road north again about nine. A light rain had fallen just after dawn and the morning was cool.

Vincente felt better, refreshed. He grinned. "I don't mind running with you. But I'm damned if I'll sleep with you again—you and your wild nightmares."

Jeff exhaled, gazing into the middle distance. "I was dreaming about Chloe. She wasn't dead. She was still alive—and we left her there."

"Madre de Diós, you are crazy. Chloe is dead. Stone cold dead. I know she was."

Jeff shrugged and nodded. He took out the map La-fitte had marked for him. "We better start looking for The Laurels. . . . It's along here somewhere. Unless we took a wrong turn during the night."

Vincente smiled. "No chance. Anytime you're deliver-ing $10,000 you'll never get lost."

A little past noon, they pulled their horses up in the roadway. The country around them was rolling pine hills, sloping off to a verdant mist-shrouded valley in the distance. They sat before the tall fieldstone gates at a winding avenue of live oaks leading to a magnificent chalet. A marble tablet, against a gatepost, named the place: "The Laurels—where love dwells," Jeff read.

"I think I'll throw up," Vincente said.

"Don't laugh. Maybe the major believed that when he wrote it."

"Then why did he run off to get killed spying for Lafitte?"

Jeff shrugged. "Who knows what happens to love when you hang on to it too long?"

They urged their horses along the lane. Nearing the house, Jeff slowed, troubled without knowing why. He reined in a hundred yards from the huge home. Something was *wrong* about this plantation. It was less imposing than the delta manor houses—most plantation houses were—but it was far more impressive than most of the estates they had passed this morning. A one-storied brick rambler set in a pine grove, its façade presented a pleasant narrow veranda with two classic Greek-style pillars on each side of a wide doorway. Apparently a place of beauty and serenity.

Jeff frowned, surveying the grounds. Maybe the oppressive silence enshrouding The Laurels troubled him. There was no activity in the middle of the day, though the gardens, lawns, fields, and house were well-kempt.

He shook his head, gazing around. No, the silence was merely a symptom of the strange malady he sensed here. At first glance, everything about The Laurels seemed prosperous and healthy. But the fact was, something was missing. There was a lack, something he couldn't figure at once, but the pervading stillness carried a tension he found almost tangible.

He shrugged. The hell with it. His assignment here was simple. He said, "Let's deliver this money to the old girl and travel."

"Where?"

"Who the hell knows?" Jeff laughed and spread his

hands. "That's why I'm so damned anxious to get started. It may be a long ride—a hell of a trip."

CHAPTER XIV

Jeff's head reeled, his heart hammered against his ribs. He felt as if he were suddenly, blissfully—but inexplicably—drunk! He was only dimly aware of Vincente's standing behind him, holding the saddlebag from Jean Lafitte. He was totally unconscious of the black butler's standing between him and the fragile blond vision in that shadowed parlor of The Laurels. The last time he'd felt this unreasonably and unreasoningly intoxicated, he'd reeked of rum, his head pained agonizingly, and he'd awakened with a mammoth hangover. He might yet waken with a hangover, but he was coldly sober.

"Mrs. Morceau?" His voice faltered, doubting.

"I done tole you, suh. This is Miz Margarith Morceau," the black man said with a hint of impatience. "Mistress of The Laurels—widow of the late lamented Masta André Morceau."

Jeff barely heard the aging Negro butler. He focused his eyes on the widow Morceau. But even looking directly at her, he could not believe this was the widow of the aging soldier Lafitte had spoken of so glowingly and with such admiration. Lafitte had told him that André Morceau had served in the War of 1812, had distinguished himself with Jackson in defense of New Orleans and the levees so vital to commerce. Even if Morceau had been a young boy at the time, he'd be pushing middle years by now! This *girl?* This young woman—Morceau's widow? How old was she—twenty? twenty-five? thirty at the unlikely outside?

"Mrs. André Morceau?" Jeff persisted. He winced, realizing he sounded as clever as the village idiot. "Widow of Major André Morceau?"

"Dat's who my lady am, suh." Impatience edged the black butler's tone. Obviously, as the late Major Morceau's body slave, he had been permitted liberties accorded few blacks. He was in his late forties, at least, his kinky cap of hair already the color and texture of third-grade cotton lint. His chocolate face was round, his body rotund. He was of medium height—about five feet, five inches tall. The servant's dark broadcloth suit was brushed, his black boots bore a military shine. He held himself erect, the way an ex–professional soldier might.

They stood for that prolonged beat, none of them moving in the shadowed room. The mistress of The Laurels had been standing alone at the inset window when they entered the parlor. Rimlighted by the yellow afternoon sunlight filtering through curtains and drapes, she had been staring out at something—nothing?—a forlorn droop to her shoulders. But when her servant announced her guests, she turned, smiling and gracious— an incredible, unearthly beauty. And this was when Jeff had decided he was 100-proof intoxicated.

Slowly she had crossed the room in shoe-length black voile dress. The flickering sunlight lost her and then provided a halo for her ethereal beauty. She raised her head, studying them as she smiled in welcome. Jeff was stunned at her youth, her fragile easter-lily loveliness, at the classic line of her gentle profile in the diffused light, the old-coin elegance of facial features, chiseled against the vague shadows behind her. He was intrigued by the arched tilt of her brows, as if she still discovered wonder and pleasure around her. Her deep, lustrous violet eyes gazed out from thick, uptilted lashes. The finely sculptured

144

cheekbones and the ceramic-glaze smoothness of her skin, the softly bruised red lips, the cleft, rounded chin, all of it struck him like three ounces of raw bourbon on an empty stomach. He had never seen such beauty before. For the first time he reckoned the answer to his restless yearning. He had always believed it was any woman he wanted; suddenly he knew better. This woman was the one he wanted above all others; he knew that in the instant he beheld her. He wanted no saucy, aggressive mistress, no black slut, no professional whore—he wanted only this woman whom he had never seen until this moment. Every fiber of him longed for her.

The butler said, "Miz Margrith is done still in mourning, she am."

Jeff smiled and nodded. This explained the black dress. But she did something for this fabric, this dolorous frock. These widow's weeds were most becoming to André Morceau's young widow. "How long has the major been dead?" Jeff asked.

"Eight months," Margarith said. "Were you friends of André? Did you serve in the army with him?"

"Masta Morceau, he a great man," the butler said. "He a strong man. He military."

"That's all right, Ponchus," Margarith Morceau said. "I know how deeply you loved the major—we both loved him." She sighed and added, almost as if speaking to herself, "That's about all we have left, isn't it?"

"Yes'm, we sho' loved that great man," Ponchus said. He seemed determined not only to make a point for their guests, but to drive it home. "He a great man. A truly great man. No ordinary man ever take de major's place."

Jeff introduced Vincente and himself. "I am one of the Carsons of The Georgics in Mississippi. But I must admit I have not been home in many years." He took Margarith Morceau's slender hand and slowly lifted it to his lips, too enraptured even to appraise her diamonds as he kissed the backs of her fingers. His kiss lingered for a moment over her faintly scented hand. She did not withdraw, but the butler spoke with some emphasis again of Masta Morceau's superb qualities, unlikely to be matched by any other gentleman.

Jeff smiled. "You asked if we knew your husband. We did not have that great pleasure—"

"It indeed a great pleasure to know the major," Ponchus said.

Jeff gave the smooth chocolate face of the black man a faint chilled smile. "We did know a very close friend of the major. . . . He was, as a matter of fact, very close to the major when the gentleman was killed. The major entrusted him with papers and money to be gotten to you as quickly as possible. My friend says to express his great regrets that it has taken such an unconscionably long time to deliver these papers and money, and that he prays he has not inconvenienced you too much."

"Of course he has not," Margarith said. "We know nothing of any papers. We were not anticipating any money."

Jeff signaled with a quick nod of his head. Vincente laid the stack of papers, held together by cord, on the dark wood table. Then he removed the considerable stacks of paper money and placed them on the polished surface. Jeff heard the butler's soft intake of breath, but watching Margarith's face, he saw a look of astonishment become disbelief, amazement, and for a beat, genuine thanksgiving.

"All of that—money—from the major?" she whispered it. She glanced through the papers, held them clutched in white-knuckled fists. "How can that be?"

"My friend told me it was in payment for a very special service rendered by your late husband," Jeff said. "I'm sorry I don't know the details."

"You must tell me the name of this friend," Margarith said.

"I'm sorry, I'm not at liberty to do that," Jeff said. "Trust me that he was very close to your husband, a very dear friend and army comrade." He added this last as a sop to the butler.

"Jean Lafitte?" Margarith asked.

Jeff's mouth sagged open. Jean Lafitte! It had been Lafitte's command that his name be kept out of it, that the very fact that Major Morceau had been involved in his last years with the pirate was the secret most carefully to be guarded.

His stunned silence was the only answer Margarith needed. She smiled and nodded. "We have known— about my husband's connections with Lafitte—for a long time. Haven't we, Ponchus?"

"Yes'm, we has. You and me. We has."

She laughed, and it was the tinkling of small bells along Jeff's spine. "Poor Ponchus. He's afraid the memory of André's life will be discolored by any reference to the work he did for the pirate."

"I assure you," Jeff said. "Jean Lafitte is no longer regarded simply as a pirate. He and his brother own a blacksmith shop on St. Philip Street near the cathedral in New Orleans, as well as the South's finest general merchandise store on Royal Street. Lafitte is accepted today as one of the most important men in the state."

Margarith shook her lovely head. "You do not need to defend M'sieur Lafitte to Ponchus and me, Mr. Carson. We are convinced that if André joined with him, there were good and honorable reasons. . . . But—all that money—my faith in the honesty of his missions falters slightly. But not my appreciation!"

"Ten thousand dollars," Vincente said. "Perhaps you would care to count it and give us a receipt."

"That won't be necessary," Jeff said.

"Ten thousand dollars?" Margarith's cheeks glowed. Her eyes brightened in a way that completely effaced the effect of the black dress. "Oh, Ponchus, think of it! Ten thousand dollars."

"Yes'm," Ponchus said. "I'm sho' thinkin'. . . best I can."

Margarith laughed. "Run tell Lilly-Belle to fix something special—we're having guests for lunch—and dinner tonight."

Ponchus nodded. "Yes, ma'am, I sho' do that. . . .

An', gen'mun', welcome to The Laurels. Yes, suh, welcome."

Margarith laughed as the militarily rigid Ponchus marched, parade-straight, from the room. "Welcome, indeed," she said. "Please. Sit down. Tell me all about New Orleans."

Jeff and Vincente sat on excellently made but aging chairs. The room was well furnished, but Jeff found part of the "wrongness" about The Laurels—that genteel poverty that characterized most of these places.

Still clutching the packet of papers, Margarith sat on a love seat and smiled at them, expectantly. But Jeff shook his head. "I'm afraid we haven't seen New Orleans for a long time." The very idea of New Orleans brought back the painful memory of Chloe's tragic death. "Vincente and I have been in Haiti for some time."

"Haiti? How exciting! Do you know, I sit here at The Laurels, and I dream of distant places. The life in Haiti must be thrilling."

"It is precarious more than thrilling," Jeff told her. "The blacks have revolted you know. They've burned all white-owned plantations, businesses, homes. They have taken over the government. Unfortunately, none of them is prepared to lead that country. They are not educated for it, they are not prepared for it, but they have taken it! They've plunged themselves into chaos. The only thing I can think is that some opportunist is going in there—and make himself dictator."

"How thrilling you make it all sound. And you were there—in the midst of that?"

He told her a romantic lie he supposed she'd want to hear. He had left his uncle's plantation—the beautiful old magnolia-graced Georgics—expecting to be employed by an established firm in Cap François. But upon arriving, he'd found the firm dissolved, their assets liquidated by the new government. But he did not regret that, he told her. He had never been intended for plantation life. This at least was God's truth! But not quite for the reasons he suggested. He told her he needed the excitement, the crowds, the unexpected changeableness of daily life in a great city. You can get sick of a plantation of darkies, even when they revere you, he told her.

She laughed and sighed. "I can certainly agree with that—especially when you are a widow, trying to run a huge plantation. Though of course all my people are wonderfully loyal and hardworking. And there is much to be said for the pleasant life of a plantation."

He agreed, and spoke of a happy boyhood, long afternoons riding across green meadows, fishing, hunting, listening to the plaintive songs of the happy darkies in the mellowing dusk. The lie was happy because his memory was diametrically the opposite, filled with rage, hatred, and frustration. As he mouthed the prettified fiction of his past, the bitter, hated truth flared like inextinguishable fires deep in the flammable storerooms of his mind.

Hell, even his name was a lie, an accidentally gifted appellation that came because he had fallen asleep in an empty carriage behind an inn on the outskirts of Natchez. He'd been running, as well as a fourteen-year-old boy could run with a shackle hobbling his ankle. He'd rebelled against the cruelties and restrictions of slavery from his earliest childhood. He'd hated his master Baxter Simon and that hatred had been returned a hundred-fold because Bax Simon liked to believe all of his slaves loved him and were happy, except this white-skinned, redheaded rogue, Bricktop.

Bricktop! This was the only honest name he had. And Bricktop's pleasure had come from defying Willow Oaks plantation regulations regarding all slaves. He especially loved violating the prohibition against black males' entering the women's quarters. This place was strictly off limits unless Bax Simon or his prematurely senile father decided on some stud-and-wench combination that would, in their calculations, "improve the bloodline and increase profits."

Jeff—then known at Willow Oaks as Bricktop—didn't give a damn for improving bloodlines; he would not reject any willing chalice proffered by panting wenches. Because

149

he'd reached puberty early and had been exceptionally endowed, he found many wenches willing to risk the whip in order to suffer the exquisite delight of his ebullient lust.

There had come that time when Bax Simon set a hair trap and Bricktop had rushed happily into it. Even with three big black bucks, a length of lariat and a halter, Bax had not been able quite to subdue the redheaded boy. Bricktop had broken free and run. When he was recaptured, after having sunk into exhausted sleep in a ravine, he had been discovered with his fly still unbuttoned. They'd dragged him back to Willow Oaks where Bax Simon supervised a lashing that left Bricktop beaten raw, bloody, and hanging by the heels when he passed out under the whip.

For some days after that he had lain quiet. Some of the tension that had always existed between him and his hated master relaxed. Bax Simon was smart. He knew slaves and the slave mentality. But he had never allowed in his calculations for a naturally rebellious nature, a quick, bright intelligence, and an overly developed sense of injustice. Rage simmered in Bricktop's mind until he realized hatred would only beget hatred. There was no damned sense in thinking unless he planned a way to change the existence he loathed. One avenue appeared open—he ran again. This time he was smarter. He slept only at night and then tied by his belt in high branches of a tree. It took them a week to run him down. They might never have captured him, but a lovely chocolate-skinned little wench smiled and he'd climbed into the hay with her.

When they got him back to Willow Oaks—shackled and spanceled in the flatbed of a wagon—Baxter Simon had personally heated the branding iron in the white-hot coals of the smithy forge and burned a large *W.O.*—for Willow Oaks—into Bricktop's back to brand him forever as Baxter Simon property. Now the red-headed rebel could run to the ends of the earth, but he could not escape that brand. No matter where he went, he was a fugitive slave, and those who might harbor him did so on pain of death.

Screaming at the top of his lungs, Bricktop had struggled during the branding. He had grabbed at the iron. His raging mind ordered him to wrest it from Simon's grasp and drive it into that hated face before anyone could stop him. But Simon was too smart—no slave ever attempted any covert trick that Simon had not already confronted and defeated at least once before. The branding iron scarred the palm of Bricktop's right hand.

From that moment, a state of undeclared war existed between Bax Simon and the slave Bricktop. Bax felt he was a benevolent despot, yet he joined this fray willingly and with gusto. The conflict with the rebellious boy drove out all boredom from his days. The young slave fought, and Bax reacted. The driven boy planned, and Bax devised counteraction. But finally, Simon recognized the rebel was a disturbing influence among the docile, bovine herd of slaves; Bricktop kept the plantation in an uproar.

Difficult as he found it to believe, Bax sometimes felt that the slaves were secretly pulling for the rotten little troublemaker. Simon was blocking a coffle to drive to Natchez and the summer slave vendues there. He'd already determined to sell off Bricktop's mother—he decided to be shed of the colt as well as the mare. He shackled Bricktop in the Natchez-bound coffle.

Bricktop knew he was bound for hell. Bax Simon had planned to sell the white-skinned mustee as an extra fancy in New Orleans, but by now Simon was determined to sell the boy to the cane fields. Though Bricktop was even then a spectacularly handsome and intelligent youth, Bax Simon's code of honor forbade his selling the redhead as anything but a born troublemaker, a maverick, an incurable runner. Nobody would want a runner for anything except for labor in the Louisiana cane fields. These men shackled their coffles and marched them under the whip into the delta where they had to be in superb physical condition to stay alive more than a year. One year and death! Bricktop saw this ahead of him when he was fourteen and boiling inside with the need to live, the unyielding, unquenchable will to stay alive, the burning desire to live free!

Even when he knew he was hell-bound and doomed, Bricktop could not surrender. Every night on the long trek up from Carthage to Natchez on the Trace, he worked at the staple that secured his spancel into what he'd found to be a decaying beam. By patiently digging with his fingernails until his fingers bled, he managed to work that staple loose late one night.

He ran. He fell often, dragging his shackled ankle. He shuddered, knowing that by dawn Bax Simon would be on his trail. Like the shepherd who'd leave the flock of ninety-nine to run down one black prodigal, Bax Simon would hound him to earth. Baxter Simon was resolute, determined, obstinate, stubborn, unyielding. He had never lost a runaway slave; he never intended to lose one.

Distracted by pain, frightened, trembling inside, and listening for Bax Simon behind him, Bricktop made his way to a barn behind an inn on the Natchez Trace at the outskirts of the slave-market town. He climbed into the rear of an empty carriage to hide and fell into exhausted sleep.

Baxter Simon had always drawn sensual and almost erotic pleasure from his unequal battle with Bricktop because he'd known all odds were stacked comfortably and entirely on the side of the slave breeder. The branded boy had no chance of even small victories. If the rebellious little bastard wanted to beat his red head against the wall until it was a bloody pulp, let him!

But on this fateful morning outside Natchez, destiny nudged the scales just a trifle, tipped them ever so slightly in Bricktop's favor—gave the boy his first advantage over his master in his short, harried existence! The carriage belonged to a retired schoolteacher named Henry Carson. He and his wife were driving back to their home in the North after having attended a secret abolitionist meeting in the least likely site of all—the second largest slave-market town in the South!

Putting into action his beliefs—so easy to express in flowery language in secret meetings—proved just the sort of challenge Henry Carson had been seeking all his uneventful life.

At first, he'd thought the sleeping boy wearing manacles in the rear of his vehicle was white—perhaps a pitiful young escapee from some cruel backwoods jail. It wasn't until Henry saw the raw letters blazoned on the child's back that he realized what he had on his hands—a downtrodden, exploited slave!

Carson covered the boy with an old tarpaulin in the rear of the single-seated buggy. He stopped downtown in Natchez, left his wife in her seat, and strode into a general store to buy a file. When the joking proprietor asked why he'd need a file, Carson replied loudly, and laughingly, that he was about to file a runaway slave's shackles off and take the slave North to freedom. The storeowner was still laughing at the gentle, gray-haired old man's jest when Carson sauntered out of the store bearing the file like a battle staff.

The redhead repaid his benefactors when the Carson carriage was attacked on the Trace by backwoodsmen who considered all strangers as fair game for robbery. Bricktop lay unnoticed in the rear of the buggy when the bandits came upon the Carsons. Carson's bravery deserted him and his wife was helpless against the two red-necks. For the first time, Bricktop considered the options: plainly this was a matter of their survival—his and the Carsons—or the road agents profiting over their dead bodies. The answer came almost instantaneously, and from that moment there was never any question. Bricktop would survive—live one way or the other. Later he added to this—he would live well.

He was husky—outraged—the highwaymen were bearded white farmers like Bax Simon. The advantage came mostly from surprise. He lunged up from the vehicle, grabbed one road agent from the rear, and broke his neck. The other bandit fled in panic when he saw his companion was dead and that Bricktop was holding the dead man's gun on him.

The Carsons took Bricktop to Philadelphia—they gave him a name—Thomas Jefferson Carson—a basic education, and good, simple food. His native intelligence enabled him to cover a surprising range of studies in five years. Pneumonia killed off Henry Carson and his wife within a few days of each other during a bitter winter. They left Jeff the few hundred dollars they'd saved.

Jeff's inheritance financed a monumental binge that lasted from Philadelphia to Pittsburgh. He ended in Louisville with three whores on his string. He found the life of a pimp pleasant and easy. His women hustled eagerly for him as long as he permitted them to enjoy his extraordinary and inexhaustible virility. But Jeff had crossed the king pimp of the Louisville waterfront and had to run south for his life.

Jeff gave his girls half his money and bought a ticket for New Orleans on the first steamboat sailing. Aboard the side-wheeler, the nineteen-year-old youth—handsome and dashing—met the George family. The youngest daughter, Minerva, was a stunner and Jeff seduced her in a stateroom before they were past Owensboro. When he learned how wealthy old man George was, how many slaves he owned at The Georgics, Jeff left the boat with them at Natchez to ride overland to the plantation where he was to marry Minerva in a brilliant and well-attended wedding. Unfortunately, one of the invited guests was the owner of the famous Willow Oaks plantation. When Baxter Simon showed up, Jeff was fought to earth, stripped, exposed as a slave to Minerva—who fainted—and her family who in disgrace agreed to shackle Bricktop in a barn until Baxter Simon could return him to Willow Oaks the following morning. But that night, still held spellbound in his thrall, Minerva helped him escape on one of her father's best horses . . . and here he was, two years later, lying to the mistress of The Laurels about his beginnings.

He listened politely as Margarith said, "Flowers are

my passion. I put on a straw hat and work with my black boys in the flower beds every day."

They walked about the mansion and Jeff viewed the rhododendron, the wan morning glory, the azalea, the lilac, wisteria, hibiscus, and pasture rose, pale against golden forsythia. He walked beside her along the six-foot-high hedge of Barbados cherry—glossy ovate leaves, rose-red flowers, and scarlet fruit the size of cherries, which she told him were used for preserves and cool drinks. A 100-rooted banyan was her pride and joy. He lied politely that he too loved flowers, though he seldom pulled his gaze from her exquisite face.

Though she said flowers were her passion, he noted, as they promenaded in close proximity, a slight trembling of her hands. Because of his unique experience with women as anxious to be bedded as he was to bed them, he took this faint tremor as sign of another passion—one which had likely been fearfully neglected since the death of her husband. He smiled and let his gaze trail admiringly across the intoxicating structure of that body beneath her black dress. Her lack was one for which he felt totally capable of providing relief, an illness for which he could prescribe, a void which he could fill.

He had no idea what she had been saying for the past few minutes, but he did hear her say, ". . . there is such a feeling of contentment here at The Laurels. Even the slaves seem to share it."

Ponchus summoned them in to the midday meal—dinner, as it was called in a world where the evening meal was supper. Jeff felt as if both he and Mrs. Morceau were released from a ritual that constricted both of them—the polite lies which etiquette and custom required all strangers to exchange. He could sense the wrong in the atmosphere of this quiet old plantation, even if he could not yet pinpoint its cause. And his own fantasy of a happy youth spent on a Mississippi estate had been so false that the only truth in the entire disquisition was the name of the state. He realized that—for one reason or another

155

—she was as guilty as he. They were both lying to each other.

CHAPTER XV

Jeff slept that night in a guest room across the rambler-type house from Margarith Morceau's boudoir. He smiled wryly, certain the arrangement was more Ponchus's decision than his mistress's. Vincente was bedded in a smaller room near his. The boy had already discovered a pale tan house-wench who made Paradis seem further removed than ever. Out of sight, Evangeline was gradually paling in Vincente's pragmatic mind.

Jeff and the young mistress of The Laurels spent the afternoon in spirited dialogue—he was never after sure what they'd talked about, only that he'd lied a lot and they'd laughed together! Around five, Ponchus had shown him to his room, sent in buckets of tepid water for his bath in a brass tub which Ponchus revealed had once been reserved for the sole use of the late Major Morceau. Jeff found the room spacious. The huge oakwood bed, chests, and other furniture had been made by a Laurels plantation cabinetmaker. Again there was the sense of genteel poverty—well above the level of want—but nevertheless real. The major had left his third young wife hanging by her lovely nails. Jeff sighed, shaved, changed his linen, and found a fresh shirt. He was splashing pine water on his cheeks when Ponchus brought in his lightweight suit, which Ponchus had had pressed for him in the kitchen.

Dressed, Jeff hurried out to the living room where he discovered Margarith there ahead of him in a fresh, far lovelier, black dress.

Supper that night was almost formal—served by three wenches under Ponchus's watchful supervision. The dining room was lit by tall bayberry candles whose mild fragrance refreshed and cleansed the room. Jeff barely noticed the food—chicken-and-rice soup, salad, fried chicken, asparagus and beets—and he experienced some difficulty in following the thread of conversation, but he was delighted and entranced by the fragile beauty and nearness of his hostess. He wondered what she would look like with that black dress discarded, her underthings thrown aside, her body bared to his eyes. And heart pounding, he wondered how soon this miracle would come to pass. He said, "What?" often and blankly when he became aware he was being addressed directly. But he smiled a lot and no one seemed perturbed by his air of distraction.

After supper, in the comfortable living room, Margarith played the spinnet. She began with light and lilting tunes but went on as though involuntarily into sad love ballads and haunting melodies that heightened Jeff's growing need to hold her close and closer, to defend her from all assaults but his own.

All this time the oppressive silence from the slave quarters, barns, craft shops, and the fields persisted. Margarith brought him again from a heated reverie when she said, "Perhaps tomorrow you might like to ride out and look over our plantings?"

Jeff hesitated. He'd not intended spending even this one night at The Laurels. But since he'd looked for the first time into Margarith's thick-lashed violet eyes, he had been performing only through some volition other than his own.

He met her gaze, but her eyes fell away under his. Her suggestion—a ride around the plantation, dinner tomorrow at noon, a cool afternoon on her veranda—might lead them to her bed, which was the only firm destination remaining in his fragmented itinerary.

"Then you'll stay?" she asked.

"We can't impose—"

"Impose? After your overwhelming kindness, we can't do enough to repay you."

"I only delivered a message—"

"And money! Oh, if you only knew how debts can mount on a place like this with nearly sixty slaves! Especially when you've never been allowed to handle your own petty cash before! Poor André. He said he never wanted me to bother my head with figures." She laughed. "I promise. I won't burden you with my woes if you'll stay."

He probed for some sign from her—he was certain he was experienced enough that he would detect and decode the most subtle invitation!—welcoming him to her bedroom later in the evening. After Ponchus was safely asleep, of course. He laughed at the not too fanciful idea of old Ponchus's sitting outside his young mistress's bedroom with a loaded gun across his knees.

Margarith was gracious—but she was as pleasant and friendly toward Vincente as to him. Her charm had no secret messages disguised in it that he could find. When she finally rang the bell and had Ponchus conduct them to their separate bedrooms, she was lovely, winsome, most cordial—and agonizingly alluring—but correctly and politely distant and remote.

Jeff suffered no nightmares in the comfortable bed that night. No evil dreams of his running on rubbery legs in molasses, while Baxter Simon gained on him, branding iron white hot. He did not relive that painful moment when Baxter Simon's bullet killed Chloe in that cabin outside New Orleans. No guilty imagery of leaving Chloe, suffering but still alive, to die cruelly at Baxter Simon's hand. No desperate frenzy to bring him starkly awake, chilled and trembling.

He dreamed. Oh! he dreamed. In his fantasy, he saw his bedroom door stealthily opened only enough to permit

Margarith and a small, flickering candle to sidle through. She was clad only in a filmy nightgown. She came to him and his hands caressed the soft, unblemished flesh under the fragile cambric. He was happy to fondle that rose pink and creamy skin, to hold those full, delicate, and pink-tipped breasts. But she was frantic for him. She caught him in her hands and led his painfully rigid erection to the heated chalice between her shapely thighs. He would have been transported beyond belief except that as he mounted Margarith, a uniformed Ponchus arrived at the head of a company of U.S. Army regulars, outfitted with musketry. He came awake dissatisfied and empty bellied. Only the rigid staff survived the dream. His brawny spike stood inflexible, quivering with need.

It was hours before he got back to sleep. Once, he almost got out of bed for the sortie across the late-night house. Could he want anyone so badly and she be unaware? Didn't women always want what he wanted? Why would this woman be an exception? He didn't know. Perhaps she would not. But he wanted her so terribly, he knew better than to spoil it all by some precipitous attack in the middle of the night. She was grateful to him, but she was a gentle girl, and he a stranger to her.

For whatever reason, real or false, actual or imagined, he resisted the almost overpowering desire. He did sleep, finally, and fitfully. He awoke at dawn, frustrated, red-eyed, more than faintly irritable—though he had only himself to despise. He managed to stay in bed until seven. He got up then, washed and shaved at the earthenware basin, dressed.

He regarded himself from head to foot in the long pier-glass mirror. He studied his rake-hell reflection sourly. If he wanted this loveliest of women, why did he procrastinate? Because she was the loveliest of women, and because he wanted her with a savagery and helpless need unknown before? Why did he hesitate like some timid swain? Why was he afraid to let her know how he felt about her—how anguishedly he desired her? Did her widow's weeds impede him? Marriage, active and real, never hindered him before. Why was he afraid she might view him with disfavor? He was satisfied he must look good to the beautiful widow—young and attractive, wide shoulders, curly red hair, slender hips, long legs. Many women had begged for his favors. Many more had paid for them. He was attractive to women. This was not simply conceit; he had the triumphs and the trophies to attest to it.

He let himself quietly out of the bedroom. He went along the silent, early-morning corridor telling himself that he would bid the widow Morceau farewell today and move on. Where? He hadn't the damnedest idea. But he couldn't go on staying under the same roof with her, sharing his bed only with his brawny and aching staff. He was alive—her elderly husband had been dead for eight months. Unless she found him detestable, there should have been some favorable reaction from her by now.

At the foyer entrance to the parlor, he hesitated, astonished. Across the room, in the vague and diffused early sunlight, Margarith sat, in crisp black dress, her blond hair radiant as old gold, on a deep, overstuffed chair. She poised on the edge of it, speaking earnestly to Ponchus. The black servant-for-life stood before her, bent slightly forward at the waist, seriously whispering. They were in the midst of some very urgent dialogue. Surprised even at finding either of them awake at this hour, he turned to escape as quietly as he'd come.

But at that instant, as if warned by some inner instinct, the lovely Margarith turned and spied him in the doorway. She caught her breath, bit her lip. Her face flushed pinkly to the roots of her golden hair. She reached out nervously, touched Ponchus's arm to silence him. Ponchus straightened and heeled around guiltily.

Jeff stared at them. Obviously, he had been the subject of their heated conversation. But what would they have to say about him they were afraid for him to overhear?

Ponchus recovered first. He said, "Good mawnin', young masta, suh. Do hope you slept well, suh. Breakfast will be served for you and Mistress Margarith in the dining room in just a few moments, suh."

Walking, as if on parade, Ponchus strode past him, his white teeth gleaming in a false and exaggerated smile.

"You're up early," Margarith said. She frowned slightly, seeing his red-rimmed eyes, his tension-taut face. "Didn't you sleep well?"

He tried to smile, watching her. "Maybe it's just that I'm not too accustomed to sleeping alone."

Margarith drew a deep breath and nodded, not quite looking at him. "I'm sorry," she said. "I knew—even when André would have been ill to suspect it—I knew he always supplied bed wenches from the slave quarters for solitary male guests. I admit I thought about it. I started to suggest to Ponchus last night, but—" she sighed out the deep breath, "I decided you—would not want such an arrangement."

"It was not the arrangement I had in mind," he said. He watched her narrowly as he spoke. If ever she were going to react—favorably or with disdain—this had to be the moment. But it passed, and she merely smiled. "You needn't be polite with me, Mr. Carson. . . . My husband has been dead eight months. I've had to face more . . . unpleasant facts of life . . . than the proffered hospitality of a bed wench for one's guests."

He spread his hands, ready to surrender. For hell's sake, had her natural instincts died along with her superannuated husband? She couldn't be more than twenty-five —her sexual needs were ascending, not waning. Unless, as he suddenly feared, she found him detestable, unattractive.

"He has been dead for eight months," Jeff said. "It could not have been easy for a young and lovely girl like you—"

"I don't know how I would have managed without poor old Ponchus," she said.

"That's not exactly what I meant, either," he persisted, throwing caution aside. "You must have been lonely— very lonely—often."

"Yes. I loved my husband very much. I suppose I might not have been able to endure it, except that he was away so much the months before he died."

Jeff felt his jaw tighten so fiercely that a small muscle worked along the grim straight line of it. Was she laughing at him? Why was she purposely misunderstanding everything he said? But before he could speak again, Ponchus entered the room behind him, cleared his throat nervously, and announced that breakfast was served in the dining room.

Jeff offered Margarith his arm. She laid her fingers on his jacket sleeve. He felt the ice-and-fire impression of her slender fingers through the fabric. His heart lurched at her touch. What would it be like to have her reach for you, hold you, fondle you with those hands? He looked forward to breakfast with dread, afraid he would throw up if he swallowed one bite of food.

She sat at the end of the linen-covered table. Jeff sat at her right. He shifted his knee until it came in contact with hers under the table. She jerked her leg away and looked up at him, nervous and pink faced. "Forgive me," she said. "I'm sorry. I didn't mean to bump you."

"You didn't bump me," he said. "I pushed my leg against yours."

She laughed softly. "How gallant of you to say that. You would want to put me at ease."

"Damn it. I wanted to touch your leg."

She laughed. "Oh, you don't know how wonderful it is to have someone like you here, Jeff . . . I hope I may call you Jeff. . . . You say such amusing things. You make me laugh—as I haven't laughed in years."

"Not since your husband died," he said with some savagery.

"Not in years," she said, looking directly at him.

At this most inopportune moment, Ponchus interposed himself like the late major's tombstone between them. He poured steaming coffee into Margarith's cup, went around Jeff and filled his cup. Jeff went on looking at Margarith, trying to decide if she were laughing at him.

"I know I must be dull company for you," she said. "I never had many beaux, like other girls. My mother died when I was young. I had the responsibility of my father. He was heartbroken, like a shadow rather than a real person after she died. Then he decided the burden was too much on me and sent me off to a finishing school for young ladies. . . . Oh, it was more a convent. We saw young men only at formal dances, so heavily chaperoned that one could hardly dance for the *guards* as we used to call them. . . . Then, my father very ill, I returned home. He had . . . arranged my marriage to André. I was seventeen. André and I were married two years—before he was killed. . . . I'm afraid I never learned to be clever—or entertaining."

"I think you're something much more wonderful than clever, or entertaining," he said. "You're real and lovely—and breathtaking."

"How kind of you to say that."

He sagged helplessly. There was no way to let her know he was flirting with her; she had no coquetry. Inwardly he grinned. She knew only direct honesty. He wondered if he might not just ask her to bed? This would be honest enough for her. No indirection, no deceit—the honest statement of fact. He was going out of his mind with desire for her.

"I have something—most urgent to say to you. I promised I would not burden you with my woes, but Ponchus insists I must speak to you."

"Of course." He watched her over their steaming plates of scrambled eggs, ham, and grits. Neither of them touched their food. He wanted her badly, but she was deeply troubled and he tried to keep this in the forefront of his mind, but it was not easy.

"I want you to take over my plantation for me . . . oh, not as an overseer. We have an overseer—Mr. Henley Lewis. You'll meet him today. As Ponchus says, we badly —desperately—need someone who will take Major André's place . . . a man the slaves will respect and obey. . . . You do know something about handling slaves, don't you?"

He nodded but did not meet her eyes.

She smiled. "I was sure you did. Your life at The Georgics must have trained you for handling Negroes— and running a plantation. But I also know you find plantation life dull and uninviting. I'm afraid that's what life would be for you here at The Laurels. But Ponchus insisted that I ask you. You impressed him beyond measure when you delivered $10,000 intact to us."

"It might have been 20,000 when I started out."

"Yes. But both Ponchus and I know better. We trust you. We want you to help us—if only for a little while. I desperately need your help. I—I'll do anything to get you to stay."

He drew a deep breath, held it. She'd said the magic word.

CHAPTER XVI

Neither Jeff nor Margarith had touched their breakfast when Ponchus burst into the dining room.

"Missy!" Ponchus was breathless. His eyes showed the white rims of distress. "Masta Lewis. He in de parlor, Missy. Terrible upset, something awful. Say he got to talk to you dis instant."

"All right, Ponchus." Margarith nodded. Jeff saw her cheeks go pallid, saw the pain flicker across her shadowed eyes. But she tilted her head and forced a smile, glancing at him. "Won't you come in with me to talk to my overseer? I realize you haven't agreed to stay on here. But this may show you how hopeless it is—even if you decided to stay—It should make it easier for you—to refuse."

Jeff didn't want to tell her that her insoluble problems with this plantation, which he'd suspected as he entered the front gate and even before he met her, would bear no weight in his decision to stay or leave. His remaining here was up to her, and her willingness, or refusal, to join him in bed—her room or his. She had troubles enough this morning without facing that issue. He said nothing, merely nodded.

Henley Lewis prowled the front room. His butternut jacket was splotched, his corduroy pants squealed with every step he took. His run-over boots were edged with cow dung.

Henley Lewis nodded precipitously, anxious to get the amenities out of the way. He was a thin, balding man of forty, slightly built, his long face narrow, hawk nose prominent above a gray-rimmed, tight-lipped mouth and ragged mustache. Faded blue eyes stared mistrustfully from a sun-leathered face. He kept turning his black felt hat in his hands.

Margarith introduced Jeff to Henley Lewis but the overseer barely gave his mistress's guest a glance. Lewis was a bubbling cauldron of self-righteous rage. He was not to be swerved from the accusations and complaints buzzing like hornets in his brain.

"You jes' got to make up your mind, Missy," he said. He twirled that hat in his fingers. "Either you let me handle them niggers the way I know they got to be handled —the way we handled them when I was a prison guard— or you may as well sell off this place. Ain't no way we can make a go of it with things like they are. That nigger Clitus—him that I begged you to let me whup good a month ago—that Clitus has got them other blacks all riled up this mawnin'. Won't a damn one of them lazy

165

apes go out in the fields to work again today. They sayin' now that nobody but they Masta Major Morceau owns them, nobody but the major got no right to tell them to work."

"Oh, well that's simply ridiculous," Margarith said. Jeff watched the line of her fragile jaw tighten resolutely. "They know better than that. They know the major is dead. . . . We'll have to go down and talk to them."

"No, ma'am, that won't do." Henley shook his head and twirled that hat faster.

"Why not?"

"You've *talked* to them too much already." Lewis's voice crackled with frustration. "They see you—a gentle lady. They know good and well you ain't goin' to lash 'em. Know you'll keep me from handlin' 'em way I handled them in prison. Prison or plantation, ain't no different. They's got to be rules, and them blacks is got to respect the rules and the white folks that make them rules. Nothin' else won't work. . . . Now, my stake in makin' them blacks work is my percentage of any income on this here place. Long as you yourself are the onliest one concerned, you can lose your shirt if that's what you want to do, bein' softhearted with them niggers. That would be up to you. But, ma'am, if'n I cain't make them blasted darkies work, they ain't no profit, from lumber, or cotton, or nuthin' else on this here plantation. They ain't no profit, I make nothin'. You know very well you couldn't run this here place without me. . . . You got to stop interferin' . . . you got to stop makin' my job tougher'n it is. . . . Now, we don't need to *talk* to Clitus and them niggers. You an' me got to *talk*. We got to decide right here. Do I stay on here, like I worked for the major? Or do I leave? We got to decide that right here this mawnin' . . . we got to decide you'll leave me handle them niggers the way I was trained to git work out'n 'em."

Margarith exhaled heavily, as if she'd been holding her breath the entire time the overseer had been speaking, shoving his face toward her, nodding furiously. She shook her head. "Of course you're not going to leave. Of course I need you. Of course I couldn't run this place without you."

"Well then, you got to agree to stop interferin'."

"I don't know, Mr. Lewis! I just don't know! I agree, the slaves have slowed down, grown surly, even defiant since my husband's death, but—"

"That's your fault, ma'am. Might as well place the blame right square where it belongs. I tole you and I tole you it wouldn't work for you to put on yore sun hat and go out an' work alongside them niggers every day. They didn't think you was good—they thought you was *funny*."

Margarith flushed red. "I just wanted them to know how important this work—these crops—are, to all of us."

"That's it. You got some fool idea niggers can *think*. That they'll appreciate you being kind an' all. Well, they ain't smart enough to think, but they is jus' smart enough to know to jump when they's tetched up proper with a whip."

Margarith shuddered. "I've seen them when they've been whipped. It's so—cruel."

Lewis spoke with great patience, as if his mistress were a retarded child. "A nigger has got one reason for workin'. Jes' one. That's somebody a-standin' over him with a whip. You too softhearted, ma'am! A nigger runs, runs away like that black Adam. Does we brand him when we runs him down and brings him back? No! Does we whup him, lay his bones bare like he deserve? Oh, no! We ties him up for one night, and we asts him nice an' polite, please not to run no more! . . . That nigger Adam is the worst, most dangerous darky we got— always 'cepting Clitus that keeps 'em all stirred up. And I could straighten 'em both out with a whip, like'n you can with a mule or airy other animal. Blacks is animals. They's just like them other apes from Africa, 'cepting they got no tails. You got to treat 'em as such. Can't be softhearted to no nigger. You does and they takes advantage."

Margarith nodded. Her violet eyes were hazy with tears. Her fists were knotted before her. She walked slowly to the window and stared through it. Beyond it, Jeff saw the elaborate and ornate headstones of the family cemetery on a distant knoll. Hell, was she looking for answers up there? He tried not to see how firm and sleek her trim hips were, even under the black fabric of her mourning dress, but thinking about that pink flesh bared—to his hands and his eyes—he sighed heavily. Neither Margarith nor Henley Lewis appeared aware of him. Margarith's thoughts were turned deeply inside, and the overseer watched her narrowly, awaiting her surrender to his demands.

"I better tell you this, ma'am." Henley Lewis's voice battered at Margarith across the shadowed room. "We don't make the right decision—this mornin'—we got a black revolt on our hands. I ain't tryin' to alarm you. But I am tellin' you the truth. We can't control them blacks no longer less'n you agree to let me take over—my way."

Margarith turned and nodded again. Henley Lewis almost laughed in his triumphant satisfaction. He nodded curtly toward Margarith and Jeff, then turned to leave the room. But Margarith's voice stopped him. "We'll come down and talk to them. One last time, Mr. Lewis. . . . If it does not work, I'll step aside. I won't interfere with you again."

He looked as if he might curse. Instead he merely shrugged. "Talk an' you want to, but it ain't goin' to do airy bit of good. Makes no sense at all."

He strode from the room. For some moments Margarith did not move at all. Finally, she came across the room. She nodded toward the love seat. When Jeff sat down, she sat beside him.

But she did not speak of their nearness, of herself, of her need for him to help her save The Laurels. Instead she began to talk softly, almost as if to herself, about the steady decline and decay of this fine old plantation.

Money had grown scarce at The Laurels even before

Major Morceau was slain on his secret mission for Jean Lafitte. The major had never confided in Margarith—he didn't want to burden her with his troubles. But she had learned of their financial difficulties in many ways. And it was clear enough to see that the major was desperately worried.

The major had made some ill-advised investments in cotton futures at the trade mart in New Orleans. He lost a great deal of money. Likely, it was to insure Margarith's security, to recuperate his losses—as well as the lure of adventure to an old war dog, plus the secret and guilty weariness of an aging husband with a teenage wife— which had pressured the major into his last, fatal venture.

Finally, when the major was reported dead and his body returned to The Laurels for burial, Margarith had been forced to mortgage the plantation. All the responsibilities fell upon her shoulders—debts he had even attempted to keep concealed from her tender eyes. She was in no way prepared to discharge such onerous obligations.

Matters deteriorated swiftly. The only white man on the plantation was Henley Lewis, the overseer and former prison guard. He was continually insisting she sell off the likeliest slaves for immediate cash and auction any blacks who gave him trouble, opposed him, or to whom he took a disliking. He despised all darkies unless they worked docilely and mumbled servilely in his presence.

The first fact of life impressed upon Margarith after the death of her husband was the state of war between her overseer and the blacks. The slaves hated Lewis. He demanded a free hand in dealing with the Negroes. Knowing this free hand meant daily public floggings, hanging recalcitrants by the heels overnight, and hunger as a punishment, Margarith had resisted.

Financial conditions worsened. The Negroes worked painfully slowly, if at all. A cold-faced wench could spend three hours to iron a single shirt in the kitchen. A black work crew could chop one row of cotton between dawn and sundown. Lewis kept telling her there was no incentive for the blacks to work unless he stood over them with his whip. She permitted him to whip only the laziest or the surliest. Every lash only increased their sullen hatred of the overseer, their defiance of the young mistress, and hardened their will to resist. The little money realized from the cotton crop went out to pay long overdue bills.

Margarith had been forced by circumstances to permit the overseer to handle all aspects of indiscriminate sales of slaves to itinerant buyers. She hated these sorry slave dealers with their scabrous coffles. She tried, by not looking at them, to pretend they did not exist. She doubted that Lewis ever turned over to her the full amount he received for the slaves he sold off .

The major had had the power of life and death over his slaves. He accepted this as a divine right. He did not question his status as a man meant to exercise the life and death power over lesser people and the black animals. He was as good to them as they would permit him to be. He punished and reproved when he saw the necessity. The slaves revered him.

The slaves had accepted that they were the chattel of Major Morceau. They belonged to him, body and soul. He had the right to sell, trade, whip, punish, or filet a slave if he wished. But when he was dead, they detested the overseer for attempting to exercise power they did not believe he had—unless his orders came from the major as they always had in the past.

They agreed they had belonged to the major. When he was dead, they belonged to no one, as far as they could see, certainly not to a cruel overseer who looked upon defiance as a crime and obedience as a sign of weakness to be despised and exploited. Lewis, the ex-prison guard, expected a slave to be naturally rebellious— as any darky was naturally lazy—and he mistrusted the docile as much as he did the fractious. To him, quiet workers were like the jackass, just waiting to break the traces.

Trouble mounted daily. Each morning a battle was

waged between unyielding overseer and sullen slaves. Recently, in order to force the males to work, he'd sold off the "wives" of the most vocal troublemakers. He cut food rations below subsistence levels to all who refused to do what he considered a day's work. And because servile obedience and docile laboring infuriated him, when they gave him what they believed had to be a full day's effort, he demanded more. The slaves were now ready to go on a hunger strike. Margarith had seen this coming for days. If there were not increased amounts of food for them and their children, they would not work at all. If they worked at all, it would be on terms and conditions dictated by their self-appointed leader, a black named Clitus.

This was the terrible way things stood this morning, she told him.

Jeff gazed down at the distracted girl. She was a courageous lady trying to take over a job that had been too big for the late and lamented major. He said, "All right. I'll stay on for a while. See what I can do to help you. I do know something about niggers." He hid the bitter twist of his lips. "You can tell Lewis to let me handle the blacks out there today."

Her violet eyes misted with tears. She reached out toward him, then let her hand fall to her side. "I don't know what I can ever do to thank you."

He grinned. "We'll think of something."

He put out his hand and she took it. She got to her feet, brushed away the signs of her tears and patted at the golden perfection of her hair. She straightened her dress as they went out of the room and crossed the foyer toward the wide front door, which Ponchus held open for them.

She smiled and nodded conspiratorily at Ponchus while she set a wide floppy-brimmed sunhat on her curls and tied it with a huge bow under her cleft chin. Jeff saw her wink happily at the elderly butler.

The gray-haired Negro smiled broadly. "Praise de Lawd," Ponchus said. "Thank-ee, young masta. Thank-ee."

171

The Negroes were gathered at the edge of the slave quarters in the far-reaching shade of a chinaberry tree. They sprawled on the ground, sat, or stood, but all were silent, watching sullenly.

Jeff walked with Margarith down the incline from the manor house, followed by the butler Ponchus, marching to his own drummer, and Vincente, who had hurried out, still eating, from the dining room. Henley Lewis stood in the sun some yards from the blacks gathered in a menacing knot in the shadow of the chinaberry tree. Margarith called Lewis aside and they spoke gravely, tautly for some moments. Ponchus stood behind Margarith, a foot or so from where they had their discussion. At last, Lewis simply threw up his hands, as if tossing the whole matter back to Mrs. Morceau. He returned with Margarith and Ponchus to where Jeff and Vincente waited. He gazed at Jeff, really seeing him for the first time, but he said nothing.

Margarith led them down to where Clitus stood some steps in front of the quiet blacks. Clitus was a young giant—three or four inches taller than Jeff, heavier in the chest, shoulders, and legs. He was a handsome man, but his features were contorted now with chilled hatred. He barely bobbed his head in greeting when Margarith approached him. "Ain't goin' to do no good—nothin' you can do or say, Miz Margarith, ma'am. We ain't workin' for Mister Lewis. . . . We ain't workin' for nobody till we gits full rations."

Margarith drew a deep breath. "I've tried to be kind to you, Clitus—and to all of you, because you're my people—"

"No'm . . . we Masta Morceau's people. The masta is dead."

"Everything that belonged to the master, now belongs to me, Clitus." There was no sign of weakness or fear in Margarith's voice. Jeff grinned, admiring her.

"We'uns bein' starved, Miz Margarith. We bein' whupped—for no cause. We bein' worked too hard." Clitus's voice remained hard, unyielding.

172

"Maybe there has been too little food, Clitus. You were getting what Mr. Lewis believed you earned. I have asked that none of you be whipped—unless I say so. But as for you all working too hard, I'm sorry, Clitus— if you had all simply worked as you should, there would be no trouble. Mr. Lewis is paid by percentage on the cotton we sell. You know we had the poorest crop we ever had this year . . . and I think you know why, Clitus."

"Ain't gwine be no different. Ain't gwine be no better— not till changes made here. Changes I tell you." Clitus straightened, tall as a young tree. He thrust out his chest, and the blacks behind him spoke in a sour chorus.

Jeff stepped up beside Margarith then and touched her arm. He stared at Clitus, and the black man shifted his position, setting himself and meeting his gaze. Jeff let his mouth twist into a disdainful smile, and he moved his gaze beyond Clitus, speaking to the assembled workers. "I have been asked to run this plantation for Mrs. Morceau, your mistress. Not as overseer. Mr. Lewis will continue to oversee your work. But his orders will come from me."

"Who you, white man?" Clitus said.

"One thing I don't have to do is explain myself to you, boy. I say something, you move. You don't move, you suffer. If I ever hear you talk back to Mrs. Morceau as you just did here today, you suffer."

"Somebody got to stand up for our rights. And that somebody is me."

"No. You're a black. You're a slave. You got no rights." Jesus, Jeff thought, who knows those words better than I? They're burned into my flesh.

"I don't know who you is, white man," Clitus said. "But this I know. Ain't none of these people goin' to work till things are different."

Jeff grinned coldly at him. "Things are different, right now, boy. So you can go on out to the fields. You people go to work till noon—you'll be fed a big picnic meal— right here under this tree at noon."

Some of the people mumbled, agreeing, but Clitus held up his hand. His voice shook. "Who say?"

"I say . . . I already told you, Clitus. You don't talk back. We do what we think is best—for you—for this plantation."

"Nobody makes me do nothin' no more." Clitus stared at Jeff, then glanced over his shoulder, letting his gaze rake his people. They waited in silence.

"All right," Jeff said. "We've talked enough. But you figure you're a big boy. Figure you got some rights. Tell you what. What's your name?"

"My name Clitus, white man."

"All right, Clitus. Here's my offer to you. You beat me—in a fight. Here. Right now. You beat me, you never have to work again in your life. You can set on your tail as long as you live."

Clitus stared at him, then measured him, then he laughed, showing his teeth. "Yeah, man!"

"Sound good, huh? Then there's what happens when I beat you—"

"If'n you beat me—"

"If I beat you today, you go back to work with the crew. Now. But then, every day after this any one of these people don't work, unless they're sick, I'll beat you again."

Clitus scowled, chewing that over, not liking the taste of it. Then he looked at his own clenched fists, at Jeff. Jeff took off his jacket and tossed it to Vincente. He glimpsed Margarith, standing with her fist pressed against her lips, and Lewis, ill with doubt, Ponchus, shoulders sagged round. Clitus bawled "Yeah, man!" again. He turned, grinning at the crowd.

As Clitus turned back, Jeff hit him straight in the face with everything he had. He felt Clitus's wide-nostriled nose smash under the impact. He saw the big man's dark eyes glaze over. In Clitus, he saw himself hurrying down the gangplank at Barataria, caught by surprise by Dominique You's huge fist. But he also knew he lacked the battering-ram power that You possessed. Clitus was more

174

surprised than hurt. He had to move while the big man was stunned.

He struck Clitus in the left temple, and again in the right. He could almost see the agony well in the black man's eyes, knew the way Clitus's stomach walls were crumbling, the way his nerve centers were scrambled. Clitus shook his head, trying to clear it. He reached out wildly for Jeff. But Jeff knew what Clitus was seeing—a dark, moving blur.

He hit Clitus as hard as he could with his right fist, clipping his jaw. This time, Clitus's knees sagged, his whole body quivered. But Jeff knew it couldn't end until Clitus was sprawled in the dirt at his feet.

With his left, he struck the right side of Clitus's jaw. Clitus's arms sagged to his side now. His knees buckled. But he did not fall. Jeff drove his fist into his face again, sent another right across the big jaw. That did it. Clitus sank to his knees, sprawled to his face at Jeff's feet.

Hiding the fact that his arms ached all the way to his armpits, that his knuckles were raw, his hands numb, Jeff sneered at Clitus's prostrate form with a contempt he did not feel but which this crowd had to see. He reached out, took his coat from an overwhelmed Vincente. He jerked his head at one of the slaves. The black ran, fetched a bucket of water, and poured it on Clitus's head.

Slowly, Clitus sat up. Blood leaked from his nostrils, his lip was cut, the side of his face swollen and bruised. He stared up at Jeff, his agonized face pulled with respect and awe. He whispered, with no hint of malice, "You fights dirty, masta."

Jeff smiled. "I don't fight unless I have to, Clitus . . . then I fight to get it over fast. . . . You want to try again?"

"Naw, suh." Clitus managed to smile as he shook his head. "I'se had 'nuff."

"You've had enough—for today, Clitus. But hear me well. Anybody don't work today, you going to have to fight me again. Somebody don't work tomorrow—we'll get together, you and me—and every day till you know what I'm talking about."

"Naw, suh, masta. I knows. These folks, they gwine work—and we gwine have a picnic—at noon. I knows we is." Clitus got up slowly, shaking lingering cobwebs from his mind. He smiled. "I knows we is—'cause I knows you a man mean what you say. . . . Yes, suh, masta, I knows you do. . . . Come on, you niggers, le's git to work."

CHAPTER XVII

When the work crew came in from the fields at noon, long tables were set up under the chinaberry tree and piled high with food. These tables were made of planks, set by the black carpenters across sawhorses and covered with white cotton sheets too old for further use in the manor house. The boards were crowded with the food prepared in the big house kitchen—sliced hams, barbecued pork ribs, fried chicken with plenty of crisply fried gizzards, hearts, and kidneys, huge black pots of black-eyed peas, earthenware pitchers of red-eye gravy, corn bread, collard greens, and rice; all topped off with large pots of coffee heated on fires set near each table, and dozens of sweet-potato pies.

The meal was served by the house Negroes who stopped complaining about having to work for the field hands when Ponchus read them the riot act. "These heah folks been workin' hard. This heah's young Masta Jeff's own party—an' nex' one I heahs complainin' gone feel my hand acrost the back of they neck."

Children came running from everywhere. The yard and barn workers, the animal tenders, the craftsmen and seamstresses all joined in the picnic.

The field crew straggled in when the noon bell rang. They came in silence, expecting nothing. But they straightened and walked faster as they smelled the freshly brewing coffee, the ham, barbecue, and fried chicken. Plank seats, set on nail kegs, were lined along the tables for them.

Margarith watched it all with delight edged in trepidation. But she relaxed and felt better when Henley Lewis rode in and reported to her. "Crew worked well," he admitted with some shock. "Don't reckon it can last, but they worked good today."

Margarith was most astonished and breathless in her relief when she saw how amiably Henley Lewis accepted Jeff as the new master of The Laurels. Her sharpest fear had been of Lewis's rage at the change. She knew him to be a cold and vengeful man who never forgot a slight, or personal injury, a man who jealously guarded his domain as overseer. But she was relieved to see Lewis was satisfied to have someone else accept all responsibility, make the decisions and, probably, someone to blame for any orders he now gave the slaves.

Henley reported to Jeff while the slaves were eating. They ate silently at first, slaves afraid to believe a promise kept, but soon they were laughing, joking, shouting at each other.

Margarith watched them, delighted, yet filled with dread. These blacks were constitutionally a happy people. God knew, they could not endure slavery without some inner hope and saving humor. She had come from a town family. They'd never owned a slave. She'd hated slavery from the first day she'd arrived here at The Laurels. She'd grown despondent and hopeless as conditions deteriorated after the major's death. She had not heard

177

black laughter—as she heard it around this table today—since before her husband died. Like Henley Lewis, she was afraid to believe it could last.

Henley talked to Jeff about the crops, the slaves, the work which badly needed to be done, the blacks who ought to be weeded out through sale or auction. Jeff heard him out, agreeing with most of the overseer's suggestions and plans.

As Henley prepared to leave him, Jeff said, "You might have less trouble with big Clitus if you made him the work foreman."

"Work foreman? That troublemaker? Hell, if I have trouble with Clitus, I'll whip him. He's got it coming."

"That's up to you. But I've learned proud men resent the whip."

"Men, yes. But these are blacks we're talking about. Slaves. Animals."

"Yes. I agree. But Clitus could be a big help to you—as work foreman."

"What in hell would he do that would help me?"

"Tell his people when to start and stop work, when they can take off, for what reason, settle troubles among them. When those workers get hot and tired out there and start fights, he could stop them fast. Things you shouldn't have to do. Make it easier on you."

After a moment of deep thought, Henley nodded. "Yeah. Yeah. All right. I'll do it. Can't hurt none. Might help."

After their lunch, the slaves sprawled in the shade, eating huge, quarter-slices of yam pie, finishing off the coffee, gnawing on barbecue bones or chicken legs, eating chicken livers as if they were peanuts. When Clitus returned from talking with Henley Lewis, the workers looked up to find the big youth's bruised face stunned with disbelief, but smiling. "All right. We's lazed around long 'nuff. Got cotton to chop. . . . Who say? I say. . . . Boss man made Clitus work foreman. So Clitus say. That who say."

They got up, talking among themselves, amazed at the

new changes, belching, laughing, joking among themselves. When they passed the tree where Jeff and Vincente sat astride horses in the shade, ready for an inspection tour of the plantation with Ponchus as guide, the workers touched their hats, nodding toward Jeff.

"Got us a new man on de place."

"New man wid balls."

"Man wid balls."

"New man—wid balls—on de place."

"Yes, Lawd."

When the crew had passed, going toward the sun-braised fields, Vincente said, "Why don't we ride on out of here—now?"

Jeff's scowl challenged him. "I can't."

"I know. And I know why you promised to stay . . . it won't work, *amigo*. This young woman . . . she is a very *gentle* lady. *Muy dulzura.*"

"Out of the mouths of babes! What do *you* know about 'very *gentle* ladies'?"

"I know they don't like the studs—like you and me. That is why there is *la puta*—why there are whores like my sister Perla—it is to them that men go when they are married to the very gentle ladies."

"Maybe the gentle ladies just have to be handled different."

Vincente shrugged. "There is a far better reason why *you* should not let yourself get involved with this very *blond,* very gentle lady. . . . I would say it aloud, but you have vowed to kill me if I do."

"My black blood? That's why I must stay—why I must take what I can, as I can. . . . I live with a sword point fixed always at the base of my throat, ready to pierce me through. The sword of my black blood. The hatred of Baxter Simon who still believes he owns me. The hidden brand marks on my back, which would reveal me as a black man to anyone. I can never truly rest. I can sleep only lightly. But by God! I can make love with a free heart, because to die in the saddle is the finest dream of every swordsman!"

179

"That's fine for you, *amigo*. But what about her? What happens when she finds out? Some ladies have—strong guts inside—they can take great hurt and recover. I do not think this gentle lady is one of them."

"Whose side are you on? Hers or mine?"

"On yours, *amigo*. Always. But there are many *damas*, many women. When this one is hurt, I do not think you walk away—how do you say—unscathed."

"Well, damn it, I'm staying. She needs my help—our help. She has terrible trouble here."

Vincente laughed bitterly. "She has *no* trouble, *amigo*, compared to the trouble she will have once she has fallen in love with you, I think."

Ponchus joined them at that moment. Jeff silenced Vincente with a sharp downward slash of his hand. Vincente shrugged and fell silent. Jeff glared at him. Look who was acting as his conscience now! the boy pimp, who had trained his own sister in ways of whoredom, the con artist, the street rascal. But as they rode across the extensive acreage of the farm, Jeff was conscious of an emptiness in his belly, a sense of insufficiency.

Damn Vincente! He was nothing but a smart-talking street arab from Havana. He ought to be sent back there immediately. He refused to listen to the brat. He had never wanted any woman as he wanted the gentle, protected—and perhaps unattainable—Margarith! She did need him here. And even if she did not, he couldn't simply ride away from her. No other woman would ever satisfy him unless he had Margarith—for unless he had her, she would never be out of his mind, though he might well be out of his!

No. Unless he had her, Margarith would remain that resisted temptation that haunts us the rest of our lives. Perhaps Vincente was right—it might not harm him to resist a temptation here and there. But to ride away from Margarith without even letting her know how fiercely he wanted her? This was contrary to all reason! And as to her learning about the brand weals on his back, about his black blood—no one would learn that truth. And so this was a fear without foundation. She would not be hurt, because she would never know.

He did not see Margarith until supper time. Ponchus proved an excellent guide, an intelligent and knowledgeable man who had worked closely with his late lamented master. Ponchus had been close enough to Morceau that the major shared his dreams, ambitions, and plans for The Laurels with him.

They rode across fallow fields, land which Major Morceau had left purposely unplanted so it could regain its strength and vigor. Here, the major proposed to build his own lumber mill, which would process the pine, cypress, oak, and other commercial woods growing so profusely on plantation property. Further along the fast-running creek, the major had set out the foundation for a grist mill. "It war' the major's hope to make The Laurels absolutely self-sufficient," Ponchus said. "Dat's what de major say—dem very words—'absolutely self-sufficient'."

"Why didn't he do it?" Jeff said. "He had all the materials—except maybe metals and nails—he had labor going to waste."

"Seemed like always something else coming up," Ponchus said.

Jeff grinned. "Sure. A war to fight somewhere. Or another wife to marry—or bury."

"Masta Morceau—he a great man," Ponchus said. But he too smiled.

When they'd inspected the cotton acreage, Jeff decided more land must be prepared and ways found to channel water in from the stream to irrigate. He made a mental note to speak to Overseer Lewis about this. The food gardens were more encouraging. Teenaged boys and women tended the beans, field peas, okra, beets, onions, carrots, corn, potatoes, and peanuts. They worked at a faster pace than the men, more willingly and steadily— perhaps because the products of their work fed them as well as the white folks.

Jeff found the cattle herds larger than he'd expected.

Swine roamed the wooded areas living on snakes, berries, roots. There was no way to take a hog census, but the sows in the mud pens looked fat and healthy, as did their brood. Chickens, geese, turkeys, and guineas ran screaming mindlessly from their path when they rode into the barnyards.

He noted that the craftsmen worked—if not at an inspired tempo—at least with adequate interest and results. Work clothing, underwear, candles, woven fabrics, repairs, and smithing all progressed satisfactorily, as did the animal tending and feed and grain handling. Jeff expressed himself surprised at the excellent state of the farm. "Yas, suh, young masta," Ponchus nodded and swung his arm. "We keeps runnin' fast as we can, but we's standin' still—like we doin' all our runnin' in mud up past our ankles."

The last site visited was the slave quarters. Here, Jeff discovered signs of deterioration which had to be remedied at once. He met Henley Lewis at the barns as the work crews returned from the fields in the hazy dusk. A deep sense of calm pervaded the plantation, accented by the ringing of the sundown bell, which called the slaves in from their work.

"I want crews put on the slave quarters in the morning," he told Lewis. "Whitewash the outer walls—but also whitewash the inner walls. Then use a clear varnish on every floor. Repair any roof that leaks, reglass all windows."

"Why you want to waste time on that now?" Lewis said. "That don't make us no profit."

"It makes us no profit right now," Jeff said, "but if these people take pride in the houses where they live—"

"They don't! You know niggers. Animals. Fix them windows. They break 'em that same day—throwin' trash out'n 'em."

"Maybe they won't when you tell them I said that for every broken window from now on, the family in that house will spend a week cleaning up the roads, lanes, and yards."

Lewis smiled, nodding. "Yeah. That might work."

"When the insides of their houses have white walls and clear-stained pinewood floors, a lantern or even a candle will brighten the place up better. They'll feel better. They'll work better. You'll get your profit."

He heard Ponchus whisper, "Amen, young masta."

By the time Jeff finished bathing in the major's brass tub, shaving, and dressing, supper was announced. He found his trousers, jackets, stockings, shirts, and linens had all been laundered, ironed, and placed neatly in the oak chiffonier, which had been built and stained on this farm.

His heart pumped faster as he went along the corridor toward the dining room where he would see Margarith again. It had been a long day. A hellish long day!

Margarith wore black, but the fragile fabric accented her pale blond loveliness. For the first time, Jeff found Margarith ill at ease, blushing easily and often, seldom meeting his eyes directly. Her hands on her knife and fork trembled. Was this lovely creature only human after all? Was this gentle lady attainable despite Vincente's predictions?

Secretly, Jeff had feared he could never have her. She had been strictly reared, overly protected, had attended a cloistered girl's school, tended an ill father while she should have been dancing and flirting, and at seventeen married to an aging man. Her beauty was all the more perfect because it was so fresh and untouched. Untouchable? He didn't know. But he did know at this moment he wanted her more than he had ever wanted any woman.

Margarith seemed as nervous as a hummingbird, as ready to flee as a butterfly on a shaking rose. He said, "Are you all right?"

"All right? Of course—I've never been happier. I've never been so delighted to have anyone in my home as I am to have you—and Vincente." She tried to smile, failed. "Ponchus says you've taken over in a way the major would have approved. This means Ponchus approves the changes he says you are already ordering."

"Nothing too drastic, I hope," he said.

"You make whatever changes you see indicated," she said in a firm voice. "That's all up to you. No matter the cost. Thanks to you, we can afford new projects."

"The changes I see needed won't cost much in actual dollars," he said.

"I want you to do whatever you think should be done," she said.

"Well, to start, I think the major's idea for a lumber mill and a grist mill on the creek are good, and I think we ought to start on them at once."

She nodded emphatically. "Then we will."

Jeff felt Vincente's gaze fixed on him, chilled and disapproving. Clearly, Vincente felt the fox had been left to guard the hen house. Had the kid actually thought Jeff would ride away from The Laurels and from this lovely vision so near that his knee could brush hers—and would have, had he not feared he would frighten her away?

As soon as he finished dessert of bread pudding, Vincente excused himself. At first, Jeff thought displeasure and disapprobation prompted Vincente to absent himself from what he saw as the scene of a ruthless seduction. Vincente was so unalterably opposed to Jeff's touching Margarith Morceau, it occurred to Jeff that Vincente might somehow let Margarith know the truth about Jeff's past and his bloodlines. Damn him! He'd kill him if he did. . . . It was hell when you were afraid to trust your closest associate with the truth about yourself. The fact was, you could trust *no one*. When your life depended upon carefully guarding a secret, the first law was never to share it, to eradicate anyone who did share it.

He felt himself drawn tauter, wondering what to do about Vincente. Then he glimpsed the boy crossing the far edge of the veranda with Jenny, the high-yellow house wench. So this was why Vincente hurried from the site of Jeff's latest conquest. He was after quail of his own. Jeff sighed heavily, able to relax for the moment and to address his fullest attention to the beautiful girl in black at the table beside him.

"I've just been ill all day," Margarith was saying. "When I think of your challenging Clitus! He's so huge! So powerful! He looked like a giant beside you! I was afraid he would kill you."

Jeff smiled, pleased to see her respond to his smiling. His smile never failed him, no woman ever resisted its charm and appeal—or its invitation. "He might. Someday. When he learns to fight dirty . . ." his voice trailed off. Through his mind flashed the ugly memory of his killing Green Mike, the king pimp of the Louisville waterfront. He shook it from his mind. He'd been attacked, the slaying had been self-defense. Anyhow, all that belonged in another world, light-years removed from Margarith Morceau's candlelit dining room. "I knew poor Clitus was a country boy. I knew he was strong, big. But I figured he'd never had to fight just to stay alive."

She shivered, her eyes pained. "I hate to think of your ever having had to fight—to stay alive." She sighed. "Perhaps I should be thankful. It taught you to be self-reliant, to handle slaves."

From the bodice of her black dress she drew a sheet of paper. She opened and straightened it on the table. She glanced at it, smiling, pleased. Then she turned it for him to read. It was one of the letters he'd brought her from Jean Lafitte. It was unsigned. It stated that the bearer could be trusted and was most highly recommended to aid her in any undertaking. Jeff grinned. That Lafitte! Letting him think the Widow Morceau was aging, but arranging, as far as he could, Jeff's entry and acceptance here. Hell, this omen was good enough for him. Lafitte's intervention had to be fate taking a hand, and he was certain nature never intended him to go very long without a woman to love. . . .

They left the dining table under Ponchus's benign eye. Jeff touched her elbow and turned her from the wanly lit room out to the darkened veranda. They found the darkness sensually scented with gardenia and bay shrubs. He moved his hand up her bare arm and turned her to face him.

She caught her breath but did not struggle. He pulled her body close against him. He felt the erratic thundering of her heart, the fullness of her breasts, the fevered heat at her thighs. He turned up her face and kissed her. Her eyes closed but her lips did not part. Kissing Margarith was somewhat like bussing an extremely lovely and delicate ceramic statue.

"Am I that unattractive?" he whispered.

"What? Unattractive? I've never met a—more attractive man—or one more self-assured," she said in her honest, open way. "I—I let you kiss me."

Jeff grinned helplessly. "Yes. You *let* me kiss you. It would have been nice if you'd kissed me."

For a moment she melted against the bulge at his crotch. He swore he could feel the heated pressure of her upon it. But she grew restive, nervous, and, he realized, actually frightened. She pulled away from him, breathing raggedly. Troubled, he released her. "I—I'm sorry," she said.

"Sorry? For what?"

"For the awful cardboard thing you must think me. . . . It's just that—I—I can't! I'm truly sorry. I'm afraid of overpowering lovers—of aggressive lovers."

He laughed. "Is there some other kind?"

"André was another kind," she said. She stared through tear-blurred eyes at her trembling hands. "He was a gentle, understanding man."

"For hell's sake. He was *old!*"

"Perhaps. But I'm afraid he's spoiled me for all other men. . . . The way you held me . . . it frightened me. . . . I'm sorry—I could never respond to such boldness— everything that André was not. Please forgive me."

He shrugged. "I forgive you." His voice was empty. "I sure as hell don't understand you. But I forgive you."

She reached out, closed her fingers on his arm. "You— may kiss me if you want to," she said. "As kind as you are, I know I owe you that."

186

He gazed down at her. "You owe me nothing, madam." Jeff bowed low. "Good night. I promise you, this won't happen again." He smiled at her, turned and walked away, stomach empty, cock hard, and gut aching.

CHAPTER XVIII

It was *déjà vu*.

She came to him as she had in his dreams the first night at The Laurels. His bedroom door sliced open and Margarith came through it, clad only in a filmy gown. In the flickering moonlight, she came across the room to him. . . .

It had been a long, brutal day, filled with tensions between him and Margarith. She had tried to be her natural self at breakfast and failed completely. Her hands shook so badly she could not hand him a cup of coffee. She asked if he had slept well, and when he only grinned crookedly at her, she looked as if she might cry. He spent the rest of the meal trying to put her at ease. But as he was leaving the table, he repeated the vow he'd made to her the night before, hoping to settle the matter and leave her in peace. "I made a mistake last night," he said. "Please believe me, it won't happen again." She did burst into tears then, and she fled from the room crying out, "Oh, what a stupid little fool you must think me!" He left his own breakfast unfinished because he was not hungry, but mostly because he didn't care to meet Ponchus immediately after having made his beloved mistress weep.

He passed a busy day; he had Ponchus send food out to him where he was showing the carpenters how he wanted the grist mill set up on the creek. He was pleased to find they understood how to dam the creek, to build a stone spillway and set the mill wheel in it. Work began that afternoon on the new building.

At the slave quarters, he found the old men, teenaged boys, older children, and all the women working with mops, brushes, and buckets of whitewash under Ponchus's direction. He had dreaded the moment when he'd first meet Ponchus, knowing the aged butler must know by now of the unpleasant scene at the breakfast table between him and the widow Morceau. But the butler greeted him warmly; obviously, if he was aware of what happened —and he had to be!—he didn't blame Jeff, or consider it a serious matter. Ponchus was fiercely loyal to his mistress. Who hurt her, Jeff knew, had Ponchus to deal with. He loved the militarily tough old man for this but had not welcomed a confrontation. There was to be none, and for this he was thankful.

By dusk every cottage in the quarters had been whitewashed inside and out. The place already glowed whitely, looking different. Carpenters had repaired all roofing and broken windows. In the morning, Ponchus promised, the pinewood floors would be varnished with clear lacquer until they shone like new wood fresh from the trees. The slaves were pleased with what was happening, and gratified that one of the first changes the new boss man made improved the quality of their own lives. They grinned shyly at Jeff, nodding their heads, trying mutely to express their appreciation.

He looked forward with no real excitement to meeting with Margarith at the dinner table. He was glad that Vincente was there to share it with them. When Vincente was anxious to escape immediately after dessert, Jeff denied him the privilege. "Surely you can be polite enough to wait until Mrs. Morceau excuses you?" he said.

Both Vincente and Margarith winced, though both for different reasons. Vincente was rampant with need to discover again tonight with Jenny the delight of their bodies. Margarith knotted her napkin in her fist, hating herself because obviously Jeff did not want to be alone with her.

She hastily finished off her dessert and coffee, excusing Vincente. The youth grinned at her, bowed over her hand, and fled the room. She gazed at Jeff, pale and uncomfortable. "Would you care to sit in the parlor? I—could play the spinnet for you—if you wish?"

Jeff knew better. He could not sit in any room with this delectable creature without reaching for her—for those breasts delightfully stressful against the fabric of her mourning frock, for those lips that needed to be kissed, that would hunger for kissing once they learned what kissing could be. But this was not to be for him. He knew now he could not have her. She had made this clear—she could "never respond" to a man like him. He should have been able to laugh. You could never attract them all; it was sad but true, the one you wanted most might find you far less than attractive, as Margarith had let him know she did. Everything her husband was not. Well, thank God for that! But he could not laugh. At this moment he did not see how he could go on without her. Perhaps—as Vincente had suggested—he should get away, as soon as possible. Meantime, he could not laugh at losing her. But he could not stay near her either. He'd never been aroused by self-flagellation.

He smiled and bowed over her hand. The hell of it was, though she was fully dressed, in mourning, she seemed naked despite her clothes. He had to get out of there, away from her.

"Forgive me," he said. "Ordinarily, I'd love to hear you play the spinnet. But tonight I'm too tired. It's been a long day."

Her eyes filled with tears, but she tilted her little cleft chin and nodded. "I know you must be tired. It was thoughtless of me." She bowed her head, turned slowly, and walked through the open door. Jeff wanted to run after her. But he knew better. What was new about *his* running after her? He'd done that since the first moment he beheld her. There could be good between them only when she came to him, even if he had no comfort in his bed except that unexciting companion, his fist.

When she was gone, he went out the tall door to the veranda, and across it. He walked for a long time in the darkness. He heard voices from the quarters, he heard night animals skittering, the distant cry of a panther, like a woman in distress. The living room was dark when he returned up the long lane from the trace. A small lamp glowed yellowly in her bedroom. He let himself into the house, went to his own room.

Despite his nocturnal hike, the long day of dealing with problems of the big farm, he was restless, unable to sleep. In his mind he conjured up the image of Margarith's naked body—the full, shapely breasts the color of ripe peaches and tipped with succulent cherries, the flat planes of her belly, the triangle at her thighs, the chalice there—waiting—practically untouched by an aging man fool enough to go away on some military adventure and leave a treasure like her unguarded in his house! Margarith and Ponchus revered Major André Morceau's memory, but he could not share their admiration—in fact, he felt a cold contempt for the "gentle" man who had "spoiled" Margarith for all other men!

Hell, the aging bastard had starved her and had trained her to accept starvation as the norm for gentle women! Maybe the son of a bitch had actually believed it—many Southern men put their white women on pedestals and seldom touched them sexually, preferring to "use" black wenches for their "animal" desires. Jesus! what a way to live.

His eyes burned, but he could not sleep. Still, he had thought he was dreaming when his door opened and Margarith let herself in, her way lighted with a small candle.

Jeff stared at her. The fragile gown only accented her

nakedness. Her breasts *were* creamy, cherry tipped, not as large as he'd thought, but more shapely, more succulent. Her old-gold hair was loose about her face and shoulders. Just looking at her with her hair let down aroused him painfully. He felt himself lurch to erection, blood engorging his stiffening rod.

"Jeff."

"Yes."

She waited. When he did not speak, she whispered, "Please don't make me say it—I have come to you. You may—do whatever you wish."

He sat up. He even swung his legs around, pulling the cover from himself, revealing the high-standing rigidity of his towering cock. She caught her breath, retreating. Obviously, she'd never seen anything like this—perhaps she hadn't even known men raised such erections. She could not pull her gaze from him. "Why have you come?" he said.

"I told you," she whispered, as if strangling.

"No. Why have you come in here—to me? Like this? I'm not what you want—not what you've been taught to want."

"That doesn't matter," she whispered, voice quivering. "You want me. You may have me—it's the least I can do. I've no right to expect you to stay here and help me—for nothing. . . . You want me . . . you may have me."

He shook his head. "Sorry. I don't want you."

"You're lying. I know you want me. My—my God—I can look at you—and know you want me."

Grinning crookedly, he tapped his rigid cock with the back of his hand. "He wants every woman he sees. You owe me nothing. You don't have to worry about me. Please, go back to bed. I've already told you I regret having upset you."

"You think me prim, prudish. You laugh at what—what André and I had together. . . . I'm only what I am. But if you want me—"

"But I don't."

"We can't go on with this terrible formality between

191

us. I need you here—I never even realized how badly this place needed a man like you—until I saw the changes you have made already. . . . I *want* to repay you."

He nodded. "You have repaid me."

"I? How?"

"By coming to my room. Believe me, nobody more than I knows how difficult—what a fearful thing—this must have been for you. But you did not have to. I told you. I know now how you feel—about men like me. Brutal men like me with rough desires. . . . I'll want you, Mrs. Morceau, only when you can come to me and say *you* want me—as you never wanted anyone else."

Tears welled in her eyes and spilled along her cheeks. "Don't you see?" she whispered. "That isn't going to happen. . . . I never knew anyone like you. I know that you could never really want me—except to use— as you've used how many other women?"

He grinned at her in the flickering candlelight. "I'm afraid that's none of your business."

"Oh, God, how stupid I am! I didn't mean that! I only meant, I can't lie to you—I can never say I want you."

He smiled and bowed, aware that she still stole amazed glances at his erection, and that she would see it in her dreams. It might scare hell out of her, waken her screaming, but she'd see it. "Then you should be able to sleep well. Until you can say it, I won't want you. And so you owe me nothing, you can offer me nothing, and I wish you a pleasant good night."

Tears spilled from her eyes. She waited another moment, but when he did not move, she turned and went slowly out of the room, the candle guttering. He stared down at his inflexible cock, thinking, I'm going to beat hell out of you, you lying bastard. It ain't that I blame you. It's just the only way I'll get to sleep tonight. . . .

CHAPTER XIX

Jeff found the tensions between himself and Margarith Morceau intensified at breakfast the next morning. She was seated at the table when he came in. She was wearing a most becoming black dress cut in a low V at the bodice, suggesting the warm cleavage between her breasts. She caught herself as her gaze flew to the bulge at his crotch, and she was completely unnerved at her involuntary and hated action. Inwardly, Jeff grinned. It had been a long night for her; she looked drawn and sleepless—but she had not forgotten.

He forced himself to talk lightly of the problems of the farm, his plans for changes, the needs of the slaves. But she appeared distracted. Though she nodded often—frequently at the wrong times—he knew she scarcely heard him.

"Will—you be in—for dinner?" she asked.

"I don't know," he told her. "Don't wait for me. There's a lot I want to do, I may not get back until supper."

He found that the work on the floors of the slave cabins had begun, and Ponchus promised it would be completed before noon. Jeff saw that most of the farm work around The Laurels was directed by Ponchus. Though Henley Lewis was overseer, the white man in charge, Ponchus ran the house and the plantation, probably as he had when the major had been alive. He saw that the cabins were painted and repaired. He supervised the house slaves. When there were questions among the craftsmen or at the barns, they came to Ponchus for a ruling. And he never failed them. He dropped in at the big rooms where spinning and weaving of rough tow and cotton was done, where the slave women's dresses were sewn, as well as the shirts and trousers for the men of the farm. He was in charge when hogs were slaughtered, when meat was cured, calves were birthed, slaughtered, or weaned. He carried it out with such ease that he made it look easy, and especially as if he were not usurping any powers which should belong to white people.

Ponchus was a smart old fellow. When the cotton was picked, baled, and sent off in the rumbling cotton wagons, it was Ponchus who found work for the field crews. Jeff suggested the yards around the manor house could be neater, and a crew was put to work up there in less than an hour.

Despite the emptiness in his belly and the ache in his loins, Jeff was pleased with his accomplishments. The slave quarters looked vastly better. The blacks put on cleaner clothes oftener, and he saw the women sweeping two and three times a day with their twig brooms. He sent a crew to thin out a pine grove and to haul the logs to the site of the new lumber mill. There was an air of industry beside the creek. The grist mill was already taking shape, and the carpenters were laying out the foundation lines for the lumber mill. There was yet a great deal to do; but clearly they were accomplishing much, and Jeff had a real sense of accomplishment—everywhere except in the bedroom of Margarith Morceau.

He sat slumped in his saddle in the shade of a live oak watching the workers set huge fieldstones in a cement mixture at the grist mill, but in his mind he was seeing Margarith's breasts.

A yell brought him rudely back to reality.

"Carson!" Henley Lewis's voice startled Jeff so that he sat up, shaking his head, looking around. The overseer's sweated face was contorted with rage. Jeff exhaled. He'd been afraid things were going too well. "It's that damned black Adam again."

"What's he done this time?"

"Same's before. The bastid run again. Workin' out there in the field, quiet as could be. With Clitus overseein' for me, I can get around, visit some of the other worksites. When I got back, Clitus told me Adam asked permission to take a shit in the woods. Adam didn't come back. The bastid. He's run again. Just wanted to tell you, I'll have to take some men and dogs and run him down."

Jeff nodded. He didn't share the overseer's hatred for Adam's running. He himself had run. Slavery had become unendurable, and he had run. Jesus, he pitied the poor bastard. Running, when he didn't have a chance in God's world. Listening for the yelping of the hounds and the yelling of the hunters behind him. Hiding from the slave patrollers. Afraid to sleep, afraid to round the next turn in the road for fear of who might be waiting up there.

He was thankful no one suggested he join the chase. Even the black men recruited by Lewis seemed anxious to go. The hounds, given the scent, yelped in anxiety to hit the trail. Vincente decided to ride along for the excitement.

He returned early to the house. Somehow the pleasure had gone out of his day, all the feeling of achievement had dissolved. He could think only of his own running, his terror. Ponchus sent in buckets of hot water for his bath in the major's brass tub. Jeff scrubbed himself fiercely with soap, lathering his body, but he could not feel clean. Adam's flight had brought back to him the precarious nature of his own life. Even soaking in the major's brass tub, he was running. Somewhere behind him, Baxter Simon was on his trail. Simon had never lost a slave, he never meant to lose one. And even if he escaped Simon, he could never escape the brands scarring his back. But the thought of what might happen

195

to him if he were caught pressed in upon him. He would never have Margarith then! He would lose his freedom. He would likely die because Simon had long since given up wanting Bricktop returned to Willow Oaks. He wanted him caught; he wanted him dead.

In a deep depression, he realized he could not stay here. Despite the fact that everything he wanted in life was here at The Laurels, he must be moving on. The danger would increase the more contented and careless he became here in this place. What would they do when they learned he was a mustee—a fugitive black, running as poor Adam was running, and doomed—ultimately— as Adam was doomed?

He shuddered, getting a mental image of Margarith's lovely blond face at that future moment when she learned the man to whom she had offered her body was not a white man at all, but a black living out a masquerade.

The kindest thing he could do for her was to clear out.

He went out to join Margarith at supper. Already sunk into deep depression, he found her fragile loveliness more than he could take. He felt tears choking his throat. She was so incredibly lovely, so eternally lost to him. He wanted her above all other women. He could never have her. He must not touch her at all.

He made no effort to smile or to be charming. His mood was as black as his blood. He wanted her to despise him. He had sent her from his room last night hating him. He did not want her to come back. He knew that this time he could not send her away. Jeff Carson might, but it was too damned much to ask of Bricktop, the run- away slave whose cock was enormous and whose days were numbered.

"You've accomplished so much," Margarith said. "In such a little time. I'm so proud."

"Well, maybe we don't have too much time," he said without smiling. He pushed his food about on his plate. He didn't want it. He wanted *her*.

She winced, bit her lip. "I know you must want to leave," she said. "It must be so boring for you here—

after Haiti! How I envy you. But—how we'll miss you—and your great energy and wonderful ideas, when you're gone. . . . I truly wish there were some way we could keep you. Something we could offer you. You've never even discussed what percentage you expect for your work."

"We don't have to talk about it now."

"But I want to." She exhaled heavily. "I want to do all I can to keep you. As long as I can. I feel so helpless when I think of your leaving."

"Don't," he said. "I'll have things arranged so that Ponchus can run them for you before I leave. I promise you that."

She winced. "I know how badly you must miss—all the pleasures you could find in a city." Her hands shook. She hid them in her lap.

He glanced at her coldly. "Perhaps Ponchus could arrange a bed wench for me tonight?"

"No!" The word burst across her lips almost as an involuntary reaction. Her face burned red to her hair line.

He grinned without warmth. "I'll work as hard as I can, Mrs. Morceau. But you can't expect me to live like a monk just because you choose to exist like a nun."

"I know that, but—" her eyes filled with tears, "—I just don't want you to!"

She would not lift her head to look at him. "I understand," he said. "Of course. Not in your house."

Now she burst into tears, crying openly. She got up and ran from the room. Jeff sagged in his chair, chilled with a sense of depression. He was not aware that the cotton-haired Ponchus was in the room until the butler said, "Missy real upset lately. She been mighty lonely since the major passed on. I sho' was hopin' that having young people here—a nice young man like you in de house would lighten up her mood some. . . . Reckon we just got to give her time."

"Reckon," Jeff said. He sat unmoving, staring at the backs of his hands on the table. . . .

Henley Lewis, Vincente, the slaves and the hounds

returned around nine o'clock the next morning. Lewis was driving an open flatbed wagon. The first thing Jeff saw was the shackled black man in the wagon bed. Adam looked to be in his early or mid-twenties. He was almost as tall as Clitus, but he was thinner. He looked desolated, his eyes as harried as a hunted rabbit's. The very sight of the poor devil Adam, displayed so proudly, made Jeff ill. How easily—Jesus God, how easily—he could be in that wagon, shackled as Adam was shackled. Adam was a despised black man who caused trouble. And Jeff realized that was exactly what he was—a Willow Oaks buck on the run, no more, no less.

The big white man who returned with Henley Lewis and Vincente roused Jeff's instant and total hatred. He rode a fat-backed white horse, sitting upon the animal as if he owned the world and held mortgages on the universe. Jeff recognized him instantly as that most hated of all white men, the arrogant slave holder, the landed gentry.

Margarith came out of the manor house wearing a sun hat. The floppy brim concealed her face. She stood near Jeff. The landowner rode directly to them, swung down, and tossed the reins to a waiting slave boy without even glancing to see that the servant would be there. The white man expected him to be there. He did not look at Jeff, but laughed loudly and caught both of Margarith's hands in his. "How lovely you look this mawnin', Miss Margarith!" His voice boomed. "It's no wonder I love you so immoderately . . . no one ever saw a lovelier vision than you, Missy."

Jeff watched Margarith disengage her hands from the man's big paws. Another aggressive lover, he thought—everything that André Morceau was not. Margarith said, "Mr. Meador Coffee, I want you to meet our new farm manager, Mr. Jeff Carson of The Georgics—in northern Mississippi."

Meador Coffee almost looked at Jeff. He laughed and shook his hand, watching Margarith. "Know some plantation owners over Mississippi way, Mr. Carson. Do you know a plantation owner named Baxter Simon—breeds slaves on a plantation known as Willow Oaks?"

Jeff felt his heart lurch and sink, seeming to slip its moorings. "I've heard of him, sir."

"Grows a hell of a fancy slave, Bax does. See him often on trips down to New Orleans. . . . So you are going to run the major's farm, eh? Well, that's fine. I've been trying to get that job, haven't I, Margarith?"

Margarith bit her lip. "Have you, Mr. Coffee?"

"Now don't start that formal stuff with me. Mr. Coffee! My good lord. I tell you, Carson, I been tryin' to get Miss Margarith to marry me. Only reason I ain't downright insisted, I figured a gentle lady like her would need a year of mourning. . . . But then—after that—well, I can tell you, little lady, with us owning The Laurels and Tanglewood plantation, we'll have the world by the tail."

Jeff glanced at Margarith. She looked ill. Pallor had spread across her cheeks. Her violet eyes showed her distress. She stared at Jeff, shaking her head. He merely smiled. "I'm sure you'd be very happy—owning half the state," he said.

Meador Coffee's laughter boomed out. Jeff sighed, seeing that the match, miserable as it seemed in prospect, was not impossible. Coffee was in his early thirties, a landowner. Coffee said, "Lost my own wife, dear Annabelle, almost two years ago now. . . . She run away from me . . . damnedest thing I ever heard of. Good family she come from. They was as broken up and as puzzled as I was. . . . Well, that's all behind me now, and I look forward to happiness with my Miss Margarith. Eh, Missy?"

Margarith did not speak. She looked around as if trapped. Jeff walked away from them. He went to the wagon where Adam was shackled. He said, "You all right? You hurt?"

Adam stared at him, his black eyes deep in tears. He shook his head, but did not speak.

Jeff became aware that Margarith was standing close

at his elbow, and that he was joined at once by Meador who stood close behind her. "What you reckon to do about this nigger?" Meador said.

Jeff glanced at Margarith. She was too miserable, too confused to say anything. Jeff said, "Think he's had enough. We'll lock him up—"

"Lock him up!" The words burst as a protest across Henley Lewis's lips.

But Meador Coffee raged. "Lock him up. No, sir! I figure I got something to say about that!"

"Do you?" Jeff's voice was harsh. "You don't own The Laurels yet."

"But I own the next plantation down the road. What affects the niggers at The Laurels affects my niggers at Tanglewood."

"Still, I'll make the decisions about Laurels blacks," Jeff said.

"Now wait a minute! How about that, Miss Margarith?" Coffee said. "You going to let this stranger come in here an'—"

"Whatever Jeff says, Meador," Margarith said. "Whatever he says. That's what we'll do."

"You locked him up before," Henley Lewis raged. "I can't see that. I can't be taking off to run him down every time he lights out running. We got to stop him."

"That's right," Coffee said, nodding fiercely. "Lewis and me talked it over. After all, I'm the one found the nigger—over at Foxmoor Plantation."

"Same as last time," Henley Lewis said. "He run straight there like a stallion with the scent."

"On the way here, Lewis and I talked about what to do about this nigger runner. We decided he's got to be branded. I demand you brand him." Meador straightened.

"You—demand?" Jeff stared at him.

"That's right. I know what's right, and I know what's got to be done. And I demand that it be done. My slaves know what happens here at The Laurels. You don't brand this nigger, my niggers know it, and it makes 'em harder to handle. Well, I won't have that. This here

200

nigger boy run, and he's got to be branded—as an example. There just ain't no other way to it. You can't be soft with a nigger. You put a brand on him, he thinks before he runs again. Other niggers see you branding him, they get a lot quieter too."

Jeff felt the illness roiling in his stomach. He looked at Margarith, but she kept her head lowered. She would not look up at him. He heard Coffee's hated voice raking him. "You come in here, Carson, a stranger. You stay awhile. How long? Who knows? You move on. But we got to make our homes here. We got to be able to handle our niggers. We can't be soft. We can't spoil 'em. I told Miss Margarith last time this black run, she ought to've branded him then. But she was too softhearted. I can understand that. Her a gentle lady an' all. But, by God, you can't make our jobs tougher handlin' our niggers. I'm a lifetime friend of Major Morceau. I can tell you if he was here, he'd agree with me. Ain't that right, Ponchus? Ask Ponchus. He's a good nigger. He'll tell you."

Ponchus met Jeff's gaze. His eyes were almost as agonized as Jeff's. After a moment the cottony head bowed, nodding affirmatively. Jeff exhaled heavily. He shrugged, then nodded his own head toward Henley Lewis. The overseer smiled coldly and slapped the reins across the rumps of his team. The horses moved away, the rest of the sad procession followed. Meador Coffee glanced at Jeff, then strode away toward the smithy with the crowd. Jeff started to follow, but Margarith touched his arm.

"Never," she whispered. "I could never marry him."

"That's up to you," he said. Sickness roiled inside him. He could not shake from his mind that he had run like Adam and, like Adam, was branded. He hated the very idea, and yet he knew the men down there would expect him to brand the Negro. He was master of The Laurels. Branding was his privilege.

"You must believe me," Margarith insisted as if this

were the most urgent matter in her life. "That loud, brutal man."

"There are a lot of us around," Jeff said. "Real animals."

"Oh, Jeff, please!" Her eyes filled with helpless tears. She put out her hand toward him, then let it drop at her side.

He turned away, then hesitated, speaking across his shoulder. "Why did Adam run away—why always to the Foxmoor plantation?"

Margarith looked up at him, eyes wet. "That's where his—woman—is," she said. "Henley got furious at Adam, and so he sold off Adam's wife to Lissa Malraux over at the Foxmoor. He said Adam would forget her—his woman. But he won't stay away from her."

Bile gorged up in his throat. Christ in heaven, Jeff thought bitterly, and *I'm* to brand the poor devil because he loves his woman, because he can't stay away from her?

CHAPTER XX

When Jeff walked into the smithy, Adam was already secured to the wall. His arms were stretched as far as they could be pulled and were tied off with ropes about his wrists affixed to large spikes in the wall studs. His legs were likewise spread-eagled, ankles shackled and the shackles hooked to wall spikes. "Can't have a nigger kickin' when you put the brandin' iron to him," Henley

Lewis was saying as Jeff entered the open building.

Meador Coffee flicked a glance across his thick shoulder as Jeff walked in. "You missed all the fun, Carson. Had a real scrap gittin' the bastard tied to the wall. Son of a bitch. Cryin' and carryin' on. Took three of us men and two bucks to get him out'n that wagon and tied up. But he's fixed fancy an' waitin' for your iron now."

Ponchus walked slowly into the smithy and stood beside Jeff. He said, "We rang de bell, sent de word. All de slaves be here soon, Masta Coffee."

Meador Coffee nodded and smiled at Ponchus. "You're a good nigger, boy. Too bad they ain't more niggers like you. Polite and all. For ever' good nigger, you got 1,000 bad'uns. But yore sure a good nigger, Ponchus. Always told the major I'd like to have you workin' for me."

"Thank-ee, masta."

Meador laughed. "Reckon we both know the major'd never part with you!"

Ponchus forced another smile. "Naw, suh, masta. De major a real fine gen'mun."

Meador put his head back laughing and clapped Ponchus on the shoulder. Jeff saw the cotton-haired servant recoil inside from the touch. "Lots of us real fine gen'muns—when you gits to know us. . . . Wish you'd speak a good word to Miz Margarith in my behalf . . . git her to agree to marry up with me—you can come over to Tanglewood with me. Happy to have you running things over there. You speak to your mistress about me, you hear?"

"Yas, suh, masta, I sho' do that." Ponchus bobbed his head.

Meador looked around. The slaves were gathering at the open ends of the smithy. Their faces sagged when they saw black Adam strung to the wall and spread-eagled. "Soon's all them slaves git here, Carson, we gits on with the fun," Meador Coffee said. His gaze raked across Adam. "Reckon you jes' can't hardly wait, huh? You damn black runner. We goin' teach you to run. Goddamn runnin' nigger! Ain't nothin' worse'n airy running nigger. Yore new masta's gone brand you. Right on your forehead. A nice *R* branded there for all folks to see. You ain't goin' ever wash that brand off, nigger. Never be able to sell you. Nobody wants a nigger that's so bad he's got a *R* branded right in his forehead. But by God you won't go runnin' off to Foxmoor ever' time you git the hots."

Adam sagged against the wall. He was crying, tears spilling along his rigid cheeks, his nose running, his full lips quivering. He was shaking and would have fallen to the ground had he not been secured with ropes and shackles to the wall. He shook his head, but he did not speak.

By this time the work crew had come across the grounds and crowded just outside the smithy. They talked and whispered among themselves, staring at Adam. Meador Coffee let the slaves get a good long look at the man sagging against his ropes, crying. Then he heeled around. "Looks like all the black folks is here to witness this here branding. That branding iron hot yet, boy?"

The black smithy, a big man gone to fat, was older than Ponchus. His hair was a sooty gray. He wore only a leather apron and butternut pants rolled up to his calves. His creamy chocolate skin glowed with sweated reflections of the glowing white coals. He nodded. "Be ready any minute now, Masta Meador."

Meador turned to face the crowd of blacks. "You heah that, you folks? Now all you folks know they wasn't never a fairer, kinder white man on this earth than old Major Morceau. Am I right, folks?"

The blacks nodded, mumbling, shuffling their feet. They did not look at Coffee, though obviously all of them knew him and had known him for most of their lives.

"Me, I'm a lot younger than your dead master. But I count myself as one of his closest friends, an' I pride myself that I pattern myself, and the way I handle my darkies, after the way Major Morceau dealt with you folks. Fair, but firm. He never liked to brand a black man. Ruin him for selling. But sometime the major was forced to brand a black boy—for running. Sometime they ain't no other way you can show a black runner you mean business but to touch him up with a brandin' iron. . . . It don't give nobody no pleasure. But it got to be done. A black boy breaks the rules, he jus' naturally got to be punished."

Meador Coffee stood silently, glaring out at the cowed herd of blacks at the rim of the smithy overhang. Jeff saw that Coffee considered these slaves as already part of his property, and he was letting them know how things would be under his domain. He said, "Now we cotched this bastard where he had run. I happens to be over to Foxmoor plantation visiting with Miz Malraux, the fine lady what runs Foxmoor, got word from one of her house servants that they was a strange nigger a-hidin' in the quarters. Well, I went down and got him." He jerked his head. "Twas this here boy. Second time he's run from here in jus' a few weeks. Now you folks can see how it is. We cain't have that. A goddamn runner. You folks is got to work if you goin' to eat and be clothed and tooken care of, the way we do for you. A runner. Upsettin' everybody. Not doing his work—cain't nobody else work when they out runnin' him down with the dogs. Ain't none of us wants to brand this boy, but it got to be done. I jus' want you all to purely see why—and why it might happen to you, you don't act way you should an' all and do what you tole."

Meador heeled around then, staring coldly at the spread-eagled black Adam. "You understand why we goin' brand you, boy? You understand it got to be done? Answer me, goddamn it."

Adam nodded his head, crying harder.

"Noddin' youah head won't do it, boy! Answer me! You answer me when I speak to you, boy, or I'll whip some manners into you soon's you branded. Now answer me! You understand we doin' this because we has to—to teach you a lesson you purely got to learn?"

His body wracked with sobs, Adam nodded his head

and managed to whisper, "Yas, suh."

The smithy said, "This yere iron's spittin' hot, masta."

Meador Coffee nodded, smiling. He bowed his head slightly toward Jeff. "There you are, Mr. Carson. You're the present master of The Laurels. You put the brand to him."

Biting back the bile that gorged up in his throat, Jeff went to the huge fieldstone furnace. He stared at the white-hot branding iron, with its inch-high *R* glowing fiercely. Why in hell was he letting this arrogant farmer push him into an act that was heinous and repulsive to him? But he knew it was not Meador Coffee doing it, it was his own insides, his desire to live as a white man. You behaved like a white man twenty-four hours a day, you accepted his privileges, you assumed his methods.

He clenched his fist to keep his hand from shaking. He felt all eyes—of white and black—fixed on him. He realized that neither Henley nor Meador Coffee suspected the anguish roiling around inside him. It was a white man's privilege to brand his slaves, his divine right.

"Goin' to teach the bastid runner, huh, Mr. Carson?" Henley Lewis said.

Jeff managed to nod. He was afraid he was going to be sick. The branding iron weals, long healed, burned savagely, and he felt as if he would vomit at the memory of burning, seared flesh. What would happen when he did touch this white-hot iron to black Adam's forehead, and he smelled that cooking meat as he had that night in Baxter Simon's barn when it had been his own skin searing?

Suddenly Vincente said, "Wait a minute, Mr. Jeff! You promised me! Last time we had a brandin', you promised next time I could brand the black. You know you promised me."

Jeff felt a flood of relief rush through him. It was as if a blast of cold, fresh air blew through the hot smithy and cooled his face. He managed to smile paternally and nod his head in assent. "All right, boy. This time. Go ahead."

He stepped back, retreating until he could press against the roughness of a peeled-log upright. He swallowed back the bile, chewed hard on his teeth. Thank God for Vincente. The boy had been a godsend in Havana when he helped make his first assignment for Lafitte a success. Vincente had saved his life on that bayou trail. He was already deeply in his debt. Now, Vincente had likely kept Meador Coffee and Henley Lewis from seeing his weakness, seeing him throw up when he tried to brand black Adam.

He pressed against the upright, his eyes glazed over, not looking at anything. He smelled seared flesh, heard the intake of breath among the slaves, the snort of approval from Meador Coffee. He knew it was over. He turned and stalked out of the smithy. He pushed his way through the crowd of silent blacks and walked toward the house.

He crossed the veranda, went through the dining room, and hurried along the corridor, sick at his stomach. He closed his bedroom door behind him. He just managed to pull the earthenware slop jar from beneath his bed. He thanked God the servants had cleaned it, put in fresh water. He heaved, the vomitus gushing up his throat, spewing into the chamber.

He got shakily up from his knees then. He went across to the dresser, rinsed his mouth and washed his face in the earthenware basin. When his nerves had quieted, he rang for a servant, told her to take the chamber pot out and clean it up.

He stood a moment at the window watching the crowd disperse. He saw Meador Coffee walking toward the manor house ahead of a small black boy leading the fat-rumped white horse. Meador would stop at the house, but he didn't give a damn what he did as long as he didn't have to see him. He didn't want to see anybody.

He pushed up all the windows in his room and lay down across his freshly made bed. He tried to laugh. It sure as hell wasn't easy being a white man. But he could not laugh. He could not stop Adam's screaming, which went on and on and on inside his head. After a long time, he fell asleep.

He did not know how long he'd slept when he heard a knock at his door. He opened his eyes, lay there listening. He didn't want to see anyone.

"Jeff?" It was Margarith's voice.

"Yes?"

"Are you all right?"

"I'm just resting. I'll be back to work soon."

"Oh, Jeff. You know I don't care about that. I want to talk to you." She waited. When he did not speak, she said in a sad, breathless little voice, "Please, Jeff, may I come in?"

"The door's unlocked," he said.

She entered the room and closed the door behind her. She studied him, troubled, her own cheeks showing the pallor of inner illness. "I know how you must hate what you had to do."

"Didn't your fiancé tell you? Vincente branded Adam."

"Fiancé? Oh, Jeff, how can you accuse me of anything like that?"

"He considers himself at least your fiancé . . . don't know what you have to say about it. . . . He's a strong-willed man. . . . He forced me to take part in something I hated—with all my heart."

"I know." She came to the bed. "What are we going to do?"

Jeff scowled. "About what?"

She bit her lip. "I'm sorry. It's so strong in my thoughts, I just imagined you were following the train of my thinking—about Adam? What can we do about him? Will he stay here—now that he's branded?"

"I don't know. Poor bastard. He's doing what God put in him to do—going to his woman with a hard-on—and we brand him for it."

"Next time, Mr. Lewis and Mr. Coffee may whip him—or geld him."

"They might. Unless we stop them."

"How are we going to do that?"

"I can tell you what I'd do, and I'd do it without thinking twice about it. Adam may be a fine boy. But a buck without a wench can be a dangerous animal. He'll sneak off looking for his woman, because that's his instinct. He might even hurt somebody, trying to get what he needs. . . . But gelding won't make him a good nigger, it will only make him a ruined nigger."

"I don't want them to do that. I don't want them to hurt him anymore. If the poor boy wasn't bad before, they're making him bad—they're making him dangerous. But they can't see that." She touched his arm, beseechingly. "Please. Tell me what to do."

"I'd get rid of him."

"But Meador said nobody would buy a runner. And if they did, they'd only mistreat poor Adam—as Meador and Mr. Lewis are mistreating him now. How would that help?"

"It would help if you sold him to Foxmoor—where his woman is. Or if you gave him to Foxmoor."

She stared at Jeff in awe and then burst into laughter. "How good you must be inside," she said.

"No. I'm just an animal, like Adam. I know what would quiet me."

"It's what you would have done—if they hadn't pressured you into branding him, isn't it? If I had stood behind you, supported you."

"Don't blame yourself. I didn't have to let them brand him."

"But you did! There would have been nothing but trouble with Mr. Lewis and with Meador Coffee if you hadn't."

"Well, I'm sick of talking about them. Giving Adam to Foxmoor might lose you some money, but it'll solve Adam's problem."

She caught his hands in hers. "I'm going to do it." She pulled him nearer, slipped her hands on both sides of his head and kissed him. "Oh, my wonderful love," she said. "There—is that bold enough for you?"

"You're going to get in trouble doing things like that.

We're not all *gentle*men like the late André."

"Don't you understand? I want to get in trouble—with you. Oh, I do, Jeff . . . I do. I tried to fight against loving you, wanting you. But I have wanted you—from the first moment I saw you. . . . I knew then what I'd been waiting for all my life. . . . You rode in here, laughing and kind and wonderful—and all the emptiness and bitterness just went out of my life . . . but I was afraid of you. . . . I tried not to want you . . . I couldn't help it. I'm saying it, Jeff . . . I've come to you. . . . I'm saying it . . . I want you, Jeff . . . as I never wanted anybody else."

He tried to smile. "In the middle of the afternoon?"

"I don't care. I can lock the door . . . I do want you. Now. Don't laugh at me."

"I'm not laughing. But I better warn you . . . it may not be me you want. Somebody told me once in New Orleans that the gladiator killings stirred up sex desires something wild in ancient Rome. . . . The whorehouses were overrun after lions spilled Christian blood in the Colosseum."

She laughed at him. "Oh, Jeff, you know that has nothing to do with it! Do you think branding that poor black boy excited me? You excited me. The first time you spoke to me—I went all hot and wet—down there. Just the sound of your voice could do that to me! I did try to fight my desire for you . . . I admit that. It overwhelmed me. It scared me . . . but it's you I want . . . only you . . . please, don't make me wait anymore."

He laughed, reaching for her. He pulled her in close between his legs, looking up at her. "Even if you're lying," he said, "I don't care. . . . I'm only human . . . looking at you, I'm human as hell. . . . Just let me lock the door."

She kissed him. "I locked it. I hoped you wouldn't notice. I felt so bold—like some common hussy—but I locked it."

He put his head back, laughing. She pulled at her dress, breaking the small rows of buttons down her spine.

The black dress slipped over her soft smooth shoulders, down over her body. She worked it across her hips, let it fall to the floor, and stepped out of it. As she worked frantically with her underthings, Jeff stared at her. Now he was seeing Margarith as she might have been if she'd never met André Morceau—her eyes bright, her lips pulled in laughter. Margarith Morceau worked the last of her undergarments loose and threw it from her. She stood before him, naked and beautiful. God, how beautiful she was!

He drew her down to the bed beside him. He kissed her gently, forcing her lips apart with his tongue. He pressed his tongue between her teeth and she opened her mouth to him. Clearly, she had never been kissed like this. Lord, he thought, have you got a lot of wonderful things to learn!

His hands caressed her breasts. Her small, pink nipples tightened, round and hard under his touch. . . . When he suckled them, she moaned, writhing on the bed. His hand slid across the smooth heap of her stomach, into the dainty hairs of her mons veneris. She was panting for breath, and when he touched her, her hips writhed and she flared into a savage orgasm under his fingers. She was truly starved.

She lay quietly then and let him learn her body, fondle and caress her, arousing her again. She whispered, "Undress. Please. I want to look at you."

He removed his clothing, with her trembling fingers aiding him. She wanted to pull off his undershirt, but he caught her hands. She persisted, but he knew her too well already. His hands on her breasts, probing at her labia, and she forgot his undershirt.

Margarith tried to enter into the carnal spirit of Jeff's lovemaking. But she was either terribly innocent, or else wholly ignorant of the ecstasy possible in vaginal catering and gratification of physical desires. But he was not disappointed. In fact, he found her charming if not proficient. She was fresh and new, almost untouched—and certainly unprobed as he would probe her—and she wanted to please him. He discovered added pleasure in leading her into the niceties of sexual foreplay. This was all new to her, but it was also a completely new experience for a bogus white man who in a few short years had graduated from the streetwalkers of Pittsburgh and Louisville, and the bed wenches of Mississippi, to those self-professed Southern virgins and beyond to the luminous red-velour parlors of New Orleans.

There was no question of her fevered desire and none of it was feigned. As he loved her, her hands stole down along his body and closed on his erect penis. He heard her sharp intake of breath. He drew her closer under him, pushed her legs wide apart and raised her knees. He came down upon her, found her violet eyes wide, her mouth parted. She was holding her breath. He eased himself into her vagina and she gasped aloud.

He thrust deep. She cried out and then lay still—almost rigid—as she must have with her husband. She was suddenly inhibited, and though he drove himself to her, she did not rise toward a climax. He stared down at her, puzzled and frustrated. Breathless, she admitted she'd trained herself never to permit herself an orgasm with André—she'd been afraid he might have been shocked and horrified if she had. He might have thought her common, a slut.

"Oh, no," he said. "You won't do that to me . . . you're going to love it—you're going to love me." He whispered in her ears, kept whispering as he loved her until almost involuntarily she writhed her hips and pumped frantically against him. His own savage need for her, combined with her divested repressed desires, brought them upward to a shattering climax. He hung to awareness enough to see that she fully shared the frantic ecstasy of complete fulfillment.

He sagged upon her, remaining inside her heated body. He felt the muscles of her vagina constrict, loosen, and then tighten again on him. His response to Margarith was totally unique. He'd had many women, but none ever lifted him to such pleasure. God knew nothing was more perfect than the ideal coupling of a man and woman—it was the greatest pleasure vouchsafed to human beings on this earth. Making love with Margarith was that perfect pleasure—what God must have had in mind in the beginning.

Her tightening muscles were driving him insane. He forgot to be tired, forgot exhaustion, forgot everything except the heat and excitement of her body.

He wanted to rage aloud with laughter. He felt stronger than any god. He felt truly free and whole for the first time in his life. So this was what the running and the struggling was all about—to find a love like this, finally to learn what it was really meant to be.

He moved faster, driving himself deeply into her again. He heard her cry out, but it was as if from a great distance and through the thunder pealing inside his own temples. He didn't know what she was saying.

He lay panting, staring down at her while the blood quieted in his temples, the pounding ceased in his ears.

"My God," Margarith was whispering—only her whisper was an anguished wail.

"What's wrong, Margarith? What's the matter?"

She laughed and cried at the same time, clinging to him. "My God, my God. I've never—done it—before. All those years married—and I've never really been . . . fucked . . . before. . . ."

CHAPTER XXI

Jeff would have willingly spent the whole next day in bed, but the bustle of plantation activity which began in the false dawn awakened him and convinced him that he could not in good conscience sleep through, as devoutly as he might wish it. He had renewed activity here at The Laurels, and it was his responsibility to keep that momentum rolling forward, no matter how whipped he'd been left by an afternoon and night with Margarith. She'd agreed to leave his bed for supper only when he convinced her they had to consider appearances. She insisted she was sleepy at seven-thirty that night and by eight o'clock she was in his bed. She left him at five, and protesting, only because she agreed Ponchus might be distressed to find her in Jeff's bedroom. She clung to him, kissing him. Now that she'd learned what making love was truly all about, she was going to spend the rest of her life making love—to him.

She'd bit her lip, blushing. He couldn't see her blush in the dark, but he felt the fevered flush of blood into her soft face against his chest. "I know you think me *brazen*. But I never talked like this with anyone else. Even if I'd wanted to, I'd have never dared. Oh, Jeff, I'm not a flirt, or empty, or a hussy, but I do love you! I do. Or maybe I am forward to tell you—to show you like this—but I don't care. It's true. I do love you. I've never loved anyone else. I'll never love anyone else and I do love you . . . and if that's brazen, then I'm brazen.

"Oh, I won't change," she had said. "You might, but I won't."

He had kissed her fragrant hair—and yawned helplessly in the middle of his kiss. She'd cried out—he was already tired of her. "My God, girl," he said. "You've got to let me rest a little—fifteen minutes maybe? Are you trying to kill me?"

When she was gone, protesting, he'd fallen into a stunned sleep. There were no memories, no fears, no nightmares, no dreams. But the cooks busy in the kitchen, the field crew shuffling past toward the fields, the dairy workers, the animal and grain tenders at their labors wakened him. All of them were contributing to the welfare of the big farm; it was a total effort; he had accepted the responsibility of making it pay. Maybe no one could, but he had to try. Yawning, his legs as shaky as a new calf's, he got up, bathed, shaved, and dressed.

He joined Vincente at the breakfast table. Vincente looked swollen eyed and tired too. His self-satisfied smile made Jeff want to laugh. Vincente had discovered the wonders of heated black flesh.

Ponchus entered from the kitchen with hot food. He smiled broadly. "Mornin', young Masta Jeff," he said. "I trusts you slept especial well?"

Jeff's head jerked up. But there was no knowing look, no teasing light in the old man's black eyes. Jeff sighed and smiled at Ponchus. If the old man knew Margarith had spent the afternoon and last night in his bed, he evidently approved. This astonished Jeff because he'd been certain Ponchus would resent any man's touching anything that had once been one of Major Morceau's possessions—and that's what the teenage wife had assuredly been.

" 'Scuse me, suh," Ponchus said, filling Jeff's cup with hot coffee. "Miz Margarith tole me what you think she ought to do about Adam."

"What are you going to do to that poor bastard?" Vincente wanted to know. "Wasn't branding him enough?

215

Good God, I threw up afterward. I never want to have anything to do with that again."

"Thanks, Vincente," Jeff said. "I appreciate all you did—for me."

"If I'd known then what I know now," Vincente said, "nobody could have forced me to brand that poor devil's face. The smell of seared flesh, his scream. Good God! What else are you going to do to the poor bastard?"

"Young masta has a wonderful plan," Ponchus said. "Missy said if we had listened to him, we need never have branded Adam. They gone give Adam to Miz Malraux over to Foxmoor plantation where Adam's woman is stayin'."

Vincente grinned. He nodded enthusiastically, but before he could speak, Margarith entered the dining room door. Jeff and Vincente stood, but neither was able to speak at once. Ponchus set the silver coffee pitcher down carefully, his ebon eyes wide. "Missy," Ponchus whispered. "My, my, Missy."

"Do you like it, Ponchus?" Margarith said. She spoke to the butler, but her eyes were fixed on Jeff's face anxiously. She twirled slowly for them to inspect the bright cotton print dress she wore—colorfast prints were the newest things from the mills of England and Massachusetts.

"You look powerful pretty, Missy," Ponchus said. His eyes brimmed with warm tears, and he nodded smiling. "Never saw a flower what looked fresher—or prettier."

"You don't mind—that I've ended my mourning?" she said.

"Couldn't nobody mind a lovely lady like you lookin' so lovely, Missy," Ponchus said. "The major hisself would be happy seein' you look so pretty and young."

"I didn't know you *were* so young!" Vincente came around the table, inspecting her. "You're young enough for me!"

Margarith laughed and kissed him. "I've got dresses older than you, boy. I'm a big girl—ask Jeff."

"She's a big girl," Jeff whispered. He had not taken

his eyes from her. He had never seen anyone who looked so lovely—except Margarith herself standing naked for him in yesterday's afternoon sunlight. God, how he loved her! He wanted to take her in his arms, kiss her, caress her, and try to make her know how deeply he loved her. But he did not move. He went on standing where he was.

Vincente held her chair for her at the head of the table. Margarith sat down, still smiling. Almost immediately, Jeff felt the hard pressure of her knee against his under the gleaming white linen tablecloth. He grinned, and she gazed at him innocently. No matter how much she protested, she was a little devil, a born hussy, a flirt. It was as if she'd been in a cocoon, and his loving had released her—a bright butterfly.

Margarith said, "Right after breakfast, Jeff, I want you to talk to Ponchus. Tell him all the work you planned to do today. Ponchus can handle it all for you. Can't you, Ponchus?"

"I do what you wish, Missy. Anything you wish," Ponchus said. There was no servile toadying in his tone, but a genuine love that didn't recognize race or condition of servitude.

Margarith laughed. "Thank you, Ponchus . . . I want you to take over the plantation today for Jeff—just as you used to do for the major. Jeff and I are going to take the chariotee and drive over to Foxmoor." She laughed, looking at Jeff. "I want to show you off—my new farm manager—" she made something sensual and intimate of the words, "to my oldest and dearest friend in the world, Lissa Malraux. She'll be pea green with envy." She laughed in anticipation. "Anyhow, I'll make it all up to her. I'll give Adam to her—as a present. She'll love to get him. He's only twenty-one plantings old, according to the major's records, and he's one of the best workers we've got. . . . I'm sorry about that terrible brand on his face, but that won't affect the way he works, will it?"

"Or the way he makes love," Jeff told her. Even the militarily correct Ponchus smiled with them. . . .

The stable boys brought the chariotee around to the

217

front entrance of the manor house. The light, fringe-covered, four-wheeled, two-seater pleasure carriage had been a wedding gift to Margarith from the major when she came to The Laurels.

Adam was brought from the barn where he'd spent the night in shackles. Ponchus had tended the seared flesh of Adam's face. It was bandaged with fresh cloths and covered with a soothing salve, which had been renewed all night on Ponchus's orders. Adam walked slumped-shouldered. Ponchus had told him he was being taken to Foxmoor to live, but Adam had been lied to before, by experts. The fact that Ponchus was also black didn't encourage Adam much, or lift him from his deep fit of depression.

Because Adam obviously didn't believe he was being transported to Foxmoor, Ponchus had his ankles spanceled, his arms shackled to the rear seat-rest of the chariotee. While this was being done, Henley Lewis rode in, his face contorted, his pale eyes glittering. "Why, Missy, we can't afford to *give* away our bes' working niggers."

"He's not working well right now, Mr. Lewis," Margarith said.

"That's because you didn't let me handle him, or give me time to straighten him out. We let this buck and that wench git too attached. I've always declared that was a prime mistake—lettin' bucks and wenches act like married humans. What we got to remember is that niggers is animals, Miz Morceau, and when you treats 'em like humans that's when you begin to have trouble with 'em. You treat a nigger right—like you'd treat any good animal—and you got good workers. And that's what they's for. The Bible itself tells us that the sons of Ham was born to labor. It's when we forgits what we should learn from the good book that we starts havin' trouble with blacks."

"I've made up my mind," Margarith said. "I didn't want to sell Carrie to Mrs. Malraux. I let you overrule me. But Adam is my gift to Lissa Malraux."

Henley Lewis remained seated rigid and angered in

his saddle as the chariotee pulled out of the drive into the lane with Jeff handling the lines. Margarith sat sedately beside him until they reached the trace. Then she thrust her bottom over, hard against his hip, and sighed expansively. "It's ten miles to Foxmoor," she said. "It may take us hours to get there."

She chattered happily as Jeff let the animals canter along the hard-packed road.

"Did you ever see a more beautiful day?" She turned and smiled at Adam across her shoulder. "Won't Carrie be surprised? Won't she be happy to see you?"

"Yes'm." Adam tried to smile through the faint mist of tears clouding his black eyes.

"Don't cry, Adam. You're going to be happy at Foxmoor. You'll be with Carrie again. Mrs. Malraux is very nice, very fair, or I'd never have let either you or Carrie go over there. . . . And you'll be with Carrie again—all your life."

"Yes'm."

Margarith turned back, her own eyes clouded with tears. She covered Jeff's hand with hers. "Poor Adam. He doesn't believe in anything anymore."

"There's a lot of that going around," Jeff said.

"How can you say that?" Margarith lifted his hand, held the back of it against her mouth. "I know I do. After yesterday. Last night. I believe in Christmas. In Easter. In the Father and the Son and the Holy Ghost . . . that used to scare me when I had to say in church that I believed in the Holy Ghost . . . but I don't mind him at all now since I've got you."

"You've got me," he agreed.

"I know." She nodded in happy satisfaction. "Isn't that wonderful? . . . But I don't want any other woman ever even to touch you. Won't you get awfully tired of that?"

"Probably."

"I won't let you get tired. I'll learn all sorts of new things to keep you interested."

"Oh, you will, huh? From whom?"

"From you, of course. I'll learn everything from you

because you're the Father and the Son and the Holy Ghost I believe in." She breathed in deeply, glancing around at the green, sun-splashed rural world. "Oh, won't Lissa just die with jealousy when she sees you? She'll be pea green with envy. . . . Lissa thinks she's the belle of the whole parish . . . it's common gossip that husbands of some of her *best* friends sneak in to visit her at night—and did, even before her husband died. In fact, it's rumor that Lissa caused poor Roget's death!"

"Loved him to death, did she?"

"Wait till you see her. Really, I shouldn't take you over there. You'll forget all about me. . . . But they do say she kept poor Roget all upset—nights, the things she did to him, things they said she learned in *Paris*—so he couldn't sleep. And then he was *jealous* all the time. It was enough to kill anyone."

He drew her soft hand up to his lips and kissed its cupped palm. She closed her fist on his kiss. "I feel like a very young girl," she said. "Wonder if Adam would mind if we stopped—just for a little while?"

He laughed at her. "Would you do that to poor Adam? The way he's already suffering."

"I'd do that to anybody," she said amiably. "I want you terribly, and I don't *care* who knows it. . . . My life seemed so long and empty and useless until you came along." She gazed at him, her eyes glowing. "I didn't even *live* until you came along, laughing and those eyes teasing me. Lissa always talked to me as if my life was *over* since André's death—and I'd come to accept that."

He smiled. "We'll make up for all that," he promised.

She slipped her arm through his and pressed his bicep fiercely against the soft downy fullness of her breast. "But I've so much to make up for. Just think I let that ninny Lissa Malraux—"

"Your best friend—"

"My very best friend—I let that stupid thing convince me my life was over and in the grave with André. Almost like those women in India who fling themselves on their husband's funeral pyres because their lives are ended. I just can't wait to show that Lissa Malraux that my life has just *begun* . . . that André is dead, but I'm not . . . I'm alive. I'm nineteen years old, and I'm alive, and I mean to live and to find happiness despite the disapproval of all those stupid neighbors who might think I should suffocate and quietly dissolve in my widow's weeds."

Jeff laughed and drew her into the circle of his arm. She kissed his throat, licking at it with the tip of her tongue. "You haven't even *started* to live," he told her.

"Oh, yes, I have." She sighed. "I wish now I'd let Lissa Malraux tell me some of those things she learned in Paris. But I was too *prim*. I was shocked. I didn't want to listen. No wonder Lissa was sure my life was over. And how angry and shocked I was when male neighbors —husbands and sons of those prim women who'll be shocked to see me out of mourning—wanted to *sneak* in to visit me at night at The Laurels. I know Lissa let them sneak in to her at Foxmoor. But I never wanted them—and I hated them for thinking I might want them."

"No wonder I frightened you the first time I wanted to make love to you."

Margarith giggled. "Oh, no. You know why I was afraid—because I knew I'd go absolutely wild if I let you touch me, and I *knew* you'd think I was a little slut. . . . From the first moment I saw you, Jeff, I wanted more. I was thinking about marriage—about marrying *you*—about being really married for the first time."

"Marry?" The word had an unaccustomed sound, an odd taste on Jeff's lips. Marriage was the least thing on Jeff's mind, likely the last thing he wanted. And there was always the danger. How long could one keep his *wife* from learning about those branding-iron weals scarring his back? Would Margarith be so ardently declaring her love for him if she knew that he was a branded buck —just like the boy in the rear of the chariotee that she was delivering to Foxmoor plantation as a gift to her best friend in the world?

Margarith shivered as if chilled. "What's the matter?

Am I too forward? Haven't you thought about marrying me—at all?"

"I thought about it," he said, voice low. "But I never thought it would be possible—in this world."

"Well it is! I don't care who you are, or what you are, or where you came from. I love you, and only you, and if I can't have you, I'll have nobody. . . . Oh, damn it! I wish we hadn't come on this silly trip. I wish we were home in bed right now—then I'd make you *know* you want to marry me as much as I want to marry you—*almost* anyhow—and that would be good enough for me. . . ."

CHAPTER XXII

A day without guests was rare indeed at Foxmoor plantation. In fact, Margarith told Jeff as they approached the fashionable showplace overlooking the wide arm of a river, Lissa often admitted she ran a high-class inn for the itinerant young plantation idle—belles and dandies who, with nothing to do to occupy themselves and running from boredom, drifted aimlessly across the face of the well-to-do South. There was always a party in progress, in the planning stages, or just winding down at Foxmoor. Lissa was never bored. There were always new faces, new loves, new gossip, new intrigues. Lissa was frightened by only one prospect—an empty house in which she rattled around unattended, except for black servants who existed for her in the same way the furnishings did. She dreaded loneliness. Most of all she dreaded being left alone with her own thoughts.

When Jeff, Margarith, and black Adam arrived at Lissa's home, there were uncounted numbers of people there, the bright young belles gathering light and male attention on the shadowed front gallery, crinolines like tiny colorful islands between the tall columns. When Jeff pulled the polished little chariotee into the drive, they all stopped whatever they were doing—hoping to escape the ennui which most of them had packed along with them like fresh linen—to greet someone new. They crowded around Margarith, kissing, petting, and chattering over her. Most of the guests had already inspected Jeff before he was introduced—the girls excited by his slender hips and prominent crotch, his long legs, auburn hair, and go-to-hell smile; the young men hating him on sight for all the same reasons.

Margarith clung to him, staking her claim clearly for all female eyes to note and take warning. Only Lissa Malraux gazed boldly into his face, surveyed his lean body and heavy crotch, and tipped her red tongue across her full lips in anticipation. Margarith had not exaggerated: Lissa was lovely; she stood out among the other young women like a bright rose among black-eyed susans. She was full lipped, full breasted, full in the hips, but she carried it all with grace and an inner knowledge that she was not only lovely, she knew how to help you enjoy every atom of that loveliness.

Margarith made her presentation of Adam, and Lissa understood at once why Adam was being given to her—he'd only run away to Foxmoor anyhow. She laughed and kissed Margarith. She said Carrie was working in the house and sent a servant running to fetch her. Jeff unlocked the shackles and loosened the spancels. Adam got down from the chariotee, tall and lean, massaging his wrists and stretching. They heard Carrie cry out. "Oh, Gawd! Oh, my Gawd! It's you, Adam."

Adam forgot his agony, the branding, the depression in

which he'd passed the long night. His mouth stretched wide with a smile. He held out his arms and Carrie hurled herself into them. Jeff was slightly astonished at the fact that Carrie was small—little over five feet tall, and heavy hipped, large breasted, and of a deep chocolate color. But Adam was transported; he could not have been happier than he was swinging Carrie up in his arms.

The young belles and dandies stood by watching Carrie sobbing and Adam laughing and crying, lifting her off her feet to kiss her, as if they were observing the antics of lively monkeys in a zoo.

"Look at that!"

"Isn't that simply charming?"

"Why, they act almost human, don't they?"

One young man said with a supercilious smile, "They're more than human when they get together—a buck and a wench . . . only thing like it is a stallion and a mare . . . or maybe Lissa Malraux—and lord knows who!"

They went into wild peals of laughter. For the first time Jeff became aware of Meador Coffee in the party. He was older than most of the other guests, but he was as fashionably dressed, and obviously had been drinking heavily most of the day. He moved in close to Margarith and took her arm possessively. "Still think you're making a mistake. You can't be sentimental in handling these blacks. You think you own them, but they own you when they can push you into doing stupid things like this. Giving up a good worker just to make him happy, for hell's sake —just like he was human."

There was a punch that was only lightly spiked; there was corn whisky in a rear library; there was opium imported through New Orleans for those who wanted to smoke it. But Lissa told Jeff, "I wouldn't touch it! I want to know what I'm doing. . . . I enjoy it more that way."

Jeff saw Margarith only infrequently the rest of the afternoon. He was plied with drinks and was soon wandering around in that same roseate glow in which most of these young people spent all their waking hours.

They drank and drifted about the large house and the

cool grounds most of the afternoon. When Jeff infrequently encountered Margarith, she looked at him beseechingly, but always with Meador Coffee's huge hand clamped upon her arm. She even tried to sit with Jeff at dinner, but Meador inserted himself between them, and anyhow, Lissa told him she'd saved the place for him at her right. Talk was loud and empty, most of it concerning the peccadilloes or perversions of people he didn't know, or ever want to meet.

It was a prolonged meal; each course served by Lissa Malraux's starched and servile maids was more special than the last and had to be "at least tasted" by everyone. When it finally ended, Margarith broke the death grip Meador Coffee had on her arm and caught Jeff for a moment alone as one of the guests began playing his violin in the parlor. "Come to my room," she whispered, "as soon as you can. I've got to see you—alone."

"With this house full of company? Aren't you afraid they'll talk?"

"Oh, damn them," she whispered. "If we don't give them something to talk about, they'll make it up. And anyway, I don't care about them. None of them is very smart, and no decent person would believe anything they said anyway. . . . And anyway, I don't care."

It was well after midnight before the mansion was reasonably quiet, with only sparse traffic in the wide corridors. Those who were abroad were more intent upon being discreet than inquisitive. Jeff went along the darkened third floor hall to the room that Margarith had let him know, through Carrie, was to be hers for the night.

He opened her door as stealthily as he could and only far enough to allow himself to sidle through into the faint illumination of the candlelit bedroom. Margarith lay awaiting him, naked on the bed. She put out her arms to him, the motion setting her breasts to quivering in a way Jeff found irresistible. He went to her erect and ready as he lay down beside her.

She kissed him frantically as if he'd been long away

225

at war and she'd never truly expected to see him alive again. "Oh, God," she whispered. "What a long evil day. I'll never do this again, as long as I live."

His hands closed on the down-soft globes of her breasts. "It's all right," he whispered, "we're together now."

"Thank God . . . I've been talking to Lissa—about some of the things she learned in Paris. I can't believe some of them . . . do you want me to show you?"

He laughed. "Maybe we better wait until we get back to The Laurels. No use waking up the whole house."

She kissed him. "Have I told you recently how much I love you—how wonderful you are?"

She parted her mouth for his kiss. As he pushed his tongue into her sweet-tasting mouth, she moved over closer on the bed, pressing herself beneath his body. Without moving their locked mouths, he lifted himself and pulled her up under him, pressing her legs as wide apart as he could. She moved up to meet him, whispering unintelligible words. She reached down, caught his cock and guided it into her, gasping as he penetrated her. Suddenly her hips were whipping against him fiercely.

Possessing Margarith was all new and fascinating again, as if he'd never had her. The smoothness of her skin against his hands sent charges through him. He could hold back no longer. He drove himself to her, wild with passionate need. She locked her ankles at his waist and thrust her hips upward to receive him. He thought in a fleeting flare of recognition that his long time of running was finally over—he had reached Eden.

He forced himself to bite back the spasms that wracked him. Already he knew that Margarith would respond as long as he drove himself into her. He brought her up to orgasmic eruption over and over, and only when she was weakly protesting did he lose control, letting himself go and pouring a broadside into her. When he fell away from her, she whimpered. "Don't go. That was best of all."

"I must go back to my room," he said. "You know I must."

"But you'll do it to me tomorrow, when we get back to The Laurels?"

"We won't have Adam along to chaperone us," he said, kissing her bruised mouth. "I may not wait till we get home."

"Indeed you won't," she said, yawning helplessly. He blew out the candle and stole from the room.

He heard movement and whispers in other rooms along the corridors, but was astonished that in only few instances was it men talking with the young women. Then it struck him that most of the young white men would not think of imposing their base desires on the young belles. If any of them were rampant with need, they'd find a convenient black wench.

He went quickly back to his room, shaking his head. He knew these people were the cream of the Southern aristocracy, the sons and daughters of the landed gentry, wealthy, spoiled, pampered, waited on hand and foot. But he shook his head again, grinning. He sure as hell didn't envy one of them.

When he touched his own door, he heard a whisper of furtive, muffled sound from within the room. His hand on the knob froze. Fear pulsed through him. Fear! To stand in terror of the least whisper of secretive noise, to wonder what is behind a closed door, this was his curse, his destiny.

Sweating, he eased the door open and stepped inside. He exhaled heavily. A window was open, but a small candle glowed on his bedside table. His bed was turned back, white sheets gleaming in the faint light, untouched, wrinkle free. Perhaps it had been his imagination? God knew Margarith had whipped him into a state bordering on complete fatigue.

Still troubled, his instincts warning him that something was wrong, he undressed, tossing his clothes across a chair. Without knowing why, he left on his undershirt. He went to the bed, lay down upon it. As he leaned over to blow out the candle, Lissa Malraux stepped from his closet. "I wanted to be sure it was you," she said, voice casual, "and that you were alone."

He stared at her through a haze of exhaustion, knowing why she was here. She wore a dressing gown, but it was even more transparent than the diaphanous gown beneath it. Her breasts were of classic proportions, flaunting taut nipples against the alabaster outthrusting of flesh. Her stomach rounded into the dark heat of her muliebria. She walked toward him, her feminine glow mocking the faint fire of the candle.

Lissa sat beside him on the bed. She smiled, tracing her third finger around his lips lightly. "Were you with the little married virgin? I can't believe it! Oh, not of you—of her. I had no idea a rugged devil like you'd appeal to her, or, *mon chéri*, that a man of your qualities would find her intriguing."

He did not move, watching her. He was dead tired. He did not see how he could find the energy to force an erection. But he had not counted on all the lessons Lissa had mastered so fully in Paris! He began by trying to think of some way he could turn her down gracefully, but her heated mouth, her tongue, her exploring fingers were not still, and suddenly he found himself putting up the boldest front.

"Oh, my God," she whispered. "I never saw anything like this on a white man. . . ."

If you only knew, he thought sardonically. But he also was aware Lissa Malraux would not care that he was black or white. She hadn't said she had never seen one like his before—only that she'd never encountered one of such colossal proportions *on a white man*. He pushed her down, letting her go on nuzzling until he knew he was ready, even for Lissa Malraux. But when he moved to push her down on her back, she stripped away her gown and got down on her hands and knees, her breasts suspended like grape clusters. "Do it—dog fashion," she whispered. "It's the only way I'm sure I could take anything that enormous and wonderful, and oh, God, I mean to have it—one way or the other."

He gave her what she asked, and more. What could he do? After all, he *was* a guest in her house, wasn't he?

CHAPTER XXIII

In the weeks that followed, Jeff was truly and completely happy for the first time. Inspired by Margarith's selfless, greedy, jealous, and high-hearted love, he discovered a warm new meaning to life, and a motivation to succeed beyond his wildest fantasies. He no longer cared that he would never rake in millions as a Lafitte minion trading black slaves smuggled into the country through Barataria and Pensacola. His driving ambition was to make The Laurels a showplace—a model of what a well-run farm could be, a place of real accomplishment. He could have Margarith, and he could build a plantation that would be the envy of all the landed gentry.

He recognized the danger in drawing attention to the plantation, and through it to himself. Baxter Simon was a friend of Meador Coffee; he was well known among the slave owners in the area. As the news of the good fortunes of The Laurels spread, certainly the word of the redhead directing that success would reach Bax Simon. He put all this out of his mind in a feverish thrust of activity. He was overflowing with vigorous healthy vitality and infectious good spirits. It was exciting being just over twenty years old and holding the world by its tail! He grinned, seeing the big farm bustling with activity, the fields spreading outward with new crops, turning lushly green, and to see the craft shops working full tilt again, the new mills grinding out food, fabrics, and wood products.

Coming in at night too tired to sleep—even after having sent Margarith spinning into exhausted and sated slumber—he would make plans for the next day, next week, next year. And that in itself was thrilling to him. He had drifted from day to day before, afraid to plan ahead, fearful of what lay around the next corner. He was too busy now to care about trouble. Once a problem at The Laurels was solved, a project completed, he found himself dissatisfied, wanting to expand, to reach toward something else that might look impossible, but which would exalt him when he achieved it. He would clear new fields for cotton, some of the older lands devoted to cotton would be put into peanuts, corn, yams, or vegetables to feed the slaves. With more hogs, he could slaughter and smoke them for sale as well as improve the slave diet with more ham, fatback, and sow belly. More cattle would provide beef, increased amounts of sweet milk and clabber. He would teach every slave at The Laurels a craft, a trade, or show him how to excel in agricultural production. Hell, old Bax Simon was content to raise fancy mustees and prime blacks for the slave market—blacks who were like sleek animals who knew nothing. The Laurels' slaves would be self-sufficient; they'd know something more than climbing the nearest wench or swinging a hoe in a cottonfield.

Still, fear must have been always deep in the crannies of his mind. He worked faster and faster, as if the devil were on his tail. The days were not long enough to accomplish all he'd planned the night before. But the new grist mill was working a full ten hours a day. People came in from as far as forty miles away—a rough two-days' travel—to admire and study it. They saw it turning out meal, flour not only for the slaves and the storerooms and the big house, but for sale to neighbors and comnercial firms, who came in and hauled grain products away.

The talk of the region was the new-fangled steam-driven power saw he'd bought and installed in the new lumber mill. There was always a crowd of men, land-owners, small farmers, lumber men, and plain curious watching the steam turn the wheels, moving the belts and spinning the large saw, which debarked a log and then sliced it into precise board widths and lengths. Before many weeks passed, Jeff's mill was selling finished lumber to dealers who came from as far as a hundred miles away to buy from him. He pleased the slaves by using the steam and belts to grind sugarcane for juice and syrup. The blacks who had always turned the cane grinder by hand power or by driving oxen in an unending circle sat laughing and drinking the sweet liquid, which spewed from the grinder as it never had in the old days.

The project that pleased Jeff most was entirely too new and untried for the farmers and gentry who arrived to marvel over the grist mill and the power saw. He would show them the concave cement slues that ran from the new dam at the grist mill out to the fields, where the water was run out through smaller, perforated runners to irri-gate the crops. Though The Laurels fields burst into a rich, lush green seen nowhere except in the silt-rich deltas, the farmers nodded and smiled and returned to the steam-powered saw.

Although Jeff—with Ponchus working closely with him —spent eighteen hours a day on the farm with hard tiring work, he did it by choice because he enjoyed it as he enjoyed nothing else—except the hours spent in Mar-garith's arms. He drew real pleasure from seeing the farm almost wholly supported by produce and products from their own acreage. He exulted in that primitive gratification of being truly self-sustaining, self-supporting —and on the way to showing a profit.

Jeff grinned at Ponchus, who sagged in a chair near where Jeff worked on the books. "No real gentleman would work this hard, eh, Ponchus?"

231

Ponchus yawned helplessly. "Leastwise I never saw it, young masta."

"Good I'm not a gentleman, huh?"

"Yas, suh. You sho' ain't."

Jeff laughed. "It shows, huh?"

Ponchus sat forward, serious. "You sum'pin' lot finer, suh . . . you all man, masta. All man . . ."

Few of the blacks shared Ponchus's energy for work. Under Clitus, the work crew cooperated, but slaves, Jeff realized, were never going to see any reason for breaking their backs in the hot sun, even when they could see the progress and green results of their labors. It seemed to him that some kind of honestly operated sharecropping would work better than slavery, but he was realistic enough to know the time was not ripe to suggest freedom for slaves; sharecropping would seldom be honestly carried out when one man kept the books and the other man couldn't read. And anyhow, sharecropping would demand that white men accept blacks, not as equals—God forbid —but at least as human beings. It wasn't about to happen, and so the South was doomed to limp along at 40, 50, and 60 percent labor efficiency at the best—and he shoved it all from his mind as unprofitable. When you couldn't change something, there was no sense wasting time thinking about it.

Things were going well at The Laurels—and he was proud of his achievements. He felt good about The Laurels, knowing he had diversified the crops, developing new ones, and expanding into lumber and grain milling. The farm was no longer solely dependent upon cotton and the cotton economy.

Meador Coffee came over often from Tanglewood plantation—too often for Jeff, who disliked him, and for Margarith, who became ill thinking Jeff might believe she cared for the planter and be made unhappy. In her selfless loving, Margarith wanted only that Jeff be happy— she didn't care about anything else—and any matter which might make him unhappy distressed her.

232

Meador Coffee was the one person who was the least pleased about Jeff's outstanding success in moving The Laurels so rapidly and solidly toward the profit column. Oddly enough, it never occurred to Meador that Jeff might be a love rival where Margarith was concerned. Sex never intruded into Meador's Southern-gentleman consciousness where Margarith was involved. She was a white gentle lady, and thus existed on a high pedestal where sex smelled of magnolias and meant a chivalrous kiss on the fingers at most. It never entered Meador's mind that Jeff might be sharing Margarith's bed—or even that he might want to. Jeff was accepted as a white gentleman by Meador Coffee. Coffee felt that if Jeff entertained any base sexual impulses toward Margarith—as unlikely as this was!—he would certainly find release in the female genitalia of some Laurels black wench, as Meador, or any other gentleman, would have done and secretly preferred to do.

No, Meador's sole frustration and impatience with Jeff was the way Carson actually worked and sweated to make the plantation a commercial success.

Jeff's success with the big farm troubled Meador Coffee because Coffee coveted the major's holdings as he did the major's lovely young widow. Coffee had always believed that when he came to an indebted, impoverished, mortgaged, panic-stricken Margarith with his serious proposal of marriage—after a suitable period of her mourning, of course—she'd be constrained and impelled to grab him as she would a lifeline. Now he was not so sure. He found it easy to bad-mouth Jeff Carson around the countryside, in plantation parlors, and tavern drinking rooms.

Henley Lewis was the only real fly in Jeff's ointment. He accepted the petulant, complaining overseer because he figured that there had probably been mosquitoes even in Eden.

Henley Lewis was after Jeff constantly to agree to the sale of some twenty of The Laurel's slaves. Some of the black herd—male and female—detested Henley Lewis so deeply and bitterly that their hatred could not be allayed even by the new sense of achievement and peace engendered by Jeff's arrival and totally fair management. Jeff resisted until a notice came from Cole & Son, Slave Auctioneers, Natchez, announcing a general sale of "small numbers of prime workers, healthy animals from many of the finest Southern plantations." Jeff agreed to permit Lewis to block a coffle for the trek to Natchez.

He was not surrendering to Lewis's persistent pressures. Jeff agreed to the slave sale because he felt that Margarith would be safer with a cash balance in her bank account. He had used much of her money for the steam engine and power-driven saw. He wanted to do what was seldom— if ever!—done on the big plantations. He wanted to pay cash for the fertilizer and seed for next year's cotton crop. With this done, and money in the bank, Margarith should be in good shape, no matter what happened. If he were going to be a realist, he had to accommodate all his plans to the ever-present peril in which he passed the days and nights of his life.

A final reason for selling off some of the slaves was that among them were many who would not or could not learn simple crafts, trades, occupations, or fulfill household duties. They were all healthy, comparatively young, and they would make good workers for less-demanding employers than The Laurels, where he wanted all of his people to be masters of some trade.

Jeff worked hard all day, but he found the motivation when he came in to Margarith each evening, or when she drew him to her in the false dawn before she'd let him leave her bed in the morning. Jeff knew his entire exultant happiness at The Laurels was based not on the achievements and accomplishments, but on the life he'd established with Margarith. They had each other; they wanted nothing more. If some nights he sprawled exhausted, Margarith would lie quietly beside him until it occurred to her to practice some of the exciting things Lissa had learned in Paris and disclosed to Margarith in whispers. Jeff soon forgot to be weary; he could have told Margarith he'd learned all Lissa's secrets in New Orleans, but he did not; Margarith especially loved the exotic flavor of her passions.

Margarith was a jealous and devouring lover; in any other woman Jeff would have found this distasteful; in Margarith it was charming. He grinned, recalling the morning they had left Foxmoor after delivering Adam as a gift, and his spending the night in sexual activity beyond the call of reason.

Lissa had spoken to Margarith, but her hungry eyes were fixed on Jeff. "Now, Margarith, you hurry and bring that lovely hunk of man back over here to see me, or I'll have to come to The Laurels to see him."

Margarith had kissed Lissa warmly, laughing. "You do, darling," she said, "and I'll have Ponchus sic the dogs on you."

Lissa did come to The Laurels. She showed up one day, lovely and busty in crinolines, her eyes dancing with secret messages for Jeff's private decoding. But Margarith insisted that Lissa sleep that night with her, saying they had "so much to talk about, so much to catch up on."

Each of them spent a sleepless stalemated night waiting for the other to fall asleep so she could escape to Jeff's room across the house. It didn't happen. Jeff slept well, awoke refreshed and sardonically amused at the tension between the two exhausted, hollow-eyed young women. Lissa was in a rotten mood through breakfast and left for home early,

Margarith did not mention Lissa, but he knew she was jealous. She wanted no other woman to touch Jeff; she would have liked it better had they not even looked at him in that hungry, sexy way Lissa had.

The days and nights at The Laurels moved forward in a happy progression. Jeff found new excitements in Margarith every night. He found himself dreaming ahead to her in the busy day, anxious to get home to her.

Margarith was indeed every beautiful thing he could ever want, Jeff mused, as she lay naked close beside him.

She was always dreaming up new refinements in the arts of love. The ecstasy that Margarith gave him was unique. Nobody ever stirred his imagination or lifted him to such heights as she did. He truly loved her. Sleeping with other women would always be fun. Making love was the greatest pleasure he'd found in life, but with Margarith it was on a new and more enchanting plateau—it was a world in which they laughed and loved as Adam and Eve must have in their world apart.

He became aware that Margarith was toying with the bent golden cross hanging about his neck. He had told her that Helen had given him the diamond-studded talisman as a good luck piece. She hadn't minded that he had meant so much to another woman when he first told her; now she cared. She got up, naked, from the bed, disappeared from the room, and returned bearing a dress sword in its scabbard.

"I want you to have this," she told him. "It should bring you much more good luck than that little thing." She smiled. "Anyway, I want you to have it, and keep it. It will be such a bother to you wherever you go that every time you curse it for getting in the way, you'll have to think of me. . . . Will you keep it? Promise?"

He kissed her, laughing. "I promise."

"I want you to have it as a symbol of my love for you . . . there we are—your sword and my sheath." She smiled. "André gave it to me. I didn't understand why. But I know now it was symbolic with him. If that's true, it is *really* symbolic when I give his sword and sheath to you. . . ."

CHAPTER XXIV

When Jeff told Henley Lewis that he and Vincente were accompanying the overseer and his coffle on the overland trek to Natchez, Lewis's face sagged and he shook his head back and forth almost convulsively. Jeff suspected Henley wanted to arrange all sales and pocket any kickbacks or side money he could set up. This didn't mean that Henley Lewis was totally dishonest. He was simply amoral in an amoral world. This kind of stealing was done by every overseer, and Henley counted his knockdowns as bonuses.

He stood, twirling his hat in his fingers, enumerating the reasons why it was wasteful and unnecessary for all of them to be away from the plantation at the same time. Jeff grinned inwardly. They were going to have an honest accounting of monies and this outraged Lewis; it was a development barely to be countenanced.

Jeff foresaw few difficulties in traveling with this small coffle on the road. The caravan comprised three wagons. One, handled by Vincente, carried provisions and supplies. Lewis would drive a flatbed with ten young black boys and men aboard, and Jeff's flatbed was to accommodate ten females. Each of the three drivers was armed against "nigger stealers," who haunted the roads to Natchez according to Lewis. The slaves being transported by wagon was another sore point with Lewis. He hated the thought of pampering blacks. Every coffle he'd ever taken to Natchez had walked, shackled. Jeff vetoed this; he wanted The Laurels slaves to look their best. Besides, he was anxious to get to Natchez, dispose of their coffle, and return to Margarith.

They departed in the false dawn amid tears and shouted farewells from assembled slaves. Margarith had spent the night crying in Jeff's arms as if she'd never see him again. She stood at the living room window and watched the wagons rattle along the tree-canopied lane to the northbound trace.

Despite Jeff's optimism and careful planning, many obstacles arose in the handling of the coffle of slaves. It was a long, tiring distance. Most of the blacks had never been off The Laurels property before. Though they found the trip itself exciting, many were depressed. The threat of the unknown, the loss of loved ones left behind, the sudden disruption of their way of living settled like a pall, and some became physically ill. Jeff served three good meals a day to the coffle, moving them on their stomachs like one of Napoleon's army companies. The ill and depressed did not respond to Jeff's kindnesses, or his jokes and promises of a new life in exciting and different surroundings. They were the dullest of The Laurels slaves and they could stir little hope inside themselves for a better day. They did straighten up under Henley Lewis's threat of the whip, and perhaps under the delusion that in leaving The Laurels they were escaping the continual fear of flogging. Jeff sighed and admitted it: Lewis kept them moving. Maybe this explained why the overseer saw himself entitled to any kickbacks and left-handed compensation he could arrange. He viewed it as well-deserved.

They stopped at ordinaries and taverns along the way where Henley Lewis was recalled from previous treks and was well received. Jeff found these dingy establishments unkempt and depressing. He would have preferred sleeping in the stables with the slaves. He grinned self-deprecatingly, attributing this desire to his earliest training as a Willow Oaks buck.

They came into Natchez, that city of split personality, of two faces—one haughty and one amoral. The resplendent Natchez wealthy and high-born looked out from mansions set on the high bluffs overlooking the river. Below, at Natchez Forks-in-the-Road, people lived in squalor, and crime, slave barracoons, auction markets, and whorehouses flourished.

Despite his long months as slave handler and buyer for Lafitte, Jeff had never become inured to the stench and degradation of the slave barracoons. Cole & Son, Slave Auctioneers, was neither the largest nor yet meanest of the slave vendues. It was no cleaner, no filthier, no uglier than the other slave jails. But Jeff felt himself sickened at the sights and smells. He admitted a part of his illness came from his awareness that he could easily —almost with a toss of the dice—be among those poor devils. He had been born to their lot, but he'd managed to escape it. Yes and by God, he'd die before he'd be enslaved, or be shackled in this horror again.

As the coffle approached Cole & Son's slave stockade, they could hear the continuous keening from within the high walls, a dirge of agonized despair. Jeff felt that old nausea at the putrid effluvium that rose sour and sickening, as if from open latrines, from the slave cells and yard.

Fred Haymeyer—Cole & Son were both long dead—welcomed Jeff and company to Natchez. A thin, red-bearded man, he was totally unconscious of the overpowering stench and the unbroken wailing of despair from the barred yards. He smiled broadly, shook hands with Jeff and Vincente, clapped Henley Lewis on the back, and untactfully demanded to know what kind of under-the-table arrangements ole Henley was demanding this trip?

Descending into this inner ring of the inferno, they added their twenty slaves to the crowd of miserable, shackled beings awaiting the auction. The Laurels blacks were sickened by the odors, terrified by the sights and sounds. They clutched at Jeff, begging to be allowed to go back home with him.

Ready to vomit, Jeff forced himself to finish his business with Haymeyer. When he'd determined his stock was as comfortable as possible in this putrid barracoon, Jeff left two wagons and horses in Cole's stables and drove with Vincente and Henley Lewis in the third uptown into Natchez. They moved slowly through crowded streets, forcing aside aged colored crones hawking cane juice, homemade brushes, lice combs, and cornshucks brooms. Black men pushed fish carts or carried croker sacks of food or fabrics on their bowed backs. Washer women strutted with baskets piled high with wash. Through this babble of small-time commerce passed wealthy planters, riverboat men, carriages, coaches, prostitutes, businessmen and tradesmen, farmers, backwoodsmen, and a few freed persons of color.

Soon after they registered at the Planter's Hotel and ate supper in the hotel dining room, both Vincente and Henley Lewis clamored to visit Miss Fifi's House under the hill. This place was whispered about, recalled, and reviled hundreds of miles in every direction from Natchez. Some there were who said they didn't know what Baptist ministers would sermonize about if it were not for Miss Fifi. She filled the church pews with hundreds of the same men who had patronized her cribs the night before. A man could slake his appetites, whatever diversity or perversion they indicated, at Miss Fifi's. Vincente paced, impatient to be on his way. Jeff refused to accompany them. Vincente thought he must be ill to turn down an orgy after long days on the dusty road.

"Just tired. Want a bath." Jeff hated to admit, even to himself, because it sounded so prudish and foreign to him, that he wanted no woman but Margarith. A whore turning a trick held no fascination for him.

He sent them along to Miss Fifi's, washed up in a hip bath, and then fell across his bed. Sounds from the street rose and blew in on a river breeze through his window, but the sound faded, growing dim and distant, and he fell asleep.

He was awake and up at dawn. The day was busy. He

had a breakfast of buckwheat cakes, ham, eggs, grits, and coffee in the hotel dining room, then went to Cole & Sons to check on the food served his slaves. The slop was so poor, watery, and rotten smelling that Jeff insisted on marching his people out for breakfast. Haymeyer raged, appealing to Lewis to explain the dangers, and refusing to accept any responsibility for lost slaves. "You sp'ilin' your nigras," Haymeyer said. "You ain't helpin' 'em none. They your nigras and you can do what you see fit. But you makin' it tough for them to adjust theyselves on farms where they goin' to be treated like what they is—animals."

Jeff sighed to himself and nodded. But he still marched his herd out and fed them food brought by Vincente and black employees of an uptown café. Well, the poor devils needed one decent memory from this trauma. The smells and sights of the barracoon sickened him and he escaped it as soon as he could.

He walked uptown to a jewelry store and asked to see rings, bracelets, and necklaces. One diamond seemed to have been mined, cut, polished, and set for Margarith. "It's two carats," the jeweler said, squinting through his loupe, "set in solid gold."

It was the gentle, almost fuliginous depth of the diamond in repose that captured Jeff's fancy and determined him to buy it. He held it up and twisted it so it grabbed at the lights.

When the ring was shifted so that it caught even the faintest glimmer of light, it seemed to come alive. Its multifaceted surface abruptly fulgurated, flashing brilliantly in a warm, wanton, undisciplined display of inner fires. It sparkled in the vaguely lighted showroom and reminded him of Margarith's face—quiet repose fragmented by sudden bright smiling. He spent $500 for the ring.

As he departed the store, a fat gold watch caught his eye. A gold vest-chain was attached to its thick stem. He thought about Ponchus, the selfless way the aging servant worked, Ponchus's loyalty to him and especially to Margarith. What in hell would she have done without

Ponchus? He bought the watch and had both purchases gift wrapped. By now the jeweler smiled obsequiously, bowed him out of the shop, held the door for him, pleading with him to return the next time he visited Natchez. Jeff walked back, reluctantly, to the barracoon.

The stockade bustled with activity. Landowners, slave traders, and other flesh peddlers inspected the slaves prior to the auction. Blacks were lined in an open-fronted shed and told to shuck down their cotton shirts and osnaburg britches. Naked, they were checked for piles, enlarged testes, bad teeth, weak chests, fissures, weals, and other disfigurements.

Jeff watched the inspections, searching for those qualifications he recognized as requisites in a good slave. Ugly blacks sold poorly. Deeply black men and women went slightly better. Good musculature and posture were musts for field workers. Slaves to be trained for housework were usually lighter in color, supposedly mentally brighter, with pleasing face, supple body, and good coordination.

He frowned. The twenty slaves he'd brought from The Laurels did not attract especial or favorable attention. He found himself pitying his herd when they were forced to undress, squat, and pull apart the cheeks of their buttocks and were put through the other degrading paces by prospective buyers. Could he have silently endured this dehumanizing treatment? He would never forget the misery of being pawed over, his gonads hefted, his penis milked. Baxter Simon had enjoyed displaying the red-headed mustee. Jeff had been a child then—half-paralyzed by terror. Could he submit to this indignity now or would they have to kill him to render him servile?

He was surprised—and pleased—when each of The Laurels slaves brought an excellent price. None of the women went for less than $800 each. A few males were sold as prime animals—going for almost 2,000 each in the confusion, excitement, and infectious rivalry of the auction. After deducting commission and expenses for Cole & Son, Jeff found he was heading home to The Laurels with almost $20,000 for Margarith's account.

Henley wanted to delay in Natchez another day or two after the slave auction ended. They had worked hard. They deserved a little vacation. Ponchus could handle things at The Laurels. Vincente agreed wholeheartedly. He planned to spend at Miss Fifi's both the days and most of the money he'd taken from Fabio's road agents in the bayous. Jeff shook his head. He was anxious to get back to Margarith. He wanted to see her face when he handed over the returns from the slave sales—solid security beyond her wildest expectations. Security she'd have no matter what happened.

He was also in a hurry to taste the fruits of her gratitude, admiration, and devotion! He wanted to get home!

Lewis and Vincente were vocal and profane in their protests. There was no sense in hurrying back home. What awaited them there but the same rut, the same labor they'd escaped for a little while, the same stubborn black faces?

Finally, Jeff agreed to take the wagon in the hotel stables and permit Lewis and Vincente to follow—after their money and their passion expired—in the other two vehicles. Lewis and Vincente grinned, slapped each other on the back, shouting like kids released on the last day of school.

"Look out, you whores," Vincente yelled. "Part your legs and set yourselves. Here comes Vincente."

On the return to The Laurels, Jeff made only those stops necessary to rest, refresh, and restore his horse. Because of the money he was carrying, he set his pistol on the seat beside him and slept with it under his pillow at night.

He saw many suspicious and threatening-looking characters on the lonely trace south. In taverns, he heard horror stories of highwaymen besetting travelers and leaving their stripped bodies to the buzzards. He had long ago learned that many backwoodsmen, ordinarily hard working and Sunday God-fearing, looked upon all strangers and every outsider as intruders, a person less than human whose murder would not even trouble a redneck conscience. When a stranger trespassed a man's territory uninvited and unwanted, he had nobody but himself to blame when he found that trouble. He was asking for it.

But on this trip, as he had on others, Jeff rediscovered a truth—the most evil of men were the least courageous unless all odds were imbalanced heavily on their side, as the numbers had been when Fabio's thugs attacked him on the bayou road. Road agents studied his size, reckoned his age, strength, and will to resist forcible robbery . . . and let him ride past unmolested.

He was anxious to get back home. Home? Back to The Laurels and Margarith's arms and all her fanciful sex games. He found no pleasure in being parted from her. Always before he'd willingly accepted almost any female for a one-night stand. Now none of them would satisfy his needs. He wanted Margarith. He loved the way she was ready and anxious to perform with him at any time of the night or day. He smiled, looking ahead across the miles, feeling his growing anticipation, and slapping the reins to hurry the tired horse.

He recognized the first familiar signs of the plantation lands ahead and his heart lurched. After his long absence from The Laurels, Jeff for the first time realized how exciting and heartwarming it was to be coming home. Home! To wake up in his own bed with Margarith's naked body beside his. To taste her lips, to fondle her shapely breasts, to find her vagina fevered and waiting for him. This was the most satisfying feeling possible to a man. It was entirely new and unique and wonderful in his experience. He was home!

He slapped the reins across the horse's sweated rump. Darkness smoked in around him. He had pushed the poor animal to the limits of its endurance; the horse was exhausted. He probably should have spent one more night on the road. Thank God he had not!

He was almost to the tall gates of The Laurels when someone stepped from the brush growing close against the trace.

Catching his breath, Jeff grabbed up his gun. Then

he recognized one of the black boys Ponchus assigned to sit on the front steps all day to watch for guests. "What are you doing out here?" Jeff demanded.

"Mista Ponchus, he sent me out here, suh. Said I was to watch for you. He say to tell you . . . a man is up to de big house a-lookin' and a-askin' for you. A man named —named—" The boy, unable to remember the name, burst into tears.

"Simon?" Jeff said. Going taut, Jeff stared toward the manor house. For a long beat, he sat, locked, stunned with panic, unable to think. He drew a full, hurting breath. It was like trying to breathe deep under water. "Simon? Is that the name?"

"Yas, suh." The boy nodded, sniffling. "That sho' am de name. Yas, suh. I scairt waiting out heah in de dark. Can I ride in to de house wid you now, masta?"

CHAPTER XXV

Jeff sat taut and unmoving on the wagon seat. He gripped the gun in his fist and stared toward the wanly lit manor house.

His mind churned, sorting for an answer where he was already convinced there was none. He wanted to race up that lane and stop Baxter Simon before that swine spoiled everything between him and Margarith. He wanted above all else to keep her love, and this meant concealing the truth about his black bloodline. He shook his head, sick.

245

He was already too late to keep Simon from revealing his slave origin, his bastardy, his unpardonable deception.

He looked about, like a trapped animal, seeking a way out. Baxter Simon had destroyed everything for him here, but thanks to Ponchus's warning, he was still free. He could run, and keep running. Margarith would despise him—she would anyway!—but he could insure his freedom as he always had in the past, by staying ahead of the vengeful Bax Simon, by circumventing the law, by continuing to masquerade behind his white skin. He stared at the gun in his white-knuckled fist. He had the cash Margarith desperately needed—in these times, a real fortune! He had to get that money to her, or to Ponchus, before he could run. He also had gifts he meant to deliver, somehow. They might not want a ring or a gold watch from a bogus white man, a fugitive slave, but he wanted them to have them. He wanted them to know how deeply he loved them, even if he had deceived them. No. He could not run this time. Not yet.

The lowering night wind cooled the sweat beading his face. The real answer was the mind-bending, yet inescapable one he'd kept out of his conscious mind as long as possible. He had to face it now. The only way to escape Baxter Simon this time was to kill him. Slaying Baxter Simon would not recover Margarith—it would drive her farther across that unnavigable gulf than ever—but it would end forever this terrible deadly game of pursuit and flight between him and his hated owner. He meant to die before he was returned to bondage, but murder would buy him at best only temporary surcease. Except for this frightened black boy, he might have hidden along the road and ambushed Simon when he left The Laurels. But the boy was a witness against him. A black's testimony was unacceptable at law against a white person but it was totally valid against another black. If he slew the bastardly Simon inside the house at The Laurels he could not be saved— self-defense was no plea for a black man who killed a white. Both Margarith and Ponchus would be required to testify against him. He would only

246

mpound the injury he'd caused Margarith by pro-
nging this nightmare in court somewhere. If he killed
mon and ran, he would only trade Simon's obsessive
rsuit for murder, for which the law would hound him
entlessly.

"Kin I ride in with yo', masta?" he heard the boy
eading in the deepening gloom of night.

"That man—Simon—is he alone?"

"Yas, suh. Rode in on he hoss a while back. Alone he
as. Yas, suh, masta. . . . Now kin I ride in wif yo'?"

Jeff shook his head. "Neither one of us is going to
de in."

"I scairt, masta."

Jeff touched the boy's bony shoulder trying to reas-
re him. "Hell, so am I."

"Ha'nts out in the dark like this, masta. Spooks."

"Could you be brave if I told Ponchus to order you a
veet potato pie with two-inch meringue on it—just for
ou?"

The boy hesitated, licked his lips. "Don't see no spooks
und yet."

"All right. I want you to run up this lane, go to the
arn, and have them saddle up my own horse and have
ready out there. If they hear you run past the big house,
ll skin you. Go to the barn. Have my horse saddled. Can
ou remember that?"

The boy nodded. Jeff patted his shoulder and told him
» get going. He watched the little fellow race, lost in
e mists of early evening. Alone, he led the tired horse
ff the lane and secured him in a plot of grass in the
eep shadows of a magnolia tree.

Holding the gun at his side, he crossed the yard. Before
e reached the drive he could see Baxter Simon's bulky
ιadow striding back and forth, arms slashing, gesturing
ι the lamp-lit parlor.

Stealthily, Jeff crossed the drive, moved through the
ιsmine to the tall window. He could hear Baxter's savage
ɔice clearly. "Some things make me purely ready to kill,
Iiss Margarith, ma'am. Nigger stealers, lyin' niggers,

247

biggety light-skinned niggers passin' as white—pretendin' they's purentee humans. Can't tolerate 'em. Them and any white woman takin' up with a nigger. I don't believe that really happens, but it'd make me sick if ever I saw it. Can stand most anything else. But some things are a crime before God. And that's the way I looks at a mustee a-passin' hisself off as a white man."

Jeff shifted his gaze to Margarith and his stomach roiled. He bit back the bile that gorged up into his throat. Margarith was not crying—not yet. He wished she would. Her eyes were shadowed, wild, verging on hysteria. Anyone but a man as insensitive to others as Simon was would have seen her distress. But the big man went on talking, justifying, blaming, explaining.

"I didn't come here to hound that Bricktop—or Jeff Carson as you know him. But he's a slave of mine—for life. I owns him like you owns the blackest slave in your quarters. He's a Willow Oaks buck, a black. That's all he is."

"Jeff must be white—as white as you are."

"White?" Bax's laugh was bitter. "He's fooled plenty of people, ma'am, pretending his name is Jefferson Carson —Thomas Jefferson Carson. Well, his name is Bricktop. He was born to a slave wench of mine, and that makes him my slave."

"Oh, God," she whispered. "Oh, my God."

"You ought to be thankin' me for gettin' here and warnin' you, ma'am," Bax Simon said. "That mustee nigger Bricktop, he purentee polecat. He's a bad nigger. He's a runner. I put welts half-inch high on his back naming him a runner. But he's my property and I mean to have him back."

"He isn't here," she whispered, barely able to control herself.

"Then you tell me where he is. An' I go and git him, and I take him back to Willow Oaks where he belong. I let no slave run and git away on me. Sets a bad 'zample for the other blacks, they see one git away. I takes him back. I puts the whip to him, and they see what happens when they try it—if they try it."

Simon bent over where Margarith crouched in the big wingback chair, cowering, though he did not see this. Simon believed he was within his rights and he was close to his quarry; he meant to end this chase. It was not that Baxter Simon was inherently evil. In his own estimation, certainly he was not. He had been wronged by a runaway nigger and he meant to redress that wrong. He was obstinate, opinionated, inflexible, stubborn, and unwavering, but by his own lights, he was justified in any action he took to recover lost property. That he might be evil was one thought that never penetrated his cranium. He saw himself as a God-fearing member of the landowning gentry, endowed with a divine right—the power of life and death over his slaves—just as any sovereign was endowed with his birthright. He accepted his God-given status, with all its responsibilities, obligations, demands, inconveniences, and restrictions. He never had occasion to consider that this same divine right which created kings also brought forth criminals, scoundrels, knaves, and beggars—and not infrequently from the same seminal fluid shucked into similar depositories. Baxter Simon no more questioned his sovereignty over the lives and destinies of his 400 slaves than he did the direction in which the sun arose on any given Sunday. To Baxter Simon, as to any plantation owner in his acquaintance, his slaves were no more or less than valuable animals, to be kept healthy, reasonably content, well fed, servile, and ready for sale. He drew no pride, no satisfaction from driving or abusing his Negroes. He held the power of life and death over them, but he'd tell you he preferred life—because he preferred profit, and there was no profit in a dead nigger. Bax Simon was a product of his time, place, conditions, economics, environment, as surely as was his lowest slave, though he never considered himself and these subhuman beings in any such context. Social, financial, and authoritarian position was his birthright. He accepted it. He never questioned it—for the very questioning implies self-doubt, and he never doubted. He was by birth a member of the dominant class. It was God's will that he be deferred to by other white people and never crossed in any manner by the black. This was all unquestioned, unquestionable. This inborn sense of superiority informed every action, every thought, every response of Baxter Simon to every situation.

"I've had that boy Bricktop since he was born," Simon was telling Margarith. "I was maybe fifteen when he was born—on my place. . . . Hell, by the time that mustee was thirteen he was built like a jackass, you'll excuse me, ma'am, for bein' indelicate in the presence of a genteel lady. Why, he could of been put to stud at thirteen. And he could of been sirin' me purentee prime fancies to sell at vendue all these years. He's purentee white on his face and hands. Not a sign he's a nigger. But that boy is branded on his back. I know! I put them brands there. He runned. He went north somewhere—stayed a few years—then he got biggety enough to think he could come back south and git away with livin' free—like you or me, ma'am, or any other human! If he'd of stayed home and behaved hisself, I'd've got plenty o' white suckers out'n him an' some mustee wenches. Worth five, six thousand each, easy. . . . So you can see, ma'am, why I'm so all-fired ragin' against him for runnin'. He's cost me plenty, not reckonin' in the time I had to waste chasin' him down."

Margarith's voice shook. She was on the brink of despair. "If he ran so far—so long—why couldn't you just let him go?"

Simon growled and slashed his arm downward. "I tole you! He's mine! He's black, he's a slave, and he's my slave to kill or keep as I see fit. Best reason I know is that this Jeff Carson—Bricktop—belongs to me. He's my nigger. He's been my nigger since he was born. Now, I mean to have him back. You tell me where-at he is, I go and fetch him."

Jeff stepped through the tall window. Margarith had been pushed to the edge of hysteria. He could not let her be badgered any longer. That she knew his secret now and must hate him didn't alter the depth of his love for her—nothing ever would.

"Here I am, Simon," Jeff said. "Come and fetch me. But I warn you. This gun's got a hair trigger. Turn around nice and slow."

Baxter heeled around, shaken, grabbing for the gun at his belt. By the time his palm struck the gun butt, he was turned and staring at the gun in Jeff's fist.

"I'll just take that gun," Jeff said. "You put it on the floor. Kick it toward me. Nice and easy. We're going to teach you some manners yet."

"Oh, Jeff," Margarith whispered. Her voice drowned in its own despair.

Baxter knelt, placed the gun on the carpeting, and shoved it with the toe of his boot toward Jeff. Jeff picked it up and pushed it under his belt.

Baxter said, "I warn you, nigger. You got any idea what they'll do to you—shootin' a white man?"

CHAPTER XXVI

Nowhere on earth did birth, custom, habit, and personal power reinforce in a man such total arrogance and self-assertive infallibility as in the plantation country. Born to presumptive eminence, a man was deferred to, danced attendance on, and fawned over until his procacity just naturally hardened into overweening insolence.

Jeff stared at Simon's brazen, haughty face and the aggressive stance of his body. The slave breeder looked directly at the gun fixed on him, in the hand of a man who hated him, and was not cowed. To Simon's imperious mind, the mustee holding the gun was not even a man at all, but a black slave, less than human, born to servility, subserviency, and obedience. To this moment, it had never entered Bax Simon's conscious mind that a slave—even a rogue black—would dare oppose him seriously. The slave mentality was programed to prostrate itself, to cringe in self-abasement after perhaps a quick show of bravado or the flaring obstinacy a stallion might display before it bowed to a superior intellect and stronger will.

Jeff laughed incredulously at this haughty man trying to stare him—and his gun—out of countenance. "You arrogant bastard," he said.

Simon stepped forward, not in the least intimidated by the gun held by one of his own herd of blacks and supremely confident in his caste superiority.

"Don't you know, Bricktop, that if you kill a slave owner, the law will hound you the rest of your life?"

Jeff shook his head, laughing, "Your stupidity is exceeded only by your conceit, you ignorant bastard. Do you think I give a damn whether it's the law or you chasing after me?"

Simon didn't even hear him; there was nothing his runaway nigger could say important enough to merit the least attention. "I'll make you an offer, Bricktop. And don't push me, because I've damned little patience with uppity niggers. Now, you put away that gun, I'll be lenient with you. All I ask is that you return to Willow Oaks quietly."

Jeff nodded. "That's right, Bax. When I return to Willow Oaks, it will be quietly—because I'll be dead."

"That's up to you, boy. But you are going back. You're not makin' it no easier on yourself actin' biggety like this." Baxter kept his voice pitched at a tone of reasoning, but tension seethed beneath it. He was outraged that one of his blacks would defy him in the presence of another white person, even a woman. "Now give me that gun, boy. The longer you hold out on me, the harder it's goin' to be on you when I git you back to Willow Oaks."

"The hell with you," Jeff said. "You're so brass-minded I can't even get through to you. I'm not going back to Willow Oaks with you, Bax. You stupid ass, don't you realize I'll kill you before I'll surrender to you?"

"Give me the gun, boy. Let's get this over with." Simon stepped forward again.

"All right, Bax, that's far enough." Jeff retreated to a wall. He yanked a cord alerting the servant's quarters. After a moment, the corridor door opened and Ponchus stepped through.

Ponchus stopped, his face sagging, his eyes showing his agony. "Oh, masta, I tried to warn you."

"It's all right, Ponchus, bring me some rope."

Ponchus looked at the gun in Jeff's hand, at the imperious Baxter Simon, at Margarith crouched in a chair, lost inside her own mind. He nodded and swiftly retreated.

Baxter Simon's voice stopped Ponchus. "Just a minute, boy. You aid an' abet this nigger, it'll go hard with you. I'll put the whip to you my own self. I'll lay yore bones bare. Now you git out there, git a few blacks to come in here and help me disarm this buck, and we'll forget the rest of it."

Ponchus shook his head. "We got no niggers here at The Laurels that would dare attack they masta."

"This mustee their masta!" Simon's voice thundered, raging. "He's a black—just like you, boy. Just like the lowest bozal on this farm."

Ponchus nodded. "Yassuh, that might be, masta, but cain't make our people believe that. Masta Jeff's got de gun, I best do what he say."

"You take one step to obey this rogue buck, boy, and when it's over, I'll hang you up and whop you bloody. Hear me good, boy, 'cause Baxter Simon is a fair and good man—but I don't never forgits a uppity or a disobedient nigger. You wanta stay alive and well, you do what I tells you."

Jeff gestured downward sharply and impatiently with his left hand. "The hell with it, Ponchus. The stupid bastard's right. I got no call to mix you up in this. Forget the rope, I'll handle it the only way good ole Bax here will let me."

He walked away from the wall, the other three people fixed in a tableau. Standing in the open doorway, Ponchus watched, eyes wide with terror. Margarith sat rigidly in her chair, her agonized gaze fixed on Jeff. Simon permitted a faint, twisted smile.

When Jeff came close, Simon reached out to accept the gun he expected Bricktop to surrender to him. Jeff backhanded him across the wrist. Baxter, stunned with pain, caught his arm. For the first time, he seriously considered that he might be in personal danger. "You black bastard," he said, "you'll pay for this."

"Turn around," Jeff said. "And turn slow, Bax. You think your wrist is hurting, I ain't started to hurt you."

Baxter stared along his nose at his slave, but he could not hide the pain that flared across his mind in waves, making him grimace. He turned slowly.

Jeff heard Margarith's despairing whisper. "Oh, Jeff . . ."

When Baxter was turned away from him, shoulders squared defiantly, Jeff turned the gun in his hand and cracked the slave breeder behind his left ear. The sound was dull, sickening in the silent room. Simon buckled to his knees and fell prostrate across the carpeting, face down. He did not move.

Margarith leaped up from the chair, her cheeks gray with pallor. "Oh, Jeff, you've killed him."

Jeff shrugged. "Maybe . . . it's going to have to happen sooner or later, anyhow."

"I git de rope now, masta," Ponchus said. He hurried away.

Jeff turned and looked at Margarith. Her eyes brimmed with tears. She tilted her head. "It's true, isn't it? What he said?"

"That the only true name I have is Bricktop? That my mother Mary was a bed wench at Willow Oaks, and my father some white man passing through? That my mother was a mulatto slave?" Jeff did not spare himself. Why should he? Any love that Margarith Morceau had felt for him was dead, slain horribly by the things Baxter Simon had told her. Jeff Carson no longer lived for her. He was Bricktop, a runaway nigger. He was no longer a human being, or a man to love. He was an animal, part of Baxter Simon's slave herd, and nothing more. "That's all true, Margarith. But it is also true that I love you—as I never loved anyone in my life."

Margarith sobbed. "Oh, God, Jeff. Oh, my God, Jeff —a slave—a black—how could you?"

"Do you want to see the brand scars on my back? Will that finish it all?"

She shook her head, crying. "I don't need to see them. . . . Loving you"—she shuddered in visible revulsion, "when I had my arms around you, I felt the weals on your back. . . . I didn't know then what they were . . . only that you didn't want your back seen . . . knew you were sensitive . . . I never thought . . ." Her voice trailed off and she gestured helplessly.

They stood for a long time in the funereal silence of the room. He said only, "I love you, Margarith."

She only shook her head, inconsolable. He was black in the eyes of the law and society. She had loved him deeply. She hated him now and she could never forgive him. Her response was almost like a stereotyped reaction in some tent-show melodrama. It *was* a stereotype because *she* was a stereotype, the end product of all the South had become, believed, and taught itself in 200 years. She belonged in this place where blacks were considered animals, feared as subhuman. She was what her family, friends, school, and churches had trained her to be. A black, a runaway slave had violated her, deceived and betrayed her—covered her with *vile*.

She hated him bitterly because she'd loved him totally, with all her heart and mind and body. He had lied to her, used her, defiled and degraded her. How could she face Lissa Malraux, or any of her friends again? How could she look into her own mirror? . . . Oh, God, how could she live without him, even now? Yet, there was no question. No matter how deeply she had loved him, she could not want him now. He was dead to her, as dead as though buried in a grave deeper than the major's. He was a nigger.

Jeff blinked back tears and straightened his shoulders. "I'm sorry. I hope someday you can forgive me."

She sobbed, pressing her fist against her swollen lips, but she did not answer.

He heard Ponchus enter the room behind him. He took the lines the servant had brought. He looped the rope about Siimon's throat, tied it off at his ankles. The least movement of Simon's head or feet would strangle him. He secured Bax's wrists in the middle of his back, used the rest of the rope to truss him up, to vent some of the hatred raging inside him.

Margarith had not moved. She went on standing immobile, staring into some lost dimension. Jeff said, "Well, even if the bastard gets free, he'll be too sick to follow me for a while."

From outside the window, Jeff brought the canvas bag of money, the small jeweler's boxes bearing his gifts. He gave them to Ponchus. "This one's for you, Ponchus."

Ponchus nodded, thanking him. The aging black man's eyes were filled with tears. He did not try to speak.

Jeff looked about the room. He walked over to where Margarith stood, body rigid, set against him. "Good-bye, Margarith."

She did not reply. Her eyes welled deeper with tears, but she remained unmoving. He reached out, took her arms in both his hands. He turned her to face him. She shivered but did not protest. "I love you," he said again. "I'll always love you." A repressed sob wracked her. He pulled her against him. He turned her face up and kissed her. It was like kissing a statue of ice. She was dead to him, and their love was dead. In her world it could never be, and in her mind, she denied it. It had never been.

CHAPTER XXVII

Jeff rode his horse out of the gates of The Laurels for the last time. A pale wafer of waning moon filtered silvery patterns on the moss-dripping oaks. Jeff slowed his horse, stopped the animal and sat slumped in the saddle in the middle of the silent, shadowed trace. Empty-bellied with longing, he stared back up at the faintly illumined manor house. Here he'd found love and purpose and contentment. He had achieved a great deal in a very short time. He had been happy for the first time in his life. And now he was doomed never to see the lovely old estate again, or any of the people there. He felt overwhelmd with loneliness, with an unshakable feeling of sadness.

He shook the depression from his mind. He had lost everything but his freedom. His whole mind had to be directed toward insuring that he remained free. He glanced north along the trace, the tiresome lonely way he had come from Natchez. Riding that way he might meet Vincente. But he'd also meet Henley Lewis who could report his direction of travel to Baxter Simon.

He gripped the reins, steadying the horse. He was sorely tempted to head north. He could ride wide of the trace. He could make it to the nearest port on the Mississippi and go by riverboat to Louisville, St. Louis,

Cincinnati. The whole world of the North was open to him; a land where blacks were rare, but where those men of color were free.

He shivered slightly, recalling his own life in the North —as Henry Carson's adopted son, and the years after both the Carsons were dead. No one suspected he was black, but he saw those others who escaped slavery in the South through the abolitionist underground. They arrived north, their black faces like curious masks to the whites who wanted them freed, but freed and left to live in the South. No matter what the Quakers said, blacks were no better treated, no more welcomed, less cared for—and their lives became far more precarious—than in the South. Unskilled, terrified, different because of black faces, black bodies, and unintelligible dialect that fell on impatient, uncaring ears, they were worse than segregated; they were shunned, isolated. They were gawked at as curiosities, as black-faced freaks, and left to fend for themselves in an alien world. When a black man stole, killed, or assaulted in order to get food or heat for his family, his presence was deplored, his criminality exploited, his person despised. That an enslaved black—lured by the siren promises of Quaker whispers of freedom—preferred Cincinnati, New York, Pittsburgh, Detroit, or Chicago to the unrelenting toil in Mississippi was not surprising. But that they adapted, overcame, and persisted in those cities was astounding.

He would not have the problem of blackness in the North. He was accepted as white in a world where Baxter Simon's claim on him had no validity. He could return to his old life as pimp and whoremaster. But could he? The evil and danger of that life repelled him. That subworld was a place of old dangers, quick death, betrayals. He had believed Green Mike was his friend until the king of the pimps arrived, armed and backed by thugs, to kill him. . . .

All of that—pimping women among the dregs of humanity—belonged to another world, and he remembered the cold winters, the constant peril, the whining girls, the drunken, murderous men. He had known a better life, and he could not go back to those old ways. At Barataria, he had been accepted by the hierarchy of Lafitte's organization; ahead had lain the opportunity to become a millionaire as slave smuggler and slave trader. At The Laurels, he had lived the life of the landed gentry; he had seen the rewards possible to a man willing to expend energy. He had been clean, waited on, respected—loved. He could not go back into the cold world of the old days on the prowl in the North.

He looked south—toward New Orleans. The crescent city beckoned like the hope of heaven. It was a metropolitan area where he would be lost and assimilated among whites, Creoles, and quadroons. He had a few thousand dollars—enough for a stake in some new enterprise. He would work, he would drive himself, he would make himself rich. He would never forget Margarith, but he would discipline himself to live without her. That looked to be all he could ask at the moment—to learn to exist in a world in which she could not be.

From the gathering gloom, sudden rain pelted him, the wind rose. Chilled, he turned up his collar, hunched up his shoulders, prodded his horse, and headed south on the trace. . . .

Riding, he let his mind trail back to the last moments with Margarith. He felt ill that he would never see her alive again. But he had seen she was already lost to him, and that made his departure less agonizing, if no easier. There was no sense delaying at The Laurels. She was dead to him. He could never have her again no matter what happened. All they'd had together was over.

He coughed, chilled and miserable in the rain. The last view he had of Margarith was of her standing unmoving, immovable in the lamplit parlor.

Ponchus had helped him get his things together in the bedroom where he had spent his nights in Margarith's arms. He shuddered, filling his carpetbag. He'd be glad to get out of a room where she had been a part of him, where everything reminded him of her. He took up the small waterproof bag that held the few thousand dollars he'd accumulated. He didn't bother to count it; he didn't care how much or how little was there. He tossed it into the carpetbag.

Ponchus said, "Where you gwine be, Masta Jeff? Poah Masta Vincente. How he gwine know to find you?"

Jeff shrugged. "It's safer for you not to know where I'm going, Ponchus. Even if I knew for sure, it would be better not to tell you. If you don't know, good ole Bax can't ever force you to tell."

"Yassuh . . . we gwine sorely miss you heah, masta."

Jeff nodded, not trusting himself to speak. Ponchus said, "That's a most scrumptious new watch, masta, and I gwine always wear it." He turned to leave. "I get your hoss brought up from de barn."

"Ponchus—"

"Yassuh, masta?"

"Nothing. Have my horse brought up here. Thank you."

When Ponchus was gone, Jeff scribbled a quick note. He wrote. "If you think the whores are great at Miss Fifi's of Natchez, be sure and try the girls at Madame Hortense's Riding Academy in New Orleans."

He folded the paper and stuffed it in among Vincente's fresh linen. Then he returned for the last time to his bedroom. He looked around to be sure he had all his belongings. He saw the sheathed sword Margarith had given him.

He took it up, hefting it. He decided he could attach it to the side of his carpetbag for easier toting. Then suddenly, he knew better. He flung the sword and sheath on the bed where he and Margarith had lain together. She would find it there. It might relieve her white mind to know the black man relinquished all claims to her. Her gift of sheathed sword was to a white man named Jeff Carson, not to Bricktop, fugitive nigger.

Carrying his carpetbag, he walked out. He crossed the foyer and went out the front door. A small black boy held a lantern. He grinned at Jeff. Jeff took the reins from

Ponchus and said, "This boy has earned a sweet potato pie, Ponchus. With a two-inch meringue. See he gets it, first thing tomorrow, will you?"

Ponchus nodded, smiling. "Yas, suh, I sho' do that." He sighed heavily. "When that Mist' Simon wake up in theah, I delay him for you—all I can."

Jeff had lifted his foot to the stirrup to mount. Now he hesitated and spoke over his shoulder. "Why not untie him and put him in bed, Ponchus? He thinks all servants love him, and he'll be grateful that you tried to help him. . . . When you get him in bed, you can send all his clothes out to be laundered."

Ponchus grinned widely, his white teeth gleaming in the lantern light. He nodded. "Yas, suh, Masta Jeff, I do that. I understands—an' I sho' will do that."

They'd stood there a moment longer in the ring of lantern light. Silence enshrouded them, a deep, late-night, graveyard stillness. Not a candle showed in the slave quarters. The house was quiet. In the parlor Margarith remained unmoving, lost, torn between the world in which she had found her only true happiness and the world ahead in which she had to live—alone, a white woman defiled by a nigger.

Jeff extended his right hand. Ponchus took it in both of his, gripping it tightly. His full lips quivered. Jeff said, "I know Miss Margarith can't ever forgive me. But I hope that someday you can, Ponchus."

Ponchus smiled, pressing Jeff's hand. "Ah has no problem in this world forgivin' you fo' havin' black blood in yoah veins, young masta."

261

CHAPTER XXVIII

New Orleans! Jeff rode into the crescent city in the gathering dusk of a rainy afternoon. Gas lamps glowing like silvery globes in the mists, the lamp of shops, and lanterns of liveries gave the town a mystical, magic beauty. The lights gleamed like gems, tossed by some profligate fist. Even coughing and hacking with a cold, Jeff felt the excitement of returning to the queen of the levees.

Along the piers, wanly lit vessels from every port laid to, secured and riding at anchor. Beyond them, strung by wet lines in the mists, keelboats, flatboats, and river craft bobbled like floats. The river smells of delta mud, decaying fish, and rotting weeds rose to mix with the aromas of the cargoes from the ocean-going brigs—coffee, bananas, leather, mahogany, raw hides, salted meats, rums, and tars.

Jeff slowed his horse, plodding toward the *Vieux Carre*. He was in no hurry because he had no destination. Since the night he fled The Laurels, he had been sick with a cold. Now his fever added to the sense of excitement and unreality of his return to New Orleans. Grogshops and restaurants beckoned, offering ales and pralines and peanuts and shrimp and snails in every kind of savory sauce. In his fevered view, all these establishments were not different, but merged into one, filled with a babble of strange tongues, raging with raucous laughter that was not many voices but one voice.

The streets were crowded with incoming traffic, and Jeff did not understand why until he heard a man yell at a loaded wagon rumbling past, "Decided you could come back home, did you? Think the plague is over, do you?"

The man on the wagon laughed and yelled back. "Hell no! Decided we'd druther die of the plague in New Orleans—than live healthy away from her."

Jeff exhaled heavily. So he had returned to the city at the tag end of another yellow fever epidemic? Each summer, the inhabitants of the lovely old town either suffered the threat of Bronze John and the added misery of hordes of swamp mosquitoes, or they fled to high ground. They believed the plague rode in on the summer miasma from the rotting bayous; they saw the pesky mosquitoes as insult added to injury by vengeful gods. They burned bonfires all night, fired cannon at one-hour intervals along the Esplanade. They hauled the swollen, blackened bodies to be cremated in rumbling tumbrels. They ran or they brazened it out; they laughed a lot, prayed a lot, drank a lot, and cursed their lot. But few ever determined to move away. Where would one go if he left New Orleans?

Jeff rode through the wagons, coaches, carriages, and buggies. The chattering along the streets attacked him like the cries of magpies, the screaming of blue jays, the chittering of monkeys. He passed over the canal which separated the American part of the city from the old French quarters, the *Vieux Carre*. Despite the long summer siege of the plague, the gala spirit of this mercurial city was hardly dampened. Here was the flavor of the Spanish, French, Creole, and backwater America. Here, when General Jackson paid off his troops after the War of 1812, more than 2,000 prostitutes had swarmed in, coming from everywhere and nowhere to where the money was.

The deeper he went into the old town, the less real the world seemed to his fevered mind. The iron-grilled patios seemed to hang out over the cobbled streets. Blacks, whites, Creoles, mestizos, griffes, quadroons lazed along the banquettes in the early night. Voices hailed Jeff, laughter seduced him. He saw a gaslit sign ahead, "Hotel La Dauphine," and he headed toward it, hoping he would make it before he plunged headfirst from his saddle.

He shook his clotted head, trying to clear it. He felt as if someone had crammed wads of cotton up through his nose to his forehead and temples. The pressure was so intense that he felt his head aching at the nape of his neck. It had started in the chilled rain as he rode away from The Laurels. The rains came and went intermittently, and the sicker he got, the less he could differentiate between dry and wet. He rode, miserable and damp, either chilled or his clothing steaming in the humid heat of a relentless sun.

Riding south, he had determined only that eventually he would reach New Orleans. He was in no hurry; he was too beat and lost to hurry. He could not look ahead for looking back hopelessly toward Margarith.

Sometime after midnight he had come upon an ordinary, set like a gloomy old barn in the middle of nowhere. A lantern hung on a spike over its front door promised food and lodging. The place was dank, smelled of ale and mildew, but Jeff was too exhausted to care. A slavey —a white girl, but barefooted and wearing a checkered dress, her hair lank about her heart-shaped face—was curled asleep behind the bar. She told Jeff the owner had retired for the night, but since they had one room unoccupied, she'd been left to wait for one final night traveler; she would register him and try to make him comfortable.

She asked if he wanted food. When he said he did not, she asked for two dollars—for the room, for stabling his horse, and for service. He was too congested to quarrel over the price, or to inquire the reason for a tax for service. He felt as if he were walking in a nightmare anyhow, and since none of was real, it did not matter.

He tossed three dollars on the bar and tried to smile when he told her to buy herself a new chemise. He ordered a hot toddy, and while she was preparing it, he took his horse around to the stable. He found a black boy masturbating on a pile of hay. "When you get through there," Jeff said, "would you rub down my horse, feed and water it?"

The boy looked up through glazed, bemused eyes and nodded. Jeff walked unsteadily back into the dimly lit barroom. His hot toddy was waiting, almost boiling hot and strong with whiskey. He drank, watching the girl go about closing the place, blowing out the lantern and locking the front door. By the time he finished his drink, the big tavern room was lighted only by the two candles the girl held, awaiting him at the foot of the stairs.

She went ahead of him up the narrow stairwell. They went along an even narrower upper corridor. Sounds of snoring and grunting and the squeaking of rope bed supports reached out at them through every closed door. She pushed open a door and entered a small room close under the unceiled roofing. The bed was pushed under the slant of the roof, which was too low to allow a man to stand. A single window overlooked the stables. Open, the window drew all the odors of ammonia and horse offal mixed with smells of wet leather and grain and animal sweat.

The girl melted tallow in the base of a saucer and then set one of the candles in it on the table beside the bed. Jeff waited, but she did not leave. She blew out the other candle. She set it on the saucer, and then, yawning, she pulled her dress over her head. "What are you doing?" Jeff said.

She wore only a shoulder-to-crotch cotton shift under the dress. She was working it down over her shoulders as she answered. "You might as well have it. You paid for it."

He laughed helplessly, coughing. "So that was the dollar for service?"

Naked, she stood unself-consciously in the lamplight

and scratched at her body. She nodded. "When I looked at you—and that there bulge at your crotch—I was goin' to do it anyhow. But the owner gits mad if I don't collect. Usually, he gits madder if'n he don't git to watch."

Jeff grinned, feeling as if he were spinning deeper into the nightmare. "How does he watch?"

"All these rooms got little holes in the walls," she said in a casual way.

"Well, look. I'm tired. I think I'm getting a cold. Why don't you just keep the service dollar and go on to bed?"

She turned slowly, letting the candle light gambol across the planes and rises of her nudity. "I ain't pretty enough?"

For the first time Jeff looked at her. She was young, still incomplete, but he could not deny she was pretty. But it did not thrill him to be furnished a slut to be used for release and relief as one would use the bed chamber. Besides his head ached, he was exhausted, and by no stretch of the imagination was she Margarith.

She smiled when he hesitated. "You do look plumb tuckered. Why don't I jus' help git you ready for bed?"

Jeff shrugged. He sat down on the bed which sighed under his weight, the ropes whimpering. She knelt before him, and slightly fevered, he watched her full young breasts bobble as she worked off his boots. She pushed him out on his back, unbuttoned his shirt and his fly. His belt was too much for her and he had to reach over sleepily and loosen it. He hoisted his hips and allowed her to pull off his trousers. She removed his shirt, but when she touched at his undershirt, he said, "No. We'll leave that. I'll sleep in it."

She withdrew from the periphery of his vision, and he thought she had gathered up her meager clothing and departed. But then he was aware she'd set the earthenware basin beside him on the mattress. She washed his face, neck, and armpits. He sighed, luxuriating after the long ride, the terrible tensions at The Laurels. It was good to be pampered. He smiled as she removed his underpants and spread his legs to wash his crotch with the damp

266

cloth in her gentle hands. She was gone another moment and then she was kneeling on the floor, washing his feet and ankles. She patted him dry with a clean-smelling towel. He thanked her and turned to plunge into exhausted sleep. He must have dozed off. He came awake with the candle still burning, his legs parted and the naked girl lying with head on his belly, nursing at his glans. He didn't want her. He didn't want any woman. But her mouth was hot and eager, her tongue furious in its hunger. He felt himself respond. He heard her gasp of pleasure as his spike thrust upward, quivering in its rigidity.

He lay fevered, half-waking, half-asleep, but fully roused, as if in the depth of some memorable wet dream. The girl got up and came down upon his upstanding member, working herself slowly, and then frantically. He was aware that she rose four times to wild orgasms, toppled forward, her breasts crushed upon the muscles of his chest, her face pressed in against his throat, until after a few moments rest, she began pumping herself upon him again. Finally, her eager passions, her fiery pudenda, her savage pumping drove everything from his mind. He clutched her, pulled her to him, sank himself as deeply and savagely as he could and they reached a climax together. Afterward she sagged beside him, and he fell asleep almost at once. But when he wakened with the first light of dawn, she was back between his legs, suckling greedily. . . .

He grinned, remembering her. He didn't even know her name. He had given her an extra five dollars and she begged him to take her with him—she would undress him nightly, care for his clothing, cook for him, mix him toddies. She would make herself invaluable—she would be his slave. "I'm tempted," he told her gently. "But I've got to travel fast, and you couldn't keep up."

She stood out in front of the tavern in the hot morning sun and waved good-bye until he was out of sight on the road south.

Rain pelted him several times during the day. He felt

worse even than he had the night before. He pushed his horse, trying to reach New Orleans before illness forced him to hole up somewhere. He felt his only safety would be in the crowded city; he would be assimilated, he would be lost in the crowds, he would be secure. Stopping only to feed, rest, and water his horse, he pushed forward, never looking back across his shoulder, but riding fast.

There was almost a sense of unreality as he rode into an area some miles north of New Orleans which was strangely and strongly familiar to him. He eased up on the horse, sagging in the saddle, looking around.

It was hot and temporarily dry in the mid-afternoon, the sky an azure blue, touched with lamb's-tail clouds and fringed with gray thunderheads on the distant horizon. He was not passing people on the road. This had to mean he was approaching the urban area. It was like *déjà vu*. He had been at this place before and recalled it for some extraordinary reason.

Then he saw the gates of a long avenue of live oaks leading to an imposing villa set well back from the road. The mansion was bright in carefully manicured lawns. It was in the French Colonial style—one-storied, with wide veranda. There was an atmosphere of calm, of restfulness that called to him like a siren's song. It was Poinciana plantation—Helen Latimer's place!

No wonder he recalled it so well! He'd met Helen when her carriage was temporarily stalled up the road. He'd been in a rush to get to New Orleans then—racing from the near-fatal fiasco of his attempted marriage to Minerva George of the Georgics. He'd escaped with his life, only because Minerva had aided him in loosening the shackles and stealing one of her father's best horses. Minerva had learned the truth—Jeff was black. But in the night as he awaited death, she had also learned she loved him too much to let them kill him—even if he was black and lost forever to her. . . .

Thank God he had delayed for a day and a half at Poinciana plantation in Helen Latimer's bed. She had wanted more—her sexual appetites were insatiable—but he had delighted and satisfied her as her husbands, her lovers—paid and unpaying—her black coachman, and colored butler were unable to.

He gazed longingly along the quiet avenue where young black boys slowly swung twig brooms and undisturbed birds chirped. Helen would be pleased to see him. He could count on gourmet meals, hot baths, comfortable beds, and a grateful hostess.

He shivered suddenly. Helen would be too happy to see him. She would devour him in his present fevered condition. He did not believe he could make polite conversation with her, the light pleasantries, the gallant flattery, the gentle lies. Oh, God, it was too formidable a task. Not even hot baths, excellent food, and exotic romancing was worth it. He didn't want to talk with anybody—not even Helen. He sank his heels into the horse's flanks, speeding him past the elegant estate. He rode fast, and he did not look back. . . .

He found the *Vieux Carré* recovering from the panic caused by the plague. The epidemic had claimed victims without distinction of class, status, financial condition, or color. Slaves died, sprawled across swollen, blackened bodies of their masters. Panic-stricken, the city regressed into a jungle, people fighting to escape, looting, pillaging homes as occupants fled or lay dying in their own black vomitus. But finally the horror had subsided. As Bronze John had come, he departed, taking with him a last few victims, like stragglers on a road. . . .

He entered the small Hotel La Dauphine and paid the clerk two dollars for a room. The man studied Jeff nervously. "You ain't got the plague, have you, mister?"

Jeff shook his head. "I don't think so. I just got into town. I caught a hellish cold on the road. I got some fever, but I don't think it's the plague. . . . I'll be all right if I can just sleep a little while. . . ."

"I hope so. We sure hell don't need nobody dying of the plague in this place."

A black youth about seventeen accompanied Jeff to his second floor room. Even fevered as he was, Jeff found the room pleasant. It was at the front, and boasted its own iron-grilled balcony overlooking Dauphine Street. He ordered a bath, and the boy promised to have it sent up. Jeff gave him a dollar and said, "You know where Madame Hortense's Riding Academy is?"

The boy grinned hugely. "Ever'body knows Madame Hortense's Riding Academy, masta. I even knew where it was—'fore I knew *what* it was."

"I want you to go there."

"Yas, suh!" the boy laughed.

Jeff tried to smile with him through his illness. Jesus, blacks had it made, especially here in New Orleans. Most of them lived as freed persons of color. The wages they were paid were criminally unfair, but the blacks had something the white people of the city could never have, they had each other, and they had Congo Square. They really lived on the Square with their hot shrimp creole, their gumbo, pralines, fortune-telling, and easy sexing.

He gave the boy an additional three dollars to buy himself a brief canter at the riding academy—where horses were unknown and the studs were part of the floor show. "You tell Madam Hortense herself, you understand, that Jeff Carson is in town. Tell her . . . I'm a little under the weather . . . but as soon as I'm better, I'll come to see her. Don't you forget that, you hear me?"

"Masta, for what this heah three dollars is gwine buy me, ole Clyde ain't never ever gwine forget *you!* I tells her—to her face. Then I gits some of that good poontang she sells, even if I do have to ride a black girl, on account they lets white men ride black wenches, but black men ain't allowed on no white ladies."

"It never made sense to me either," Jeff said. He removed his shirt and boots and sprawled across his bed. A black boy and tan wench brought hot water for his bath. The wench asked if she should stay to soap his back, but barely aware of her through fevered eyes, Jeff shook his head and sent her away. Locking his door, he bathed, luxuriating in the hot water. Then he fell across his bed. The wind, drenched with jasmine, soothed his body. He fell asleep.

From some incredible distance he heard a faint knocking. Getting up, more fevered than ever, his throat parched and head clogged, he put on his shirt and opened the door. The black youth, Clyde, stood there grinning like a Cheshire Cat. For a moment, in his illness, Jeff didn't even recognize the boy.

"It's me, masta, Clyde. 'Member? You sent me off to get pestered at the Ridin' Academy?"

"Yeah. Oh, yeah. Come on in."

The boy entered and closed the door. He was carrying a folded copy of *The New Orleans Picayune*. Clyde said, "I got my hay raked, masta, a real forkin'!" He laughed. "I plumb grateful."

"Did you see Madame Hortense?" Jeff staggered back to the bed and sank down on it.

"Yas, suh. First, that big fellow, Lancer, he wasn't gwine let me noways near the madame. But I tole him your name. He went up and come back and fetched me in to her! I never seen her before. I never seen no lady like her before!"

"What did she say?"

"She recollect you most warmly, young masta. Say she wondered what happened to you. She say she be looking ahead to your visit. In meantime, she say, she want me to give you this paper. Most important for you to see what is in it."

Jeff nodded. He took the paper, trying to tell himself that despite his fever and chills, it was a good day. He was safely in New Orleans again, out of the reach of Baxter Simon. He had friends here, he would make more friends. To hell with fear and running.

He could barely focus on the newspaper. Reading even the headlines made his head ache, feel as if it would burst, or send his eyeballs erupting from their sockets.

He had turned only half a dozen pages, scanning the headlines, wondering what it was that Madame Hortense was trying to tell him, when he saw it.

The display advertisement was six columns wide, by ten inches, bordered with a quarter-inch black rule. He shivered, suddenly overwhelmed by cold as he read it:

WANTED!
DEAD OR ALIVE!
BRICKTOP—FUGITIVE SLAVE!
ALIAS JEFF CARSON
This mustee—six feet tall, redhaired, white—has brand marks W.O.—for WILLOW OAKS PLANTATION —on his back. Is armed, must be considered dangerous. Passes for white. Any information leading to his apprehension and return should be given to local law authorities, this newspaper, or sent directly to MR. BAXTER SIMON, WILLOW OAKS PLANTATION, CARTHAGE, MISSISSIPPI.
REWARD—$1,000.00
DEAD OR ALIVE!

CHAPTER XXIX

Jeff read the blatant ad again, feeling sickness boil in his stomach. He threw the paper from him and fell on the bed, fevered. Bile gorged upward into his throat. He managed somehow to pull the foul-smelling chamber pot from beneath the bed. He vomited into it.

When he had the strength and will to move again, he got up, yanked the cord summoning room service. The boys and wench who appeared looked at his pallid face, his haggard eyes, closed their noses to the putrid odors of his room, and refused to enter. He begged them to send Clyde.

The black youth entered the room fearfully. He agreed to remove the chamber, to empty and wash and return it, only because he felt a great gratitude and friendship for the young masta, even though he could not hope for a gratuity that would suffice to fight the plague should he become infected.

"Damn you," Jeff said. "I haven't got the plague. I'm sick at my stomach. Get that pot and get out of here—and I hope you spend the rest of your life pounding your fist."

He was asleep when Clyde slipped back into the room and returned the scalded pot beneath the bed. Clyde found some change on the dresser and took it, assuring himself the sick man would want him to have it were he awake, and if he didn't awaken—as Clyde suspected he might not—he would have no need for money anyhow. Considering this, he returned and took another dollar.

Jeff slept fitfully through the night. Asleep, he dreamed of Margarith, and awake he found her haunting him. He could not get her out of his mind. She had trailed him all the long miles from The Laurels. She would follow him as long as bands played love songs, as long as women passed in the street who held their blond heads tilted, as long as he would recall eyes like wet violets, lips bruised and shapely, and tricks from Paris learned in shocking whispers, and practiced in delight and eager passion. Margarith . . . oh, God, Margarith.

He slept and wakened, slept and wakened. He was aware of morning sunlight and afternoon heat. He vaguely smelled the jasmine in early evening; from the streets and courtyards he heard distant laughter. He staggered across the room, managed to get Clyde to approach as near as the corridor door. For five dollars, Clyde brought a bottle of bourbon and a jar of hot gumbo soup. He shoved them inside the door and fled.

Jeff sat shakily on the side of the bed. He opened the whiskey and took a drink. The liquor spewed, sprayed, whirled, and burned in his empty stomach and came gushing back up, bringing vomitus with it. He vomited until he was heaving, dry and agonized.

He decided that maybe the gumbo would line his stomach enough so that he could get the food value and restorative qualities of the liquor to stay down. He went out on the balcony in his underclothes. He sat on a chair and opened the jar of hot gumbo soup. The first spicy aroma almost overwhelmed him, but he persisted. He took one of the large spoons full of the soup. As he took the second, he knew it was a mistake. He dropped the jar to the cement flooring where it smashed. He hung out over the balcony vomiting.

The sight was not unusual enough to stop traffic on Dauphine Street. A few passersby glanced up at him disinterestedly. A boy hawking newspapers tried to sell him one. Jeff pulled himself up, staggered back to bed. He lay across it, afraid he was too ill ever to sleep again. But sounds and smells retreated, and he slept.

When he awoke it was morning and Vincente stood at the foot of his bed, staring down at him. He did not know how long the boy had been there. Then he realized the room had been cleaned, scrubbed, and freshened. He managed to smile, "Where the hell you been? It took you long enough."

"What the hell's the matter with you?" Vincente said.

"Something I caught from white people," Jeff said in bitter self-deprecation. "It's called heartbreak."

Vincente shook his head, nostrils distended. "Sure is messy."

"Sure as hell is." Jeff smiled—and began to recover. . . .

It was not that easy, or all that sudden. Vincente was a good and patient nurse. He spent part of each afternoon at Madame Hortense's Riding Academy. But he usually waited until Jeff was asleep—or pretending to sleep—before he took off. He came home each evening, full of gossip, straight from the horse's mouth.

One afternoon, he returned with Dominique You in tow. The vast-bellied man seemed more corpulent than ever, too gross now even to attempt the role of Falstaff, though his laughter boomed through the walls and shook his huge body. His black eyes, deep set in that round red face, darted, taking in the surroundings.

"We were afraid the plague had you," You said.

"We?" Jeff said.

Dominique You laughed. "Over at madame's Riding Academy. As you know, I am her most frequent visitor when I am in town, though as a customer, I pay only for the floor shows starring that black sex machine named Lancer. I can get a charge watching him satisfy half a dozen nymphs and stand rigid as a flagpole waiting for more. But I don't believe in paying for something I can't use anymore, eh?"

"How are things—down at Barataria?" Jeff asked hesitantly.

Dominique You shrugged. "I would lie if I said we didn't miss you down there, Jeff. You had earned a real place in the organization, boy. I reckon it'll always be hard to find young men who are as honest as you, and as smart. Honest and smart don't always go together. A young fellow is smart, he spends most of his time planning to make a quick killing—at the expense of his boss. I could tell 'em, if that boss is Lafitte, they're going to end up on the wrong end of a killing. But they're too clever to listen. You weren't like that . . . we miss you."

"I'd like to be back," Jeff said.

Dominique You shook his head. "Would do you no good to return. We gave it a lot of thought—the pros and cons of sending you away from Barataria. . . . Lafitte thinks you would cost the organization more than you would deliver . . . as long as he thinks that, you'd have no future with us."

"I know that. But I must find something—and I want something that will pay me well."

"Of course you do." Dominique You nodded his balding head. "Maybe I can tout you on to something.

Not much happens in Louisiana that I don't hear of—ahead of the newspapers."

"I know slaves best. But it worries me. What would Lafitte say? If I'm competition—with knowledge I learned at Barataria?"

You laughed. "Lafitte would say, go with his blessings. If you shipped in slaves, he might blackbird you. But that would in no way be personal—it happens wherever a Lafitte ship encounters another slaver. But as for the rest of it, he would bless you. We knew when René Beluche taught you that we could not remove that knowledge if the day came when you left Barataria. . . . I admit, we never expected you to learn so much, so well. But we could not be fools enough to expect you to discard what you have learned."

"Thank you." Jeff said. "I don't know what I'll do. But in order to get along, for a while it will have to do with selling and buying slaves—since that's all I know."

"Good for you, my boy. Meantime, I'll keep me weather eye out for some good opportunity. As for immediate advice, why don't you let your mustache remain when you finally shave after your illness? It's black. It makes you look older—it will help until people forget that advertisement and the thousand-dollar reward."

When Dominique You was gone, his gleaming carriage rattling along Dauphine Street like a solitary parade, Jeff pulled himself out of bed. He went across the room and peered at his bearded face in the shadowy mirror.

Dominique You was right. A mustache would make him look older. It would afford a good disguise. It added a touch of class, a certain dash, a bit of élan. Yes, a mustache would do something for him. He had always been accepted for what he was not—a young Southern gentleman. His good looks, his tailored clothing, and the favorable impression he made with his easy smiling and perfect manners had helped him pass not only as a white man but one of the superior class. Well dressed, he was certain he could go anywhere in New Orleans with impunity. Few people were going to associate the well-groomed, well-fed young planter-type with a fugitive slave named Bricktop.

He laughed, watching the reflection of his smile that had charmed so many females right out of their pants. The diamond-encrusted cross glittered on his chest. His good luck talisman! He would become rich. That's what the white man's world was, wasn't it—a land of opportunity? Well, he'd grab that opportunity whenever it showed the tip of its head! He'd use any white man—or white woman—in any way he could to further himself. Damn 'em. They had all the odds in their favor—let them beware! No more fortunes delivered to deserving widows without a full cut off the top! Beware, you white bastards. The whites misused the slaves. In his way, he'd get revenge on the whole white race for the misery of the blacks. . . .

Madame Hortense, proprietress of the Riding Academy, finished off her morning soufflé and cafe brûlot. She wore a pale lavender negligee and was heavily made up. Her brilliant red hair was lacquered into place and her fabulous jewelry sparkled on her fingers and wrists.

When a knock sounded at her door, she said, "Come." She smiled, saying it—the magic word in this place. She had opened her academy with herself and one other girl to supply male demands. Now she had dozens of girls, fresh young virgins coming in from the rural areas all the time —blacks, whites, Creoles, lovely tawny quadroons. She herself no longer indulged in sex except for pleasure. She'd seen so much, done so much, that only extremes of perversity aroused her anymore. Perversity—and the sight of a true and manly staff such as the boy entering her room possessed. Lancer was the son of a bozal off a Cuban slave ship. But he was handsome, chocolate brown, with thick, bared chest and exceptional genitalia. The only comparable such equipment she had seen on the youth Bricktop—the fugitive slave who called himself Jeff Carson. She sighed, pushed all pleasant reveries from her mind and said, "Yes, Lancer. What is it?"

"Hit's that gen'mun from Willow Oaks, Missy." Lancer winced faintly. "De one that's always a-wantin' to finger me, and tryin' to buy me to take to he place to stud fo' him—de one wid dem mean eyes. Dat Masta Baxter Simon, ma'am. He say he wants to see you."

"All right. Send Estelle in and tell Mr. Simon I'll see him in five minutes."

She used the five minutes to renew her makeup and to ascertain that not one brassy hair was out of place, that her eyes were correctly shadowed for morning, that her gown was free of wrinkles.

When Lancer ushered in the swarthy, well-built young planter, Madame Hortense smiled and extended her bejeweled fingers for his awkward kiss.

"I do hope you recall me, ma'am . . . Bax Simon of Willow Oaks plantation, up Carthage way."

"Oh, I do recall you. One of the new slave breeders. I recall you once pestered—as I believe you so quaintly call it—a young quadroon of mine named Chloe. You were so taken with her, you wanted to buy her. You also wanted to buy Lancer. I can save you a great deal of time. Chloe met with a tragic accident two years ago, and Lancer still is not for sale, at any price." She laughed. "Now, what did you want to see me about?"

"Got a couple things on my mind, ma'am. . . . First one is easy to talk about. I'm chasing a nigger. His real name is Bricktop. He's a slave of mine. A mustee. Goes under the name of Jeff Carson—"

"I believe I saw your advertisement."

"Yes. Well, I had him. But the devil clubbed me with his gun butt and managed to escape."

Madame Hortense concealed her faint smile behind her bejeweled hand. "And what has this to do with me, Mr. Simon?"

"I figger this nigger ran south to New Orleans. Just a hunch. You see, he was up north where he was safe. But he didn't like it up there. He wanted to come back south."

"Maybe he has a secret wish to die."

"What?"

"Nothing. Go ahead. You think he's here in New Orleans?"

"Yes'm, I do. Got lots of good reasons for thinking it. But if he is here, he'll be looking for a whore—and since you got the finest place in town—and he likes the best of everything, likes to live high on the hog, he does, like he was as human as you and me. He's got to be considered dangerous. And he's as horny as he is dangerous. I wanted to ask you to be on the lookout for him."

"I certainly shall look out for him," Madame Hortense promised. "Now, what was the important matter?"

"Important? Why, ma'am, gittin my hands on that thieving, sneaking, runaway nigger is the most important thing in my life. . . . This other matter, hit's a bit more personal, and I don't know if I can discuss it with you—a white lady and all."

She smiled at the backcountry aristocrat. "There's nothing on earth you could say to me, Mr. Simon, that I have not heard a hundred times before."

"Yes'm." Simon's face colored. "That's why I wanted to come straight to you. Well, ma'am, it's like this here. Tell you the straight truth, though I been married once—to a Christian white lady—I never cared to bed down with her, nor nary other white woman. Somethin' plain repellin' about all that pale white skin, if you'll forgive me, ma'am. . . . It never mattered before. When I come here, you always had some nice tan or chocolate gal that I could pester. No worry about her bein' white or pure or nothin'. . . . Got so, I'm skairt I can't ever even do it with a white lady . . . you know?"

"You simply can't get a hard-on with a white woman?"

Simon blushed furiously, looking ill and shamed. "To me a white lady is almost as sacred as the mother of dear Jesus. You know? Doin' something carnal with them . . . I just cain't do it."

"As long as there are dark-skinned and russet beauties," the *madame* shrugged, "I'm afraid I don't see your problem as very serious."

"No ma'am. Not until recent . . . Sunppose I did take it in my head to marry again? I'd have to marry a white lady. . . . But suppose I jus' couldn't force myself to—do it—even on our wedding night? . . . She might expect that."

"She might." *Madame*'s smile was dry, twisted.

"I wondered if you—"

"I don't—pester—with customers anymore, sir."

"Oh Gawd, *madame!* I had no such carnal thought! I figgered maybe you had some white woman here that you could get to help me—help me get that sick feeling out of my mind? I figure if I could force myself to do it with a white lady—even a paid whore—I might be all right, in case I do ever marry up again."

Madame Hortense rang for Lancer. He must have been loitering just outside her door—he did this sometimes when he was nervous about her safety—for he entered almost immediately. *Madame* said, "Is Lou Ella busy, Lancer?"

"No'm, not just this minute, she ain't."

"I want you to take Mr. Simon up to her. Now, Baxter, you just relax. It's going to be all right. You explain to Lou Ella, just as you have to me. . . . She will help you. Or," she laughed and kissed the tips of her fingers," you can't be helped on this earth. . . ."

Mr. Baxter Simon had been gone from her chambers no more than five minutes when another knock disturbed Madame Hortense's morning meditations and money counting.

"Damn," she said when Lancer appeared in her doorway. "What is it now?"

"Masta Jeff Carson, Missy. He out here."

Madame Hortense chewed at her rouged underlip. "Get him in here, quickly."

"Yas'm." Lancer went out the door, opened it again immediately, and ushered in Jeff Carson. Madame Hortense caught her breath, shocked at how pale and thin the youth looked. "I do hope you haven't lost weight

280

everywhere," she said, making that word a heavy *double entendre*, and smiling.

Jeff kissed her, and she clung to him for a moment. "I don't know," he said. "I fell in love—and she rejected me. It's a little hard to get over."

"Best way to forget one woman is with three women," *madame* said.

Jeff grinned, teasing, "With you watching secretly?"

"You wouldn't deny an old woman her only pleasure, would you?" She tapped at his arm. "Did Lancer warn you? Baxter Simon is here—in this house. He's with Lou Ella right now, trying to overcome his fear and revulsion of white women's nakedness."

Jeff winced. "So he followed me straight here, huh? Didn't fool him much. I guess he's lived with slaves so long and so intimately that whatever they do, he's seen it done a dozen times before."

"I like your mustache," Madame Hortense said. "It should help you fool people looking for Bricktop—the slave. It wouldn't fool Baxter Simon, of course, but should deceive any stranger into believing you a handsome young gentleman."

"I hope so." Jeff glanced at himself in one of the *madame*'s dozen mirrors. "It was Dominique You's suggestion that I cultivate it."

"And a good suggestion . . . We all love you, and wish the best for you, Jeff." She studied him. "And I have a suggestion. Why don't you dye your hair black. With black hair and a black mustache, you might even fool old Bax Simon, for a few minutes anyhow."

"That's a good idea. Wonderful," Jeff said. "But how could I dye my hair black?"

"My dear boy." *Madame* laughed and rang for her beauticians. "How do you suppose I keep *my* hair a flaming red—as old as I am? You'll walk out of here with black hair in less than two hours. . . . But I don't think you should walk out. I think you should honor my offer. Three women will drive one woman out of your mind every time. They'll keep you so occupied you can't think. . . ."

Screams broke across her words and brought the *madame* up straight on her chaise longue. She grabbed the cord, ringing for Lancer. But before she could pull it, Lou Ella threw open the door and burst in raging, screaming out her hatred. The *madame*'s voice lashed out, "Lou Ella. Control yourself! What in hell is the matter with you?"

"I'll tell you what's the matter. It's that stupid backwoods rube you sent in to me. Goddamn him, he threw up on me—just laid there and vomited all over me . . . son of a bitch, I oughta kill him . . . but first, Hortense, I wanta know—is this your idea of some kind of fucking joke?"

CHAPTER XXX

Madame Hortense's suggestion that he bed down three of her choicest quadroon wenches to drive from his mind the anguished memory of the blonde he'd lost, won Jeff's serious consideration. It was easy to believe that *madame* had accumulated all truths about life over years of dealing with people from every strata of human society—at their most vulnerable. She was venerable without being fusty. Her business, associations, and interests kept her blood surging, her eyes and ears alert, her mind youthfully receptive. As to her actual age, she was so thickly plastered with mascara, rouge, and powders that one could not even hazard a guess. Her figure was laced fiercely in corseting and never permitted to sag. Jewels glittered at her ear lobes, her breasts, throat, wrists, and fingers. She had been sole proprietress, and therefore mother confessor, of her famous Riding Academy for more years than she'd permit recounted in her presence. And there was in her faintly accented and cultured voice that charm and clarity which disavowed her vulgar finery and brassy red hair and hinted at a mysterious past in which she may well have been a fascinating lady of quality. He trusted her suggestions. He had been ill and alone for a long time. Though he feared nothing could make him forget Margarith, he was forced to admit he was as horny as hell. . . .

It titillated *madame*'s sharply honed sense of drama to have the dogged hunter Bax Simon and his unyielding quarry Bricktop under the same roof. With Lancer as near to her as the bell-cord in her fingers, she was assured the dramatics would remain under control. But there was always the thrilling possibility that something might go wrong, that they might enter the same doorway, meet in a corridor, or somehow encounter each other.

She was not sadistic—at least not in a way in which Bricktop's suffering would amuse or enthrall her—but she admitted to that delicious feminine trait of finding eroticism in danger. When Bricktop's auburn hair had been dyed by *madame*'s own personal beautician to a Creole ebony, she spirited him to a room on the third floor where a huge bed and three quadroon succubi awaited him, and where, through cleverly concealed louvers, she could watch the performance. It took promise of quite extraordinary erotic thrills to get *madame* off her chaise longue these days, a *partouse par excellence* to persuade her to climb a flight of stairs, a sexual circus of exotic proportions to please her once she had made these incredible sacrifices of her creature comforts.

Madame was not disappointed in the carnal display, but Jeff was. It was not the sexual and mental release he had anticipated. It was fun—the three minxes were proficient, expert, and once they saw his audacious eminence, anxious to please. Further, *madame* had not exaggerated. The tawny quadroon girls would have been choice in any seraglio. They were young and fresh, but in no sense virginal. They sought to rouse him with their hands, nipples, tongues, and toes. Rousing him, they attempted to destroy him through sheer physical assault. But it was the girls, the professionals, who whimpered and sobbed out in delight.

Jeff was returned to Madame Hortense's private suite and into her august presence, whipped, paler than ever, almost staggering with fatigue. But there remained in his eyes the haunted look of the desolated man —the anguish of loss, rare in the male, but scarcely even understood by the female of the species, who being hardier, tougher, more pragmatic, always keeps open secret exits even when she dedicates herself totally to one lover.

"I hope you enjoyed yourself," *madame* said. Her eyes glittered like the diamonds and sapphires illuminating her body, and she licked the tip of her tongue across her murrey lips, eyeing the slender young stud. Oh, God, if only she were two weeks younger!

Jeff laughed at her. "You know whether I enjoyed myself or not. You watched every stroke, and you know you did."

Madame shrugged, neither denying nor confirming his accusation. After all, it was *her* academy. "I'm going to have a good hard talk with my girls. They are *required* to give more pleasure than they receive, and I don't think it worked that way today."

"Don't blame them," Jeff said with a faint smile. "If *you* enjoyed it, what the hell?"

"I never stayed in business all these years by enjoying it, my dear boy. Though I *did* enjoy it."

"I'll bet you'd still enjoy it." His grin challenged and charmed her.

She laughed at him "I refuse to remove my corset to find out, you young pillager."

Jeff kissed her lightly. "Is it safe for me to leave—concealed behind a dashing mustache and Creole black hair?"

"Yes. Quite safe. We think we have bought you at least temporary safety—from a direct attack by Baxter Simon, at least."

"I thank you, with all my heart—and I forgive you for watching me fuck."

"I watched you *get* fucked, my dear boy," she said. "You put neither your heart nor your mind to it—and it was still a better *partouse* than my patrons pay hundreds to see." She reached out, closed her bejeweled fingers on his arm. "Dominique You says you are looking for some enterprise which might offer you a challenge—and a chance at riches."

"Yes. I believe I am as smart as any rich man I've ever known. Maybe not as lucky to be born to wealth. But I have energy and ambition—yes, I am looking for something."

"There is this place," she said. "I have never even entertained the notion of taking a partner. In fact, I have *resisted*. I have opposed force. But I would sell you half an interest in an enterprise that would supply your physical needs, indulge your favorite hobby, and make you a millionaire many times over in a few years." When he hesitated, she shrugged. "I don't need your answer now. I see in your face, you want some enterprise with *respectability*. Though I fail to see what is more *respectable* than catering to the needs of repressed, deprived, and thwarted men. I find it almost an holy crusade, eh?"

"Almost," he said, smiling.

"Ah, but you, young bucko! You must *impress* someone who would not be all that impressed with a millionaire whoremaster!"

"I don't know what I am going to do," he said. "Only that I am going to be rich. As rich as any white man. Rich enough I never have to fear *any* man again."

She smiled. "Still, for now you must be careful. We have removed Bax Simon from the scene—for the moment. While he was still weak and sick from his vomiting and ashamed of his unmanliness, I gave it to him straight. I warned him that I could swear never to let a word of what happened between him and Lou Ella out of the Riding Academy. I would never speak of it. I would forbid that it be mentioned. But I told him I had gossipy black servants, and that if he stayed in town now and was taunted by friends, and acquaintances, or enemies up around the St. Louis Hotel, he might *never* overcome his fear and revulsion of white women. . . . But, I suggested, if he went back to Willow Oaks plantation up at Carthage—and went immediately, so the gossip spread and died before he returned to New Orleans with his next coffle—and if he practiced sex with every white woman he could find in Mississippi, he *might* cure himself of this fearful sickness. He *thanked* me for the kindness and wisdom of my suggestion! He was too ill and too shamed to protest, and so while he was in this sad shape, confused and uncertain, I ordered dear Lancer to escort him in my own carriage down to the foot of Canal Street. There, Lancer was to book Mr. Simon passage north on a Mississippi night boat. Poor old Baxter! He'll be back home in Carthage before he fully comprehends what has happened to him."

Madame Hortense accepted Jeff's grateful kiss and then settled back, laughing, on her chaise longue. It had been an interesting morning. She felt better than she had for years.

Jeff walked out of Madame Hortense's Riding Academy convinced he was entering a new world, with a new look, a new identity, but with the same old driving purpose to thrust himself to the top of the white man's realm. He felt tired, shaky, and exhausted, but never more secure. He determined to mumble his surname as Laforche in the immediate future. As Smith was common across the country, so was Laforche an ordinary name in the Creole parishes contiguous to Orleans. Thomas Jefferson Laforche, suh. He would evade the question about similarly named acquaintances by admitting that his father had emigrated from the area to northern Mississippi before he was born. Hell, this much might even be true. A black-haired, mustached Creole named Laforche looked older, more elegant—and certainly in no way resembled Brick-top, fugitive nigger.

He found the world a better-looking place even than when he had entered the *madames*'s front door. Patches of sky showed cerulean blue beyond the overhanging balconies, the high courtyard walls, the tile roofs. Within this new periphery, the haunting memory of Margarith persisted, the gentle blue of her eyes, the fragrant texture of her blond hair, the smooth rise of her breasts, the exciting warmth of her accommodating body. But he had walked out of that world in which Margarith existed. He would not look back.

He strode through the narrow streets, past the shops and the street vendors hawking their shrimp and scampi and peanuts and pralines. He walked into the hotel room to find Vincente dallying with the black chambermaid. In fact, Vincente had the wench by the ears, on her knees between his legs. Not recognizing the mustachioed, black-haired Jeff at once, he leaped guiltily to his feet, certain he was being accosted by the girl's jealous lover.

Jeff laughed at him and insisted that he continue with his performance. The wench, her bodice open and her dark breasts exposed, her mouth bruised, objected to taking it in her mouth with a gentleman looking on. "Do it," Jeff told her. He brought a gold eagle—worth about twenty dollars, which exceeded the girl's value on the vendue table—from his pocket and placed it in her hand. "This is yours—if you earn it."

She smiled, nodded, and reached for Vincente again. Watching them, Jeff felt himself aroused as he had not been by the three quadroon beauties who excelled this wench in every way. Growing hard, he locked the corridor door, removed his boots, trousers, and outer shirt. He sat on the side of the bed, vicariously enjoying the fury with which Vincente thrust himself between her lips.

It was a brief, violent storm and Vincente slumped back in his chair. Jeff said to the girl, "Come here." She looked at him, eyes widening at the sight of his unsheathed sword and came to him on her knees, intent upon only one thing, earning that gold eagle she clutched tightly in her fist. . . .

Jeff lazed around the hotel and the *Vieux Carre* restaurants for the next week. He read the newspapers, the reports of cotton futures, the lumber sales, the shipping of tar and hides, the auction of blacks. There was potential for wealth here; he had only to find that enterprise into which he could pour his whole heart, mind, and furious energy. Meantime, he saw no point in pushing his luck while Simon's bold ad was current. But his mirror assured him he bore faint resemblance to a red-haired runaway nigger. He did have the dashing elegance of a young Creole fop, and finally he decided to take the bull by the horns.

Jeff could not deny a sense of fear as he sauntered uptown to the St. Louis Hotel. Here was the center of New Orleans business, trade, and social worlds. Here gathered the slave buyers, sellers, and traders from all across the South. He dressed impeccably, trimmed his mustache and brushed his hair. He set his Panama planter's hat at a jaunty angle and walked into the morning sunlight with an audacity he certainly did not feel.

The familiar overhanging iron balconies and narrow streets seemed to press down upon him, to crowd him on the banquettes, and he found himself nervously studying faces of every passing stranger. He attracted no overt attention, either on the streets or in the lobby or bar of the swank St. Louis Hotel. Escorted women did glance admiringly under lowered lashes; there was envy in the faces of less physically endowed young aristocrats whiling away their leisure in the bar.

He entered the saloon off the lobby of the St. Louis Hotel and walked directly to the bar without looking left or right. He ordered a gin and tonic and sipped it. When his eyes became accustomed to the cavernous darkness of the large room after the metallic sunlight of the street, Jeff saw the place was crowded with men. Instinctively he knew most of them were present for the afternoon auction of prime-quality slaves. Convinced that Baxter Simon would have no animals on the vendue tables, he relaxed and tried to enjoy his drink.

He drifted into a conversation with a medium-tall, stocky-chested man who drank his whiskey straight and then chased it by throwing his head back and swallowing half a glass of iced water.

The man mentioned his name but Jeff missed it in the subdued hubbub of the room. Since he mumbled his own assumed alias, he did not pursue the matter. The man was a Georgia cotton planter who expected to diversify by raising blacks for sale. "The cost of everything forces me to it," the man said in a syrupy thick accent. "It's a case of push coming to shove. Now the folks really makin' the money these days are them that are sellin' slaves to other folks. You agree, suh?"

"I agree entirely, sir," Jeff said. He bought his new friend a drink, watched him down it, shudder, and then follow it with a gulp of water. The planter insisted upon buying Jeff a drink and then invited him into the restaurant to lunch as his guest. Jeff accepted, feeling this was taking his first small step in his exploitation of white men. It was a long way from a lunch to riches, but it was also a long way from the fugitive fleeing of a ragged slave boy. Hell, you had to start somewhere.

"Want my mind clear," the Georgia planter said. "Picked me out some prime specimens to bid in. Want you to look at them with me, see you don't agree I've made some fine choices. Was hopin' there'd be some Willow Oaks stock up for auction, but the quality that is here appears prime."

When the auction was announced, almost the entire company in the bar and restaurant crowded into the hotel ballroom. On the band dais, tables and display space had been set up. The Georgia planter remained silent until the fifth buck was marched in and placed on the block.

"Look at that buck. A real stud, I'd swear. What you say, suh?"

"I want you to forgive me, but you did ask my opinion," Jeff said.

"What? Oh, yes, suh. Yoah opinion is jus' what I want." The planter was flushed, troubled. "What's wrong with that buck?"

"Nothing, probably, if you want a good field hand. He looks strong, and his eyes are clear. From here, his teeth look all right. I suppose you checked for piles, whip weals, or other blemishes?"

"He ain't got none of those," the man was practically whispering, overwhelmed with doubt and admiration for Jeff's apparent knowledge.

"If there's anything I know, it's nigger flesh," Jeff said. "I can tell you what to buy—for what purpose. Now this boy is no good to you as a stud. He's too black, too ugly. See the slanting forehead, the ridged brows, the out-shot jaw. He's a bozal. I don't want to tout you off of him, but he wouldn't give you salable suckers no matter what wench you mated him to."

"Oh, lord," the planter whispered, drawing a line through a name on his pad. He winced as the buck was knocked down for almost $1,500. He said, testily, "He brought a good price for a bozal."

"There are plenty of men here who buy in the excitement and fever and competition of bidding," Jeff said. "They count on that for their profit. And there are plenty of men who look at a buck's thick chest and wide shoulders and decide he'd make an excellent stud . . . but there's a lot more to it. The best prices you'll get are for the light-skinned fancies. If you're breeding slaves, you want handsome bucks and pretty wenches—not the thick, ugly blacks you'd get from that boy. He might be great, intelligent, and worthy, but he's sure hell ugly. And you don't want that in a stud black."

The planter fell silent, torn between a desire to utilize the knowledge Jeff seemed to possess, and the fear that he was being gulled by some stranger who liked to sound important but was full of hot air. After Jeff disapproved two more of the selections the planter had made after careful inspection the day before, he grew angry and remote. But when Jeff suggested that he bid on a slender, tan youth that he had passed up the day before with only a glance, the planter made his first bid and stuck with it until he won his prize for $900. "You got yourself one hell of a bargain," Jeff told him. "Sure, the boy's slender. He's only about seventeen—at the most. But look at the bone structure. He's going to be big, without being stocky or gross. He's got good coordination, and he's a good-looking boy. You buy a lovely wench and they'll give you salable suckers."

The planter grinned happily and exhaled, relieved. He wanted a parcel of ten or twelve bucks and wenches as starters. By four that afternoon, Jeff had helped him select a gaggle of blacks that had the planter giggling and talking to himself with delight. Jeff warned him there was many a slip between the auction and action; he had to transport these blacks to Georgia, keep them well, healthy, reasonably content and not allowed to become too attached to each other. "Yes, suh!" the planter said. "I can handle all that. I feel like I made a real start here today, thanks to you, mistuh. How much I owe you?"

"You don't owe me anything," Jeff said, knowing damned well he was going to be paid for his knowledge as he once had been paid for his favors by grateful women. "It amused me to keep my hand in. I was happy to help you—and I believe I really have."

"I *know* you have!" the planter chortled. "Hell, I can't wait to git them bucks and wenches back home to Georgia and paired off. Now, le'ssee. I spent $20,000 here today. I could've spent 30—and come out a loser. Thanks to you, I'm on my way to a successful trade in blacks. Even a commission of 10 percent hardly covers what I owe you. But I insist you take $2,000—and my eternal gratitude."

Jeff accepted the planter's $2,000 and eternal gratitude. The Georgian wrung his hands in parting and then hurried off to collect his herd and prepare to ship them east.

Jeff smiled to himself and walked into the bar. He was on his way. He did know slaves. He hated to see the blacks on the vendue table, but his hating their mistreatment wasn't going to stop it. Somebody was going to profit. Men were growing rich. By God, he might as well be one of them.

He pushed his way between the tables, headed toward the bar when someone behind him at the bar yelled, "Hey, Bricktop!"

The words struck Jeff like stones hurled against his back. He did not stop or even betray by any overt sign that he had heard the raucous voice, but he felt his spine turn to ice. He kept walking, but he felt as if every eye in the big room was fixed accusingly on him, as if they all knew he wasn't Thomas Jefferson Laforche at all, but was a runaway nigger, masquerading among them as a peer, an equal, as a white man.

CHAPTER XXXI

Jeff sauntered toward the bar, not betraying by the least flinching of his body that he'd heard the man yell his slave name. But the few feet between the white-draped tables to the mahogany bar was the longest distance he ever traversed. Time slowed, stood still; he felt as if he were plodding knee-deep through bayou mud.

He leaned against the bar, ordered a Saratoga—gin and tonic water. Drink in hand, he casually turned to survey the room. He brushed lightly at his mustache with the back of his index finger.

He stared down into the flushed face of a slender, almost effeminate young cotton-country aristocrat. The fellow had bounded through the crowded bar in Jeff's wake, yapping at him like a pampered poodle. The youth looked to be in his early twenties. He was smartly outfitted in an expensive custom-made shirt, with monogram, ruffled front and cuffs, tailored suit of forest green, and planter's hat to complement his costume. The manly duds served only to accent his lack of manliness; he did not look virile, he looked slight, short, and pretty in an offensive way. His hand-tooled boots gleamed dully, his manicured hands looked as soft as a girl's. His light brown hair, already thinning on top, grew thick down over his collar. His features were delicately hewn, his small mouth petulant, his patrician nostrils flared, his astigmatic eyes glittering. He was trembling with rage. He was also intoxicated.

"Why didn't you answer me, boy?" The young dandy spoke so loudly that conversations died, noise faded into silence, as all eyes fixed on him and Jeff.

Jeff had met so many of these insolent, haughty young cotton aristocrats that he could burlesque their mannerisms perfectly. He gazed in chilled hauteur along his nose at the green-suited popinjay. "Do I know you?" he inquired.

"Maybe you don't," the boy shouted. "But I know you. I am Antoine Belmare, of Belmare Place, Mississippi, suh, and I count Mr. Baxter Simon as one of my dearest friends."

"I am not Mr. Simon, sir," Jeff said in that chilled, unrelenting tone.

The boy almost choked on his own bile. "Of course you're not—You're his slave—Bricktop, his mustee slave!

I've heard him describe you often enough. I know you. I know Baxter almost caught you at The Laurels. Besides, I met you. Up at Miss Lissa Malraux's home. Foxmoor. I saw you there. I know you!"

Jeff took a long sip of his tonic water. The very insolence of his action nearly unmanned young Antoine. Jeff glanced beyond the youth, pointedly staring over his head as if Belmare were beneath his notice. "If there are any of you gentlemen who admit friendship with this—with M'sieur Antoine Belmare, I suggest you remove him from my presence before I forget that I, at least, am a gentleman."

"You! A gentleman? A bastard mustee. A nigger. That's what you are."

Jeff looked around one more time. "Are there none of you who will remove this—person—from my presence? I came in here for a quiet tonic. If the room has become so low and vile as to permit trash among us, then I for one shall discontinue my long association. . . ."

Some of the raw threat under the chilled words ate through the alcoholic fog numbing Belmare's brain. He shifted his jacket up on his narrow shoulders, glanced over his shoulder. When he found three young men several paces behind him, unmoving, unsmiling, he was drunk enough to draw reassurance from their support.

"I challenge you, Bricktop!" Antoine said, voice rising, fluting. "Oh, your hair is dyed black, you're wearing fine clothes, but underneath you're a branded, runaway nigger. . . . If you're not, sir, I challenge you to remove your jacket and shirt and show us your back."

The three men pressed slightly closer now, or perhaps they were pushed nearer by the men crowding around.

When Jeff did not move, Antoine cried out, "Any of you gentlemen care to bet? I say this is a runaway nigger named Bricktop, masquerading among us as a human, a white man. I've got $3,000 says he has the letters *W.O.*—for Willow Oaks—branded on his back. Who'll join me? Who'll demand this man prove his identity?"

Several of the men spoke among themselves. They

pressed nearer, watching Jeff. Jeff finished off his drink, set the glass on the top of the damp, gleaming bar. He gazed with contempt at Belmare. He said, "I owe you nothing. No explanation. No proof. I say I am Thomas Jefferson Laforche. I say I do not have to prove it."

"Then we'll prove it," Antoine shouted. "We'll tear his shirt off."

"I have a better plan," Jeff said. He lowered his voice and studied his nails. "But it will cost you money. It will cost you gentlemen $10,000 to see my back." He laughed, looking around.

"Done!" Antoine Belmare shouted. "I'll put up 3,000! Who'll join me?"

Jeff's chilled, calm voice cut across Belmare's. "One moment, sir. There is one more proviso. This is the supreme insult of my life. I'm tolerating you, you simple-minded toad, only to prove I at least am a gentleman. When the $10,000 has been placed on this bar, I'm quite willing to remove my shirt. But . . ." his voice hardened, raking across the men before him. "Each man who joins you, M'sieur Belmare, in putting money on that bar, also joins you in this insult to my dear, beloved mother, God rest her soul. And so, each of you will—when I have proved my gentility, my origin, my patience with gutter trash—you will prove your courage by meeting me—in-dividually—in St. Anthony's Gardens where you will defend your so-called honor, or die. Go ahead, gentlemen, I invite you, place your money on the bar."

Even those men who had pressed closest, now retreated as much as six or seven paces. Suddenly, Antoine Belmare found himself isolated in a cleared space. He shook visibly, unable to retreat or advance. He glanced at the three young friends who had urged him into this adventure. They had moved back and were lost in the ring of on-lookers.

"Go ahead, sir," Jeff said. "Place your money on the bar."

"Well. Now wait—just a minute."

"No, sir. I'm not waiting a minute. Not a breath longer.

You have insulted my family, my mother, and me. I can endure an insult, by considering its source. But my dear mother can no longer defend herself from the insults of trash like you, and so I must act in her behalf."

"Now—just a minute, M. Laforche! There could be some mistake!" Antoine cried.

"There may be. But you must pay—to find that out."

"No. I apologize. Perhaps I was wrong."

"It is too late to apologize, my frail friend. Either you put your money on the bar, or you go on the bar yourself. Now which is it?"

Antoine retreated a step. "Now—you keep your hands off me. These men won't—"

Jeff laughed. "I invite any of them—individually or collectively—to join you in this insult to my parents." He waited, looking around. "Your money, sir."

Antoine cried out involuntarily. He heeled about to run, but Jeff snagged his shirtfront in his fist and hoisted him, kicking and wailing, straight up off the floor. Driving his left fist up under Antoine's crotch, he hefted the youth up on the bar. Antoine was crying openly, begging someone to help him. Embarrassed for him, the men in the crowd turned away. He sobbed, staring at them helplessly. "What can I say?" he wailed. "What do you want me to say?"

"You've said too goddamn much, you little prick," Jeff said. "Haven't you even common sense enough to understand that? That there is *nothing* you can say that would remove the smear upon my mother's name? What you are going to do, you little bastard, is wipe that smear off the floor of this room, so that you and these men will never forget it is wiped forever away."

Antoine only shook his head, crying helplessly.

Jeff caught the boy's green jacket and ripped it off his back. Holding it before him, he tore it down its seam in his fists and flung the parts to the floor. Crying, Antoine gestured helplessly. "I've got money, take it. Take all of it."

"Every word you speak adds to your infamy," Jeff said.

"Are you so crass, so low, so vile, you believe you can *buy* back an insult to my mother?"

"Oh, no, suh. No. I'm sorry I said that. I regret it."

"I'm sure you do. But it's also too late for regret, m'sieur." He caught the youth's monogrammed shirt at the collar and ripped it downward, jerking it from his belt and off his thin shoulders. Then, before Antoine could move, he clapped his palm behind the youth's head and slapped him off the bar so he sprawled prostrate on the floor.

Antoine lay cringing on the floor, like a hound expecting to be kicked.

Jeff said, "Now, *m'sieur*, you have your shirt and your jacket as rags to wipe up the insult against my mother. You will wipe your way across this room, across that lobby, down the steps, and out into the street. From there, you'll go your way, but I promise you this. If I ever encounter you again—anywhere—you shall eat your own teeth."

Antoine got up to his hands and knees, clutching the torn fabrics in his trembling hands, trying to smile through his terror. "No, suh. I vow to you. You'll never be troubled with me again, suh. Nevah. I sweah."

"I've warned you, Belmare. You've already talked too much. Now get to scrubbing."

Antoine nodded and once started nodding, looked as if he could not stop.

He began to scrub furiously with his shirt. The men who had laughed and drank with him earlier turned their backs and moved aside, making a wide path for him to crawl through. Crying, sniffling, but not daring to stop or look back, Belmare worked his way across the bar and through the lobby.

Jeff watched him a moment, then shrugged, shoved his way roughly through the onlookers and chose a table near the wall. A waiter brought him a gin and tonic, but for some moments Jeff sat, not touching his drink. He was too filled with fury to keep the liquor down, and his hands shook so badly that he held them in his lap under the table.

Gradually, some semblance of normalcy returned to the room. Men crowded at the bar, sat at the tables. A few nodded toward Jeff as if wishing to convey their sympathy for the ordeal he'd been subjected to. Jeff stared straight at them until they looked away, uncomfortably. He knew the snobs well enough to know they admired only one thing, and this was arrogance outstripping their own.

His waiter returned after less than five minutes with another gin and tonic and a note folded on the tray. Jeff said, "I didn't order that."

"Naw, suh, masta, you didn't. Hit's from that gentleman yonder. He also instructed that I give you this note, suh."

"All right, put it on the table."

The waiter placed the glass and the folded paper on the table and backed away, nodding and smiling. Jeff sensed that every man in the room was eyeing him covertly. He unfolded the note, laid his hand on it, flatly.

The note was etched in that careful Spencerian hand that was the symbol of the well-educated gentry: "Sir, may I join you at your table for five minutes? I have no wish to insult you, or to prolong your ordeal. However, what I have to say may prove most interesting—and rewarding —to you. Sincerely, Julien-Jacques Gischairn."

For a long beat, Jeff stared at the note. He looked up and met the warm smile of a man who appeared to be between thirty and forty. His face was pallid, with a look of unhealthy dissipation and complete evasion of sunlight and fresh air. His eyes were dulled by long-practiced personal excesses. His hair, which grew half over his close-set ears, was prematurely graying and brushed at an angle across his pate to cover spotty baldness. Adding to the man's unusual quality, which included an almost vulgar air of extreme wealth and studied disdain for ordinary mortals, was the small gold-and-diamond earring glittering at the lobe of the gentleman's left ear.

Jeff hesitated. The man looked effeminate, an aggressive pervert. He had troubles enough without having to dissuade a persistent pederast. But as the man continued to smile, as if he could wait patiently over extended durations for what he wanted, Jeff began to see more in him. He saw opportunity. Suppose the man was a screaming Miss Nancy? Who the hell cared? To each man his own diversion, his own religion, his own tastes, his own pursuit of gratification.

The fact was, Jeff was looking for a wealthy white man who might provide him the opportunity he avidly sought. If he had to trade a few caresses in exchange for a chance at riches, what the hell?

He inclined his head in a mocking nod and Gischairn leaped up, upsetting his chair. He came bounding with springing steps between the tables. He beamed, nodding and smiling.

He hesitated across the table, awaiting Jeff's invitation to sit down. Jeff nodded his head and Gischairn smiled, almost weeping in gratitude. The waiter pulled out the chair and Gischairn sat down, settling himself comfortably.

"I suppose you wonder why I thrust myself upon you like this?" Gischairn asked with a wide smile, which revealed a sparkling gold tooth. When Jeff shrugged, Gischairn's smile widened. "Even if you don't give a damn, sir, let me tell you who I am . . . I'm no one really . . . I've never turned my hand in my life toward honest labor . . . I shudder at the thought. I once sold slaves. Can you believe that? I made the millions I needed to enjoy myself, and then I retired to a life of excess. The slave trade became dangerous, messy, with pirates and lawbreakers. One cannot bring slaves into this country without breaking the law. I saw all of that I cared to. I had enough to live most comfortably two lifetimes. Once in a while, I wish I had my hand in. You know? But then I come down here to an auction, and I get my fill of it, and I return to my dissipation."

"Very interesting."

"I realize how boring it sounds to you so far, my dear fellow. But don't be hasty to judge me. I sat directly behind you and your friend from Georgia—he of the grits-strained accent. I've admired few men as I admired you, as you handled this poor clod's buying of black flesh. I never knew a man who knew more about the qualifications of good slaves—for the market."

"Thank you." Jeff shrugged again. His insides had calmed down enough that he could trust himself to take a drink. He did, a long pull at the chilled tonic.

"Well, even so, I merely noted your talents and skills and intelligence, and let it go at that . . . until I saw you handle that despicable little nancy of a plantation brat, Mr. Antoine Belmare. Then I realized I was looking at a man of incredible courage."

"Oh?"

"Yes. It took courage above any I have encountered in a misspent life to do what you did, to face that little bastard and his friends and back them all down. Courage. Incredible courage. My God, incredible courage."

"Why?" Jeff's voice chilled. "Do you think I am Brick-top—the fugitive slave?"

Julien-Jacques Gischairn put his head back laughing delightedly. "I don't know. But I can tell you this—I'm not going to put *my* money on the bar to find out!"

CHAPTER XXXII

"It was at that moment—at the instant I knew I'd found a young man of great courage and daring, combined with the creativity, even, of swagger and bluster—it was at that bright moment I determined to return to the slave trade." Gischairn nodded, smiling. "The only obstacle now is your availability, your willingness to join me as a full partner. If you agree, nothing can stop us from making millions—millions."

Jeff stared at the urbane, sophisticated, Machiavellian, and subdolous gentleman. He realized he'd never encountered quite such a singular personality in all his travels. Through his mind flashed the memory of the fat Cuban pederast Solano; but Solano was fat and gross. This man was sleek, fastidious, and aware. He not only admitted what he was; he flaunted it. The diamond ear-bob winked at him, like an elfin third eye.

He gave Julien-Jacques Gischairn a sour smile. "A full partner?"

"Full. Fifty-fifty. You will provide the courage, the daring, the skill; and I, the capital, and the influence and trickery necessary to circumvent the law profitably. An unbeatable combination, sir. Unbeatable."

When Jeff continued to sip his drink and refrain from making any reply, positive or negative, Gischairn leaned across the table, smiling like some obscene doll. "Why don't we have dinner? Talk about it?"

Jeff smiled. "I can't lose anything, having dinner with you, can I?"

"Nothing except your reputation, sir."

"Shall we go?"

Gischairn leaped to his feet. "Delightful. The daring. The courage. The go-to-hell in every breath you take. Beautiful. Beautiful."

The *maître d'* leapt to attention when he espied Julien-Jacques Gischairn and guest approaching. He bowed them to a secluded table that afforded a clear view of the large dining room. "The one thing which interests me most in this world, dear Jeff, is people. I sit here and simply marvel at people. Even the meanest, the lowest hold a fascination for me. I can't believe it—simply credit it that with all his experience, God can turn out so many failures."

Jeff laughed. Gischairn ordered drinks and the head-waiter trotted away. When the menu was brought, Jeff glanced at Gischairn. "I defer to your expert taste in food. Why don't you order?"

"That's where you've made a mistake," Gischairn said. "I suppose I look like a gourmand—at least a dilettante. The fact is, I've found there are few true gourmets. Just as there are few true opera devotees. Many people just fake it. They don't understand what's happening, and so they force themselves through the ritual with a great flourish. They order strange and exotic dishes and sit gagging them down with insipid smiles splitting their stupid faces. Well, I've found there's nothing better than a rare slice of beef, butter-browned potatoes, a salad with the house dressing, and some dessert to tickle the palate and evoke nostalgia for that better time when we were children and didn't have to pamper ourselves because others pampered us."

"I'll drink to that," Jeff said. "I don't know what the hell you're talking about, but I'll drink to it."

Gischairn handed the menus to the waiter. "Bring us the evening special, Vonnie. I don't want to know what

302

it is. Soup of the day, salad with house dressing." He laughed. "People will be peeking covertly to see what we're eating and whispering to their waiter to bring them whatever the handsome young man and the old *queen* are having." He laughed and then gestured, hands spread. "I realize your hesitation, part of your doubting, are occasioned by your suspicions of my—tastes? Eh? Perhaps you consider me a limp wrist? Is that troubling you?"

Jeff shrugged. "I don't hold a man's religion against him—as long as he doesn't try to force it on me."

Gischairn leaned forward, persisting. "But you think you'd be less than comfortable, associating your future, your fortunes with a man with what society considers perverted tastes, eh?"

Jeff laughed. "I told you. It doesn't matter. The only thing that concerns me is that this whole elaborate business is simply leading up to your inviting me up to your hotel room—to look at some filthy etchings?"

Gischairn laughed with him. "I assure you, my dear boy, I am far more subtle than that. . . . But I would like to settle the matter, because I can foresee a mutually profitable partnership, if—when—we can trust each other. I don't confess—one always has to confess to homosexuality, to boast of it is inadmissible. Anyhow, I'm not a homo . . . not entirely." He laughed. "Though you will learn through rumor that I am a two-headed axe."

"You cut both ways?"

"You'll certainly hear that. The fact of the matter is, I am a connoisseur—a dissolute connoisseur—but a connoisseur of beauty. Beauty admits no sex. Many men are far more beautiful than the loveliest woman you have ever seen. On the other hand, there are women whose gentle beauty breaks your heart."

"I've just encountered—and lost—one of those," Jeff said.

Gischairn nodded vigorously, as if some suspicion had been verified in his mind. "I knew it! You were—preoccupied. Almost distracted. What is more distracting to a

303

young man than a faithless woman? So she broke your heart, eh?"

"I'll get over it."

"Of course you will. I speak from experience. I loved deeply—once. By now I've learned—not to love at all. I love beauty. My love is transient, but so is beauty."

"I'll drink to that," Jeff said. "Again without having the least idea what you are talking about."

"There is a remedy for a hangover that calls for the hair of the dog that bit you," Gischairn said. "I've found it is not really a remedy at all, but the alcoholic's crafty way to start a new day's drunk with a clear conscience. Still, applied to a broken heart, the theory works. The best way to vomit up an old love is to ingest a new one—new women can make you forget familiar ones."

"I've already tried the hair of that dog."

"With indifferent success, eh? Well, come along to my home. As I said, I am a connoisseur of beauty. What I didn't tell you is that I am a collector of beautiful women—as some men collect ceramic miniatures of Christ's agony."

Jeff laughed. "So that's your twist on the old filthy etchings routine, eh?"

Gischairn shrugged. "I appreciate your suspicions. I understand them. But I am patient. Since I encountered you here today—quite by chance—I have determined to return to the lucrative slave trade, which grows more profitable every year! Why, when I was involved in the traffic of slaves, a prime buck brought eight or nine hundred dollars. I still walked away from the table with my millions. But, my God! today a prime stallion will bring up to five thousand dollars on the vendue tables here in New Orleans. Breeding top-quality slaves has become a fashionable game with these stupid cotton farmers. I need a partner. A young, vigorous, courageous, and creative partner. If there is *any* way I can prevail upon you to join me in this enterprise, I shall attempt it. . . ."

Gischairn's home was the most imposing on St. Charles

Avenue—that street of churches and millionaires. Within its courtyard, flowers, subtropical plants, and willows spread in profusion. Everything was manicured to perfection. Not a fallen leaf littered a flower bed or a cobbled walk. The house was marked by extravagant ornamentation and curved, flowing lines popular in eighteenth-century France. Inside the mansion was a breathtaking elegance and quality of furnishings, every stick and fabric imported from France. Huge canvases dominated the walls—French masters, originals by David, Ingres, Gericault, Jean Gros—in handcrafted framing. The paintings alone qualified Gischairn as a millionaire. At least, so far, he had not lied—silver candlesticks, polished brassware, subdued globes of blown glass glowed with gaslight. There was flourish and every creature comfort known to the ultramodern world in which Gischairn passed his days. Jeff was totally impressed; he made no effort to conceal his amazed approbation.

To the butler who took their hats, Gischairn said, "Bring liqueur to the parlor, Jamie, and then ask my little beauties if they would care to join us."

The black servant nodded and retreated, silent on thick Persian carpeting. Gischairn bowed Jeff into a deep armchair and sat in its twin across a small, fragile-legged table. The servant appeared, as silent as a wraith, served the small tumblers of after-dinner liqueur.

Jeff lifted his glass to his lips and stopped. Entering the room from the foyer were three of the loveliest tawny-colored creatures he'd ever seen. Their beauty was in their totally dissimilar similarity. Jeff admitted he had to drink to that because he didn't know what in the hell it meant, only there was no other way to explain the quality of their dusky comeliness. They were quadroons, and none was more than eighteen, but they were complete, mature in symmetry, grace, and elegance. Any flaws, minor as they might be if they existed at all, were completely concealed by ministrations of beauticians. Their radiant pulchritude had been polished and glossed by applications of science and indulgence of Gischairn's great wealth. Jeff stared openly at the exquisite garland embellishing the ornate interiors of Gischairn's home. Gischairn smiled, pleased at the response he'd evoked from his young guest.

"My God," Jeff whispered. "What a hobby."

He and Gischairn stood. They bowed over the slender hands of the lovely young ladies. Gischairn indicated the sofa and chairs. The girls sat, smiling at ease, and apparently totally happy. The butler brought them drinks, their preferences set on the tray and turned for selection.

A clever, experienced, and interested host, Gischairn directed the flow of the conversation, leading the three girls to chat easily and warmly about themselves and their lives *chez* Gischairn. Each was involved in the study of history, current events, grammar, home economics, which included basic arithmetic and something which Gischairn called sexuality science. This meant, he explained, that these girls were learning to be excellent wives, mothers, lovers—a trinity devoutly to be sought, but seldom found, in marriage. Being willing, beautiful, and even deeply in love were not in themselves adequate qualifications for excellence in marriage. Besides those classes designed to improve their minds and personalities, they also studied the arts, music, and fashion design. They admitted, with some humor and delightful smiles, that they had little free time. But all insisted they were happier than they'd ever dreamed they might be, and so grateful to Gischairn that they would die to please him . . . And what did Gischairn get out of this philanthropy?

"Satisfaction. Envy." Gischairn's mouth twisted into a malicious smile that seemed to please his taste buds. "Jaundiced deference, my dear boy. The elite of this city gaze with sick, envious eyes when I appear at any formal gathering—party, state affair, the opera—with yet another lovely miss, like a singular orchid worn on my lapel. Perfection. Loveliness that renders their own women dowdy even in their own regard. As I told you, I am a collector of beauty. But it is more than beauty you are looking upon. It is the inner quality—which I can help

306

them enhance—that makes beauty glow outwardly from within. These girls are the loveliest of creatures because they know and accept, casually by now, their own incredible loveliness; it is a part of their nature, their sweet good humor. They don't flaunt their beauty, they wear it easily. There is even a humility in their bearing, as if they are *enchanted* to please *you*. They have learned to find interests outside themselves, to be too concerned to be selfish, petty, or self-centered. I am famous as a curator in the science of perceived beauty, and I am accorded grudging respect. But mostly, thank God, I am envied. Unlike my girls, I can indulge my own pettiness and selfishness." He tugged at his diamond earlobe and put his head back, laughing.

"In a few months, a few weeks, a year at the outside, each of these girls will have married. They will marry wealth. Not simply a rich man—many rich men are clods who know only how to work and cannot appreciate beauty. They will marry one of the *privileged* rich, if you know what I mean—a man who has stopped even counting his money. When one of my lovelies leaves me, I find another rough gem to polish, finish, exploit briefly. All I do, really, is assure their birthright. Their beauty demands equity. I simply help them assume what is their due."

Unobtrusively, Gischairn eased the conversation from the girls to their guest. Soon, without knowing how it happened, Jeff found himself reciting a censored version of his heartbreak at The Laurels. In his laundered version, lies from the envious jealous turned his blond amour from him, sent him, ill, to New Orleans to forget. He did not feel his tale merited tears, but he saw them brim in the gentle black eyes of the tawny-skinned quadroon girls. For Gischairn it was an easy transition from this, into the pleasure it should afford his sweethearts to see that their guest was kept too occupied, too pampered, too delighted ever to look backward again in despair.

Jeff's admiration for Gischairn's masterful psychology soared. The suggestion that perhaps their guest might enjoy what they called The Lesbos Tableaux, came not from Gischairn, but from one of the girls. This was met with completely unself-conscious approval from the girls whose last inhibition had been gently polished away. Gischairn agreed, clapping his hands, as if the idea might never have occurred to him but met with his total approbation. The girls retired, Gischairn enjoyed a handmade Havana cigar, Jeff had one more drink. Finally, the butler entered and invited them into "the theater."

This proved to be a room made circular by heavy red damask draperies. Four or five—obviously the audiences were never large in this theater—deep and comfortable leather chairs were placed near the stage. This raised area was a circular, red-covered bed nine feet in diameter. Curtains were fragile, filmy, transparent; they parted as Gischairn and Jeff sat down.

Jeff caught his breath and felt his loins tauten, his testes ache, his rod stiffen. The Lesbos Tableaux had everything except total nudity. The translucent robes heightened and accented the nakedness of the girls. As the filmy curtains parted, the girls were revealed, like lovingly formed statues, one girl on her back, a second standing over her, head and shoulders back, breasts upthrust. The third girl was crouched over the face of the prone girl and she had her face pressed into the mons veneris of the second, her arms embracing the girl's hips. To Jeff's stunned amazement, and agonized enjoyment, they seemed not to move at all, and yet they changed positions in a fluid motion that increased in tempo until each girl was raised and released in orgasm.

When it was over, Jeff was trembling and sweated. He was aware, through a haze, that Gischairn was applauding politely. Dazedly, Jeff joined him. The filmy curtains whispered, closing, and the girls were gone. For some time, Jeff and Gischairn sat without speaking. When his host suggested it had been a long and tiring day, Jeff agreed and permitted the quiet butler to lead him to one of the most elegantly appointed bedroom suites he'd ever entered. No one mentioned sleeping arrangements, and though he ached in his groin, Jeff said nothing. He could not believe that Gischairn was insensitive enough to heterosexual needs to ignore his internal agony. He was right. Black girls appeared with hot water for his bath; they offered to lave him, but when he refused, they remained to shave, powder, cologne, and massage him. He knew he was being prepared for an unusual sacrifice. He only hoped Gischairn didn't show up when that corridor door was opened.

The black servant girls—each small, dainty, and chosen for her dark pulchritude—were gone. He lay down, aware of nothing but the savage pulsing of blood into his penis. He breathed irregularly, exhaling through his mouth, reliving the agonized delight of the floor show provided by the three quadroon lovelies. My God! they had driven each other crazy, but they had sent him out of his mind.

The servants had left small candles in silver candleabra, sedately glowing. He heard a whisper of sound, and two of the quadroon beauties crossed his room, approaching his bed in sheer nightgowns. He was afraid to speak for fear he might break the spell, afraid to reach out for fear that, like butterflies they'd flee if he tried to hold them.

They lay down beside him, kissing him, caressing him, massaging him. They seemed to understand that the tableaux had left him tense and ready to erupt. They did not get down to the serious business of loving him until with hot mouths and probing tongues, they had helped him find a quick release. He permitted them to make all advances; it seemed this was the lesson they had learned. Both girls were appalled and pleasured by his size and heft. It was not long before they forgot their lessons, and he forgot everything except their hands and mouths and vaginas struggling to service, to be serviced, to please and to be pleased. Long after he was physically exhausted, the two succubi were using every stratagem known to femininity to finesse one final erection, one last shared moment of ecstasy. They were not to be denied. . . .

Gischairn resumed his discussions of his proposed

partnership when Jeff came down to breakfast at ten the next morning. He awoke to find the quadroon beauties gone, but the black serving wenches ready with hot bath water, shaving utensils, and cologne. . . . He came down to breakfast refreshed, invigorated, but he would have lied had he said even the quadroons had driven Margarith and his need for her from his mind.

"Over the months—and years—since I was actively engaged in the slave trade," Gischairn said, "I have gone over and over in my mind the ways in which the business could be handled most profitably. Admittedly, I have invested in shipping—import and export—most profitably. But there was always missing the erotic satisfaction of dealing in human beings. I withdrew from these mundane enterprises, but I was never able to put the slave traffic from my mind.

"I know to the penny the cost of buying and outfitting a proper schooner with provided space amid-ships for transporting slaves. I know that for under $4,000 such a sailing ship can be bought and outfitted, supplied a crew. I know the cost of slaves in Cuba. With a knowledgeable expert like you to do the selection and buying of the blacks, we should realize a profit of two or three hundred percent on every black we bring in to the New Orleans slave vendue."

"I agree," Jeff said. "But you are overlooking the risk factors."

"Not at all. I considered them most carefully. That's why I resisted my temptation to return to the slave industry—until I encountered you. You are speaking, I am aware, of the threat of the U.S. ships patrolling the gulf and the Mississippi, and Lafitte's blackbirders prowling the shipping lanes."

"That's part of it. Blockade running gets tougher every year. I know. Lafitte is able to do it with ex-pirates manning his ships."

"And don't forget the infamous Commodore Louis Aury who works boldly from his island headquarters off the east coast of Florida near the mouth of the St. Johns

River. Are either of them better men than you? Does either of them have more courage, more cunning? I think not. It's because I plan to go into competition with Lafitte and Aury that I need you. Together—with my handling of the bribery of customs and coast guard people, and you bringing in the *merchandise*—we cannot fail. I will guarantee you at least $100,000 as your share of the first delivery you bring in to me. Isn't that worth a risk, or two?"

CHAPTER XXXIII

A fair wind stood them into Havana harbor. . . .

Jeff stood, legs braced apart, far forward on the white-scrubbed deck of the *Julia*—his ship! The salubrity of seductively scented and langourous zephyrs rode out to greet and enchant him from the gentle tropical island that emerged out of the sea like a lush green jewel. His mind shuttling from memory to anticipation, Jeff urged the ship to a speed impractical in these calm waters and unseemly in this unhurried world.

He admitted from that first morning at breakfast in Julien-Jacques Gischairn's mansion an increasing excitement over the prospects of the enterprise proposed and outlined by his host. The guarantee of a fortune from his very first delivery of slaves to the New Orleans slave market fascinated him, and he could think of little else. If there were no other way to blot Margarith from his mind, he would buy his way free of her. He would work so hard there would be no place for her memory; he would drive himself until he lost her in fatigue. While his planning and his fantasies regarding his new career did not wholly erase his longing for Margarith, he promised himself a day when that surcease would come. Meantime, the more he looked along the path to great wealth, the more he wanted Margarith. He could buy her the world, he could buy her forgiveness, her forgetfulness, her love. And all the time he knew he lied to himself. . . .

No, he couldn't buy Margarith, but before God, he could buy any other women in the world, and he would buy them, as he needed them, as he bought fresh linen.

In the meantime, there were a thousand things to do, and every day was too short. But it was when he threw himself wholeheartedly and with all his boundless energy into his new enterprise that he found time, progress, and tangible accomplishment slowed to a snail's pace. Finding, purchasing, and remodeling a merchant ship was not simply a matter of a financial transaction. It was a slow, secretive, and tedious task. Where he had thought it might take days, it consumed weeks and months.

One dealt with ship's candlers and carpenters, men who could be told everything except the truth—that they were being hired to convert a vessel for use as a slave ship. These workers could not be allowed even to guess the truth; final shackles and chains would have to be fixed in place by the ship's crew when it was at sea. Importing slaves into the United States had been outlawed by anti-slavery legislation of 1807. More importantly, a supplemental statute of 1819 provided awards for informers. This combined with the fact that the act passed by congress on May 15, 1820, declared importation of slaves into the United States to be piracy and punishable by death, increased the need for stealth and deception where outsiders were involved.

Outlawing slave importation in 1807 actually served only to increase the price of slaves and place a premium on bootlegging the blacks. When the law was passed, there were about 1 million slaves in the country. Each year after that, about 20,000 slaves were smuggled across its borders.

After the antislavery law was enacted, prices and profits in the trade soared. Still, informers could and did collect for delivery of a suspected slaver. Carpenters sometimes supplemented their meager incomes by turning informer. When caught, slave traffickers were actually hung unless they were highly placed in status or were rich enough to grease palms and hire attorneys.

Because Gischairn had been involved in apparently legal import and export, and because he began a subtle and rewarding approach to the customs officials, they were able to transform a merchantman into a vessel suitable for carrying slaves. Still, the conversion had to be conducted cautiously, and it was time consuming.

Jeff drew plans for the space " 'tween decks" on the double-decked schooner to be prepared about six feet in height. Black men would be shackled at the ankles in pairs. Each had to lie on his back. The shackles would be secured by chains or rods nailed to deck and bulkheads. At one time, standing space between decks had been less than four feet, and for the ten-week voyage, each man was allotted deck space of sixteen inches in width by five and one-half feet in length. But almost 15 percent of each human cargo died on these voyages. Inhuman conditions along with inhuman brutality meted out on this middle passage often cut in half the number of usable animals finally delivered. Such wasteful loss of profit brought about enlightened treatment and increased areas between decks.

Jeff and Vincente inspected the progress daily. Jeff suggested to Gischairn that they should transport goods needed in Cuba on the voyage out. Disinterested in any probable profits, Gischairn invited Jeff to make any arrangements he wished and to pocket the entire profits of his venture.

With Vincente to translate for him, Jeff wrote a letter to Don Cipriano, mentioning to the affluent and influential friend of Jean Lafitte that he was outfitting a ship for a voyage from New Orleans to Havana, and inquiring about exports from the States in which Cuban merchants might be interested. Don Cipriano replied by personal courier. Whatever manufactured fabrics, whatever grains and wood products were available at attractive prices, Don Cipriano would welcome, and he would purchase dockside at Havana upon the arrival of Don Jeff's ship.

Jeff began to haunt the trading marts, the exporters, and the grain firms. Weeks before the *Julia* was ready to sail, he had cargo committed. He had invested almost all of his personal cash. He knew Gischairn was waiting for him to borrow capital, but Jeff managed to load his ship with rice, wheat, sweet potatoes, corn, peanuts, pecans, cottonseed oil, and paper products. One thing his industry accomplished: any lingering suspicions were allayed concerning the ship being used for illegal traffic in slaves. Before he sailed, he was even surprised to gain added revenue for transporting mail and valuables. But by the time the ship was loaded, he realized that stowing all these products aboard was only the first step—the shipping lanes were infested with men who made their fortunes from plundering merchantmen. He spent the last of his money on three small brass cannon, which he mounted fore and aft on the *Julia*.

They passed from the vernal equinox through the autumnal equinox and the vicious hurricane season with the *Julia* riding at anchor in the New Orleans harbor. Jeff thanked providence he was not at sea as he had been when a hurricane struck Captain MacFarland's ship as they transported slaves from Havana to Barataria.

During these months of delay, Lenora, the daintiest and most passionate of the three quadroon girls residing with Gischairn, married an incredibly wealthy landowner. Gischairn, hiding behind her family, financed a wedding which was the scandal and envy of Louisiana for months. But the effect in the Gischairn household was one of loss . . . they missed Lenora. Before Jeff sailed, however, Gischairn introduced into the group a sixteen-year-old beauty that would have broken his heart, had it not been broken already.

As the moment for sailing approached, Gischairn became impatient, nervous, and uncharacteristically emotional. "Remember, Jeff, we want to deal only in the prime animals—the fancies, the extrafancy. You may expect to pay more—I've allowed for that. Once we get them here, I'll hold them for my price. We'll never have to sacrifice to panic selling. They'll pay my price, or they won't touch my stock. But, in order to do this, we must purchase only the cream."

Jeff shook his head. "I think you know better than that—unless you're trying to saddle me with an impossible task. You cannot force a slave trader to sell you only his prime and fancy stock. He's smart too. He's been in business long enough to know he must profit from the transaction, and he'll refuse to be left with culls. . . . You're going to have to trust me. We're going to be forced to accept some ordinary blacks. I'll be as careful and as tough as I can, but I won't have you sitting here expecting miracles."

"My dear boy! I do trust you. We can use a few ordinary laborers. I can discount them off if I have to. I do trust you!"

Gischairn's plan for smuggling the merchandise into Louisiana sounded foolproof, though Jeff knew better than to count his money unntil he'd slipped past the last Lafitte lookout. "Aury, and sometimes even Lafitte, bring the herds of blacks in through Florida—landing somewhere around Pensacola and marching them overland. My plan is a lot more workable, with less risk. I own a plantation which has fallen into disrepair downriver from New Orleans. It belonged to my parents, and their parents. While you're gone, I shall have the place renovated and stocked with a few blacks to keep it up. You'll sail with your legal exports. When you're in Cuba, you might buy some woods, tobacco, cigars, sugar—whatever you can. I want you to *look* like a legal ship—we've paid off the customs people, but we've got to give them a way out. If they can see you're hauling tobacco and other products, they can pass you without the close inspection that would reveal the blacks. You don't have to bring the slaves up the river all the way to Algiers, across from the *Vieux Carre*. That would be foolish and unprofitable. That's why I'm opening the plantation at Palm Villa. You will anchor in the river. Blacks from the plantation will row out, and you will use your own lifeboats, and you will unload your slave cargo at my plantation downriver. We'll keep them there, feed them, make sure they're healthy, and we'll bring them into New Orleans only as we wish to auction them off. There, I've removed as much risk as possible."

"Yes. All I've got to do now is keep the customs people off my ship, stay clear of Lafitte's and Aury's blackbirders, and unload them downriver."

"If there were no risks there would be no incredible profits. I wouldn't be interested—and I wouldn't need you. . . ."

Jeff was busier, working eighteen hours a day, as the hour for sailing out approached. Sometimes for as much as two hours at a time he was too busy to think about Margarith—or fortunate enough that no one, no word, no fragrance, no passing thought, brought her back to his mind. But he did not forget her. He tried, he wanted to, but he did not.

Finally, in January, came the day to weigh anchor. Gischairn had hired an evil-looking character named Augsberg—Captain Rupert Augsberg, sir!—as the *Julia*'s executive officer. He was advised that he was, of course, master of the vessel at sea, but he was answerable to Jeff under all circumstances. Augsberg recruited a ship's company even less prepossessing than himself. Jeff had no way to investigate, but he had the hackle-prickling suspicion that Augsberg and his men knew each other better than they allowed. He suggested to Gischairn that they might even be a complement of Aury's sea rats between voyages. Gischairn only laughed. "I'm confident you can handle them," he said.

To add to his presentiments of imminent wrong, Jeff was astonished to see Dominique You waddling across the pier and up the gangway to wish him bon voyage. You asked no questions. He could not have been more affable. He drank to Jeff's great good fortune and went away smiling and waving his pudgy arm. Jeff was left with the troubling question, how had You learned of his project? What did he know? Where had he learned it? Had he been alerted by Lafitte's Cuban contact, the wealthy Don Cipriano? He sweated over it but found no answers.

He stood, with Vincente, at the railing, listening to Augsberg call orders for casting off and hearing them repeated, shouted forward and aft.

Gischairn arrived dockside in his finest carriage with all three of his quadroon beauties in attendance. The girls wept and threw kisses. Gischairn stood fluttering a white silk handkerchief. The ship's owner and his retinue drew all attention from the gleaming *Julia* as she slipped her lines and sailed with sleek grace downriver.

When the schooner moved out into the wintry gulf, Jeff had Captain Augsberg assign three gun crews. The captain passed his order down through the chain of command and a fat, insolent bosun's mate reported to Jeff with the men. Jeff ran them through gun drills three times a day. He was pleased to find them proficient gunners, even expert. They could disintegrate a pelican out over the water. His suspicions of their claims to being ordinary seamen from merchant ships deepened, but since their own safety depended on how they handled themselves and the guns when confronted, he decided the hell with it—he didn't give a damn what Sunday schools they came out of, as long as they didn't attempt to appropriate his ship and cargo from within.

Gun drill proved to be the greatest excitement afforded in the crossing. They saw few other ships in the lanes, few signs of other ships, and yet Jeff had the feeling that they were being tailed, followed, kept under surveillance. Even when this paranoid idea made no sense at all, he could not shake it.

They sailed out of winter into the spring of the tropics. Gulls soared above them, porpoise bounced along as if mocking them and laughing at them. The sea faded into lime greens and milk blues, and the serene skies showed clouds, silky white, in every pattern known to chance.

Don Cipriano himself was at dockside to greet the *Julia* when she was secured in her berth. Vincente saw his natural father first, grabbing Jeff's arm and pointing to the handsome man beside the furbished cabriolet on the crowded pier.

Jeff stared down and found the great loading docks as they had looked the first time he saw them. Every possible foot of loading space was crammed, stacked high with crates, boxes, croker sacks, tubs, and barrels, awaiting shipment to Spain and other potentially profitable ports. Half-naked, sweated black stevedores chanted as they worked, forming an endless conveyor belt that moved to the precise rhythms of their wordless song. Jeff felt that same excitement. It was exactly as he remembered it two years ago—the same overwhelming heat, the same brassy sun, the same people struggling impotently against the ever-increasing piles of goods. The difference was Don Cipriano himself. He stood out as royalty projects against rabble everywhere.

Señor Don Cipriano Olivarez was Lafitte's confidential agent in Havana. He was a most influential man with his foot in many doors. The Spanish government in Cuba was putridly corrupt and Don Cipriano exploited this disgraceful dishonesty to his own profit. But he also employed his energies along honest channels as a business tycoon, much as Lafitte himself did in his New Orleans enterprises.

Don Cipriano came bounding up the gangplank as soon as it was winched into position. He was a middle-aged man, his hair prematurely snow white; but his sparkling black eyes—identical to Vincente's and equally brimming with spontaneous merriment—and light, springy steps suggested something of his inner strength and energies, which set him apart from his countrymen.

Don Cipriano bowed graciously toward Jeff, smiling warmly, recalling his earlier visit as Lafitte's envoy; but without Vincente as translator, they would have been unable to trade more than stilted greetings. Vincente stopped speaking and stood staring incredulously at this man who had casually conceived him and as casually abandoned him. He had sent occasional handouts when he remembered, a preoccupied aristocrat, alms which Vincente and his older sister Perla had supplemented through her whoring and Vincente's pimping for her.

For a long beat, Don Cipriano was struck dumb at the sight of his bastard son. It was as if Don Cipriano were a faded carbon copy of Vincente. Vincente had grown so incredibly, his father cried. Even to Jeff it was as if Vincente looked into a strange mirror that returned his image, but somehow aged it without otherwise altering it very much. Cipriano and Vincente were identical, but the years had deepened lines in the don's handsome face; otherwise there was the same arrogance and pride, the same thick curly hair, the same quick laughter, the same scarcely controlled potential for violence.

His eyes brimming with tears, Don Cipriano examined Vincente searchingly. Then he clutched the boy in his arms—an offspring he could not have successfully denied even in one of the Havana courts where his influence was total. *"Mi hijo!"* he wept. "My son. My dearest son. *Mi corazón!"*

Before he could endure to transact the first bit of the business that had brought him personally into this pitiless heat, Don Cipriano had to plead with Vincente to come with him to his home, as his acknowledged son, his heir. Vincente remained distant. His tilted brow inquired—without words—about those years of his childhood, the hungry days as a street arab, a ten-year-old pimp for a twelve-year-old sister: where were you, Don Cipriano, when I needed you? When my sister had no one but me to protect her, where were you then, my lord? Aloud,

Vincente said only, "I'll have to give it much thought, *patrono*."

Don Cipriano burst out, in a volley of Spanish, speaking directly to Jeff.

"What did he say?" Jeff asked Vincente.

"He pleads with you that you will use your great influence with the son of his heart to persuade him to come into his empty house as his acknowledged heir."

"Tell him that I shall use every means available to induce his son to do just that," Jeff said. "And be damned sure that's what you tell him."

Vincente grinned at him coldly. "You mean, after all these years, *amigo*, you think you can't trust me?"

"I mean, *amigo*, it has taken me all these years to learn just how far I can trust you. Now, tell your father what I said. Exactly what I said."

CHAPTER XXXIV

Jeff and Vincente walked deep into the maze of narrow old cobbled alleys twisting through a section that had merely grown older and uglier since Havana was a walled city. Despite the depressing surroundings, the deteriorating buildings, the littered walks, the empty-eyed naked children, Jeff couldn't deny a sense of triumph and satisfaction. Don Cipriano had inspected the ship manifest sheet, studied the bill of lading, and agreed to buy the entire cargo—for cash. Cipriano's own gang of dockhands were set to unloading the holds of the *Julia*. When Jeff was troubled about carrying almost $15,000 in cash, Cipriano suggested that a draft be sent in his name from Banco de Cuba to the Commercial Bank of New Orleans, where the money would be deposited in Señor Carson's account. Jeff agreed. He also agreed with Don Cipriano that Vincente should be provided a college education, training in law or medicine. Vincente had merely watched them with a chilled smile, translating precisely everything they said to express his contempt for the whole notion. He tried to tell them he was as free as the gulls, who existed on what they scavenged along the piers—one did not waste a college education on a sea gull. . . .

Vincente walked ahead of Jeff in the dank and winding streets, hurrying. When they met a mule- or ox-drawn cart, they had to duck into a smelly doorway, or flatten against the wall. Vincente laughed. He felt truly at home again.

Jeff didn't feel at home. Hackles stood along his neck as they had the first time he'd followed Vincente through these mean streets. Dark, lean men skulking like hungry cats in the shadows looked as if they'd slit your throat for a peso. Jeff had the urge to keep checking back over his shoulder.

They came at last to the hovel Jeff recalled. Here Vincente had lived with his twelve-year-old sister, who became a *puta* to help supplement the money Vincente made shining *caballeros'* boots in the streets. To increase Perla's income, Vincente had become her pimp.

They entered the arch in a mildewed gray wall surmounted by rusty iron-laced balconies. Vincente spoke in rapid Spanish to the men and women lounging in the doorway. Vincente no longer looked like the ragged street arab who had belonged among them; perhaps few of them recognized the tall, slender youngster with the arrogant manner of the aristocrat—an inherited trait from his father. In all the Spanish reeled off, Jeff understood only "Perla?" But he recognized the shrugs; their language was international. Perla was not here. They did not know her. They did not remember her. Though Vincente spoke faster, imperiously, his tone threatening, they merely shrugged.

Abruptly, Vincente heeled around and pushed through the ring of people, beckoning Jeff to follow. In the alley again, Vincente unreeled a string of street curses. "Perla is gone. No one knows where. Some swear they don't even recall Perla. . . ." He laughed coldly. "One thing is then certain. She has done well, gone up in the world from here. If she'd had worse times, or died, they'd all remember her."

Jeff shivered slightly in the brilliant sunlight. He recalled how casually they had abandoned little Perla to the tender mercies of the brutal, dehumanized pimp named Jorge. "Will we be able to find her?"

"If she lives." Vincente shrugged exaggeratedly to hide the shudder that wracked his slender body. "When all else fails I can ask her priest . . . or we can go directly to Josephina's . . . perhaps Perla has been taken into that fine whorehouse . . . at least someone there will know of her, all whores know each other . . . and I can get some relief after these days at sea."

"You can't stop to fuck—"

"Yes, I can. I'll think better if I do."

"We should find Perla first. Then we have business."

Vincente glanced at him. "Do you wish to be despised in Havana, *amigo?* Business is transacted in Havana only when one has cleared the pressures from his mind and body, or when he is too tired to fuck. . . . Follow this simple rule and you will be understood—and admired—in Cuba."

Jeff shook his head, incredulous, and shrugged. "So be it."

Vincente's sister was nowhere to be found, yet Vincente could postpone his search to buy physical release in a *casa de puta*. Since the boy had casually abandoned Perla two years ago, Jeff thought, turning a trick with a whore wasn't an unconscionable delay. And Perla was Vincente's sister, Vincente's responsibility and not his—though he'd looked forward to seeing her again. He recalled with some inner heat the way the muscles of her tight little vagina had closed, stripping one's rod almost as a woman's mouth might in *una manera francesca*. Vincente had boasted of his sister's prowess and insisted he had taught her this trick.

When the hack stopped before what had formerly been the busiest, most famous whorehouse in Cuba—patronized by the elite, the wealthy, the influential—they found Josephina's was not as either of them recalled it. The distinguished old bawdy house looked rundown, tired, passé. None of the brisk traffic flowed through its doors as before—young, old, tycoon, laborer, farmer, and *turista*.

As Jeff paid the hack driver, the man observed, "You may go where you like. But why Josephina's? Only old hags work here now—little better than you can find on the street for a peso. At Perla's—" he kissed his finger-tips, "one finds fresh new merchandise—occasionally a virgin, though such a one costs prohibitively."

"Perla's!" Vincente leaned forward, excitement glowing in his face. "Yes. Take us to Perla's."

Perla's Palace was a mansion on a street that once had been a most-respected boulevard of churches and fine family homes. The neighborhood was less fashionable now, but Perla's place was in better repair than it had been since the year of its construction. Vincente leapt from the carriage and bounded up the wide steps.

Inside, the vulgar appointments, bright colors, porno-graphic art, seductive music, and disembodied laughter added the correct atmosphere, that spice of the faintly forbidden. The manse had that *successful* look and air. Dark-skinned girls, Castille blondes, redheads, mestizos— all young but sleekly sophisticated—strolled about the corridors, smiling, looking charming, revealing a glimpse of curved breast, bright garter, trim ankle. Vincente gawked, looking everywhere at once, and licked his lips greedily as they were ushered into Perla's private parlor.

Perla reclined on a chaise longue in a translucent robe that concealed nothing but rather underlined her nudity.

She looked older, even more sophisticated than she had been as an unabashed little *puta* who thought she knew all the answers and most of the questions when Jeff met her. There were few lingering traces of the little girl. That sleek hardness lay like a ceramic patina on her heart-shaped face. The dark curls he remembered were piled on her head, secured with a sapphire tiara. Her gray-green eyes brightened and she squealed out her pleasure, leaping up from the chaise and running to them, her robe falling away enchantingly from slender body and trim thighs. She grabbed both of them into her arms, sobbing, laughing, and kissing them at once.

As Perla clung to Jeff's hand and chattered breathlessly to her half-brother in musical Spanish, Jeff surveyed her. He found her breasts plumper, still a gentle tea-rose in color and tipped with maraschino cherry nipples. The dainty triangle of black hair at her primrose mons veneris was as he hotly recalled. Jeff felt himself growing hard, remembering her when she'd been a sex-hungry child. She'd been afraid at first that he was too big for her and had nuzzled him with her hot wet mouth, her darting, licking tongue tantalizing him beyond endurance.

Remembering the way he'd lifted her in his arms, found her vulva bubbling with hot liquid, the way he had inserted his staff—at first carefully—to have her go wild, battering herself upon him and moaning in sweet agony, he suddenly wanted her now—fiercely and immediately. But he could not destroy this tender, excited reunion between brother and sister. He forced himself to sit quietly and politely though his testes constricted, though he boiled inwardly with a rampant desire for Perla.

Vincente translated Perla's incredible story as she poured it out to him. Jorge had used her cruelly, treated her rottenly, robbed her of every peso she earned. Finally, with the aid of a young baker who had a cart, she escaped and ran to Don Cipriano. He was not her father, but he was Vincente's and he had always been kind, if casual and forgetful, in the old days. She had nowhere else to go. Don Cipriano agreed at last to see her, listened to her story, cried openly, and took her in. Jorge traced her to the don's fine villa, threatened her, and made a vile scene. The next day harbor police found Jorge's dead body floating in the bay—a crime still unsolved. In her gratitude, her need for affection, and her desire to repay the don's kindness, the girl sneaked into his bedroom— his door left conveniently unlocked—likely as her own mother had. Don Cipriano had been, to state it mildly, enchanted.

Wishing to repay Perla for her great kindness, and her exciting vagina, the don boasted of her to a famous land and slave owner, Don Cesar. Years before, Don Cesar had found his wife with a black just shipped in from Africa. He killed the slave and almost murdered his wife, but she fled Cuba, escaping only with her life. He had been unable to forget her in these years. Don Cipriano swore Perla could make Gabriel forget his horn, and Don Cesar agreed to invite her to his home for dinner. Don Cipriano bought her a lovely dress, sheer underthings, new shoes and stockings and brought in a beautician. Don Cesar had been overwhelmed. At thirteen, Perla was no longer a child, but a blossoming young woman in Cuba. Don Cesar kept her for a month, buying her lavish gifts every morning.

Finally, when the don, already burdened with years, came to the sad realization that a thirteen-year-old with the French vagina could be fatal as a steady diet, he asked what she wanted most in the world. This was the easiest question ever posed Perla—except that basic one, do you want to fuck? Perla told Don Cesar she wanted to own her own whorehouse. She wanted the security, the wealth she knew she could amass as a madam. She knew how a truly profitable whorehouse should be operated—she knew instinctively what men wanted and she would cater to their wants. Don Cesar bought her a mansion, bought her all the licenses and protection she would ever need, and came to her for her tender ministrations only once a week now. But he always spent the night, too exhausted, his legs too weak to return him home after his visit.

Vincente was ecstatic. His sister, the queen of whores in Havana! The most famous madam in the land—women like Josephina paling into insignificance beside her. Vincente went on chattering until Jeff thought he could not endure another word from the boy. It was Perla who suggested that Vincente might wish to sample her wares. "Whatever you want, dear brother, it is on the house."

Vincente disappeared as if by magic. Left alone, Jeff was awkward for the moment. This was no longer a skinny little girl. This was the most famous prostitute in Cuba, the mistress of Don Cesar himself! She stared at the bulge at his crotch, reached over, and massaged it longingly. "How I have missed you!" she said. "One never forgets a lover built as you are, Don Jeff. . . . May I have it once more, in memory of old times?"

"Please do," he said. And he watched her kneel before him, proficiently remove his belt buckle, unbutton his fly, and dive upon his rigidity.

Time screeched suddenly to a halt. Her hot mouth nursed, and he hung suspended between this moment and another time in his past. When he could endure her nuzzling no longer, he lifted her in his arms and carried her to her bed. Her black eyes, tear brimmed with passion, burned with a desire he could hardly credit in a girl whose career was the flesh trade. She lay down on the bed, drew his head to her hard, pink nipples. She clutched her arms about him, holding him to her. She reached down and guided his inflexible rod into the hot cauldron of her pudenta. He thrust deeply, but as he withdrew, he felt her tighten on him as if she would crush the life from him. "Still the French trick," he said, smiling, agonized, delighted.

"Better than ever—for you," she said. "How I have practiced—knowing you would come back to me some-day, and remembering how much you loved it."

326

CHAPTER XXXV

Don Solano giggled. "Don Jeff! I've been expecting you! You naughty boy! All these weeks you've been in Havana and you haven't come near me."

"Obviously, I was in error, Don Policarpo Solano," Jeff said in feigned contrition—any diplomatic lie that might salve the wounded feelings of the fat pederast.

Don Solano wriggled sensuously, licking his mouth as his tiny beady eyes grazed over Vincente's lithe young body. "And who is this lovely creature?"

Jeff bowed. "This is Vincente. You have forgotten. Vincente was my interpreter when I met you last. . . . He has grown."

Don Solano rubbed his fat hands together. "He certainly has grown, filled out so delightfully. Come here, my boy, let me look at you."

Vincente gave Jeff a crooked grin that said he had been dealing with these queer ones since he first began shining boots in Havana. He walked close to the grossly fat man reclining on his throne of pillows. Of all things in Cuba, Don Policarpo Solano had altered least with the passage of time. He seemed not to have lost an ounce of the sagging fat, which rendered him almost immobile unless he was assisted by at least two black servants. The same sweated ringlets fringed his bald pate, growing over his small shell-like ears and across several layers of his

327

neck. His narrow forehead remained unlined, his brows thick, his eyes almost lost in sockets of suet. His cheeks bulged round and rubbery, his nose nestled small and pudgy above his petulant mouth. Don Solano reached out bulbous arms, grasping at Vincente with short stubby fingers. When he moved, the gross welts of mammary fat quivered beneath the shimmering fabric of his lace shirt.

"I am pleased to see you again, Señor Solano," Jeff lied. He had delayed visiting the sodomist. This oleaginous man's quirky mannerisms and blatancy sickened him—there was at least the saving grace of a self-deprecating, waspish sense of humor about Gischairn. Solano's breathless falsetto voice, with its effeminate lisp, repelled him. As long as there had appeared legitimate slave traders with whom to deal in Cuba, he'd avoided Solano. Now, he was here and it looked as if fat Solano had him over a barrel.

Solano managed to catch Vincente's penis and testes in his soft pudgy hand and massaged greedily, his breathing labored. "Oh, you lovely boy. Such a lovely boy. Look at those thick lashes, those full lips. Did you ever see anything lovelier?" He gave Vincente a simpering smile. "You wouldn't treat Don Solano as cruelly as Señor Carson did when last we met, eh? You would have understood an aging man's needs, eh? You would have seen how I was overwhelmed, enchanted by Señor Carson's male loveliness—such a delightful brute! One could yearn to be hurt by such a man, eh? All I asked of Señor Carson was *one* night . . . I pleaded—for one night . . . and he rejected me. . . . Oh, he treated me so callously, repulsed me so coldly. I shall never be able to forget, or forgive him. No, never."

Still clinging breathlessly to Vincente, Solano raised his glazed eyes up to stare in petulant accusation at Jeff. "You are indeed a cruel man, Don Jeff. Somehow you must be forced to pay for the cruel way you rejected me—when I existed for only one night—one night of your love."

Vincente stepped back so suddenly that Don Solano

almost toppled forward like an unbalanced Buddha. He spoke in a mocking tone of contrition—the sarcasm totally lost on Solano, who heard only what he wanted to hear. "I am at fault, Don Solano. I translated your wishes, sir, if you recall. Perhaps I misunderstood you—your true intent. I may have translated so poorly that Don Jeff misinterpreted your invitation. . . . I was so young at the time."

"You were never that young," Don Solano said in a malicious tone. "I warn you now. Be sure every word you translate for Señor Carson is precise. I want it understood that I *know* I am your last hope to buy slaves in Cuba. . . .You will deal with Solano, on Solano's terms, or you will deal with no one."

"I understand that," Jeff said.

He had been brought to this realization over many idle weeks by the cruel facts of Cuban political life. One made no move on the island unless it was correlated with the policies and profits of the corrupt elite. From the first day, Jeff saw blacks herded from arriving slave ships into the *cuartels;* the barracoons were overcrowded, but he could not find one dealer who would sell to Jeff Carson. Though Gischairn's credit was established in Banco de Cuba, the flesh dealers shrugged. They were sorry.

Desperate, the days fleeing past like shadows in this flawed Eden, Jeff went to Don Cipriano Olivarez. As to the matter of slaves for sale, Don Cipriano spread his hands in a small helpless gesture. At this movement, Jeff saw how hopeless it was. Few men in Cuba had more personal influence and power than Don Cipriano. When *he* was reduced to impotence, the opposition had to be formidable indeed. It was. "I have heard that Lafitte has threatened to boycott—harass and destroy—any slave traders who deal with anyone he does not approve. I am sorry. You are competition to Lafitte. He does not approve you. You won't find dealers in Cuba to sell to you. To go to Haiti—with the blacks in revolution and the corrupt in control of that revolution—is a risk ill-advised. I am sorry."

329

Jeff sent word to Gischairn, but he had small hope that the message would arrive in New Orleans ahead of the returning *Julia*. He could not admit defeat even when he was opposing Lafitte. Other men bought slaves here and transported them into the United States. How did they accomplish it? He set out to try to learn that vital secret. Meantime, the *Julia* rode at anchor in the bay; the crew stayed drunk on rum and fatigued on whores. They gambled and fought; they frequently landed in the stinking Havana jails from which Jeff had to bail them.

He was able to buy merchandise for the return—the best Havana cigars he ordered by the barrel, getting a price that promised a substantial profit. He bought laces, barrels of sugar, sacks of coffee—anything that was for sale at cut rates and promised to find a market in New Orleans. But none of this was the answer. This was merely marking time while he found himself daily more seduced by the languid life of the island.

He yawned a lot, even as he was planning to steal slaves and make a run north across the Gulf. He drifted into the habit of the *siesta* from noon to four. No sense fighting the languorous lassitude when everybody else was sprawled out snoring, businesses, banks, and shops all closed. He spent more and more time at Perla's. She had lovely girls, but she was jealous of him; she wanted him for herself. Even when at last he was leaving, Perla pleaded with him to spend one last afternoon in her bed—a memory for both to carry, a shield against loneliness. He went to her, wondering what could be unusual in activities they both had pursued with diligence, passion, and professionalism. He found out. Perla excelled even Perla. She devoted herself to his supreme delight. She carried him to heights he'd seldom scaled before; she carried him there again and again by exciting byways and side trips. Her passionate odyssey ended only when she sagged in fatigue, facedown into her silken pillow. He left her, admitting he had never encountered such erotic lovemaking; it was unlikely that he would meet another girl so dedicated to her art. And even through the staggering fatigue, burned the deep unquenchable longing for Margarith and Margarith's arms. . . .

He had seen less and less of Vincente as the lazy weeks passed. Vincente spent much time at Perla's Palace, swaggering about as if he and not his half-sister were the entrepreneur. He ordered people about and was obeyed. He continually advised Perla and she agreed eagerly to whatever notion he mouthed, no matter how unreasonable. He suggested changes in a system that was a golden success and his suggestions were incorporated without question.

Vincente's inflated ego made him insufferable. Jeff was relieved that Vincente spent so much time at Perla's Palace, though he was afraid the swaggering boy was going to put her out of business by laying every golden goose in the place and smashing all the golden eggs they managed to lay. But Perla was exultant having Vincente near again to direct her life. She adored him; the more impossible he became, the more she pampered and coddled him. Only the fact that Vincente found great pleasure in playing at being the extremely wealthy and handsome son of Don Cipriano Olivarez saved Perla from total ruin. Vincente loved to ride in Don Cipriano's finest carriage with his father. He relished the attention they attracted on the boulevards. One could almost read the lips of the rapt onlookers. How handsome! Father and son! Copies one of the other! So aristocratic. So handsome. He found himself receiving invitations into the best homes. Don Cipriano opened unlimited charge accounts for Vincente Olivarez in the finest tailoring shops and most exclusive clubs and restaurants. In tailored suits, Vincente was indeed handsome—his arrogant walk delighted the women and intimidated the men. They bowed to him, simpered, and deferred to him.

Jeff had decided that Vincente had found a niche large enough for his swollen ego as Don Cipriano's son, as the silent emperor behind the queen of Havana's whores. He was pleased. Perhaps in time Don Cipriano could talk some sense into the boy's head, get him into school. Jeff hoped so. But then, Vincente turned up, as if he had not even been away, different only in that he was elegantly attired, sporting a top hat and a cane. "Solano has slaves," Vincente said. "Prime. Fancy. He will deal with us—despite Lafitte and his threats."

And so they'd come to Solano's—the last resort.

Jeff stared, pleased and astonished at the prime quality of the blacks in Solano's barracoon. Exhausted by the short, servant-supported walk from his carriage, Solano panted helplessly. He invited Jeff and Vincente to seat themselves on a raised dais in a lean-to at the north end of his *estocade*. Solano sank, with the two black servants supporting his porcine body, into a bank of pillows. Then he clapped his pudgy hands and the parade of slaves began.

Each black was ordered to drop his lightweight cotton britches. Each was warned to obey Don Jeff under pain of whippings with a wide-bladed, perforated paddle wielded by one of Solano's castrated servants. Solano's pudgy mouth pursed and his bright little eyes glittered; he would relish a show of slave defiance; a whipping would intoxicate him. But there was no discord. Still in a state of shock, or recovering from illness suffered in the weeks of middle passage from African coastal "slave castles" to Cuba, the blacks were as docile as sheep, mute, as they were herded in for inspection. When Jeff remarked about the prime quality, Solano said petulantly, "If you knew Policarpo Solano, dear boy, you would know I deal only in the truly beautiful specimen."

Jeff spent two hours testing teeth, testes, reflexes, chests, legs, looking for blemishes. Solano's stock was prime to fancy. Jeff found few flaws in the males or dams. But what disturbed and surprised him most was the mild way Solano agreed to his base offer on each animal. He'd expected to haggle with Solano, but he would name a price—obviously too low for such quality stock—expecting Solano to protest and make a counteroffer. Solano merely nodded and waved his stubby hand. Jeff couldn't believe his good fortune. He had a superb bargain here, far beyond anything he or Gischairn could have anticipated.

"The only thing is, I don't trust that fat bastard," Vincente said when they left Solano's *cuartel* in their carriage. "Solano has not changed—that rhino is still the most despised *maricón* in all Havana."

Jeff nodded. "I know something is wrong. I just can't figure what. We'll just have to be alert, that's all."

Something was wrong. They found out what and how badly wrong when Captain Augsberg moved the *Julia* across the steaming bay. Lafitte's confederates had been around, asking questions. They had frightened away part of the crew. Augsberg had been able to find replacements, but the return crossing promised to be pirate infested. Their only chance, as Augsberg saw it, was to load the herd of blacks after dark and make a run for it on the first tide. Jeff agreed. Activity became feverish. Jeff sent word by Vincente for Solano to have his blacks at the wharfside by four that afternoon for transfer by longboat to the *Julia*, riding at anchor.

Solano sent back word that this would be impossible. Surely Señor Carson understood Solano could make powerful enemies by dealing openly. The delivery would be made secretly, or not at all. If the *Julia* were prepared to sail, Solano's people would deliver the 200 blacks in time to get safely out to sea under cover of night. Since this was the only way it could be worked, Jeff capitulated. He spent the day overseeing the final loading of his own merchandise as well as provender for the blacks—sacks of beans, maize, smoked pork, and lemons.

Solano cut the delivery time as close as possible. Jeff saw why at once. As he prepared to send the first of the blacks into the longboats, he saw these were not the slaves he had bought. They were the poorest of culls.

Jeff swore. He cursed even when he realized swearing wouldn't buy him anything. It relieved his inner rages and tensions. It stirred the adrenalin and it expressed not only his hatred for Solano, but for his own gullibility. How that fat sodomist must be laughing! Solano had his revenge. He had shown fancies and delivered culls—and Jeff Carson had bought it.

"Let's take them back," Vincente said.

"No." Jeff shook his head. "Go ahead, Captain Augsberg. Load them aboard. Prepare to sail. I'm going back and get my slaves."

"You can't carry 400 blacks on the *Julia*." Augsberg was calm, but he was pointing out what he felt had to be an obvious fact.

"We'll have to," Jeff said. "It's the only way we can make Solano think we're too scared to wait around—that's what he was counting on. That's what we'll let him believe."

Jeff armed Vincente and a black Cuban who had just come aboard the *Julia* as a replacement. Lopez knew the countryside better than either he or Vincente. The Cuban led them across country so they came up stealthily upon Solano's barracoon. Jeff was surprised but coldly pleased to find Solano's carriage still parked at the stockade entrance.

They moved in quietly, cracking gun butts across the skulls of Solano's guards and leaving them trussed up in the darkness. When they walked in upon Solano, his *cuartel* manager, and his black servants, the four men stared at the guns, speechless. Lopez tied up the servants and the manager. Vincente looked at Solano and said, "Leave the fat one to me."

Solano wept openly, his rubbery lips quivering, tears streaking his cheeks. "Listen to me," he cried, his falsetto voice cracking. "It does not matter that I sent you culls —Lafitte will take them anyhow! Don't you see the supreme joke when he takes your shipment—to find them culls?"

"He might not see the joke, Solano," Jeff said. "If he is going to take our herd, we'd better have the quality he expects—he taught me how to select blacks, you know."

Solano struggled, trying to get to his feet. But Vincente shoved him over. The fat man rolled upon his bulbous belly and rocked there helplessly, sobbing.

"Get the slaves chained and ready to march," Vincente said. "I'll keep Solano occupied so no signal is sent anywhere."

Jeff ran to assist Lopez in lining up the fancy and prime slaves he had chosen earlier. He heard Solano screaming, at first in rage. As they marched the slaves out of the compound and headed them across the forests toward the wharfs, Jeff saw that Vincente was beating Solano's fat buttocks with the perforated paddle. Solano's cries changed from anger, to agony, to delight, and then to squealing wails as he ejaculated under the ecstasy of the whipping. He wallowed on the floor pleading for more, begging Vincente for the one more stroke which would lift him to supreme release. . . .

Vincente arrived at dockside as the last of the fancy slaves was loaded aboard the longboats. Augsberg was sweating, anxious to get going. Jeff said, "Good work, Vincente, get in the boat and let's go."

Vincente smiled, but remained standing on the wharf. "I'm not going, Jeff. I've decided to stay here in Cuba—as Don Cipriano's son . . . and, too, my sister needs me. Perla truly needs me."

Jeff laughed at him. The oarsmen poised ready to pull away from the pier. Jeff said, "I'm glad you're staying—though I'll miss you."

"And I you, *mi amigo*."

"But—Perla *needs* you! How hypocritical can you get, Vincente? You abandoned her two years ago—to starve or be beaten to death by Jorge. She didn't need you then?"

"Not as she does now. Two years ago, Perla didn't have her own whorehouse—which needs me to run it. I cannot let Perla down, as much as I would like to return to you."

Jeff laughed. He was still laughing, despite a deep sense of sadness, as the longboat was rowed away from the dark wharf. Even when they pulled alongside the *Julia*, he could see the dim figure still standing in the darkness.

CHAPTER XXXVI

Jeff stood on the bow of the *Julia,* sensing the chill as they sailed from the calm of spring across that imaginary Tropic of Cancer line into the frosty chasm of winter. The wind chilled, freshening, waves churned, and topsails cracked like bullwhips. The *Julia* seemed to skim the water like a porpoise, becoming one with the wind and the sea, following a north lane paved with silver and gold.

Behind him, the sun dropped hotly into the sea, sending red flames shooting through the heavy clouds banked along the horizon. He watched those flaming colors, flaring as if the sea itself were afire—scarlet, crimson, and cerise streamers flickering out from the skyline into the rising blue swells of the Gulf.

He turned, and then heeled back, his pulse quickening. What had appeared to be a gull against that tormented sky, seemed now more a pelican, and then he realized it was a sail, full bellied in the wind and fixed like some sea falcon on the wake of the *Julia.*

He alerted Captain Augsberg who had already spotted the brigantine. They fixed the largest telescope on the pursuing ship, and Augsberg, in that cool tone, confirmed Jeff's worst fears. The ship was a blackbirder. It was in full pursuit. "Our only chance is to run north, and keep running as long as we can," the captain decided. "That'll

336

buy us nothing but time for a few extra prayers."

They raced the *Julia* north, full sail, running scared, her bow biting into the long swells. The ship showed no lights, the pilot steered by the stars—anything north by northwest was close enough. They were racing for a harbor, any old port where they could find sanctuary from the blackbirder.

Jeff stayed on the captain's deck all night. He watched the waves mount, the winds rise, and the clouds flood across the last traces of the stars. He heard the keening of the slaves between decks. One could almost believe they sensed the tension of the crew. But he knew better— the blacks were seasick, as he would be if he had time to think about it. He was nauseated, but he could not throw up. There was no way to vomit fear.

An impenetrable fog settled in the darkest hour before dawn, and the wind died away. They were not becalmed, but they were moving now at the whim of the winds. They laid off the fog horns, moving forward in cold sweat. When they saw a black bulk looming ahead, it would already be too late. But the sea was still, the calm unbroken; they heard no distant cries of fog horns.

It was after eight in the morning before the fog began to lift, and it was ten o'clock before the sun began to burn the wisps away. They moved forward through the smoking fog, and as it burned above the crow's nest, the warning cry came from up there: "Brigantine! Hard to starboard!"

Captain Augsberg studied the dim outline through his glass. He nodded at last. "It's her," he said. "She not only followed and overtook us in the night, she's cut us off. Some smart skipper, I'll give him that." He spoke casually, as if sitting at a bar table somewhere, recalling a mildly interesting tale.

They watched the blackbirder sail across their bow, setting herself to be carried alongside the *Julia*. They were ready for the cannon shot that went harmlessly across the *Julia*'s bow.

They went out on the deck. Jeff stared, recognizing

the *Sainte Teresa.* It was the Lafitte ship in which he had completed his final mission for the pirate. In Captain MacFarland's vessel, he'd gone to Haiti and returned Lafitte's stolen slaves.

MacFarland's Scot-burr voice rode across the distance between ships. "Heave to, *Julia.* Prepare to be boarded."

Captain Augsberg took up the huge megaphone, but Jeff touched his arm and for the first time exerted that power he had reserved above the captain's. The captain shrugged and handed him the megaphone. Jeff called, "Hold off, Captain MacFarland. It won't be that easy. I know your guns can blow us out of the sea—but that's what you'll have to do."

"Virgin's balls! You've got human lives there to think about."

"They're no good to you dead, either, captain!"

"So that's your fool's choice, is it? Knowin' in advance we can sink you?"

"But you best hear me first, captain! We've got three small cannon aboard—"

"Then heave to quietly and spare your lives—you're hardly armed a-tall!"

"Wait, captain! I know the precise location of your powder magazines. No matter what you do to the *Julia*—none of us on either ship gets out of it alive! Hear me well, man! I got all three of my cannon fixed on your ammunition magazine, captain. . . ."

A thick and sour silence hung taut between the schooner and the brigantine for a long beat. One could almost see Captain MacFarland toting the odds on the abacus of his mind. His voice slit the wind. "That you, Carson?"

"It's me, captain! I know your ship as well as any man —but you."

"All right, lad! You've struck yourself a bargain! . . . We'll let you sail past this time. But hear me well, lad! Not again! Not ever again in these lanes! By all that's holy, we send you to the bottom next time—cargo and all! And that's straight from Jean Lafitte himself!"

Jeff mopped the cold sweat from his forehead and nodded at Captain Augsberg. The sails shifted, tacking, bellying in the wind, catching at it and slipping past the brigantine.

They were in sight of the mouth of the Mississippi before Jeff breathed easily. His chest ached as if he had held his breath since the moment Captain MacFarland released them. They sighted the customs ships, but somehow Jeff no longer feared them after the encounter with the blackbirder at sea.

"Them customs boys are going to let us past," Captain Augsberg said. "They can do that—let us pass inspection at pierside in New Orleans. They do that with ships they don't suspect." For the first time since Jeff had known him, the captain laughed. "And us carrying 400 blacks of every shade and grade and sex known to man! Our holds crammed with 'em, and them customs boys waves us past."

Jeff didn't speak. He just breathed out heavily, sighing.

The captain pulled his lips into a rare smile. "I got to admire you, lad. Thought little of you when we met—you gone far up in me estimation."

"Thank you, captain." Jeff gave Augsberg his warmest smile. "I can tell you, captain, when we met I didn't trust you—and now I'd trust you with my life."

The captain smiled. "You did, lad. You did. . . . Well, you know, I've found in a long and misspent life, we mistrust—and we dislike—what we don't know." He nodded. "On sight, you looked like one of them arrogant young aristocrats I hate on sight, and I know to you I looked like a pirate, too disreputable to land an honest job. You turn out to be all of a man, and I turn out not to be half so bad, eh?"

Jeff laughed. The captain hadn't believed his little observation had earned such a hearty response, and Jeff couldn't enlighten him. He trusted the captain, sure, but not enough to tell him that far from being an arrogant young aristocrat, he was really a black slave—running from the law. Quite a few rungs below the level of the disreputable pirate. . . .

They sailed up the Mississippi in the night, all hands watching for the three yellow lights to starboard. It was almost midnight when they spotted the three yellow-glowing sea lanterns on pier supports. Beyond, the wharf was dark; above it, the land ascended to a plateau where a manor house sat, dim lights glowing in all the windows across the front.

Something happened inside Jeff at the first sight of Palm Villa plantation. He could not put it into words, any more than he could put the feeling from his mind. He had never been in this place before, and yet Jeff had the distinct and unsettling sensation of coming home—of truly, and only at last, coming home. . . .

By the time Captain Ausberg had ordered an anchor lowered and lines cast across the waters to the pier, long-boats, manned by half-naked blacks, were moving silently in the black river out to the *Julia*.

Jeff ordered the *Julia*'s longboats lowered over the side with crews in each of them. He warned the blacks through their interpreters that crocodiles infested the river, they must be careful not to fall in. What he was warning them was that they would be killed if they attempted to swim for freedom. But again, he found even the finest-looking black specimen docile and easy to handle. They were in a strange and alien land. They were frightened, ill, confused. There was nowhere for them to run. Jeff felt pity for them. He understood the feeling.

Offloading the slaves went smoothly and much faster than boarding them. The blacks didn't know what this place was, but after long months at sea, or rotting in stench-fouled barracoons, they were to be put ashore, their shackles removed. They went willingly, even hurrying down the gangplank and into the waiting boats.

A black man who introduced himself as Michel took charge of the slaves on the pier. He walked them in groups up the incline and beyond to where food and bedding awaited them.

Captain Augsberg laughed. "Well, Jeff, except for the stink of nigger musk, we're a clean ship now! Customs can't fine us for stinking! They can suspect, but suspicion ain't proof. We can sail your cargo of coffee and cigars right into Canal Street harbors, big as life."

Jeff smiled and shook his head.

"I'm letting you take her in, captain. I know as you do that Gischairn has greased all the palms in sight—nobody will challenge you. But you can do as you like—if it were me, I'd have this ship hosed down, spread with tar or something stronger than nigger musk. No sense in putting the customs people in a bad position—give them an out. If they don't smell niggers, they won't even think niggers. And we made it all the way."

Augsberg nodded. "We'll scrub down clean, fore and aft, Mr. Carson. We'll smell of tar and resins when they come aboard us. . . . But you got a small fortune here in honest cargo . . . why you stopping off here in the middle of nowhere?"

Jeff exhaled deeply. "If I told you I knew why I'm staying here, captain, I'd be lying. I don't know. I'm tired. I'm beat. I don't want to see Gischairn, or anybody for a while. . . . As to my cargo, I trust you, captain, and I trust Gischairn, and I trust the Commercial Bank of New Orleans. I'm not worried about my cargo."

The captain shook his hand and Jeff went into the pier with the last longboat. He stood on the pier until the lines were cast off, the anchor weighed, and the ship's long boats hauled the *Julia* forward until her sails caught the wind.

He tried to feel pleasure and excitement. He was a wealthy man—or he would be when Gischairn took these blacks into New Orleans vendue. There were twice as many blacks as they'd counted on. Some of these lesser blacks were bozals and wouldn't bring more than 600, tops. But what the hell, the profit on the culls would far exceed that of the brightest fancy they'd auction off. The culls hadn't cost them a dime. . . .

But he was too tired—too exhausted mentally and

physically—to feel exultant at being a wealthy man. He would soon be worth well over $100,000, and this wasn't a bad start for the bastard offspring of a mulatto bed wench and a passing stranger. But he felt no gratification or satisfaction. Not even the fact that he could well become a millionaire before he was thirty—he had eight years!—could lift his spirits. He was between the hawk and the buzzard, in limbo. He was melancholy and depressed, and he was lonely in the dark night.

He touched the gold cross on its chain about his neck, trying to draw some hopefulness from its diamonds. Nothing helped. The *Julia* was gone in the darkness of the vast river, the night silences shrouded in upon him. He took up the carpetbag and walked up the terraced land to the manor house.

Michel and a black woman named Lady Nancy welcomed him. The woman offered to fix a meal for him, but he told her he only wanted to sleep. He told Michel they would begin the next day to get the slaves into the best shape possible—groomed, fed, oiled, medicated, and clothed so they would look even fancier than they were when they were transported to the slave auctions in New Orleans.

But he was too tired to look even that far ahead. He would do all he could to polish up these slaves so they would bring good prices, go to plantations where they would find tolerable conditions. It seemed somehow important in his present mood that not one of these slaves —not even the culls—should be sold off to the cane fields. They were his niggers, and he wanted the best for them.

CHAPTER XXXVII

Palm Villa proved to be the sanctuary Jeff had been looking for. The quiet, lazy days passed slowly, and at first he was afraid he'd be pestering the slave wenches because he'd need female companionship so fiercely. But the old estate showed itself to be everything he'd dreamed a home could be—everything life had denied him. The manor house had been constructed of native brick, local timbers, and roofed with seasoned cypress from the bayous themselves. Profusions of every bright flower—hibiscus, roses, gardenias, gloxinia, amaryllis—burst from the rich earth. Every room of the mansion provided evidence of past glories, hinted at long-hidden secrets, and was redolent of cedar, linens, silks, colognes, fabrics, and recollections of loud and noisy days forever lost. He found it pleasant, secure, restful, and fascinating.

The servants warned him that visitors were rare at Palm Villa. Travelers seldom if ever came down the shell-paved lane to the plantation unless they'd lost their way. Few boats ever tied up at the cypress-wood pier along the riverbank. They were remote, isolated—not a very exciting place for a young man alone. "I've had enough excitement for a while—maybe for life," Jeff said. He shook his head. "I don't know what I'm looking for here. Maybe I won't find it . . . But I'm in no hurry to leave. I'm content. Owls calling at night are noise enough for me."

For the first week or so, he lay in bed every morning until after ten, content to rest while activity flowed all around him. Servants in the kitchen, maids polishing, making beds, cleaning, slaves exercising in the yard. He heard them, saw them, told himself to get up, to oversee it all, improve it all, to make sure the slaves going to auction were at their best. But for a while, he took no part in any activity. He did not want to. He could not push himself anymore. He was tired. The hurts were tamped within him, but they'd caught up with him, and inside, he ached.

Gradually his energy returned; the hurt became memory of hurt, the total exhaustion a weariness he could live with, and the tensions relaxed. He saw much that needed to be done and soon he was waking at dawn; he was slowly rejoining the real world of the living. He could not make himself care very deeply about anything, but he could look for something to do, to occupy his mind if not his heart, something to take him out of himself, whether he wanted to go or not.

Jeff wandered through the old house. He found himself intrigued by its solid construction. Huge, hand-hewn beams supported the patiently hand-planed flooring. These four-inch thick planks were interlocked, tongue and groove, and were secured into their joists with pegs. The ten-foot ceilings and tall windows drew the mildest zephyr and helped to cool the shadowed interiors on the hottest day. The mansion had been built lovingly, carefully, to last many generations. The place seemed to Jeff to offer the permanence he'd been seeking, a house with a proud past, a promising reach into the future. Even the bricks—made on the property in a private kiln—had a glaze and dull redness all their own. The cypress shingles were black, petrified, thicker than tiles and secured against gales.

Arable land ran for a mile or two both ways along the river and was bordered on three sides by lush bayou jungles. Jeff walked the fields, prowled the forests, and for long hours at a time, could forget he was a fugitive, a bastard nigger without roots, without hope, and with a price on his head.

During the weeks that lazed past, as he explored the plantation he began to believe he discovered himself. He had never seen more peaceful country than that which surrounded the plantation—it was like retreating deep into the primal forests of his own lost heritage—and from this peaceful silence, he drew strength. Day after quiet day slipped past, and one day he knew he was well again.

He worked with the black slaves patiently, preparing them for the coming auctions. He set up beds in one of the cabins for the ill. The smartest women were taught to change the ill, wash them, feed them. There were dozens of handsome young bucks who'd rate fancy on any slave vendue. Jeff kept these youths busy exercising, rubbing themselves and each other with oils, honing their muscular coordination. New from Africa, they were frightened and despairing. They welcomed his kindness and his attention. Through interpreters, he told them of the wagons that would come to take them into New Orleans where their physical beauty and strength would be put on display, where they would be chosen for work —in crafts, fields, houses, or among domesticated animals. The kind of jobs they won would depend on what they knew, what they learned here, and how well they applied it all. The women Gischairn had sent along with Michel from New Orleans taught the slave girls to stitch up the cotton shifts they would wear on the vendue tables.

Jeff found boxes of colored cloth in the mansion attic and had the women add designs—butterflies, flowers, gulls —of bright color to each shift. The black wenches fell in love with the pretty shifts, parading around in them, smiling and simpering, and begged to be allowed to wear them on the farm.

Jeff encouraged copulation among the bucks and the young females. He offered extra shifts with bright designs as prizes or bonuses to the first wenches who became pregnant. Most of the women who left in the wagons for New Orleans could be certified pregnant—and therefore more valuable by two-thirds.

There was little Jeff could do to improve the lot or the fate of the culls. Solano had tried to swindle him with these rejects. These second- and third-class animals —as Beluche had trained him to consider the lesser-grade slaves—had languished a long time in barracoons around Cuba, often rejected by slave traders. They were the bush Negroes, the short, squat, flat nosed, thick mouthed, vacant eyed, those with the slanted forehead, the ridged brow, the undershot jaw, the malformed legs. Jeff spent as much time as he could with them, trying to discover native talents that might mitigate in their favor at auction time. He found dozens who had belonged to a tribe of horsemen. He worked to increase their proficiency in harnessing animals, caring for them, feeding, watering, tending minor equine ills. A smart auctioneer could guarantee they'd never be doomed to the cane fields and quick death. He could play down their defects by selling them as animal handlers. Other bucks had been part of a hunting tribe, others had been warriors, some had tended sheep, goats, or cattle. He found at least a dozen with sharp, pointed teeth, men from tribes who preyed on their neighbors and ate them, boiled with roots, leaves, and leeks.

He was still working to improve the least skills of these people when Gischairn's wagons arrived for the first contingent of slaves to be auctioned. Carefully, Jeff chose the 100 with the most advanced skills, those who might be judged first class, prime and fancy.

After the first auction had exceeded all his expectations in profit, Gischairn himself made the trip to Palm Villa to praise Jeff for the excellence of his work, his selection of animals, his preparation of the stock. "You should have seen our wenches, in their shifts with the pretty bright designs on them. They looked like something extra—as if somebody cared about them, as if they were worth more than the ordinary wench. And by God, they brought

346

more. . . . Now, come back to New Orleans with me, Jeff," Gischairn said. "You've earned it. You're a rich young man. You're going to be richer. You could be the most eligible young bachelor of the season—with my backing. You could have your choice of the loveliest young females —Creole, quadroon, white, or black!"

"Am I rich enough to buy Palm Villa plantation?"

Gischairn stared at him as if trying to decide whether his young partner was joking. "My dear boy! Of course you are! For under $15,000 this entire estate—owls, bats, panthers, and all—is yours. It has belonged to several generations of my family. However, I grew up mentally healthy—I was never a maudlin, sentimental slob. . . . I hated this place when I lived here—the hurricanes put you in jeopardy and flood tides of that river can take you right off to hell."

"You make it sound perfect," Jeff said. "I'll take it. You sign it over and I'll write a draft transferring money from my account to yours."

"My dear boy! I'm in no hurry. Let me deduct the price of this old place from our profits. . . . It's yours . . . but for God's sake, don't bury yourself out here. New Orleans is throbbing with life, glowing with beautiful women . . . and we've got much to do—we can't stop this slave trade now."

"Jean Lafitte says we can. In fact, he promises to sink our next ship."

Gischairn shrugged. "I know Jean. Of course he hates competition—and our niggers made his best look dowdy. We'll go right ahead. We'll take precautions. We'll be ready for him. That's all."

"That's easy for you to yell at him from your parlor on St. Charles Avenue," Jeff said. "I invite you to try it sometime from a deck of a ship with his cannon trained on you."

Gischairn laughed. "You're just low right now. You'll get rested up. We all get tired. We all want to quit. Your depression will leave you. You'll get bored out here— you'll know when you try to crawl one of the cows it's

347

time to come into town. . . . You'll figure ways to outfox Lafitte. I'm sure of it. I'm patient. I can wait."

But it was a year almost to the day from Jeff's arrival in New Orleans from The Laurels to his return to the crescent city. He delayed at the farm. He put the south forty into cotton. He planted vegetables to help make Palm Villa self-sustaining—potatoes, corn, beans, onions, watermelons, yams. From the herd awaiting sale, he bought those blacks who appeared destined to be knocked down as cane-field laborers in any auction. They had no inkling that he had saved them from stifling, back-breaking, soul-robbing work that killed off the ablest black in less than three years. They did know Jeff treated them kindly, fed them well, and encouraged their pestering any willing wenches. They liked him. They worked hard for him. . . .

Jeff checked into the Hotel St. Louis when he arrived in New Orleans with Michel as his body servant. Gischairn had told Jeff that Baxter Simon had been in New Orleans twice in recent months—once with a sensational coffle of fancy blacks that brought record vendue prices, another time chasing down a lead on his fugitive slave Bricktop. "Your old friend Bricktop," Gischairn said with an enigmatic smile. "You remember Bricktop, don't you? Well, as usual, the lead proved to be false and Simon returned to Carthage. I think this slave Bricktop is dead by now, don't you?"

"He ought to be," Jeff had said.

Climbing the stairwell of the hotel with bellboys and Michel like pack animals in his wake, Jeff wondered if his new affluence would protect him were he to confront— and slay—Baxter Simon? His heart quickened at the idea —the only way he'd ever secure his own freedom. Or would he? Gischairn liked to say you could get away with anything if you could afford the right lawyers. This was true for white men, maybe even for freed persons of color. He was not free. He'd once held forged papers purporting to grant his manumission. But in the eyes of the law, he was black, a slave, chattel of Mr. Baxter Simon of Willow Oaks plantation. He could not marry a white woman. He could not testify in court against a white man. If he killed a white man, even to save his own life, he was denied any defense; he could be hung without trial. If he were permitted a trial by jury, no black's testimony, including his own, in his behalf was admissible against a white man. He might be wealthy by all standards of the times, but he was still black by rule of law. He was a rich nigger. This could only increase white hatreds, incense them against him. He had come a long way, the bastard son of a bed wench. He had run as hard as he could . . . but it was like running in place. He had never really moved forward at all.

Michel pressed Jeff's trousers, jackets, vests, shirts, put his clothing away. Jeff gave him a gold eagle and told him that with twenty dollars he'd be treated like a prince down in Congo Square. Michel grinned and thanked him and went out, hurrying.

Jeff fell across the bed. He lay on his back, staring at the ceiling. He heard the muted sounds from the busy street below. He told himself to go down to the bar for a drink, to have dinner. He'd come to New Orleans to be among human beings, to find himself a woman. He'd been weeks, living the life of the celibate down at Palm Villa. He considered this totally unnatural and somehow unhealthy. He decided to visit New Orleans, and if he found a woman who could interest him for longer than one quick pestering, he'd take her back to Palm Villa with him—for as long as he could stand her, as long as she could endure the isolation. This was his plan. But he did not move. He was tired. It had been a long trip up from the plantation. Maybe tomorrow . . .

He dozed off to fitful sleep. He dreamed Captain Mac-Farland's ship cannon were trained on the deck of the *Julia* where he stood alone. The huge guns mounted in the *Sainte Teresa* sideboards were fixed on one target— him. No matter where he ran, the great gun snouts trailed him, exploding, belching fire and ball and death. . . .

He realized someone was knocking on the door's thick mullions—and had been for a long time. Still sleep-drugged, he got up from the bed and walked across the room, yawning and running his hands through his hair. He almost touched the door knob when he realized he had enemies as well as friends in this town. Troubled, he found his handgun. Holding it concealed against his thigh, he opened the door.

Jeff and Ponchus stared at each other. The aging black man exhaled as if he'd been holding his breath for a long time. His mouth quivered, broke into a smile that faltered and failed. "Oh, Lawsy, Masta Jeff! Young masta! How good it is to see you. How long I been lookin' for you."

"Ponchus. My God! The last person I expected ever to see again! Come in. Come in."

Ponchus entered the room and Jeff closed the door, locked it. "How'd you find me, Ponchus?"

"Found people what knowed you, masta. Took a long time. Finally found a Mister Gischairn . . . he promise he let me know the minute when you come back to town. I was waitin' outside the lobby down there. I was hopin' Mister Gischairn would come in—he do sometime mos' every day—and then—glory to Gawd, Masta Jeff—I seen you. Big as life. Heah you was big as life—a-walkin' right into this hotel!"

"Why didn't you come on up?"

"I tried, masta . . . Lawd knows, I tried. But I'se a black man a'tryin' to git past the lobby in a elegant white hotel. . . . That ain't easy . . . I'd of nevah done it. But I bought youah room number from a hotel nigger, and I snuck up the rear steps."

"Sit down." Jeff grinned, studying the exhausted, but still militarily rigid figure. "How are you? . . . How is—she?"

Ponchus tried to smile, failed. "I doin' 'bout as well as can be expected, masta. But Missy—she in desperate trouble, masta . . . I see my Missy in hell, Masta Jeff. . . . It break my heart . . . that chile—she plain in hell and ain't nobody to help her but you . . . and I been searchin'

350

for you for weeks. For months . . . 'cause without you, Masta Jeff . . . Missy—she ain't got nobody."

CHAPTER XXXVIII

Jeff stood rooted to the floor. He stared at Ponchus, unable to credit the things the exhausted Negro was saying. There was the unreality of a nightmare about it all, and yet Jeff knew it was so incredible it had to be true. Three or four times he urged the fatigued Ponchus to sit down; the poor devil would sit on the edge of a chair, pouring out the story bottled up for so long within him. But he could not sit still. He leaped up, pacing the room, his voice dead and flat, as if he were saying things that not even he could believe, though he had seen them with his own horrified eyes.

"I gettin' old, Masta Jeff. Sometime I 'fraid I'se almost as old as I feel. I seen a lot in this life—dyin' of the most fearful kind on the battlefield where I marched beside de major. I seen sorrow and pain and hurt. But I ain't never seed before on God's earth a time of heartbreak like my poor Missy is lived through."

"But—she must have money. I left it with you—a small fortune. She couldn't have spent it—or lost it all in a year."

"No, suh. She ain't spent it. She ain't lost it. She ain't never really had it. He done took all that—all her land—all her servants. Everything, he took it from her."

"Who took it? That fellow—what was his name? Coffee? Meador Coffee? Did he take it?"

"No, suh. Poor Mr. Coffee, he tried to help Missy everyway he could. But he couldn't do nothin' . . . he was helpless."

"Who took her money? Tell me?"

"You best let me tell it straight from the first, Masta Jeff. Or else you gwine be all ragin' inside, and you ain't gwine hear it—and you got to hear it all . . . you got to know how bad Missy needs you.

"Like you tole me, the night you had to run away, I untied Mr. Baxter Simon and I helped him up to bed, and I removed all he clothes—sayin' I figgered they best be laundered for such a fine gen'mun. Well, he rages and cusses at me, but when he do git he clothes all done up fresh, he don't take off after you at all.

"That man, he plumb smitten with Missy. I heah him allow to Mr. Henley Lewis as to how he don't care for white women in bed. They makes him puke, he tells Mr. Lewis. He jus' vomit when he look at all that dead white flesh . . . an' he like the dusky wenches best. They do what he say. They don't noway talk back. An' he say he put white ladies up on a pedestal—and to him that where Miz Margarith belong. She de flower of the South, he tell Mr. Lewis. She so lovely and fresh, it plumb hard for him to believe she ever was married to Major Morceau. And Mr. Simon, he say he figger as how Mr. Morceau feel about white ladies like he do—they belong on a pedestal, and mayhap the major ain't trifled with Miz Margarith, 'ceptin' on the weddin' night which mos' white ladies is ready to endure anyhow. . . . He say that the way it is. De major he pestered the black gals and left Miz Margarith in peace.

"Mr. Simon, he stay around The Laurels most nigh on to a week. He ride all over de place with Mr. Lewis. He always tellin' Missy what a lovely farm she got, what fine herd of blacks she got, what a lovely lady she is. Miz Margarith, she like she ill after you gone. She distracted like. She starin' into nothin' half the time. She hardly hear

352

Mr. Simon what he say. But he think this is angelic—he tell her that. She like an angel—like she unearthly—like she don't belong on earth . . . and her left alone, a widow and all, to run a farm as big as The Laurels . . . she need a man he kept tellin' her . . . a man that would respect her, and hold her high on a pedestal, and run her farm to make her rich.

"Missy hardly answer him. I know dis is because she hardly even hear him. She don't care what he say. But he takes it to mean she listenin' an' she ain't gainsayin' him.

"Finally, Mr. Simon say he got to leave. He got to get on down to New Orleans—on business, he say, and he got to git back to his plantation. But he do hate to leave her, so helpless and all . . . and nobody to take care of her. He say he comin' back . . . and she just force a smile . . . an' I know she ain't even listenin' to him.

"When Mr. Simon gone, Missy ill. Like she got the brain fever. Out of her head. Crying. Miz Malraux, she come over from Foxmoor, and she cain't do nothin'. . . . Mr. Coffee he 'round all the time tryin' to keep the plantation a-runnin'. . . . Jus' when Missy gettin' a little better—a-sittin' up, taking broth—Mr. Simon come back. . . .

"Mr. Simon—he pace in front of Missy's big chair on the veranda . . . back and forth, a-talkin' and a-talkin'. . . .

"I a-standin' jus' inside the front room . . . I don't like Mr. Simon . . . I know you don't like him . . . and I reckon Major Morceau was he alive would've run him off his land . . . but de major ain't there . . . you ain't there. . . . I heah Mr. Simon say he made up his mind. He don't yet ask Missy a by-you'-leave. No, suh. He tell her. He say he been married once, and his wife a good Christian woman what died. And he had made up his mind never to marry again . . . but he had no way of knowing that God in His heaven would bring some fine lady like Miz Margarith into his ken . . . that what he say.

"Miz Margarith, she shake her head a little while. But he keep after her. She weak. She vomitin' in the mawnin's spite all we can do. She feelin' poorly all the time. He a relentless man once he make up his mind. He tell her he goin' to marry her—and help her run her plantation—and take care of her. . . . I don't know then—like I able to figger later—why Missy, lovely and dainty little Missy, ever say yes to a gross man like that Mr. Simon. . . . It make me want to vomit when she agree to marry him.

"All I could think was that Missy had been full of love for you, young masta. We all know at the plantation how you both fancy one another . . . and we happy . . . but after she find you got black blood—and she can't let herself love you no more—I think maybe she married him jus' cause she felt so bad 'bout losin' you. . . . She was a sick girl, I know that.

"She sick right up to the time of the weddin'. Wasn't nothing for Mr. Simon but that they have the biggest weddin' in the history of them parts. They let's Miss Lissa Malraux handle all arrangements—and she deliver them a weddin' like nobody ever see before. . . .

"First, they go on a honeymoon up to St. Louis. Then they come back to The Laurels. But Mr. Simon he kinda restive . . . he say they got to spend mo' time over at Willow Oaks because he got valuable black animals over there. He want to leave The Laurels in the hands of Mr. Lewis and let me run the house. But Missy, she stan' up against him, for the first time and the only time I see her stan' against him—she want ole Ponchus 'long at Willow Oaks. I know Masta Simon he hate me—I too ole to cover any he wenches and give him new suckers to sell . . . I maybe helped you in front of he eyes—he don't take no shine to me. But Missy won't have it no other way. So we go over to Carthage in Mississippi—ain't much of a town, like a crossroads—and then out to Willow Oaks, which is just a farmhouse, with hardly nothin' nice about the place. Mr. Simon, he kept tellin' Missy she can build a big new house. But sayin' that close as he come. . . .

"He lot more content at Willow Oaks, and I reckon

I know why. He got him bed wenches over at Willow Oaks. They come in to his bed every night. . . . Even if Missy know about it, she ain't sayin' nothin' . . . and I see she plain pregnant—far pregnant. She gwine have a baby—and she don't care what Mr. Simon do long as he stay away from her. . . .

"Well, we still at Willow Oaks when Missy's time come. They ain't no human doctor in Carthage—they jus' one ole white vet what tends blacks and animals. Mr. Simon don't send for the vet. He say the midwives on Willow Oaks better at deliverin' than airy doctor. Missy mighty sick, in terrible pain, but she don't complain about no doctor.

"Well, sir, when that baby was born, we jus' all plunge right down like in a nightmare. Missy a-screamin' in pain, and Mr. Simon sittin' downstairs in that worn-out old rocker of his'n, jus' a-sittin'. Finally, they come and say the baby born—a boy, and Mr. Simon gone be mos' proud when he see it.

"I upstairs. I hear him when he walk in and they show him the baby. He howl like a bear in mortal pain, masta! He rage. He curse. He threaten to kill Missy. He yell at her that he know now why she married him—to give Bricktop's bastard brat a name! He accuse her of sleepin' with a nigger—with Bricktop. He say it ain't no good she lyin' to him—that baby got red hair jus' like Bricktop, an' it got splotches on its belly that shorely mean it got nigger blood. Bricktop's blood.

"Then I see what I never expect to see in this world—full of woe as it is. He pick up that baby by the ankles and he knock it in the head. . . ."

Sobbing, the aging Negro stopped talking. He walked to the window, stood a long time trying to get himself under control. But when he continued speaking, his voice quivered.

"Then he don't even give that baby a decent burial. He throw it out the window into the yard. He tell the yard niggers to bury that bastard baby, or else feed it to the hogs—he don't give no goddamn which they do.

"All this time—even after her baby is dead—poor Missy is pleadin' for its life. She sayin' it a innocent baby. If he gwine kill something—he ought to kill her. But not her baby . . . He tell her he ain't havin' no bastard nigger baby in his house to pass as his own. Far as the world know, that baby born dead . . . that all the world will ever know. . . .

"Missy jus' went out of her mind with her grief. . . . I reckon it easier on her than on any of us . . . she jus' out of her mind . . . she don't know where she is . . . she jus' walk aroun' all day, starin' at nothin'. . . . She don't fix her hair or change her dress unless Masta Simon he tells one of the women servants to clean her up and change her clothes. . . .

"We don't ever go back to The Laurels again. We jus' stay there in that ole farmhouse at Willow Oaks. Mr. Simon he jus' raging all the time that there ain't nothin' more terrible in the sight of God than a nigger man a-pesterin' a gentle white lady—less'n it be a no-good white slut what takes up with a black buck. Blasphemy! Filth! Evil in the sight of God, he rages. He mean to kill that nigger buck what defiled his wife. . . .

"He keeps yelling at Missy that he gwine kill her too. He ought to've killed her the night he found out they ain't got no baby at all—that she been carryin' the bastard sucker of his nigger slave Bricktop.

"I find out, Masta Simon he would of kilt Missy—Gawd knows he wanted to, only 'fore he did, he found out that Masta Morceau done played him the lowest trick of all—in Masta Simon's eyes. Major Morceau he left The Laurels to Miss Margarith only long as she lives. During her life, the big plantation her'n to do as she wish, but when she die, The Laurels—slaves, property, and goods—all go back to the major's family. If Masta Simon kill Missy, he lose that big plantation.

"What he done was, he took The Laurels and he stripped it bare. He sold off every slave, all the animals, fired Mr. Lewis 'cause he didn't need him no more.

"He plan to raise slaves for de market at The Laurels.

He spends a lot of time gettin' the place ready to be another stud farm like Willow Oaks. . . . Only time we happy at all at Willow Oaks when Mr. Simon he away at The Laurels, or takin' a coffle in to New Orleans. . . .

"Poor Missy, she hardly know when he there or not. He yell at her, she cringe, but that all. He treat that poor chile worse'n airy kitchen drudge. But I see it don't matter—she sick in her mind—she don't even know where she is. When she cry, she don't even know what she cry about.

"Ever' time I tries to help her, makes Masta Simon ragin' mad. He had me strung up and whopped, jus' for tryin' to git Missy to eat a bowl of soup. He had me whopped a few times . . . but I don't mind . . . I been with the major in battle . . . my life been spared . . . I thankful for what I had . . . I ast nothin'. . . .

"Then I see we gwine lose Missy. She gwine die of grief and starvation. She don't eat nothin'. She just sit and pine. Sometime she walk around that ugly ole farmhouse a-draggin' the major's sword in its parade sheath . . . but she failin' . . . somebody got to git her away from Willow Oaks. Somebody got to git her away from Masta Simon, 'cause she dyin', and he doin' nothin' more than jus' barely keepin' her alive. If they takes The Laurels from him when she die, it don't matter to him—he done stripped it. He jus' holdin' her there 'cause he hate her . . . 'cause he gwine make her pay for what she done to him—what he call a mos' vile crime against him an' God an' white people."

Jeff exhaled heavily. He was sweated down. He saw that Ponchus was staggering with weariness. He said, "You best go to bed, Ponchus. You're going to fall if you don't."

"Please, masta. You got to promise me. You got to help Missy. You don't help her, nobody can."

"We can't do anything tonight, Ponchus. You sleep in my bed—"

"Oh, masta. I couldn't do that."

"The hell you can't. You sleep in my bed, and that's an order."

Ponchus smiled, his ebony eyes brimming with tears. "You all man and then some, young masta. You de onliest man I know what is more man than ever even de major was."

"Maybe it's my black blood, Ponchus."

"Yas, suh," the old Negro nodded. "Hit might be that."

CHAPTER XXXIX

Throughout that night Jeff never slept. He felt no sense of exhaustion. He sat in the deep leather-covered chair. The room sank into darkness when the candle on the bedside table guttered out in its own tallow. Ponchus had protested but had finally undressed and crawled beneath the sheets on the bed. Jeff heard the aging man sniffling for a few moments and then mumbling, as if he were praying. Jeff shook his head, wondering to what gods old Ponchus prayed? There must be gods somewhere if a man like Ponchus still believed. When the prayer ceased, it was quiet in the room and in the late-night city. Occasionally, Ponchus snored. He had carried his burden as far as he could tote it. He had shifted it to the younger shoulders of the mustee fugitive. He asked only the impossible. He asked Jeff to return to the scene of his greatest terror, that plantation where he'd been born, whipped, despised—and branded. Even the memory of

Willow Oaks caused Jeff's stomach to churn and filled him with a nameless dread.

Jeff sat, staring into the blankness of the dark window —and north across the night to the plantation country around Carthage, Mississippi. Mindless with grief, harried and despised, Margarith was doomed unless he went back to Willow Oaks and delivered her to safety. For a long and painful moment, he thought of her as he remembered her gentle beauty, and the sad image Ponchus etched of her in her loss and grief overtook him. His son! Their son—conceived in their love. His own son from Margarith's womb. What more to be devoutly wished? His son—only he would never see him alive on this earth. Red haired. The color of the baby's hair, the telltale splotches on its belly had signed its own death warrant. Simon had knocked it in the head, as he might any flawed animal, and thrown it in the yard for the blacks to dispose of. His hands gripped the leather chair arms. He would have sobbed aloud, but he was too full of rage for the tears. He bit back the bile that gorged up in his throat.

He felt the pressure of blood pounding in his temples. He felt as if his head would burst with the pressures building in it. Oh, God, he had thought he'd hated Baxter Simon when the slave breeder had burned the plantation initials in his back with a cattle branding iron. But he had not known what hatred was then. He had hated as a child hates. Now his hatred possessed him. It was an obsession, the kind of burning hatred that had driven Baxter Simon on his trail all these years. It was as if everything in his life, every road he traveled, every alley along which he'd run breathless, had brought him to this place. Baxter Simon had casually slain his child, driven Margarith mindless with grief, treated her as if she were a scullery slut. The question was no longer whether he'd go back to that hated, feared, and despised place, but rather, where would he take Margarith when he delivered her from Willow Oaks? Where could they go?

He laughed savagely, thinking about going home.

Home? Well, it was the place where he'd been born, where his mother had delivered him, where he'd been owned body and soul, by a man whom he hated and who grew to hate him in return. Most people thought warmly of home. To him it was a place of terror. But if he belonged anywhere—the bastard offspring of a passing stranger and a bed wench—it was Willow Oaks. From its earth he had come. Yes, even if he thought of it in horror, it was home. Returning there filled him with a fearful sense of his terrible loneliness against overwhelming odds.

It was not the first time in his life that he had felt alone, but now there was the numbing sense of helpless loneliness. In Carthage, Mississippi, he was not Jeff Carson, or Jeff Laforche, or any man entitled to a surname. He was Bricktop—fugitive slave. The blacks, whites—affluent and red-neck—would rally behind Bax Simon against him. Dangerous? God knew, he had never faced such danger where every man would be turned against him. He had never even contemplated it because he had never believed any power on earth could force him to return to Willow Oaks alive. And yet it never occurred to him that he would not go. Margarith would not know him, and if she knew him, she would despise him; yet he must go to her. All he could do was attempt to find, in that wily intelligence that had kept him alive twenty-two years, some plan which might outwit his hated enemy, might somehow free Margarith, might get him into Willow Oaks and out of it alive. Alive, that was the operative word—the only way to travel.

He was still sprawled out in the deep chair at dawn when he heard Michel's key in the door lock. The young black let himself into the room, then stopped, mouth agape, when he saw the gray-haired Negro asleep in the bed and Jeff slumped in the leather chair near the window. "Masta. What happened?"

Jeff shrugged. He yawned and sat up in the chair, keeping his voice casual. "Did you have a big night on Congo Square?"

Michel grinned. "I could die right this minute, masta,

and never have missed nothin' in this life."

At the sound of their voices, Ponchus stirred, sat up in bed. Jeff was saying, "Michel, I want you to return to Palm Villa today. Take Ponchus with you—"

"No, masta," Ponchus said. "Please, masta! I got to go with you."

"There's no sense in it," Jeff said. "It's too dangerous."

Ponchus shook his head. "I marched with the major in the battle of New Orleans, masta. He never sent me back where I'd be safe, 'cause he knowed I wouldn't go without him. . . . I've seen death, young masta . . . I ain't scairt of nothin' Mr. Simon can do."

Jeff rang the bell-cord for room service. When the boy appeared, he ordered breakfast for three—pancakes, ham, eggs, and coffee. Michel packed while they awaited the meal. Michel ate ravenously. "A man builds an appetite on the square," he said grinning. "Will I hope to see you soon back at Palm Villa, masta?"

Jeff shook his head. "I don't know. If you don't hear from me, you'll hear from Mr. Gischairn."

"I'll keep the place ready," Michel said. "And pray you a safe trip." He took his bag and went out of the room. Jeff looked at Ponchus and tried to smile.

"Well, we might as well head out. Nothing to hang around here for."

Ponchus—brushed, boots polished, body militarily erect—carried Jeff's carpetbags as they left the hotel lobby. He was a most respectable-looking manservant for a handsome young dandy whose black hair was showing streaks of auburn. Jeff decided that when he got back he'd have his hair dyed again. Then he grinned crookedly. Strike that. He was making no plans beyond his arrival at Willow Oaks. His life had begun there; it might well end there. He could no longer look ahead.

They hailed a hack outside the Hotel St. Louis and rode to the riverboat offices at the foot of Canal Street. One of the new sidewheelers was shipping out that morning at nine o'clock. Jeff bought two tickets to Vicksburg. The ticket agent was a native of Mississippi. He told

Jeff it was something over a hundred miles on bad roads from Vicksburg up to Carthage. They would pick up the Natchez Trace at Jackson, and leave it at Ofahoma, turning east. The man laughed. "You got to look fast to find Ofahoma, and even faster to find Carthage. You're likely to ride through it if you happen to sneeze."

Jeff and Ponchus prowled the pier impatiently, sweating in the blaze of morning sun until the gangplank was opened and they boarded with a gaggle of fashionably dressed travelers and their black servants. Jeff had reserved a stateroom, though the gabby ticket agent counted it a waste of money since the sidewheeler would dock in Vicksburg around nine o'clock that night.

Jeff sprawled in the lower berth and Ponchus lay down in the upper. Jeff wanted to sleep, but he could not. He was aware of the boat's fighting the swift tug of downriver current. At noon, Ponchus brought their lunch from the dining room along with a bottle of bourbon. Ponchus urged Jeff to eat, but he couldn't do it. He and Ponchus killed the bottle before the boat pulled in and tied up at Vicksburg, almost on time. The river town was loud and alive along the docks. Saloons and fleabag hotels were lit with gas lamps, and busty women smiled from the shadows and whispered sweet obscenities.

The last thing either of them needed was more alcohol, but Jeff chose the best-looking saloon and they entered. Ponchus carried his bags, walking erectly and sedately at a respectful distance behind him. When the bartender smiled, welcoming him, Jeff knew the masquerade was working—he was the model young Southern aristocrat traveling with his body servant. His good looks, his casual manner, freshly pressed suit and shirt—thanks to Michel! —and the favorable impression both he and Ponchus made convinced people he belonged to the landed gentry and was on a meaningless odyssey.

He had a pressing need at the moment for a lightweight buggy that could travel fast, even on rotten roads, and even more importantly, a first-class carriage horse. He didn't give a damn what they cost. Time and quality were the only priorities. He had whatever money he would need stashed in his carpetbag. He let the bartender understand, over a bourbon neat, what his need was, what gratuity for a good lead could be arranged—and that money was no object.

Before the bartender could make his suggestion and send him to a livery where he'd get a kickback, the man standing at Jeff's shoulder spoke to him. "You're in luck, mister. I might have just what you're looking for—if you're willing to pay what it's worth."

That voice sounded so familiar that Jeff felt the hackles stand on the nape of his neck, and his hand instinctively moved toward the handgun under his belt. As he turned, he saw Ponchus staring at the stranger, mouth agape, eyes white rimmed. Then he realized why the voice was so familiar—it was as if he himself were speaking, even down to the inflections in the tone.

His own eyes widened, his own mouth parted slightly. It was as if he stood looking into a time-lapse mirror. The image he saw was his own—in about twenty-three years! The stranger's auburn hair was fading slightly, salted. Grey flecked his tilted brows. But those go-to-hell brown eyes were as young as Jeff's, caught in a net of crow's feet. The nose was the same, the jut of the cleft chin. Their heights were almost identical. "Name's Craven, sir. Brook Craven," the man was saying.

Jeff shook his head. He didn't speak. Craven said, "What's the matter? What's wrong? What you starin' at me like that for?"

"My God," Jeff whispered. "You don't notice anything strange?"

The man laughed and shrugged. "Hell, you mean we look a little alike?"

"We look one hell of a lot alike."

"So? I been through these parts, man and boy more'n twenty-five years. Likely I could run into plenty of woods colts that bear me a strong resemblance. I been movin' around, and movin' fast, all my life. Selling leather goods, patent medicine, run my own little travelin' carnival for a

363

while. These damn riverboats, floating with their shows—the competition is too tough. I'm back to selling again. That's my real trade, I reckon. Selling a tonic at the moment—cure diseases they ain't even discovered yet."

"How about sitting down over here—just a few minutes. Let me buy you a drink?"

"How about that horse and buggy you're so hot after?"

"You got one. Is it any good? I need something light, with thin, rimmed wheels. I don't care how rough it is. I want it to move fast. And I got to have a fine horse."

"Think we can make a deal. I tell you. I'm a man likes to travel first-class. No matter how low my finances might be, I like to live like I got it all, you know? Horse I got is first-class. You can check him—have a vet check him. I know he's good flesh. And the buggy is light and strong —and fast."

Jeff sat down at a table, watching the man's easy, charming, go-to-hell smile. "Why you so anxious to get rid of the horse and buggy?"

"Mister, I'd get rid of my mother if the price was right . . . man like me—with fine tastes. Need cash. Besides, I got my heart set on a closed coach. Ain't young as I used to be—though I never let the women hear me admittin' a heresy like that. I have to travel in all kinds of weather. Sleepin' on bad roads sometimes. Storms. A closed coach to carry my clothes and my samples—and a little mattress, that's the ticket. You come up with enough loot, you got yourself the finest young horse and the slickest buggy any young sprout ever sparked his doxie in."

"All right," Jeff said. "We'll look at it. But first I want to ask you something. You ever travel up around Carthage?"

The man smiled. "I've traveled this state both ways, up and down with side trips to N'Orleans for the Mardi Gras."

"How about a plantation named Willow Oaks—did you sell leather, or patent medicine, or yard goods at Willow Oaks plantation about twenty-three years ago?"

Brook put his head back laughing. "Son, I can't honestly

recollect where I was three *weeks* ago."

"No. Listen. You'd remember this. Even if it was twenty-three years ago. If it was you, you'd remember. You stopped at Willow Oaks—they ran a nigger stud farm. Visitors spent the night, they give 'em bed wenches."

"Lots of my favorite customers do that."

"But this time—at Willow Oaks—there was a beautiful little mestizo girl. Her name was Mary. Think. She was so beautiful you took her, even when they warned you that Baxter Simon—owner of Willow Oaks—was saving that virgin to break for hisself . . . you took her. When Simon found out, he tried to kill you."

As Jeff talked, the man remembered. His face showed he remembered. He grinned, then he laughed, then he slapped his leg. "Lord, yes! I went out of that house without my shoes on—got away in my underwear, carrying my suitcase and my samples." He put back his head laughing.

"You're my old man," Jeff said.

Brook shrugged. "Might be. That Mary was plenty hot. She drove me wild. Still recall her, though I rode wide of Willow Oaks all these years. I might well of unloaded a full broadside into her—two or three times as I recall that night. She was hungry for it, and I loved it."

"Christ," Jeff whispered. "My old man."

"Well, look, boy. I may or may not be your father. Even if I am, you got plenty of half-brothers and -sisters wanderin' around this state. It don't mean a fuckin' thing to me. So let's not git maudlin. You hear? I feel nothin' toward you. Nothing paternal. Nothin'. You're just a good-lookin' kid that I meet one night in a Vicksburg saloon. Hell, you ought to be good-lookin'. You came from me and Mary!"

Jeff exhaled heavily. So this was where he came from. This was his heritage. This man was his father, this man who didn't give a damn. After a long beat, Jeff shrugged. "All right. We don't get maudlin. Where's that horse and buggy? I'm in a hurry to get started."

Brook stood up. "Down the street at the livery. But I

warn you now, boy. Don't expect no discount because you might be blood kin. That horse and buggy going to cost you $600. It would cost you 600 even if you wasn't fortunate enough to be my own flesh and blood. At least *I* ain't tryin' to take advantage of the fact that you're my son."

CHAPTER XL

"So you ain't one of these snot-nosed rich kids, eh?" Brook Craven said as they strode along the Vicksburg night street with Ponchus marching in their wake with Jeff's bags. "Had you figgered wrong from the start."

"It's a wise father that knows his own son," Jeff said.

"You got a burr under yore tail," Brook said. "Need a fast buggy and a good horse—and fast. What you running from—son?"

Jeff laughed. "You won't believe it, but Ponchus and I aren't running *away* from anything. Not this time. I'm running *back* to Willow Oaks plantation, and the faster I make it the better—papa."

Brook Craven was silent a few moments. They walked with identical long and graceful steps with that panther ease. He said, "Yeah . . . but—well, you got nigger blood."

"*You* are a wise father."

"Why you going back to Willow Oaks—where they *know* you're a nigger? Take my word for it—son. You could pass anywhere. Not just for white—but for one of these aristocratic young white bucks."

"Thanks—papa."

"Hell, I'm serious, boy. My old grandfather had one saying I live by, the only one I care for at all. He always said, never hurry to be hung."

Jeff exhaled heavily. "It's nothing I look forward to with a lot of relish, papa. But something I figure must be done. Baxter Simon is holding someone there—against her will—and I've got to get her out."

"Her!" Brook Craven swore volubly. "Might of knowed it. Has to be a *her* gittin' you to stick yore neck in the noose! You're *my* son, all right. Every mistake I ever made in my life, some wench was behind it. Hell, I been snared in every hair trap from here to Valparaiso, Indiana."

When they rolled out the carriage at the livery stable, Jeff knew he had what he wanted. The single-seater had lightweight shafts, thin, high steel-rimmed wheels, and space in the rear, which Brook had used to transport his samples.

Brook leaned, thoughtful, against an upright as Jeff and Ponchus inspected the buggy. The livery owner had gone off, shivering, to fetch Brook's carriage horse. Ponchus nodded, hoping to influence Jeff's decision in regard to buying the light buggy. A man moved just about as fast as he could hope to in a light trap like this, behind a good horse. Brook said, "That Baxter Simon always was a son of a bitch. Throwin' his weight around. Helpin' God run His world—givin' Him advice, I'd vow. Self-righteous. Jesus, it's easy to hate a righteous son of a bitch, ain't it?"

The carriage horse was about three years old, a roan with rich mane and a high-held head. It was sound of wind, strong in the withers. It appeared to have been well cared for.

"No profit in not keepin' a first-class animal in less'n first-class condition," Brook said to nobody in particular.

But Ponchus was bold enough to agree with him.

"My old masta, de major, he always say that. Major André Morceau, that was. He always say you got to treat good animals good as you treats your own self."

"Well, hell," Brook winked at the aging man, "I don't go that far."

Jeff counted out the money, telling the livery man to harness the animal in the cart. He handed over the $600 to his father. Brook took his time counting it. Then he looked up and said, "There's also the matter of the two dollars livery costs."

Jeff laughed, shaking his head. "You're a cheap son of a bitch, aren't you?"

Brook shrugged. "That's a hell of a way to talk to your own father. It ain't that I'm cheap . . . I've just had to learn to never pay anything that you can git somebody else to pay for you."

Jeff paid Brook's livery tab and Ponchus set their bags in the rear of the carriage. Jeff looked at his father—at this time-lapse image of himself. He couldn't agree with Brook that he felt nothing. A bastard didn't come across his father every day. Brook looked like a hellion, a devil-may-care who likely hadn't improved the world much, but who had gotten his kicks from every hour of the day. Jeff extended his hand. "Well, it's been real great—and expensive—knowin' you—papa."

Brook surprised him by grasping his hand in both his. Brook clung to him for a moment. "You take care, you hear—son?"

"Sure. And you too, papa," Jeff said. He watched Ponchus bob his head toward Brook and go round the buggy and climb up on the far side.

Brook went on clasping Jeff's hand in both of his for a long beat. At last, he said, "Hell, I'm headin' north. Why don't I ride along with you—at least until I find the kind of coach I'm looking for. Might be able to find just the ticket in Jackson maybe. . . ."

With Ponchus crowded in the middle, they headed east on the Vicksburg-Jackson road. This was no highway; in places it was a weed-grown plateau marked by ancient ruts. Jeff let the horse pace itself. They took turns curling up to try to sleep in the rear of the buggy with their head on the carpetbags. Brook Craven was a compulsive talker, and as far as he was concerned, the subject of priority interest in this world was Brook Craven. Before they rode into Jackson the next day, Jeff knew most of his father's history—where he was born, where he grew up, why he ran away from home, how many years since he'd seen his parents. But Brook's favorite stories were how he got the better of smart-ass locals who were always out to gull a stranger.

It was only during that brief recess when Brook decided to try to get some sleep in the rear of the buggy that Jeff was able to think, to plan ahead, to try to see what Baxter Simon would do, what his reaction would have to be. But it was not until after he bought breakfast for Brook, Ponchus, and himself that he was able to come up with even the nebulous wisp of an idea. It came to him when Brook insisted they delay in Jackson long enough to allow him to inspect coaches and a span of horses. At first, Jeff was going to refuse and angrily remind his father that time was more than money right now —it was life. But he changed his mind, nodded, and agreed. When Brook located a polished, secondhand coach and a strong team of horses, Jeff astonished his father by buying them for him.

"Look, son," Brook said. "You don't buy nothin' bein' a sucker this way. Hell, you spend all this money buying me a coach and pair, you think I'm going to be choked up with gratitude? Hell, no, I'll be lookin' around for ways to stick you again . . . you got to think on that, son." But to the coach dealer, Brook said, with a brusque thickness in his tone, "My son's buyin' me this coach and pair. Not many men got generous sons like that, huh? Huh?"

They headed north on the Natchez Trace out of Jackson. Jeff was silent, grimly quiet and lost in his thoughts. Ponchus did not speak unless Jeff spoke to him. Jeff realized the old orderly had learned that when his idol, the major, had weighty problems, he needed peace in which to chew them over.

They rode into Ofahoma and spent the night there in an ordinary. The bar was crowded; travelers still used the Natchez Trace between southern Mississippi and Memphis, though the riverboats were altering travel patterns. The Trace had been shown on French maps as far back as 1733, but its importance as a highway had been steadily diminishing since the War of 1812.

Despite the crowds, Brook struck up a liaison with a barmaid just out of her teens. She was fascinated by the charm the ex-medicine-show spieler showered upon her. She whispered her room number in his ear.

Looking at his father, Jeff noticed something different. He grinned, shaking his head. His father had used some kind of red powder in his hair—something left over from the carnival days—to conceal the gray. Jeff had to admit the old boy looked younger, more like his own twin than ever. . . .

A pallet had been placed on the floor for Ponchus, and the aging man curled up on it and was soon snoring. Jeff was to share the big double bed with his father, but he was sure Brook would spend most of the night with the barmaid. He was right, Brook did.

Jeff lay sleepless on the bed, ankles crossed, burning eyes fixed on the high, dark ceiling. His mind churned, making plans, discarding them, seeing roads that looked like exits but turned out to be cul-de-sacs in a hopeless maze. He was still awake when Brook staggered in just before false dawn. The room was cave dark but Brook fumbled around, undressing. Jeff sat up and fired the lamp beside the bed. Brook said sarcastically, "I'm a big boy. You didn't have to wait up for me."

"I've got to talk to you."

"Are you crazy? My head's out to here. My ears are stopped up. I'm dead, boy."

"I want you to listen. I want you to do something for me."

Brook Craven heard this. He straightened and twisted

around, glaring at Jeff. "I don't know whether you got some fool idea that being my son gives you some claim on me. But get that out of your head. Brookfield Wallace Craven does nothin'—nothin'—for nobody but Brookfield Wallace Craven. Now go to sleep and let me alone."

"No." Jeff got up. "You called me a sucker for buying you a coach and pair."

"Might of known it. You buy me a little gift—you figger you own me. Well, fuck you, son."

"You're going to earn that coach and pair, papa. If you don't, I'm taking them away from you. And if you think I'm not big enough to do that, you *have* wasted your life."

Mouth twisted, Brook stood in his underwear, staring at his natural son in cold rage. "You are a bastard," he said. "Personally, as well as legal. What you think I'm going to do for you?"

"You're going to be me."

"What? Where? Up there in Carthage? Boy, you *are* out of your mind. Right here in Ofahoma is where our trails part. You go east to Carthage, and me—I head north to Memphis and a new life where I got no bastard son to haunt me."

"You go north—you walk," Jeff said.

Brook cursed for two minutes without repeating himself. "Look, boy. I been to Carthage. Like you say, twenty-three years ago. I lost nothing up there. That Simon's a bastard red-neck. Them backwoods crackers use real guns—real bullets."

"Not only that," Jeff said. "There's a thousand-dollar reward out for me—dead or alive."

"You bastard . . . you'd put your own father in jeopardy like that." Brook shook his head.

"I didn't want you going into something without knowing all the angles," Jeff said. "What I want you to do should be a piece of cake. Easy. But I can tell you this—it may be the most important thing anybody ever did for me in all my life."

Brook shrugged. "Then you best get somebody you can trust to handle a big job like that."

371

"I trust you," Jeff said.

"Then you're too stupid to be a son of mine."

"Oh, I don't trust you because you're my father, but because I know how bad you want that coach and pair. Now listen to me. With that red powder in your hair you look young—you look a hell of a lot like me—enough to fool somebody who already *believes* you're me. And I see most of that red powder has rubbed off on your doxie's pillow—and that's good too."

He outlined his plan. They would travel east until they were within a mile or two of Carthage. Then they'd hide Ponchus and the buggy. With red powder in his hair, Brook would ride, hidden, inside the coach. Jeff would drive into town, let word get out to Baxter Simon at Willow Oaks that Bricktop was back. When Simon came riding in pursuit, they'd let Simon *see* Jeff leap onto the coach and haul east out of town. What they wouldn't let the slave breeder see was the place where Jeff leaped from the coach and Brook took over to sucker Simon into following him—long enough for Jeff to get into Willow Oaks and, hopefully, out of it.

Jeff realized that Ponchus was sitting up on his pallet. It pleased him that the old army orderly was nodding agreement at his strategy.

"What makes you think a fool plan like that will work?" Brook wanted to know.

"Because it's got to work."

"Why?"

"Because it's the only plan I've got. . . ."

Sleep was out of the question for any of them. Brook had sobered up. He dressed furiously and paced the room, savage with inner rages. At the first light of dawn, they went downstairs, had breakfast, and headed out east on the narrow road to Carthage.

In less than two hours they were approaching the Carthage area. It had been a long time—seven years—but rage had burned it all forever into Jeff's mind as those brand marks were seared into his back. Even the road, winding through the dry country, looked familiar. The farms they passed looked the same, older, shabbier, more desolate, but still vivid in his memory. It was all clearly etched behind his eyes where he couldn't forget no matter how devoutly he wished it—the streams, trees, and fields. He was coming home, but he viewed none of it with nostalgia. Instead, a cold ball of fear knotted in the pit of his stomach. He was returning to a hot, savage land where blacks were no more than animals, like the cows, hogs, horses, to be used casually and slaughtered at the whim of their owner. A man's black skin rendered his life forfeit.

Jeff stared at the men in Ofahoma, and those they saw in the barren yards of the subsistence farms along the trail. What made these white men superior? In God's name, what? Ugly, crooked-shouldered, scrawny—these puny toads marching around like gods. Did they hate blacks because of the better musculature, the velvet skins, the virility? Did they force them to the status of animals because they were afraid of what they might accomplish if they were allowed to live free—as human beings? He didn't know, but not knowing fueled the hatred he felt for Baxter Simon and the suffering he caused among the blacks he bred and sold.

He signaled Brook to halt the coach and pulled the buggy into a copse of loblolly pines, which concealed it from the roadway. He left Ponchus armed with two guns. He shook his head and said in a flat voice, "Give me three or four hours, Ponchus. If I don't show up, get to hell out of here—and fast."

"You be back. An' I be heah, young masta."

Jeff nodded and smiled. He walked up the incline, stood a moment marking the place clearly in his mind. The road out of Carthage made a long turn, the back road concealed behind trees growing thickly against its shoulder. He swung up on the driver's seat of the coach. Brook sat sweated, hungover, and angry. Jeff said, "Get inside. Stay down. I don't want you seen—by anybody. And for God's sake put some more red powder in your hair. Do you think you look like me with all that gray showing?"

He rode boldly into Carthage, seated on the open front of the coach and handling the horses with ease. He pulled in before the only tavern in the village and swung down. He stood for a long beat, staring around in the sunlight. He was grinning coldly, though inside his belly was empty and his nerves drawn taut.

He saw a young boy get up from the shade where he sat in front of the general store across the road. The boy sidled toward the corner of the building. He climbed on an aging horse and rode out of town, fast. Jeff watched him and the dust he stirred—on the road toward Willow Oaks. Well, it was started. . . .

He pushed open the batwing doors of the tavern and stepped inside. For some moments he was blind after the dazzling sunlight of the street. He walked to the bar. There were four or five men loitering at tables, playing checkers, drinking, whittling. They stared at him, stirred uncomfortably, and gazed at each other. They fell silent, but they did not move.

Jeff grinned at the bartender. "Howdy, friend. Nice place you got here. I used to live around here—don't recall you."

"Name's Ben Ralston," the bartender said.

"Who your folks?" one of the men at a table said.

Jeff turned, smiling. "You probably wouldn't remember them. My old man was a traveling salesman." He ordered a bourbon, neat. The bartender served him and swiped at the bar with a damp rag, making big motions. A fly buzzed around his eyes. He batted at it with the bar rag.

The bartender said, "Mister, I don't know you. Don't recollect you. At all. But I got a kindly word for you—and most of these fellows will back me up—you'd do well to get on out of this town."

Jeff looked astonished. "Why? Looks like a nice wide place in the road. A man could settle down among you folks—make no trouble."

"Look, mister, it's likely a mistake. But all these fellows

will tell you—ever'time a Mr. Baxter Simon comes in here, he gets to talkin' about a redheaded nigger he's chasing."

One of the men at the tables laughed, a chilled sound. "You look a hell of a lot like the mustee—the way ole Bax Simon describes him."

Jeff's voice chilled. "Why, that's a hell of a thing to say to a white man. Accusin' him of bein' a nigger . . . I come in here, tryin' to be friendly—"

"We're tryin' to be friendly, mister," the bartender said. "We 'uns *know* you ain't Bricktop—Mr. Baxter's fugitive nigger."

"Well, thank you," Jeff said in savage sarcasm.

"Look, mister. No offense. But only reason I figger you ain't Bricktop—spite of the way you look like him— is no nigger in his right mind would come back to Bax Simon's town. But Bax Simon is a man with a hair-trigger temper. He might shoot first and ask questions later. Or somebody else in this town might take it in his head to collect the reward for Bricktop."

"Reward?" Jeff set the glass down.

"That's right," one of the loiterers said. "Mr. Bax Simon has offered a reward for—for Bricktop. Offering $1,000—dead or alive . . . That's a lot of money in a town like this."

The bartender nodded. "Man in Carthage with $1,000 in his pocket would be a rich man. If I was you, I'd get in that coach and ride on to wherever it was you started."

"Yeah, but I was headed here. Carthage. Wanted to see the old home place. I can't believe a white man would shoot another white man for $1,000."

"Then you ain't very smart, mister. Everybody in this town seen you ride in—they seen your red hair. Ain't one of them ain't thinkin' about gettin' that $1,000—if you was Bricktop."

"I seen Johnny Lester high-tailin' it out of town—ridin' out to Willow Oaks, I vow," a man at one of the tables said. "Mister, I think you don't clear out, somebody's goin' to decide to take a chance and collect from Mr.

375

Bax Simon—over your dead body."

"Tell you what. I don't know this Bax Simon. But I don't like him—without knowin' him. Tell you what I'll do. I'll just buy some life insurance. I'll pay *fifteen hundred dollars* for your Mr. Baxter Simon—*dead*."

None of the men spoke. The loudest sound in the tavern was the buzzing of blue flies over the small trickling of beer on the bar and the tables.

Finally, one of the men at the tables said, "Maybe you just best stand where you are, mister, until Mr. Baxter Simon gits in here. He can say whether you his fugitive mustee or not. Won't take Johnny long to ride out to Willow Oaks, and you can bet Baxter Simon will burn up the road a-coming into town."

"I've got an even better idea." Jeff showed them the gun he took from his belt. "See this pistol? Brand new. Invented in England. See the extra bullets. Right in the cylinder. Rotate the cylinder. Don't have to stop to reload. . . . I could just about ruin business for this nice bartender with the bullets I got in this gun."

"I don't want no trouble, mister," the bartender said. "This fellow jus' got fractious, that's all. You walk right out, you want to. Drink on the house. Yes, suh, yoah drink's right on the house."

Jeff walked to the table nearest the door. He could see the street through the window. He laid the pistol on the table and kept his hand on its butt. He said, "I appreciate your kindness, Mr. Ralston. I hope there ain't no trouble. But I been insulted. You don't call a white man a nigger unless you're ready to fight—not where I come from."

"Tom's just fractious, that's all. We was all startled at the way you looked, mister," Ben Ralston said. "We didn't mean no harm."

"I appreciate that," Jeff said. "But I'm a man likes to be able to ride into a town without being insulted. We're just going to wait here until your Mr. Baxter Simon comes in—maybe he can apologize for your whole town."

The bartender exhaled heavily, as if he had been holding

his breath without even realizing it. . . .

Jeff heard the thunder of hooves and wagon wheels in the silent town. But even if he hadn't, he'd have known Baxter Simon was racing into the village limits by the way the men in the tavern went tense, sitting forward in their chairs. "Here comes Bax," somebody whispered.

When Jeff saw the dust and glimpsed the wagon at the far end of the street, he stood up suddenly. He held the gun on the men. He laughed. "Well, this is so long. Tell ole Bax that Bricktop was here."

Laughing, he backed through the batwings, heeled, and leaped up on the coach seat. He was laying the buggy whip across the rumps of the horses as he moved. The animals lunged forward, racing out of town. Behind him, yelling in frustration and rage, the men charged out of the tavern into the sunlight.

Waving his arms and shouting, but holding his gun ready, Jeff yelled down at Baxter Simon and the two slave patrollers in the open wagon as he raced past them.

Simon leaped up in the wagon, yelling. He pulled on the reins, turning the horses in the street. Men ran out from the tavern and the store shouting at Baxter and pointing toward the racing coach that rocked side to side, rattling out of town.

"All right, papa!" Jeff yelled. "Get your ass up here and take over. You run 'em as far as you can—and then we're quits, old fellow."

Brook pulled himself up on the seat beside Jeff. He took the lines, slapping them. "You a hell of a poor excuse for a son," Brook raged. "Putting your father in jeopardy like this."

"All you've got to do is ride fast and keep riding!" Jeff yelled. He looked over his shoulder. The wagon was pounding in pursuit. Ahead was the wide curve in the road. He waited until they were past the outcropping of trees. Then he shouted, "So long, papa."

He leaped from the coach, which was racing pell-mell, though it had to slow for the curve. He was rolling as he struck the sand of the road shoulder and he kept rolling, deep into the underbrush.

Brook Craven looked over his shoulder, watching the wagon in the distance. He laid the whip to his horses, cursing because he had to misuse his animals in this way. A hell of a thing. But he did not slow down. He kept up the maximum pace the horses could sustain all the way into Ofahoma, ten miles from Carthage.

Brook had slapped out every trace of the red powder from his graying hair. He had pulled down on the lines, slowing the horses and bringing them to a full stop outside the ordinary where he and Jeff had spent last night. He was just stepping down from the coach seat as the wagon rattled to a stop beside him. The three men in it yelled at him, guns bristling.

Brook raged at them. "What the hell is the meaning of this? Chasing an honest traveling salesman like thugs."

"Where is he?" Baxter yelled. He jerked his head. One of the slave patrollers leaped from the wagon, jerked open the coach door. Simon looked ready to sob in rage and frustration. "You son of a bitch, what have you done?" But he didn't wait for an answer. As the patroller scrambled back aboard the wagon, Baxter was already turning the lathered team and racing back along the trail toward Carthage.

Brook Craven slapped the reins across the rumps of his team and headed north. He would have gone in the tavern to wet his whistle, but he didn't want to run into that barmaid today. He'd been pretty good in there last night, and every time a woman found a good man, she got possessive. He'd find a drink farther down the Trace.

He grinned, pleased with himself. Hell, it hadn't been a bad day. Not a bad day at all. He'd come out of it with a span of healthy horses, a new coach. And there was more, the pleasure of shafting old Baxter Simon one more time. Plus, he'd learned he had a grown son, a good-looking scudder too, the spit-and-image of his old man . . . the kind of son a man could be proud of. . . .

CHAPTER XLI

Troubled by the creeping paralysis of old fears, Jeff drove the buggy into the yard at Willow Oaks.

On the seat beside him, Ponchus poised, holding a gun at his side, watchful and alert. Jeff hated exposing Ponchus to the almost certain doom of returning him here as an ally of the fugitive Bricktop. Simon already despised Ponchus. If anything went wrong, neither of them had a hope in hell of getting out alive. He didn't bother putting his regret and concern into words. Ponchus was where he wanted to be. His Missy was in that ugly old house yonder and Ponchus would willingly die to free her.

Fear—instilled in Jeff with his mother's milk on this place and reinforced through the terror of his childhood and the cruel training that his white master was next to God Himself—was difficult to dispel. Yet the challenge and hatred of Baxter Simon, and Jeff's love for Margarith, flushed through his veins too. Despite immobilizing dread, the utter exhaustion of the long unbroken race north from New Orleans, the lack of sleep, and the tensions in Carthage, Jeff was alert, drawn fine. For the first time he saw a faint glimmer of hope. Give me one break, God, just one break, and we'll make it. We'll whip that arrogant bastard in his own back yard, and we'll get her out of here.

Considering the time of day—the sun was just cresting

—the yard and fields around Willow Oaks were empty and quiet. Jeff saw the whitewashed rows of shacks in the quarters where he had grown up. Nearer were the whipping barns, the gaol for the recalcitrant—cynically called the church—the smithy, the barns, the fenced fields where the youngest children played naked in the sun. There were no families at Willow Oaks. One of Bax Simon's strongest beliefs was in refusing to allow the black animals to become attached one to another. In his own case, a mustee among blacks, his mother had known him, and he had known her. He had loved her. One of the reasons why Simon hated him was that he tried to be near Mary, and Mary wept hysterically when Simon had the child whipped for running to her at every chance.

Small black boys came running to tend their horses. Ponchus said, "You boys stay away from this here buggy. We won't be here long. We don't need nobody to tend it." The children fell back, smiling tentatively.

They rode close to the open porch that ran the length of the old, unpainted slab house. A butler came out onto the porch, the screen door squealing. Behind him came a woman. She was about thirty-six.

Jeff's eyes widened. She was the color of a tea-rose. Her crisp black hair framed her gentle face, her eyes were deep and black and stricken with resignation, even when she smiled.

"Mornin'," the black butler said. His tone suggested how rare guests were at Willow Oaks.

"It's us, Titus," Ponchus said from the wagon. "We've come for Miz Margarith. We want no trouble."

"Nah, suh, Mista Ponchus. I ain't makin' no trouble . . . but Masta Simon he be back mos' any minute. He won't take kindly to nobody takin' Miz Margarith from Willow Oaks."

Still staring at the woman on the porch, Jeff felt his eyes fill with tears. He leaped from the buggy and bounded up on the porch, reaching out his hands to her. She shook her head, retreating, uncertain, frightened—afraid to believe what her instincts told her. "Mornin'," she said.

"Morning?" Jeff caught her slender arms in his hands. "Mama. Mama. Is that all you can say to me?"

Her eyes brimmed with tears and she collapsed against him, crying. "Oh, my baby. My pore baby. You got to git away. He be back—Masta Baxter be back mos' any minute."

"Yes, mama." Jeff nodded. "We're both goin'. You're going with me, mama."

"Oh, sweet Jesus, I wish I could——"

"Mama. You can. Listen to me. Get in the buggy. You don't need to take nothing with you. Whatever you need, I buy you. . . ." He led her gently down the steps and across the ground to the buggy. Ponchus helped her up into the seat. "We goin' in a minute, mama. We goin' in a minute." He heeled around and ran back up the steps. He caught Titus by the arm. "Where is she? Where's Miss Margarith?"

"She yonder inside, masta. I gits her for you—though Masta Baxter gwine be fearful upset."

Inside, the house was as drab, ugly, and cold as its clapboard exterior. A thick-legged center table and a butt-sprung rocker near the fieldstone fireplace dominated the room. Rag carpets, made by the women slaves of Willow Oaks, were islands on the scrubbed pine floors. The furniture was bought, hauled in, but it was a tasteless collection of odds and ends—what the Simons had needed, they sent someone to the nearest town to buy. Standing slump-shouldered at a window, Margarith stared out across the rear yard, unaffected—or unaware—of the excitement on the front porch.

Jeff gazed at her emptily for a long moment in which his heart felt as if it might stop beating. She was wan, her cheeks pallid, thin, her hair frowsy about her face. It was difficult to find in this despairing woman the girl he had loved so desperately. He spoke over his shoulder, "Get her a cloak, Titus. Something to keep her warm."

"Yassuh." Titus moved slowly to obey. Jeff cursed him to hurry him. Titus only complained, whining, "Masta Baxter gwine be terrible upset."

"He'd hate to find you dead," Jeff told him. "Look sharp!"

Margarith had turned from the window and was gazing at Jeff, but he saw no recognition in her lifeless, lackluster eyes. She looked at him, she looked through him. He had no way of knowing whether she saw him or not. She was in hell, and there was no way to know whether she shared this private purgatory with outsiders—even old lovers. He went to her and put the cloak about her shoulders. "We're going now," he told her.

She did not protest, she walked slowly beside him across the room and out to the sun-struck porch.

Ponchus took her arm, led her down the steps and to the buggy where Mary sat, hands knotted in her lap, eyes shadowed with terror. Ponchus and Jeff helped Margarith up to the seat beside Mary. Ponchus climbed into the flatbed behind the seat and Jeff ran around the buggy and swung up beside his mother. He patted her hand reassuringly. But then Margarith said, "No."

Wincing, Jeff stared at her. Ponchus bent forward, patting her shoulder. "Gwine be all right, Missy. You gwine be fine."

"No."

Sweated, Jeff stared toward the road, looking for the first dust clouds that would be the warning that Baxter Simon was returning. They could drive away, but it would be hell covering the hundred miles to Vicksburg with a screaming woman protesting every mile.

"What's wrong, Missy?" Ponchus said in that gentle, unhurried tone. Jeff saw the sweat like marbles leaking from the cap of cottony gray hair.

"Sword," Margarith said in that forlorn, empty voice. "Must have his sword, Ponchus . . . it's all I have of him, you know."

Jeff moved to swing down from the buggy, but Ponchus was already on the ground. Ponchus's face muscles looked rigid, but he spoke gently. "I git his sword, Missy. I gits it. Ponchus know jus' where it is."

Titus stood immobile on the porch, staring at them.

All he could think was of the bad news he had to deliver to Masta Baxter, and the way the master always hated the messenger of evil tidings. Titus could already see himself swinging by the heels, the whip cutting his flesh. His eyes filled with tears of self-pity and spilled along his cheeks. He did not move.

Ponchus was gone only a few moments, but it seemed an eternity to Jeff. His fists gripped the reins. Mary whispered, "I bes' not go, son. Masta Baxter, he kill me—"

"He'll never get near you again, mama." Jeff said this with more conviction than he felt.

"I jus' slow you down . . . I know that man be worse on your trail now than he ever be."

"I want you with me, mama. I don't care."

Mary smiled and covered his hands with her own. He felt the calluses, the roughness of her palms. He grinned at her. "You're gonna live like a queen, mama, like a real princess."

"I don't care about that, son. I be with you . . . no matter how long . . . I be with my baby at last."

Ponchus came down the steps carrying the parade sword and its sheath. He handed it up to Margarith. She took it. Her face showed no expression. She clasped it with both hands, but she went on staring into nothingness. Jeff was turning the buggy as Ponchus vaulted up over the rear board.

Glancing over his shoulder and seeing that Ponchus was straightening himself in the bed of the buggy, Jeff laid the whip across the horses. They lurched forward, racing down the lane toward the public road.

Jeff turned the carriage toward Carthage. There was nothing else to do. They had to watch for dust signs ahead, they had to be ready to get off the trail if they met anyone.

Within a mile of the village, Jeff slowed the horses. He dreaded showing himself in that town, even if there were any chance of getting through it before Simon and the slave patrollers returned from chasing after Brook in the coach. As if reading his thoughts, Mary said, "There's a fork ahead. A bad road, but it skirts round Carthage."

Jeff laughed. He put his arm about his mother and drew her against him. "A queen," he said, laughing. "A real queen."

Mary rode, clinging to his arm, as if for whatever time they had together, she would stay as close to him as possible. Beyond her, Margarith rocked with the motion of the buggy, she squinted against the sun. She did not speak. She was lost within herself.

Ponchus stood up, holding on to the seat rest and keeping a gun ready in his fist. "Yonder a turn," he said.

Jeff pulled the lines left, turning the horse from the road into a weed-grown lane. Mary had not exaggerated; the trail was barely discernible. An aged bridge across a creek had rotted and never been replaced. Jeff got out and led the horse across the narrow, rocky creek. Beyond, the road lost itself in places, crossed a pine hammock, and wound through thick undergrowth. Ponchus said, "Road up yonder."

"The Ofahoma Road," Mary said. "It's the way they took us—to the Trace, and up to Natchez—when you runned away, son. Long years. Long years."

"I thought Baxter Simon sold you in that coffle."

Mary shook her head. "He was meanin' to. Then he got to thinkin' how you doted on yoah mama, how you kept a-comin' back to me. Even when they whup you, even when they cut you to the bone, you kept a-comin' back to me . . . even when I begged you not to come so they wouldn't hurt you no more . . . when my heart couldn't stand them hurtin' you no more . . . still you come. He make up his mind. He keep me. He let the word git out that yoah mama is still at Willow Oaks . . . he think somewhere you heah that, you come back to Willow Oaks to me—and then he got you."

Jeff drew up the buggy in the underbrush. He could see the Ofahoma Road, but knew they were concealed from it. He said, "I never heard you were still at Willow Oaks. I never knew it . . . but for a long time, mama, I was up north."

"I prayed you wouldn't hear it," Mary said. "My prayers were answered—till today. I didn't nevah want you comin' back to Willow Oaks . . . I didn't nevah want you hurt by that man no more."

"He hasn't got us yet, mama."

"That white man more bulldog than he is man. He mean and he never let go. . . . He kept me on, hatin' me. But they needed a cook, and I was the best. Gradually, I took over the kitchen, then with Titus, I took over runnin' the whole house. . . . I think that Masta Baxter liked having me close—'cause it kept fresh in he mind the way he hated you, the way he means to run you down."

In the distance a mare's tale of a cloud expanded into a thick curtain of dust. Jeff heard Ponchus exhale. "I reckon it him," Ponchus said. "They on they way back."

"Hang on," was all Jeff said. He didn't know whether he was speaking to them or to himself.

They sat silently, barely breathing. The dust increased; they heard the thunder of wheels and hooves on the ground. Birds wheeled up nervously from the underbrush. Then they saw the lathered horses, the wagon. Baxter Simon held the reins, the armed and uniformed slave patrollers sat beside him, scanning the road, the woods, the side trails.

The wagon passed so close they could hear Simon's heavy voice raging. Jeff forced himself to sit there for five minutes. Five minutes. It was more like a chilled eternity of waiting. The sound of the creaking wagon, the sound of hooves died, and still he forced himself to wait. He was sweated down and he felt the chilled drops of sweat roll separately down his ribs.

At last, holding his breath, he slapped the reins and the horse moved through the thick underbrush, returned to the trail and went up the incline to the roadbed. They were in the road, and Jeff was turning the buggy toward Ofahoma, when Ponchus said in a dead whisper, "They foxed us, masta."

One of the patrollers fired his rifle. Simon whipped the horses and the wagon lurched forward on the road behind them. The patroller fired again. The bullet whistled past Jeff's head. He said, "Get down low, Ponchus."

Jeff didn't whip the horse. Running, with the patrollers armed with rifles, would only get them killed. He drew the handgun from his belt, half turned, steadying it on the seat rest, and forced himself to wait. Simon's raging voice was clearly audible before Jeff took aim at one of Simon's horses and pressed the trigger. The sound of his gun was the loudest explosion he ever remembered. It caught Simon and his people completely unaware. Mary gasped and even Margarith cried out.

The bullet struck the horse between the eyes, killing it. The animal stumbled, still moving forward under Simon's lash. As it fell, it tripped the other horse, crossed the lines, and stopped the wagon dead. Jeff didn't stop to see this. He said, "Get down, all of you." Mary bent over and, with her arm pulled Margarith down beside her. Ponchus crouched in the bed of the rear space. Jeff whipped his horse and the light buggy rocked, tilted, shook and trembled, racing west on the roadway. The rifles blasted behind them, and the three men were still firing in frustration and rage even when the buggy was long out of range.

They rode into Vicksburg twenty-four hours later. Jeff had pushed the horse as much as he dared, and the animal responded. They stopped to buy grain and water for the horse, sandwiches and milk for themselves. Otherwise, they kept moving. Ponchus sat, hunched in the buggy's bed, watching the back road. He did not doze once, through the hot afternoon, the long night, or the eternal following morning.

Jeff made no attempt to lose himself or the buggy in Vicksburg. He drove to the docks and entered the riverboat office. The agent smiled at him. They indeed had a sidewheeler to New Orleans, a nightboat, a beautiful trip. The boat came in to Vicksburg from the north about five, took on passengers and cargo, departing at six.

Jeff winced. This gave them a four-hour delay. He could not believe that even a dead horse fallen in the traces had bought them a four-hour advantage over Simon. There was the chance that Simon might have decided they'd stay on the Trace south to Natchez. But he wouldn't waste too much time checking on that. If anything delayed him, it would be tracing them by stopping often at taverns, ordinaries, and crossroads stores. Still, this was the only passage available. Jeff nodded. "I'll take two adjoining staterooms. One for my servants, and one for—my wife and me."

The agent nodded, stamped the tickets. Jeff said. "You have facilities for animals, don't you? And space for carriages?"

"We take animals—horses, cattle, goats, hogs, even. We have some of—our best people do like their own carriages when they get to New Orleans. What we do is, you pay for shipping it, and we take it if we can."

Jeff nodded. "That's fair enough."

There was no sense sitting around biting their nails all afternoon. Jeff drove up to the town on the high bluffs above the river. At the Planter's Hotel, he rented their best suite. He was tempted to explain their dustiness, but bit his lip. He didn't owe anybody any explanations. Hotel people were accustomed to outlanders being dust covered and road weary on arrival. He ordered bath water sent up. While Mary was bathing Margarith, he went into a dress shop and bought a new frock for Margarith, underthings and stockings. He bought a dress for Mary too, but was not yet ready to flaunt his mother as a princess. She'd look better in a simple shift—the uniform of the female servant.

Margarith's dress accented her pallor. She seemed completely unmoved by the dress or other garments. But Mary brushed and pinned up her hair; she looked palely regal, if wan and ill.

By the time Jeff had bathed and changed clothes, they'd be cutting it close getting back to the docks. As they crossed the lobby, Jeff walking with his fingers clasping Margarith's elbow and Mary and Ponchus following sedately, people looked up and smiled. Jeff grinned inwardly. The masquerade was working. The more they looked like young planter and wife, with their body servants, the safer they would be.

The nightboat to New Orleans was at the pier when Jeff drove to it. He showed his ticket and they led his horse and carriage aboard. Here, ship's stewards helped them alight, transported bags to the staterooms, and tended the horse and buggy.

And then they waited. Margarith sat immobile in her chair. Ponchus was exhausted. He kept yawning. Jeff told him to go into the stateroom they'd share and go to bed, but Ponchus refused. "I wait until we get movin', masta. I cain't noway rest until then."

Jeff went out on the deck to find out what was causing the delay. A steward shook his head and indicated the loading dock where arguments over the cargo were growing heated. Jeff leaned against the bulkhead, feeling helpless. People passed him, murmuring about the delay. They spoke politely to him, and he remembered to bow deeply in return.

The gangplank finally was removed from the dock. Black smoke belched up from the smokestack. The whistle screamed. This was when Jeff saw Baxter Simon and two armed slave patrollers running across the pier toward where the lines were being cast off for the night boat.

Holding his breath, Jeff touched the handgun pushed under his belt. He stood unmoving, pressed against the bulkhead. There was no chance that Baxter Simon saw him from the pier below—he stood in shadow of the overhang. But Simon was aware they were aboard the riverboat. He was yelling, waving his arms, demanding that the steamer be halted so that he could board it. But Jeff was aware that somehow Simon and the patrollers were getting smaller, there was open water between the boat and the pier. The paddles were cutting deeply and the riverboat was picking up speed.

Jeff bit down hard on his jaw to keep from laughing aloud. Simon's next chance of overtaking the nightboat was the docks at Natchez. But that was a long, overland trip to overtake a paddlewheeler that glided as easily as moonbeams downriver with the current.

He went back to the stateroom. He caught his breath, seeing the stewards and passengers knotted outside his doors. As he hurried, he heard screams from within his cabin. His heart lurched. Margarith.

He shoved his way through the crowd, opened the door enough to allow himself to sidle through. Then he slammed and locked it behind him. Margarith stood in the center of the cabin, screaming mindlessly. Ponchus and Mary stood beside her helplessly, pleading with her, whispering to her, reassuring her. Margarith did not even hear them.

Jeff went directly to her. He caught her in his arms, pulled her against him. She went on screaming for a moment, then gradually subsided against him. She sagged, desolated.

There was no sense asking her what had disturbed her. She *was* disturbed. Even if she knew, she couldn't tell him. There was no way to reach her in the private hell where she existed.

He nodded toward Mary and Ponchus, reassuring them as Margarith quieted. He kept whispering to her. It did not matter what he said, she didn't hear him or understand him. She responded only to the strength of his arms, the gentle way he held her, the quiet tone of his voice.

After a moment he sat in a wicker chair and drew Margarith down into his arms. He did not hold her as a lover, as a woman, but as he would hold a frightened child. She pressed her head against his shoulder. He felt her body wracked with shudders, and then for a long time she was quiet.

Ponchus went into the next cabin, sagged into the upper berth and was soon sleeping. For a long time, Mary sat across from where Jeff held Margarith in his arms. When she yawned, he said, "Get some rest, mama . . . it's going to be all right now . . . I promise you, it's going to be all right."

She nodded, yawning, overwhelmed with fatigue. He

expected her to lie down on one of the stateroom bunks. Instead, she went into the other room where Ponchus lay snoring. She lay down on the lower bunk.

Jeff sat, listening to the slap and whisper of the water against the swiftly moving boat. Distantly, he heard music and laughter, but there was no reality for him in the sounds—they were like noises from another cosmos.

He heard Margarith whispering. "I can't love him . . . I can't let myself love him," she was saying. He went empty at the hollow sound of her voice. "He's black, you know."

CHAPTER XLII

Jeff had never considered the possibility that day would come when he would drive swiftly through the streets of New Orleans to St. Charles Avenue, seeking sanctuary in the rococo chalet of Julien-Jacques Gischairn. He had nowhere else to turn. Simon's friends and operatives would trace him through hotels, and more urgently, Margarith required medical attention. Her illness was too deep for him, too fearful, too overwhelming. Physically, she was debilitated, losing weight, enervated. But it was far more than somatic illness. She was lost—but lost inside herself. There was no way to reach her, no way to make her aware of you. She looked at you. She didn't see you. You spoke to her. She heard your voice, but not your words. She needed immediate and professional attention. Gischairn was his best hope. He knew the finest people of the New Orleans upper crust; he was certain to know the finest medics too.

They arrived at the mansion on St. Charles Avenue late in the evening. It was after eleven P.M., but Gischairn welcomed them warmly. When Jeff apologized for the hour, the inconvenience, the lack of advance notice, Gischairn laughed. "My dear boy! What are friends for, except to inconvenience you?"

Jeff could not bring himself to introduce Mary as his mother. He tried to, but he could not force the words. Knowing that Gischairn was barely aware of lower classes except as they might temporarily serve him, he mumbled something unintelligible. Mary curtsied and Ponchus bowed as Gischairn's gaze raked across them. Jeff felt his face flush hot with shame. Inside his mind he vowed to Mary, *I'll make it up to you. You'll live like a queen. Everything I can give you. But not right now. We need this man, we need him badly—his influence, his connections, his power.*

He studied Gischairn narrowly. Perhaps his partner suspected he had black blood, but there was the single chance he did not and that was the gamble he couldn't take tonight—with Baxter Simon on his tail, Margarith ill, and all of them with no place to hide. He had no idea what Gischairn might say or do if he had proof that Jeff were really Bricktop.

He waited for Gischairn's reaction; there was none. More than his partnership with Gischairn was on the line tonight—Margarith's sanity might well depend on how willingly Julien-Jacques Gischairn provided concealment, aid, and succor. As things stood, Gischairn would do anything for his young partner. Would he lift a finger for him, knowing he was a *nigger?* It was a circumstance he didn't have the will to face tonight.

Gischairn rang for his butler. He instructed Jamie to show Mary and Ponchus to their quarters for the evening. Then he turned his attention to Margarith. Jeff told him a highly laundered version of her difficulties with Baxter

Simon. Simon had *caused* the death of her baby, but had not knocked it in the head—the truth seemed too violent for a man like Gischairn. Simon had misused her, he had treated her badly, and he had neglected her. She had declined, grown despondent, disturbed, ill. Jeff said that when he'd first known Margarith a year ago, she had been lovelier than any belle Gischairn had ever encountered. He said no more, the rest Gischairn could see for himself.

Gischairn appeared disconsolate at the despondency and desolation he saw in Margarith. He touched the golden hair that once had shone with richness, gleamed with highlights. He tilted her chin, studied the bone structure, the pallor of the gentle cheeks, the lackluster dullness of her violet eyes. He said, "What a waste, what a foul, heinous crime . . . we'll do what we can for her, my boy. We'll do what we can."

Their arrival dampened the festive atmosphere of Gischairn's seraglio. Jeff was surprised to find that none of the three quadroon lovelies who had been fixtures here when he had first arrived was still in the house. Each had married brilliantly, Gischairn assured him. They often dropped by for tea, to laugh with him and to recall old times and, he added with a sly smile, to reminisce about their young guest, built like a stallion and with the endurance of an Atlas. When Margarith had been led off to bed, Gischairn called the three new beauties and introduced them to Jeff. They were younger—none could have been more than seventeen—and, if possible, were lovelier than the girls he'd known before them in this house. They assured Jeff they were busy studying, learning, and, they laughed, living life as the gods must have meant for it to be lived. They were like dolls, perfect to the eye, unblemished. Gischairn involved them in sprightly conversation for an hour, but when Jeff remained preoccupied, troubled, Gischairn smiled and sent them off to bed. . . .

The procession of medical specialists began the next morning at nine o'clock. The medics came singly or in pairs, some remaining for consultation with a later arrival.

Each spoke warmly with Gischairn on a variety of subjects; he seemed to be conversant in any field and interested in all. Then the doctors would visit with Margarith for forty-five minutes to an hour. When they emerged from her bedroom, faces dour, lips pursed, eyes averted, they spoke with Jeff in Gischairn's book-lined library. Their diagnosis in each case: dementia—the marked decline from former intellectual level, and emotional apathy. Their prognosis: poor.

Two specialists went a step further, calling her illness dementia praecox. One of them said this was a common form of insanity. Yes, she was legally, medically insane. Dementia praecox developed late in adolescence or in early adult life. "This is not something which simply came over her in a hurry," one doctor said. "It has been building in many ways—in ways the laity would not recognize—loss of interest in people and things, loss of effective participation in practical or social life, incoherence of thought and action, and an almost total blunting of emotion." Jeff stared at the medic. "You don't believe it has been caused by the brutal death of her newborn baby?" The doctor shook his head. He certainly did not believe this—shock at death of her child?—a contributing factor, nothing more. And treatment? Nothing one can do—outside the asylums for the insane, or the private sanataria established to treat these poor wretches.

By four o'clock, Jeff was drawn taut with tension, pity for the ordeal Margarith was enduring, and rage against medics who quoted like parrots from medical tomes, unquestioning, unyielding.

Could he hope to remove her to a place of tranquility, there to take care of her himself? The medics without exception opposed this idea. There was no hope for her recovery under such unprofessional, undisciplined, and uncontrolled conditions. Surely, he could see this? They could not endorse, support, or in any manner accept responsibility for the sanity or life of the patient under such circumstances. One doctor spoke coldly, while his colleagues nodded sagely, "I strongly recommend against

393

such action. The cost to those around a mental patient cannot be estimated, and the injury to the patient might be irreparable."

Jeff drank down two glasses of straight bourbon while he paced the parlor and waited for the last doctor whom Gischairn had invited to the St. Charles Avenue mansion. This doctor, a middle-aged Creole with a strong French-Cajun accent, said, "She is a very ill girl . . . she has been desperately hurt—and she has retreated inside her own mind from that hurt. That is why we—none of us can reach her. She has been so terribly wounded she exists in terror of every human contact—of everything and everyone. What can we do for her? Not very much, I am afraid. We can try to improve the health of her body, we can give her every tenderness, care, love, hope, patience. . . . If she responds to none of this I may—reluctantly—suggest the asylum."

He smiled, shook his head, said he was sorry, smiled again, and then taking up his derby hat, scurried away as if running from his own inadequacy.

When Gischairn entered the library, he was surprised to see Jeff smiling. "The prognosis is negative," Gischairn said. "What do you find to smile about?"

"The last doctor made up my mind. I can't give Margarith medical skills, but I can give her healthful food, tenderness, love, and care. I can do that. I'm going to do that. I'm leaving in the morning for Palm Villa."

Jeff wrote out papers that recorded the sale of slaves Ponchus and Mary, from Margarith Morceau Simon to Julien-Jacques Gischairn. They were able to prevail upon Margarith to write her witnessed signature on the bill of sale. In the meantime, Gischairn's lawyer arranged manumission papers for the two slaves he'd bought from Margarith. The lawyer left the mansion with the bill of sale and manumission documents to be recorded. When they prepared to leave for Palm Villa the next morning, Gischairn said to Mary and Ponchus, "Well, you are free, both of you. You, Ponchus. And you, Mary Craven."

"Mary Craven?" Mary said. "You mean I have a full name?"

"That's right, Mary," Gischairn said. "Craven is your surname—and you are a free woman."

Jeff drew a deep breath. He put his arm around Mary, drawing her against him. He said, "I don't know if you understood me the other night, Julien, but Mary—is my mother."

Gischairn's face remained expressionless. His voice was flat. He said, "How nice." And in a tone that altered not a decibel, he added, "You are a very lovely lady, Mrs. Craven."

Gischairn was busy the rest of that morning, and they did not see him again before the buggy was loaded and they left for Palm Villa. Jamie, the butler, and the three young quadroon girls stood on the front steps and waved good-bye. Jeff drove away, feeling chilled, thinking that he had closed the door behind him on a way of life, and that he could never go back.

The next day around noon, they approached Palm Villa. The deep silence was almost oppressive, the isolation nearly total. He saw the fences marking the northern boundary of his property and then, framed through the moss-dripping oaks, the big old house he'd come to love. Love it or hate it, this was the door to the new life opening for him. He glanced at Margarith, slumped on the far side of the carriage, staring into nothingness. He shivered as if chilled.

"We're home, mama," he told Mary. "This is your home. For as long as you live."

"This place!" Mary stared at the tall columns, the deep red brick, the lean windows, the carefully tended grounds. "All this? How'd you ever earn a place like this?"

"It wasn't easy, mama." He put his arm around her. "And I don't want you cooking, or cleaning, or dusting, or polishing. All that's done for you."

She laughed at him. "What would I do with myself, just sitting around in a great big place like this?"

Jeff grinned. "Well, you can tell Ponchus what you want

done, and if Ponchus feels like it, he can tell somebody else to do it."

"That's fine, Masta Jeff," Ponchus said, laughing. "Sounds jus' like my old days in the army."

Late the next afternoon, Jeff mounted a horse with Michel to ride out to inspect the cotton planted in the south forty. They were talking with the blacks who had been chopping in the rows among the new plants when they saw Ponchus running across the field, waving his arm. Instinctively sure something had happened to Margarith, Jeff leaped into the saddle and rode across the cotton rows to meet the breathless black man. Ponchus swung up behind him and they rode into the yard. Jeff swung down, leaving the horse with Ponchus, and ran into the house through the kitchen door. He heard Margarith's screaming even before he reached the house.

She was crouched in a corner of the living room, pallid, her face muscles rigid, her eyes wide and stark. Mary said, "She thinks *he's* killing her baby. . . . We couldn't do anything with her . . . she went wild—got unmanageable right after you left the house."

Jeff nodded and touched his mother's face. "It's all right," he said. "Go out on the veranda. It's cool out there. They'll bring you some lemonade. She'll be all right."

He knelt beside Margarith. He wasn't sure she would be all right, whether they could ever recover her from hell, only that they had to try. He remembered the medical specialist who had warned him that the ordeal of caring for the mentally unstable was destructive to everyone around her. Well, so be it. He had made up his mind to care for her, he would have to pay the price. Others around her would just have to adjust to it. Somehow he was going to make her well. He touched her face with his palm. At first she shuddered, but she didn't move away. He spoke gently; gradually she grew quiet and sagged against him, breathing raggedly.

The days passed slowly. Tension seemed to affect even the atmosphere of Palm Villa. Even when everything was quiet, Jeff saw all the servants were taut, waiting for an outburst. The superstitious blacks looked on Margarith as they would an evil spirit. They dreaded and feared an insane person. He tried to tell them she was not insane, she was miserably unhappy and ill. But he saw they didn't buy that, though they gave him a lot of teeth and much nodding.

Margarith was quiet, tranquil, almost serene, as long as he was with her. Learning quickly that he could not leave her for extended periods, he took her with him when he and Michel or Ponchus rode around the acreage, overseeing the work. She seemed happy when she was riding with them. She never talked to them. She did not respond to the texture or odor of a giant magnolia. When Michel showed them a boll of cotton that was three times the size of crops farther away from the delta country, she crushed it in her fingers to test its softness, but this was her only response.

What troubled Jeff most was her attitude toward him. Though she grew disturbed, distraught, and even unmanageable when he was away from her, she hardly seemed aware of him when he was near. It was as if her mind had blocked Jeff Carson out completely because of his color, because he was forbidden to her, because she could never love him, and she would never love anyone else. Jeff Carson—or Bricktop—didn't exist. But she responded to his tender care, his loving gentleness, and with him near, she was secure and content.

But her needs taxed him almost beyond endurance. Sleeping alone, she would waken screaming. Sometimes every servant in the house and most of them in the quarters were awake and shaken with superstitious dread before they could get her calm enough to sleep again. He solved this by lying down with her until she was asleep. Then he began to sleep with her. She lay curled in a fetal position, snug against him, and she would sleep the entire night undisturbed.

It was Jeff who didn't sleep. There was no such thing as sexual desire or heated emotions in that hell where

Margarith existed. He lay, night after night, holding her in his arms. Sometimes his hands inadvertently brushed the soft fullness of her breasts, or she pressed the mound of her mons veneris against his thigh. He'd been a long time without a woman. He was drawn fine. Every memory of Margarith's sleeping with him had fire and passion in it—and variations straight from Paris!

He felt himself grow taut. His breath quickened, his pulses raced, and his blood pounded, even when he tried to tell himself she was ill. Still, he could hardly believe she could lie so close to him and remain unaware of his need for her, his love for her. When he would assure himself she had to feel his need, respond to the pounding of his heart, the heat of his hands, he would hear the gentle rush of her deep, restful breathing. She was sound asleep in his arms.

He didn't sleep much, but he drank a lot.

CHAPTER XLIII

The days at Palm Villa were long, the nights interminable. Then with the warmth of May, there was a change, subtle, almost unnoticed. The spring suns, the rain showers, erupting suddenly from brilliant subtropical skies, the rich delta earth, everything combined to bring the cotton to a full fruition beyond the expectations of the most wildly optimistic. The sudden bursting bolls, sprouting like snow puffs on the deep green bushes, brought every man, woman, and child on the plantation running with eight-foot croker sacks strapped across their shoulders. They dragged these bags along the rows, plucking the bolls as if the utter beauty of the crop might tempt the gods or rouse jealousy in the highest echelons of heaven. They brought in the bountiful harvest, saved it from deleterious effects of rain, hailstones, insect, or souring sun. Ponchus, Mary, Michel, the kitchen workers, and the maids joined Jeff and every slave from the quarters in the south forty. No one mentioned the matter, or spoke of it aloud at all, but when they saw Margarith, wearing a floppy sun hat, dragging her croker sack, each of them said a little prayer of thanksgiving, each in his own way, each to his own gods. Jeff wanted to yell out his exultance. Instead he went on working quietly, but with demonic energy and ebullient fury—Margarith was recovering. She was getting well. It might be slow, with much hell ahead, but she was going to make it. She was going to be all right.

It was slow. Like a lonely little figure struggling up a glass hill, there were three steps and a long slide backward. She would find something to laugh about at lunch, she wept at dinner. She rode with Jeff across the lovely fields. She nodded and smiled when he pointed out the extraordinary growth of plants in the silt-rich delta earth. Later, waking from a nap, alone, chilled in the warm afternoon, she screamed, seeing her baby with its skull crushed, hurled through the window into the yard. It took the long, dark night and two or three sunny days of holding her, reassuring her, whispering to her, to stop the quivering and trembling in her body.

He no longer hoped she would turn up her mouth for his kiss, put out her arms, asking to be loved. He denied his own needs, buried them under exhausting work, drinking them out of his mind. Often he was certain she had crossed one long bridge on her way to recovery; she recognized him, she knew him, she wanted him near, she could not sleep without him beside her in her bed; but she denied she loved him, denied she had ever loved him. Baxter Simon had murdered more than her baby, he had killed Jeff Carson for her. No such person existed for her, no such person had ever existed. Something inside her mind had blocked him out. The man she had loved was dead, as dead and buried as their baby. There remained only the gentle, patient man who was her shield against hurt, her comfort, her only hope of security. But she didn't love him—she couldn't love him because he was black. By all legal reckoning, by precedent and custom, he was not a man at all, but an animal, a chattel of his superiors, his owners. There was no way on earth to change this accepted truth.

She could look at him and smile, secure. She could cling to him because she needed him. She was inconsolable when he was away from her. But he saw that the gulf between them was unnavigable; he was a *nigger*— no matter how white he looked, he was a nigger, black as Ponchus was black. He held her in his arms until she slept, then he walked out to the living room and poured himself a tumbler of bourbon and drank it straight, slumped in a high-backed leather-covered chair. Sometimes shadows covered him, night closed in around him, and he remained unmoving until she cried out, calling him.

He decided he was in a hell of his own, paying for whatever sins the gods had toted up against him. His debt was heavy; his punishment was severe. Maybe Baxter Simon was right. Maybe a slave was only an animal, a chattel without human dignity or human rights. Maybe all the running all the days of his life had brought him to this place where he must pay for going against the gods' decree—a black is born to slavery, the slave who rises against his master must be punished.

He tried to lose himself in work. The summer produced incredible bounty in his gardens, as if the rich black breast of the delta could suckle the hungry of the entire world if she were nursed and loved and tended. Jars lined every pantry counter with preserved fruit and vegetables. The cotton brought a rich profit. He opened a plantation account against which Ponchus and Mary could draw. No matter what happened, they would live safe and protected, well fed and secure at Palm Villa.

By autumn, the farm was becoming self-sustaining, and Jeff walked around in a bourbon-induced haze.

They were building a windmill to irrigate the south forty, which would be expanded to a hundred acres of cotton next year. The earth was silt rich, the rains plentiful but erratic, the sun was scorching; a windmill would give them control, and besides, it was something to occupy his mind and drive out the obsessive thought that spun inside it, harassing him: he was black, and she could never love him because he was a nigger.

One night he staggered in, took a hot bath, and fell across his bed. Margarith had been at the windmill site most of the afternoon, watching the work progress. She had come in to the manor house alone about an hour before quitting time. He had seen her only briefly at the supper table. She kept her eyes lowered, but he saw that she ate ravenously. Her appetite had returned, her cheeks were glowing with color put there by the sun and wind; she was gaining weight. Hell, face it. She was as lovely as she had been at The Laurels when she was driving him insane with her latest activity—straight from Paris via Lissa Malraux's whispers. Only now she lay beside him as if he had never loved her greedily, sent her into paroxysms of orgasmic ecstasy.

The house grew quiet. The last candles and lanterns were doused across the fields at the quarters. In the distance a panther screamed in the stagnant swamps. A boat passed on the river, coming out of the darkness, vanishing into it. He wondered if she were coming to him tonight? Perhaps she had recovered enough that she no longer needed his strength and nearness. He exhaled heavily. Perhaps if she could get along without him, he'd go up to the nearest town, to the nearest place he could find a woman. He didn't want just any woman—but he knew damned well he had to have somebody.

The door opened hesitantly, and Margarith came

through it. She paused just inside. The lamplight showed him she was the Missy from those lost days at The Laurels. Her golden hair glowed from the hundred strokes she'd brushed it. Her face looked as fresh and unblemished as a day lily. Those lustrous violet eyes caught all the light in the room and reflected it. She wore a pale lime-colored gown, so fragile it was translucent. Her breasts rose against the fabric, her nipples the soft pink that tipped the gentle rise of those fascinating globes. The dainty triangle at her mons veneris was like some alluring fire beckoning him to its heated sphere. Jesus Christ! She *was* Margarith Morceau of The Laurels again. Her beauty would have been irresistible under any circumstances, but this was like setting a banquet just beyond the shackled fingers of a starving—slave . . . God almighty knew that said it. He was a slave, his blood was black. Though he wanted her more than the next breath that would sustain his life, he could not have her. His need for her was overwhelming. He felt the stirring in his loins that was a hated passion by now. He could want her. He could suffer with need for her. But he could not have her. He could never have her again.

Her voice, low, modulated, hesitant, reached across the room to him. "I brought it," she said. "I brought it back to you."

He saw she held the sheathed sword in her hand, dragging it along the floor at her side. His heart lurched. He sat up on the side of the bed, watching her. "I want you to have it," she said. "I know why you left it for me . . . but that's over now—that's past. I want you to keep it."

He stood up and held out his arms to her. She dropped the sword. The weapon clattered to the floor. She ran to him, pressed herself against him. "I love you, Jeff," she said. "I've always loved you. I know how wrong I was, but I did try to fight loving you. It was what I'd been taught, what I'd been trained to believe. I couldn't help it, Jeff. I was a fool, but I couldn't help it. No more than I can help loving you now . . . I love you. I don't care about anything else . . . I don't care about black blood . . . I don't care. Without you, I don't live . . . nothing else matters except that I be with you."

She turned up her face, her full lips parted. He kissed her, feeling that charge of their kiss vibrating through him. "Oh, God," she whispered against his mouth. "It's been so long, Jeff. So long."

He let his hands move over her breasts, the rise of her femininity, the fevered heat of her thighs. He drew her gown up over her shoulders and let it fall to the floor. He reached out to turn down the lamp wick, but she caught his hand. "Leave it on, Jeff. From now on we can make love in the light . . . it doesn't matter about those fearful brand marks on your back. I know about them—I'm sorry because you were hurt so brutally—but I know. We're free to love, Jeff. Free. Nothing in the world is between us now."

He smiled and drew her down to the bed close beside him. "Oh, Lord," he said. "I'm afraid I'm starved for you, Margarith . . . for you." He laughed. "The first time may not count for much . . . or the second . . . hell, maybe even the third."

She smiled and kissed his throat, stroking him. "It doesn't matter, darling. We've got all night . . . all the rest of our lives."

Trying to force himself to move slowly, Jeff kissed her lips. His hands gripped her, his body touched hers, adhered, covered her. "Don't wait," she whispered. "Please don't wait . . . I want it too . . . I want it more than you ever could. . . . Oh, Jeff, I'm so wild for you. . . ."

He wanted to laugh, to deny this could be true, but he did not answer her at all. He buried his face in the soft texture of her sweet-scented hair. She thrust herself upward to meet him. He came to her with all the immense power and hunger of his body. She cried out in sweet agony, locking him to her. Her arms went up under his arms and her fingernails dug into the flesh of his shoulders as she pulled him down to her.

In their mutual orgiastic fury and mindless ecstasy they

did not hear the rustling of gardenia bushes outside the bedroom window or the boots grinding across the sill. Baxter Simon was in the room and striding toward the bed before they realized they were not alone in the cosmos.

A growl of primal rage tore through Simon's throat. He crouched over the bed, his eyes wild, his face flushed and rigid. "You slut! You white slut. Humpin' with a *nigra!* God knows, it ain't no surprise to me that this here black ape's been pestering you—even before I knowed you. Before I wed you. Before I give you my good name."

Margarith screamed out in terror, screamed and went on screaming at the sight of Simon's hated face. Simon backhanded her across the head. "Shut up! You bring anybody else in here, you jus' gits them kilt too!"

Margarith crouched on the bed. She stared up at Simon, her eyes going stark and empty. She screamed again and went on screaming. Raging at her to shut up, Simon caught her by the hair. He yanked her off the bed and hurled her half across the room behind him. He backed away then, retreating to the corridor door. He twisted the key in the lock at the precise instant that Ponchus battered on it from the hall, and Michel called, "Masta. You all right, masta?"

Simon said, "Get away from there, you niggers. And keep quiet. I warn you. I got my people outside this house. Anyone of you blacks steps out that door gets killed."

Jeff leaped up from the bed. All he could think was he had to get his gun from the chiffonier. But Simon moved fluidly, striding back toward the bed, angling himself between Jeff and any other part of the room. As Simon moved, he drew his handgun from his holster. He fixed it on Jeff. Crouched naked, Jeff felt vulnerable, helpless.

"You goin' die this time, nigger. I come for my wife. But I goin' leave her here with you—dead, you black bastard. Pesterin' a white woman—pesterin' my wife. Oh, God, how it's goin' to pleasure me to put bullets

404

in yore guts. Then her. By God, then her. I be doin' her a favor, killin' her. Always heard that when a white woman gits to humpin' a nigger, she ain't ever fitt'en for white men no more."

Behind Simon, Margarith moaned, "No . . ." It was a mindless, almost unintelligible sound.

Drawing the sword from its sheath, she came up to her knees. Holding the weapon in both hands, she sprang upward. Catching his breath, Simon heeled around. As he turned, she drove the sword into him, thrusting it with all her strength.

Staggered, bent almost double, Simon fired in a reflex action. The bullet struck Margarith in her left breast, ripping it open, blood spurting. She released the sword, driven backward by the impact of the point-blank gunfire. She toppled against a chair, upsetting it. She was dead as she struck the floor.

Jeff was already moving toward Simon. Simon's fingers relaxed on the gun butt. He dropped it. Jeff knelt and caught it up. He heard a rustling sound in the gardenia bushes hedged against the house outside his window. Staying on his knee, he fired through the window. There was a yell out there. At the same time, pistols fired in the darkness from both ends of the house.

Simon was writhing on the floor. Blood bubbled from his mouth. His eyes were wide and with both hands he caught at the sword blade, fighting it. But he could not remove it. Savagely Jeff reached over and drove down on the hasp of the sword with all the strength and fury in his arms. The sword struck the flooring and shook wildly as Jeff backed away, still on his knees. Simon did not move again. He was dead.

Jeff crawled on his knees across the room to where Margarith lay. Crying, he lifted her up and cradled her in his arms. He was holding her gently when Ponchus came in through the window.

Ponchus looked down at Margarith. He shook his head, his eyes welled with tears. "Oh, God, Missy," he whispered. "Oh, my God."

405

Tears spilling down his cheeks, Jeff looked up at the grayed old soldier and shook his head. "She's dead, Ponchus. She's dead."

Ponchus nodded. "It a bad day, masta. A evil day." His arm was torn, blackened with gunpowder. He said, "They dead, masta. The two men out there that come with him," he jerked his head toward Simon's body. "When I knowed what was gwine happen in this room, masta, I knowed we couldn't let them two men git away alive."

Jeff nodded. He did not speak. There was nothing for him to say, nothing left for him to say.

CHAPTER XLIV

The morning shone bright and fresh, alive with lush growth and wary birds. There was no grief, no pause for death programed in the infinite play of nature. Time was irrelevant. Life began, ended, replaced itself in a remorseless ebb and flow of some casual driving toward an unknowable, random future beyond the farthest horizon—because, like time, horizons also were inconstant, unreal, and indefensible.

Jeff stood unmoving as Margarith's pinewood casket was lowered into the ground. Ponchus spoke, almost inaudibly, his voice strangled, begging God to receive Missy kindly, to love her tenderly as those around her on earth had loved her, to see in her only her gentle goodness, and to forgive those sins all flesh is heir to. Long after the last straggler had returned to the farmyard and the quarters, Jeff went on standing, a solitary figure of grief, on the knoll. The sun rose blindingly, seeming to sear a steaming sweat from the fields and meadows and swamps. Three hundred feet away, at the rim of the live oak grove, Ponchus stood alone near the boll of a huge tree, waiting in silence.

The morning sky was scathless, the earth unsullied as if dawn itself were a lustration between the night's violence and the day's burial. From the muck and ordure of the silt and dung, the slaves had gathered huge roses, immaculate gardenias, unblemished magnolias, lilies, chrysanthemums, and ferns. They walked slowly forward and placed the flowers on the raw mound of Margarith's grave atop the knoll west of the manor house. The silent procession of blacks continued until the brown, wet grave was concealed, the flowers rising out of the grass like some shaggy, multicolored blanket. The slaves knelt, placed their bouquets, and then with a wordless nod toward Jeff, they turned and walked silently back through the grove of live oaks toward the brick manor house, which gleamed in the drowsy sun-drenched morning haze through the dripping tendrils of moss.

Jeff tried to tell himself it was over, life had closed another door and locked it finally behind him. But had it ended? Would it ever end? Would there be a night, a day, an hour in which Margarith would not live vividly and achingly within him? And Baxter Simon was dead, but did his virulent kind of hatred ever die, or did it spew like some purulent evil even after death? Baxter Simon was dead, but he had not died in the natural course of events; he had been violently slain . . . could that murder be hidden, or must he run forever from its reprisals?

Last night had plunged from a nightmare of horror into vertiginous insanity—an evil without end. Jeff and Ponchus had stared at Baxter Simon's body. The fresh blood could be washed up with cold water and would leave no trace. Simon as well as his two confederates could be dropped off the pier and consigned to the river and its swirling currents. Ponchus, Mary, and Michel would join Jeff in swearing to any investigator that Simon had never arrived at Palm Villa plantation. But could they hope the law would accept the word of three blacks with everything to lose? If only Margarith—or any white person—could testify, the matter could be disposed of quickly. Jeff knew that once the law got on his trail—armed with the history of Simon's relentless long pursuit—it would never end.

The fact was that every one on the roads between Palm Villa and New Orleans would know that Baxter Simon was hunting a fugitive nigger named Bricktop—a red-haired mustee who passed himself as white. Baxter Simon had set out, armed and with allies, on the road through the swamp that led only to one destination, Palm Villa plantation. Why had he not arrived? What had happened to him? Why would anything happen to him on the road through the empty bayou?

Still, the bodies had to be disposed of. Without corpses, the law would be hindered, if not halted in its investigation of murder. Ponchus withdrew the sword. It was washed clean, returned to its sheath. Then they wrapped Simon's body with a sheet to keep him from leaving a trail of blood. Hefting the body across his shoulder, Jeff carried it out to the yard where Michel stood with a lantern near the dead bodies of Simon's allies.

Jeff stared at the two dead men in stunned recognition. One was Fabio, the road agent who'd attacked him the night after he left Barataria. The other was Fabio's follower, the ugly giant Elice.

Jeff shrugged Simon's body from his shoulder, tossing it to the ground beside the bodies of the bandits. "Find these men's horses," Jeff said to Michel.

The black man nodded toward the darkness. "They tied up, masta, yonder at the barn."

Jeff nodded. Looking at Fabio's ugly, bearded face, at Elice's wide-staring eyes, he saw a way out. He ran to the barn, hitched a horse to a flatbed wagon, secured the three saddle horses to its tailgate and drove to where Michel and Ponchus stood over the dead men.

Michel and Ponchus, grasping the dead men by their boots, helped Jeff toss the corpses into the wagon bed. "I'm going to take them ten miles back up the road," Jeff said. "I'm going to leave them there."

From Simon's pockets he removed wallet and papers. By lanternlight he sought any mention of Bricktop. There was one flier promising a thousand-dollar reward—dead or alive. Jeff burned it. The other valuables and wallet Jeff stuffed into Fabio's pockets. "It's going to look like a robbery and murder," he said. "Even if they started out together, there's not a sheriff in any parish south of Orleans who doesn't know what petty thugs Elice and Fabio were—they'd kill a man for a gold eagle—and Simon always carried wads of money, had gold rings and an expensive watch. If they want motive for murder, by God we've given it to them."

"That Simon, he kilt with a sword," Ponchus said.

"A point blank gunshot ought to change the looks of that wound," Jeff said. He held the gun a few inches from Simon's belly and pressed the trigger. Michel winced at the explosion, but Ponchus only nodded his approval and satisfaction. "Take care of everything," Jeff said. "I'll be back when I can."

"I goin' with you, masta," Ponchus said. "Two of us thinkin' and hatin' and lookin' for what might go wrong lot better'n one. . . .

They plodded north on the narrow, twisting road through the maze of the bayou for almost three hours. They had covered the bodies with empty cotton-gathering croker sacks. If they met anyone on the trail, there should be no questions, but if anyone became too curious, both of them were armed.

They ground-tied the saddle horses in the middle of the trail. If the animals wandered, so be it. They would shy at gunfire anyhow; they would seek grass or water. They didn't have to worry about the horses. Standing in the bed of the wagon, Jeff hefted Elice and Fabio over the right sideboards, letting their bodies strike the ground, guns clasped in their fists. Jeff lifted Simon and let the body fall on the left side of the wagon, across the road from the road agents. Then he leaped down, cautiously turned their horse on the trail and headed back toward Palm Villa. . . .

The night that would never end had ended. Dawn splashed vivid pink across the swampland as they drove the wagon into the barn. Here they found the pinewood casket that Michel had set out for Margarith's body.

Jeff remained unmoving at the graveside. He wanted to weep, but there were no tears. She was dead. She was lost to him. He blamed himself for her death. He could not escape that fearful responsibility. When he had made love to her that first time, he had sealed her death warrant. He had not meant it that way. He had loved her above all else on earth, but his loving her must have gone against some immutable law he didn't understand— and death was the price of her loving him. Hell, every girl he touched was destroyed somehow. Jesus! He didn't want to harm anyone. He had never looked for anything but a moment of love in his headlong flight from bondage. Yet he hurt everyone, he destroyed them.

His life had been lonely and brutal. When he drew a girl into his arms and loved her, the gods snatched her away from him, vengefully and violently. He thought about Minerva George, who had loved him enough to risk her own life to save his—even when she knew he was black and lost to her. And Helen Latimer. His hand touched the battered diamond-studded gold cross on his chest. Thank God, he had taken her gift and ridden away from her before she was hurt. She had wanted him to have the cross—a talisman, a good luck charm, a token against evil. But had it been? Evil had followed him since the day Helen had locked this trinket about his neck.

Suddenly, he closed his fist and yanked the cross, breaking the thin gold chain about his neck. He stared at the bauble in his hand. Helen's charm had been with him when he found Chloe—but it had also been with him when he lost her violently, to Baxter Simon's gunfire. What had Helen told him about the cross? The Cuban priest, Father Diego, had seen the man who first owned the cross die in cold blood, slain in a duel. Jeff recalled the Cuban whore named Lolita who had found the cross on his own chest and had thought him a heavy-hung Catholic priest— ¿Católico clérico? she'd cried in superstitious terror. And now, Margarith. She lay dead under that banking of flowers, under that mound of delta earth. Why had he thought this thing a good luck charm? It was almost as if Helen had given it to him to insure he never find another love—as if in her hidden jealousy, she'd given him not a good luck charm but a talisman of evil.

He shuddered in the hot sun, even as he admitted it was all superstition. It didn't matter. But he didn't want the damned talisman hanging around his neck anymore. No. No more. He hurled it from him across the knoll as hard as he could, swallowing at the tears of rage and anguish that stopped his throat and threatened to strangle him.

For weeks he went every day alone up to Margarith's grave. But it was empty and lonely up there; there was no solace to be found. He saw the flowers wilt, turn brown, and grow putrid on the mound. He made up his mind that he would not come up here anymore, but every day he found himself walking across the live oak grove, going to the knoll. Mary and Ponchus had started keeping a small vase of fresh flowers at the head of the grave. He wanted to thank them, but he said nothing, because he had no words.

He walked back through the grove toward the manor house in the lazy morning sunlight. He saw the brilliantly polished coach, the uniformed livery men, the brushed and shiny-coated team. He shook his head, looking around, wanting to run. He wasn't ready to see anyone—not anyone. He didn't know what he wanted.

The coach pulled to a stop before the manor house

veranda. The uniformed footman leaped down and opened the tonneau door. Jeff stared, disbelieving his eyes. It was Julien-Jacques Gischairn. He remembered the last time he had seen Gischairn, when he'd admitted —implied at least—that he *was* Bricktop, the fugitive mustee. He had told Gischairn that the slave Mary Craven was his mother, the mulatto bed wench. He had never expected to see Gischairn again—perhaps he might send his lawyers to dissolve his partnership.

The doorman went on holding the door until the second passenger of the coach stepped out. Jeff shook his head. It was Vincente. Vincente Olivarez, son of Don Cipriano. Vincente!

The two men were laughing, chatting, looking around as Ponchus and Michel came out with Mary to greet them.

Jeff walked forward, feeling as if he were slogging through bayou mud up to his ankles. He still didn't know whether he wanted to see them now or not, but he had never expected to see either of them again. Ponchus waved his arm, pointing toward Jeff, and Gischairn and Vincente hurried across the sun-crisped grass toward him, arms extended. Vincente walked, then increased his steps, running.

"Don Jeff!" Vincente threw his arms around him. Jeff clapped him on the back, smiling, trying to smile.

Gischairn joined them. He extended his hand and Jeff gripped it. Gischairn said, "I heard that Baxter Simon was killed on the bayou road trying to get down here to you . . . the high-sheriff told us that two road agents killed him for his money. Strange. A man with everything Baxter Simon had—to chase after vengeance until it killed him on a lonely road in the swamps." Gischairn shook his head, puzzled at the ironies of life, the whims of fate, the hellish twists of chance. "You're free now, Jeff. But I guess you've always been free, haven't you, inside?"

Jeff shrugged. He wasn't sure that he was free now, that he would ever be, inside where he had to live with himself. He was chained to the past, to his lost love, to what he was, what life had made him. Free?

Gischairn had brought the recorded manumission papers for Ponchus and Mary. He handed over to Jeff the recorded transfer of Palm Villa. "A whole new life, Jeff," he said. "To do what you will with it. I hope you'll come back to New Orleans with me and go back to work—in our partnership."

Jeff stared at Gischairn, puzzled. "You still want me as your partner—knowing what you do about me?"

"What do I know about you? I know your mother is a lovely woman named Mary. I know you have inventiveness, courage, and daring. I wouldn't have any other man for my partner. . . . And now, young Vincente has come forward with a proposition which has excited my greed— one I don't think you'll be able to refuse."

"What are you doing here, Vincente?" Jeff demanded. "Why aren't you in school? Why aren't you with your father? Why did you leave Cuba?"

Vincente smiled and shrugged. "Well, it got to be very difficult—trying to help Perla improve business at her place. She appreciated my suggestions and followed them. But her patrone—Don Cesar—he was impossible to deal with. He accused me of ruining a successful operation, of destroying my own half-sister with my stupidity. Don Cesar and I fought—oh, only with words, but pointed and unforgivable words. . . . I was forbidden to enter Perla's Palace."

"Then why didn't you stay with Don Cipriano and go to school?"

Vincente shrugged again. "After a little while of being a young don—with nothing to do but wear fine clothes and be seen in Don Cipriano's carriage—it all got very boring . . . That's when I heard of slaves—prime, first class, and fancies—to be bought in Haiti. Cheap. Dirt cheap. The niggers down there have revolted, driven out all the whites—the lawmakers and landowners. The place is in chaos. They're hungry. You can buy slaves for a dime on the dolllar. I don't exaggerate, Jeff."

Gischairn was nodding eagerly, watching Jeff's face. Jeff looked at them, shook his head. "What's the matter

413

with you two? Buying slaves may be easy—but getting them into the States past Lafitte's blackbirders. There is just no way."

"There must be a way," Gischairn said. "And if there is, I'm convinced you'll find it, Jeff. A fortune to be made. More money than we ever dreamed about."

"And a quick and watery grave," Jeff said.

"That doesn't sound like you," Gischairn said. "You've always known that anything worthwhile is tough. There is no free lunch. There never has been. Likely never will be . . . Come back to New Orleans with me, Jeff. The girls and I—we'll try to help you forget your hurt. . . . When you feel you're ready, you and Vincente and Captain Augsberg can take a run down to Haiti—hell, just take a look. What can that hurt?"

"It can't hurt," Vincente said. "Here, Jeff. Here's your good luck talisman." He held the battered cross out in his hand.

Jeff said, "Where'd you get that?"

"Ponchus. He picked it up when you threw it away. He says you think it's evil. But have you thought about it? We know how evil things have been for you *with* the talisman—but how bad might it have been *without* it?"

Jeff smiled in spite of himself. He took the talisman. Vincente nodded, pleased, and said, "What the hell, that cross can be as evil in some pawnshop as it could out in that underbrush. Time may come when we might need to pawn it."

Gischairn laughed. "Wear it, Jeff. At least, wear it to the nearest pawnshop."

Jeff gazed at the two laughing men. They believed in life, they saw life as it was, accepted it in all its casual cruelty, its playful evil. They endured, that was the only secret. Maybe they were right. You believed in nothing, you protected yourself at least, you were seldom hurt. No matter the loss, or wishes to the contrary, the minutes tick away, the hours and days and nights pass, and life goes on whether you want it or not. You hung in there, you tried to find a laugh once in a while. Maybe this was the best you could hope. He nodded. At worst, he could run from pain, the memory of agony. He could travel fast and far, too swiftly to remember. But even as he thought this, he recognized with a faint chill that he could never outrun heartbreak. He could go on living but he could not forget. He would not forget. . . . What the hell, he didn't want to forget.

New York City, January, 1975
Indian Rocks Beach, Fla., January, 1977

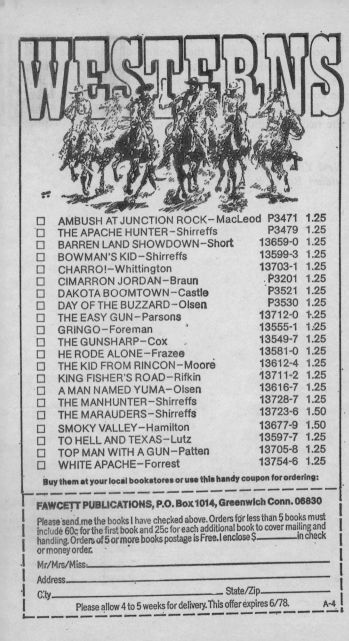

WESTERNS

	Title	Code	Price
☐	AMBUSH AT JUNCTION ROCK—MacLeod	P3471	1.25
☐	THE APACHE HUNTER—Shirreffs	P3479	1.25
☐	BARREN LAND SHOWDOWN—Short	13659-0	1.25
☐	BOWMAN'S KID—Shirreffs	13599-3	1.25
☐	CHARRO!—Whittington	13703-1	1.25
☐	CIMARRON JORDAN—Braun	P3201	1.25
☐	DAKOTA BOOMTOWN—Castle	P3521	1.25
☐	DAY OF THE BUZZARD—Olsen	P3530	1.25
☐	THE EASY GUN—Parsons	13712-0	1.25
☐	GRINGO—Foreman	13555-1	1.25
☐	THE GUNSHARP—Cox	13549-7	1.25
☐	HE RODE ALONE—Frazee	13581-0	1.25
☐	THE KID FROM RINCON—Moore	13612-4	1.25
☐	KING FISHER'S ROAD—Rifkin	13711-2	1.25
☐	A MAN NAMED YUMA—Olsen	13616-7	1.25
☐	THE MANHUNTER—Shirreffs	13728-7	1.25
☐	THE MARAUDERS—Shirreffs	13723-6	1.50
☐	SMOKY VALLEY—Hamilton	13677-9	1.50
☐	TO HELL AND TEXAS—Lutz	13597-7	1.25
☐	TOP MAN WITH A GUN—Patten	13705-8	1.25
☐	WHITE APACHE—Forrest	13754-6	1.25

Buy them at your local bookstores or use this handy coupon for ordering:

FAWCETT PUBLICATIONS, P.O. Box 1014, Greenwich Conn. 06830

Please send me the books I have checked above. Orders for less than 5 books must include 60c for the first book and 25c for each additional book to cover mailing and handling. Orders of 5 or more books postage is Free. I enclose $_____ in check or money order.

Mr/Mrs/Miss_____

Address_____

City_____ State/Zip_____

Please allow 4 to 5 weeks for delivery. This offer expires 6/78.   A-4